In the Shadow of War:

Spies, Love & the Lusitania

Colleen Adair Fliedner

Colleen Adair Fliedner

In the Shadow of War: Spies, Love & the Lusitania
Published by Sand Hill Review Press, LLC
All rights reserved
www.sandhillreviewpress.com
1 Baldwin Ave, #304, San Mateo, CA 94401

ISBN: 978-1-937818-93-7 paperback
ISBN: 978-1-937818-94-4 case laminate
ISBN: 978-1-937818-95-1 ebook
Library of Congress Control Number: 2018951951
© 2018 by Colleen Adair Fliedner

Cover art direction by Tory Hartmann
Graphics by Backspace Ink
Image of the *Lusitania* from a vintage Cunard postcard
Maps by A. Cuellar

SHRP
Sand Hill Review Press
1 BALDWIN AVE, #304, SAN MATEO, CA 94401

This novel is dedicated to the 1,198 men, women and children who died on the *Lusitania*; and to those who survived and lived the rest of their lives with the memories of that horrific catastrophe. They were all people like you and me. Their stories, their lives, this tragedy should never be forgotten.

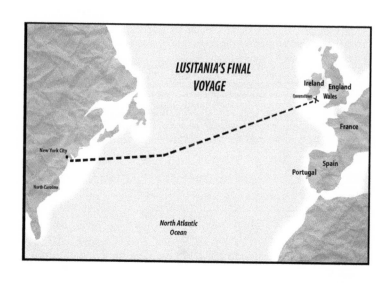

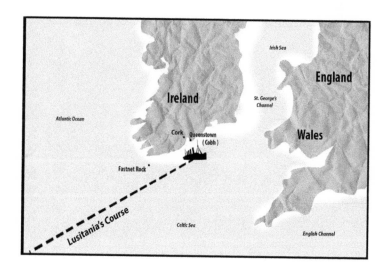

In the Shadow of War

PART ONE

Chapter 1

Manhattan, New York
February 1915

CURTIS CARLSON wiped the foggy moisture from the taxi's window with the sleeve of his woolen coat. He leaned back in the seat, gazing up at the rain clouds visible in the gaps between the jungle of new skyscrapers. As usual, Park Avenue bustled with traffic. Horse-drawn carriages darted through intersections jammed with motorcars; while a river of pedestrians holding open umbrellas flowed like a thick, black ribbon along the clogged sidewalks. Motor trucks chugged and huffed, sounding their horns at horses with mounted riders. Ah, yes. This was Manhattan. And he loved it here.

He looked forward to the day he would move to the heart of the city. It wouldn't be long before that happened. He was sure of it. His employment with Morgan and Company had gone well, and with his next raise in salary, he would move to one of those towering apartment buildings overlooking Central Park.

Curtis slid his hands behind his neck, clasping his fingers together. His life was on track. And he suspected things were going to get even better. In fact, this was likely one of the most important days of his life. Today would be his first face-to-face meeting with Mr. Morgan, Jr., who had capably taken the reins of the huge, world-famous company two years ago when his legendary father died. The monthly reviews of his work performance had been filled with compliments—lavish praises, in fact. There was a good chance he was about to receive a promotion. Curtis smiled. A big, luxurious apartment would come his way sooner rather than later. It would happen. He knew it.

As he entered through the front doors on the corner of the angular building, a blast of cold wind followed him in. The dozens of neck scarves, assorted hats and caps, and long coats hanging on the wall hooks swayed in near unison. After removing his coat and derby and placing them in empty spots among the other garments, he proceeded through the inner door and into the main workspace.

Morgan and Company looked more like an office than a bank. The secretaries, mostly young men, sat at small desks on the far side of the massive room. Curtis often quipped that the noise outside was almost rivaled by striking typewriter keys which echoed a cacophony of clatter through the marble halls; so loud one would have to plug an ear to hear, and shout into the telephone's voice receiver to be heard by the caller.

Parallel rows of roll-top desks were interspersed with potted palms and brass spittoons…not that most gentlemen used them in these modern times. Cigars were preferred over chewing tobacco, especially inside such a prestigious institution. The notable, extremely wealthy Morgan clientele were taken upstairs to the higher echelons where they lunched in the private restaurant with the partners or had tea with the heir apparent…the new king himself, the man whom only the most senior, important partners called "Jack."

Curtis made his way to his desk, placed his valise on the floor, and settled into his chair. Fumbling in the center drawer, he pulled out his all-too-frequently used metal tube of indigestion tablets and lifted the cap. One triangle-shaped tablet wouldn't do today. He shook out two, popped them in his mouth, and chewed.

"Good morning, Mr. Carlson." He swiveled around, swallowing the chalky mixture. Mr. Mumford, one of Mr. Morgan's assistants, stood beside him.

"Good morning, Mr. Mumford," he responded, keeping his mouth more closed than open, hoping the remnants of the powdery white medicine weren't visible.

"Glad to see you were early, son. Mr. Morgan likes eager beavers, you know."

Never mind that Curtis was always early. He fought the urge to remind Mumford of that fact. After a quick wipe of his lips with his jacket sleeve, he followed the senior partner upstairs to the third floor. To the holiest of holies. The "inner sanctum," or so the company's lower-ranking employees called it, was where the partners' board room was located.

Mr. Mumford opened the paneled door. "Wait in here. They'll be here momentarily. You are to sit at the chair in the middle," he instructed. "On this side of the table."

Curtis nodded, and thanked him.

"I wouldn't worry, Carlson. Good things come to those who are prepared," he said, closing the door behind him as he exited.

In the nearly three years he had worked there, Curtis had never been in the boardroom. And it was amazing. He stood quietly scanning the décor, the portraits, the furnishings. The expensive burlwood table must have been twenty-feet long. At the far end of the room hung a portrait of Mr. J. P. Morgan, Senior and father of the current Mr. Morgan. A smaller painting had been mounted a few feet away on the left side of the big window. Curtis recognized the subject as Junius Morgan, grandfather of the current head of the banking empire; the man who had begun the business decades earlier.

Curtis had only been with the company a few months when the elder J. P. Morgan had died in 1913 on a trip to Rome. The famous tycoon hadn't spent but a few brief days at 23 Wall Street before his death. Still, seeing Mr. Morgan, Sr's, portrait stirred Curtis' memories of seeing him stroll through the office in formal attire, donning a top hat and tails, with his ornate gold-crowned cane.

He didn't usually get nervous about things, but the wait was killing him. He stepped to the chair and lowered himself into his assigned seat, picked up his pencil and began to tap it on the table. Drawing in a long breath, he closed his eyes to compose himself.

Footsteps approached, accompanied by the low sound of men's voices. The door opened, and Curtis turned to see a group of stoic-faced men entering.

"Ah, good, Carlson. You're already here." It was Mr. Morgan, speaking as he walked past.

Curtis pushed back his chair and rose. "Yes, sir."

Mr. Morgan leaned his gold-topped cane against the Egyptian cabinet and took his seat at the head of the table. The seven partners selected other chairs surrounding Curtis.

Walking over to Mr. Morgan, Curtis reached out and shook his hand. As many times as he had seen Jack Morgan enter and exit the building, he had never spoken to him. "It's a pleasure to finally meet you in person, sir."

"Ah. A firm shake. I like those qualities in a young man. Shows confidence."

"Thank you, sir." Curtis held the famous man's gaze, determined not to blink or look away. Like his father, Mr. Morgan, Jr., was a celebrity. Mere mortals feared him. Peers revered him. Everyone else begged him for money. Curtis knew that both the senior and junior Morgans were known for their intimidating, piercing eyes; eyes exuding ferocity and a strength that sent a shiver clear to a person's soul.

Returning to his seat, he noted that the junior Morgan bore a striking physical resemblance to his late father. But it was more than the facial features, or so Curtis had been told. Both were relentless business geniuses, determined to get what they wanted. The Morgans gained strength and wealth with each new generation. J. P. Morgan, Jr., was every bit as infamous, loved and hated, feared, reviled and esteemed as his father had been.

Shifting in his chair, Mr. Morgan scanned the stack of papers and then fanned them out on the boardroom table. "Ah, yes. You're a Harvard man, I see," he said, drumming his index finger on a typewritten page. "*Summa cum laude.* Master's degree in business. One of their first."

"Yes. One of the first in economics, actually," Curtis countered.

"In fact," Morgan said without lifting his gaze, "You taught economics as a professor at Harvard for more than a year before

8

being snatched up by Mr. Arnold and brought on board at Morgan and Company."

"Correct, sir." Curtis smiled in acknowledgement. Mr. Ernest H. Arnold, a bespectacled, older gentleman with a full gray beard, had been one of Mr. Morgan, Sr.'s, right-hand men, and a well-respected member of the two Morgans' inner circle for decades.

The tycoon looked up, his expression hinting at a smile. "Please stop with the 'sir,' Carlson. Call me Mr. Morgan. That will suffice for now. And when you become a partner, you may call me Jack." He cast a wide grin at Curtis, as if he were dangling a tantalizing carrot before a hungry horse.

"I look forward to that day, Mr. Morgan," was all he could think to say. He fought a smile, trying to look cool and calm.

Morgan continued, glancing back at the papers. "I see you sail. You are indeed a man after my own heart."

"Yes, I love to sail! Guess you could say it's my passion. In fact, my fraternity brothers used to tease me. They called the ocean 'my mistress,' since I seemed to spend more time with the sea than with actual ladies," Curtis said, his hearty laugh louder than he'd anticipated. "Truth be told, it's been a while since I've been out sailing. When I was a student at Harvard, I had access to the school's boats."

"Yes, very good." Morgan went back to the paperwork. "You were captain of the rowing team at Harvard. Lots of honors and trophies I would imagine." He glanced up at Curtis.

Looking into the dark eyes of the fabulously wealthy and world-famous John P. Morgan was indeed extremely intimidating. Unsure if it had been a question or an observation, Curtis responded with, "Several."

"Still rowing, are you?"

"Yes, indeed. I crew for the New York Athletic Club."

"Ah. So, that's how you keep in shape, then." Morgan lifted his heavy brows and smiled. "We bankers spend our days behind a desk. No time to do much else but make money."

Curtis cleared his throat, a ploy to pause while wondering why Mr. Morgan wanted to know about his workout routine, of all things. Was he criticizing him for maintaining his exercise regime? "I am here at my desk six days a week, and I row on Sundays, when I can."

"Rowing is all well and fine, son." He leaned his elbows on the edge of the table. "But I need another good man to crew on my yacht. I try to utilize the talent from within the ranks of my employees. We're entered in a big regatta race in July. I'll put you down to man the winches. Not too many athletes on my staff here."

Relieved that Morgan wasn't condemning him for not working all seven days, excited at the prospect of becoming one of the crew on the company yacht, he grinned. "Thank you, sir. That would be... incredible. I would be honored." So, Mr. Morgan wanted to see him about joining his crew. Not a raise in salary. Curtis tried to cover his disappointment. "Thank you, Mr. Morgan." He pushed back from the table and rose.

"Sit down, Carlson," Mr. Morgan said.

Puzzled, Curtis lowered himself back into the chair.

Mr. Morgan paused, leaning back casually. "About the thesis you wrote," he said, his attention and gaze once again shifting back to the papers. "I obtained a carbon copy of it. Read it yesterday. Cover to cover. Damned boring to the non-academic, I've got to say."

"Oh." Curtis swallowed, squirming uncomfortably in his chair. "Sorry, but—"

"No apologies, son. It was brilliant. Insightful. You actually predicted a war in Europe, didn't you?" He looked up, placing his left hand under his chin.

Still confused at where Morgan was going with this conversation, Curtis simply nodded.

"A war that would involve the whole of Europe and possibly beyond its borders," Mr. Morgan added. "That's what you wrote five years ago when you were a graduate student."

"Yes. Nearly six, now."

"Uh-huh." Mr. Morgan leaned forward, his eyes locked on Curtis. "You wrote that it would be a war which would require England to become involved." He turned several pages of the manuscript and was silent for a moment. "You also wrote the United States would ultimately enter the war." Momentarily glancing at Curtis, his gaze returned to the pages. "Yes, yes. Here it is. You even called it 'The Great War.' And that's what everyone is now calling it." Mr. Morgan drew in a breath, looking at Curtis with an inquisitive stare. "How in God's earth did you come up with this hypothesis, son?"

Slightly embarrassed by the questions, Curtis straightened, looking as confident and self-assured as he could. "You see, I simply analyzed the long-standing alliances, old and new treaties, allies and their enemies in the various European countries," he explained, glancing around the table. "Then I factored in each country's gross national products, their imports and exports, and their political loyalties and long-standing associations. Of course, there were variables, as I spell out in the thesis. Things like the bloodline connections in the royals who ruled many of the countries." He shrugged. "I believe the outcome was inevitable. Very basic," he added. "It was pretty clear to me."

"Amazing," Mr. Morgan said, shaking his head. "Clear to you, perhaps, but the so-called experts in these matters said no such thing." He leaned forward, his arms on the table with his hands fanned out. "About the only thing you missed predicting was that the Archduke and his charming wife would be assassinated."

Curtis shrugged again. "Well, sir. I suppose I would have needed a crystal ball to do that, I'm afraid," he said with a smile. "But I knew it would only take one major event to trigger a war. Sadly, it was the death of the Archduke and the Duchess Sophie."

"Unthinkable...." Mr. Arnold whispered.

"There were warning signs," Curtis said.

"Hindsight is always crystal clear," Morgan commented.

"Sadly, my thesis went into the library archives at Harvard," Curtis said with a small huff. "I didn't think anyone would ever read it. So, I must say I'm surprised and honored you did, Mr. Morgan."

Morgan sat back in his chair, his eyes still fixed on Curtis. "You're a brilliant young man, you know. I have Mr. Arnold here to thank for discovering your many talents." The man had come to Harvard and interrupted Curtis during a lecture to tell him that he wanted to hire him as his assistant at Morgan and Company.

"He's also writing a book about the financial Panic of 1907, Jack," Mr. Arnold said, sounding like a proud father. "Trying to analyze the events that caused it."

"Is that so? Then you know the role my father played in that fiasco," Morgan said to Curtis. It was more of a statement than a question.

"Yes, sir…I mean, Mr. Morgan. The deeper I've dug into my research, the more I respected your father's actions. I do believe he was responsible for saving the American economy at that time."

"He certainly thought so!" Morgan said with a laugh. "He was quite proud of himself, able to convince his cohorts to work with him to shore up the United States banking system."

"I was so proud to meet him when I first started working here. When he came back from a trip abroad back in 1912 – my first month at Morgan and Company – your father made it a point to introduce himself. It was a life-altering moment for me."

Morgan looked pleased. "When do you expect to have this book of yours finished?"

Curtis blinked, lifting his eyebrows. "I wish I knew! I don't have much time to work on it. Mostly in the evenings after I return from the office. But I hope I'll have it to the publisher by the end of the year."

"Excellent, Carlson. Excellent. I look forward to reading it."

"May I say, Mr. Morgan, my research about your company's actions in 1907 is what made me decide I wanted to work with you one day. I have such admiration and respect for your late father and you. And when Mr. Arnold recruited me to join the firm, I didn't give it a moment's thought. I'm truly privileged to be here with all of you."

Mr. Van Camp, sitting directly across the table from Curtis, interrupted. "My son, Rudolph, is writing a book about the economic situation in America. You might enjoy reading it, too, Jack. We should have it to the publisher in a few months."

"Yes, very good, Phineas. Let me know when it comes out." Mr. Morgan sounded as if he were brushing him off.

Mr. Van Camp, a noteworthy senior partner, was a burly man of about fifty. His neatly trimmed beard attempted to hide much of his ruddy cheeks and double chin.

Curtis had a low opinion of Rudy Van Camp, an egotistical, obnoxious young man who performed minor duties for his father and annoyed the few women working at the company, mostly scrub women and girls who ran errands. It seemed obvious Mr. Morgan wasn't too keen on Mr. Van Camp's son, either.

Mr. Arnold, as always, was Curtis' champion. "Did I mention that my boy, Carlson, here, was also the captain of the debate team in his senior year? The Dean of the Business Department had nothing but praise for the lad. Said he won more than one debate for Harvard, he did. Beat the pants off Yale, I was told."

"Well, gentlemen. Looks like Mr. Carlson can handle it," Mr. Morgan said, glancing around the table.

In near unison, the partners expressed their agreement with grumbled "here-here's." Except Mr. Van Camp, who leaned back in his chair, arms folded across his chest.

Curtis asked, "Handle what?"

Mr. Whitney, one of the younger senior members, sat on the other side of the table. "There's to be a discussion...a sort of debate about the war at Columbia University in a few weeks," he said. "A government man, a Mr. Green, will be speaking on behalf of President Wilson regarding his neutrality position, and we want you to take the opposite point of view. To speak about why the U. S. of A. should help our business associates and friends in Great Britain and France. You see, we here at Morgan and Company believe that without American intervention, we may permanently lose our French and British allies, if those damnable Huns win this fiasco. Sounds like it would be right up your alley, Carlson."

Things moved quickly now. Several of the partners muttered their opinions in a chaotic sequence. Curtis looked from one to the other, not knowing what to say.

"The German Embassy in Washington, D.C. is making noise about sending their own representative," Mr. Burns, a partner who had been quiet during the meeting, growled loudly.

"We haven't confirmed that," Van Camp bellowed.

Ignoring Van Camp, Burns continued, "Carlson would have to go head to head with him on the German issue."

Mr. Whitney asked, "Do you think you can handle it, Carlson?"

It was suddenly quiet again.

"I...I," Curtis stammered, still trying to sort it all out. "This is certainly unexpected."

"As you know, Carlson, House of Morgan has offices in both England and France," Mr. Leighton, the youngest partner, interrupted. "It's crucial we convince the young men of America it's in the best interest of the United States to join in the fight."

"Hell, not just the United States," Mr. Morgan stated.

"Indeed, Jack!" Mr. Leighton slammed his fist on the table. "It's crucial to the entire world that Germany and its allies be defeated. We'll begin with the young men at Columbia University to make the case for America entering the war as soon as possible."

Mr. Morgan chimed in. "We need someone young. Someone who is a good orator. Someone who can address the hundreds of young men of Columbia University and convince them to speak out against neutrality." All eyes were on Curtis. "We all agreed that a learned university man would have a handle on speaking to the youthful minds." Mr. Morgan leaned forward. "Can you do it, son?"

Before Curtis could answer, Mr. Van Camp spoke up. "If he's not in agreement, Jack, I still believe Rudy can handle this. He's an expert on the matter. And he's been with this company far longer than Mr. Carlson." Mr. Van Camp sounded very defensive. Too insistent.

Waving his hand in a dismissive motion, Mr. Morgan exhaled a slow breath and frowned. "Yes, yes, Van Camp. I know your boy wants to excel here. But in my opinion, in all of our opinions, Carlson, here, is better qualified. Plus...and please don't take this personally, but Mr. Carlson makes a better-looking Morgan representative. He's young, handsome, and possesses oratorical skills. We have already decided to offer him this opportunity."

"As you wish, Jack." Mr. Van Camp's face flushed, his voice filled with anger.

Curtis hated being put in the middle like this. And this was an awkward moment, to be sure. He looked back and forth between the two men. "And a fine opportunity it is, Mr. Morgan," he managed to say, his mind whirling.

Mr. Morgan turned to Curtis. "Well, son. Let's hear what you have to say."

With that, the room fell uncomfortably silent. Again, all eyes were on Curtis.

He swallowed hard and drew in a breath. "First of all, let me say that I'm sorry, Mr. Van Camp. I certainly don't mean to cause you or your son any grief." Curtis knew that having enemies at this level would eventually backfire, and that was the last thing he wanted. "I have already formed my opinion about the war overseas." Curtis moved his gaze back to Mr. Morgan. "So, yes, I would be honored to represent Morgan and Company in this debate. I share your reasons for wishing America to enter the war. And I am confident that I can represent both of our interests…my own, and the best interests of Morgan and Company."

Mr. Morgan sat back in his chair and smiled. "Excellent…only, you will be speaking not as an employee of Morgan and Company, but as a professor at Harvard," he said casually. "A professor who is an expert on financial matters. And an author who literally predicted this abominable war."

"What?" Curtis was taken aback. "An author and a professor? But, I'm no longer a professor, and my book isn't yet completed."

"An author, nevertheless, Carlson. Your thesis is with my publisher at this very moment being set into type. It should be available for sale in bookstores quite soon."

Curtis was surprised. "Well, well! I don't quite know what to say. That's wonderful news, Mr. Morgan. Thank you so much. But I'm afraid I still don't understand. Why must I represent myself as a professor and not your employee?"

Mr. Morgan leaned back. "Now, here's the way we want you to handle this. We don't want our company involved. It would make tongues wag and newspaper reporters salivate at the thought of knowing this company was involved in promoting the United States' participation in the war."

"But how can I—?"

"You will tell them you're a college professor. At Harvard." He pulled a thick cigar from his coat pocket and tapped it on the table. "I've arranged it so that no one will be the wiser. They will believe that you still teach at our alma mater. Can you handle it?" he asked.

Chapter 2

March 2, 1915

IT WAS HARD for Josette to believe her childhood friend, Julian Laurent, was dead. Sitting in St. Patrick's Cathedral where Julian would be eulogized during the morning Mass, his death finally seemed real. His parents received the devastating news in February. Thousands of Allied soldiers had died that day. There was no way to send their bodies home or to bury them individually. Instead, a deep trench – a common grave – had been dug near the battlefield. Mr. and Mrs. Laurent brought a portrait of their son to the service – it had been painted after his graduation from Harvard. It rested on an easel near the stairs that led to the altar.

The morning air was heavy with an icy chill that crept clear to her bones. Shivering, Josette buttoned the top button of her coat. The fact that St. Patrick's Cathedral was a cavernous edifice of stone and marble and stained-glass windows didn't help, either. This was the first Mass of the day, and at seven a.m., the heating system, such as it was, hadn't yet warmed the interior of the massive structure.

Josette, her twin sister, Yvette, and their mother sat in a pew located at the far-left side of the crowded cathedral. They wore their warmest black mourning attire. Mother, always dressed as if she was off to the opera, had selected her black ensemble trimmed with white rabbit fur. Her hat had an over-sized brim and was covered with fake flowers and netting that hung to the level of her brows. Mother always dressed to impress. But then, that was Mother.

Speaking in monotone Latin, Bishop Hayes, wearing a beautiful long purple robe, struck a commanding figure. "*Sanctus, sanctus, sanctus,*" he said, interrupting Josette's thoughts. He stood beneath the large golden cross, his back to the parishioners. After making the sign of the cross, he steepled his hands at chest height.

Looking around the massive interior, Josette noticed that the early morning light beamed a rainbow of colors through the stained-glass windows, scattering a diffused glow over the nave and rows of pews. This was one of the holiest times of the year in the Catholic faith. The weeks of Lent were underway and, as such, the edifice was made even more beautiful by the addition of silky, royal purple fabric draped across the statues and crucifixes.

Wearing a serene smile, the Bishop began to speak the special eulogy prayer in English. "Many of us have gathered here in the light of God, the Holy Mother, and our Lord and Savior, Jesus Christ, to pay homage to one of our parishioners, Julian James Laurent. He was baptized in this church and served the Lord as one of our very special altar boys. We are honored to have Mr. and Mrs. John Laurent, his parents, here worshipping with us today." He paused, nodding to Julian's family seated in the front center row.

Bishop Hayes continued. "Let me open with a passage from Ecclesiastics 44, Verse 9. 'And some there be, which have no memorial, who are perished, as though they had never been; and are become as though they had never been born.'" He paused, his gentle gaze clearly locked on Mr. and Mrs. Laurent. "Though Julian's earthly remains rest with his fellow soldiers in a field in France, you can be sure he is with God. Lo, they are all with God." He raised his arms, looking to heaven. "'And their bodies are buried in peace; but their name liveth evermore.' They may be gone, these young brave men, but they will never be forgotten. And now, let us pray."

Josette hadn't seen much of Julian since he was sent away to boarding school as a teenager. And then, he had gone on to Harvard University. Glancing at his portrait again, Josette's eyes welled with tears. She opened her purse, retrieved a handkerchief, and dabbed away the moisture from her cheeks. Julian's parents had begged him not to sign up as a soldier with the British army. Mrs. Laurent said that when Julian read the newspaper accounts of how the German army had marched across Belgium, a neutral country, and laid waste to its capital, murdering innocent citizens and poisoning wells in the process, it had been the last straw for the conscientious young man.

Heavy footsteps echoed on the cold, marble floor, snapping her out of her reverie. She turned as a man wearing a long, brown coat walked by. Without so much as a glance at her, he stopped at the end of the next pew. Balding, with a thin fringe of very dark hair around the bottom of his head, he carried a huge cigar with a glowing end in his right hand. No one dared to smoke inside the cathedral. Everyone knew that. Josette was shocked.

The odd man stood there silently without genuflecting – obviously not a Catholic – and then settled in the empty spot in front of her. Surprised at his strange behavior, at the fact he was smoking a cigar, Josette stuffed her handkerchief back into her purse, snapped it closed and tapped him on the shoulder. He half-turned to look at her.

"Excuse me, sir," she whispered. "You need to snuff out your cigar."

With that, he twisted completely around and shot a foul glower at her, his eyes filled with hatred. A tingle crawled up her spine, and she drew back. She was sorry she had said anything. Those eyes. Dark. Cold. So angry. Then he turned forward again.

"How dreadful!" The words slipped out of her mouth. Josette scooted to the right, as far away from him as she could, so that her body was close to her sister's. Yvette's head was lowered in prayer. Josette tapped her on the arm, glancing at the ill-mannered lout. "Can you believe it?" she whispered to Yvette from the corner of her mouth, her gaze still locked on the back of the man's hatless head.

Yvette looked puzzled. "What in the world is going on?" she said in such a low tone, her words were barely audible.

Widening her eyes, Josette said, "He's smoking!"

Yvette drew back. "What? Oh, my heavens!" she said softly.

"Shhh," Their mother mouthed with an angry expression.

Josette and her sister pressed back in their seats. A thought ran through Josette's mind. If the man wasn't a Catholic, then he must have been a friend of Julian's. That seemed highly unlikely to her, since he was rude, disrespectful of being inside a church. And looked at least forty. Julian was in his late twenties, for heaven's sake.

She heard more footsteps approaching. Another man passed, pausing in the aisle beside the pew where the first man sat. Italians, she surmised, noting their coloring and features. This one, likely in his late twenties, had a full head of curly, coal-black hair and long sideburns. And then she noticed that he, too, carried a lighted cigar.

Josette let out a gasp. She and Yvette exchanged confused glances. Before Josette could say anything to the newly arrived Italian about the matter of smoking, the bell sounded signaling the worshippers to kneel again. Both Mother and Yvette went back to the kneeler. But not Josette. Instead, she watched as the seated man motioned to the younger man, indicating he should continue walking towards the front of the cathedral. With that, he ambled forward slowly, stopped, crossed himself and kneeled to pray near one of the enormous stone pillars at the front of the sanctuary. But why there? In the walkway? Why didn't he slide into one of the empty pews?

Josette scooted left, back to the end of the seat, stretching her upper body into the aisle to see what he did next.

The Italian who knelt in prayer wore a long, black, split-back woolen coat. It had frayed elbows and looked as if it had faded several shades. Something, a large lump, seemed to make his coat pocket jut out.

The scrub woman, who had been cleaning the vestibule area when they entered the cathedral earlier, moved in Josette's direction. She dusted a window sill, the gate across the aisle, a pillar base, and then strolled over to wipe the carved end of Josette's pew. The woman smiled.

Josette forced a smile in return. The poor young dear was certainly homely—a large nose, rutted skin covered by a thick layer of caked powder, and bright red lipstick. And then a second cleaning woman appeared. Even more unattractive, she wore baggy clothes and had her faded red hair plaited into a long braid that hung down her back. The two scrub women exchanged knowing glances.

It was all so strange. Why were they cleaning while a Mass was underway?

Still holding his cigar, the unpleasant man in front of Josette rose, stepped into the aisle, pushed past the cleaning ladies, and bolted up the aisle. The shorter of the two cleaning ladies lifted her skirt, exposing a man's laced shoes, and scurried after him.

Flabbergasted, Josette watched as the red-haired woman dashed down the aisle. In an abrupt move, the kneeling man reached inside his coat and pulled out a good-sized, strange-looking object bound with what looked like copper wire. Placing it on the floor against the marble pillar, he touched the glowing tip of his cigar to a thick cord protruding from the object. It only took a few seconds for the cord to ignite. He got to his feet just as the cleaning lady arrived and grabbed his shoulders. The pair struggled. The Italian pulled himself free and sprinted for the aisle. It was obvious the cleaning lady wasn't a woman, but a man dressed in woman's attire. He dove for the fleeing man, wrestling him to the floor.

The shock of what was happening swept through Josette's body like a lightning bolt. "It's a bomb!" she said in a near shout, as she got to her feet.

Yvette and Mother looked up with terrified expressions.

"Quick! Run!" Josette said.

Without responding, Yvette and their mother were beside Josette, pushing their way up the aisle with the other parishioners from nearby pews who had seen the commotion. The elderly, bespectacled usher who had guided them to their seats that morning, bolted past, sprinting in the direction of the explosives.

Josette glanced back just in time to see the usher's gray wig fall to the floor as he leaped on the lighted explosives.

STANDING OUTSIDE the cathedral's front entrance with dozens of parishioners who had escaped during the turmoil, it seemed quite strange to Josette that there were still hundreds of worshippers inside and that the Mass had continued.

Nearby, a rotund woman sat on the top step sobbing loudly, face buried in her hands. Her husband stood over her, trying to calm his wife. No one in the crowd seemed to know what to do next. Their faces reflected confusion, fear.

Yvette was visibly shaken. "Why? Why did they want to blow up the cathedral?" she asked Josette. "They could have killed all of us."

Josette shook her head and exhaled a breath. "I don't know, Yvette. I just don't know."

Mother looked dazed. Yvette slid her arm around their mother's shoulders. "It's all over now. Everything is fine."

"As Father would say, 'the plot was foiled,'" Josette said, attempting to lighten the moment. Yet, she knew if the bomb had exploded, the big support column would have been seriously damaged. It probably would have toppled over, bringing down part of the roof onto the worshippers below – hundreds of innocent men, women and children could have been killed.

Who were these terrible men, and why were they so calloused, so angry...such cold-blooded killers? Josette wondered. Where could anyone go these days to stay out of harm's way? Even churches were no longer safe. A sense of anger, of sudden determination rose from deep inside her. "You stay here with Mother," Josette instructed her sister. "I'll be right back."

Josette approached a nearby police officer who was speaking to a small group of people. "Pardon me, sir."

He excused himself and turned to face her. The clean-shaven young officer looked quite dashing in his crisp, dark-blue uniform. "Yes, miss? Are you and your family doing all right?"

"We're well, thank you. I have a question, however. Those cleaning ladies. And the usher. They were men, weren't they?" She already knew the answer.

"They was all New York Police Officers at their finest."

"And those men? The ones who attempted to blow up the church? Who were they?"

"The Department has been tracking them two Italians for quite a while. They're part of a group of anarchists based right here in the City."

"That's a chilling thought, sir," she said, drawing in a deep breath. "I read in the newspaper that they've been setting off bombs all over the country."

"I'm afraid it's true, miss. But we got the ones here in Manhattan dead to rights!"

"Well, then. Thank heavens for all of you brave men who risk your lives to keep us safe, and most especially the officers who kept those men from carrying out their deplorable plan."

The officer puffed out his chest like a rooster about to crow. "I'll pass that along to the men, miss. And don't you worry. Them Italians won't be planting no more bombs around here. They're handcuffed and on their way to Police Headquarters. You're safe and sound. You have the personal guarantee of Willie Crabtree, at your service."

"Pleased to meet you, Officer Crabtree," she said, politely bowing her chin. "I'm Josette Rogers, daughter of Henry Rogers. Would you please ask Captain Tunney to telephone my father at his office to tell him his family is doing well? It's my understanding that the captain and my father are acquaintances."

"Of course, Miss Rogers."

"One more question, if you don't mind, Officer Crabtree. Why do you think so many of the parishioners didn't evacuate the cathedral when we did?"

He shrugged. "I suppose since the ruckus was all the way over on the far west side of the cathedral where all of you was sitting, the folks all the way across on the other side just didn't hear nothing. St. Paddy's is like a gigantic cavern, isn't it now?"

"Yes, but—"

"If you'll excuse me, I've got to get going. I'll be sure to give your message to Captain Tunney." With a tug on the cap's brim, he descended the stairs to a waiting police vehicle.

Josette stepped back to where Yvette and their mother waited.

"*Mon Dieu, Mon Dieu!* Mother muttered. We forgot communion." She blinked several times, looking like a confused child. "We should go back inside, *n'est pas*? To finish."

"Let's go home," Yvette said, taking their mother's hand. "Come with me."

"I'll hail a taxi. Mr. Herrmann wouldn't be here with the car to pick us up for quite a while," Josette said.

The threesome made their way to the curb in front of the grand cathedral. The police cars were gone. The sidewalk that had been roped off to the public was now open. The ever-present throngs of pedestrians pushed their way along Fifth Avenue at a hurried pace, late for this or that, as if nothing had happened. Life, it seemed, had already returned to normal.

And yet, as she and her sister helped their mother into the back seat of the taxi, Josette knew it might be a long time before life in New York City would truly be normal again. Too many men were unemployed. People, and especially the immigrants, were starving. According to the *New York Times*, Italian anarchists had turned their anger towards Catholic churches; a gruesome way to express their bitterness against the wealth of the Catholic hierarchy. The church's wealth, the anarchists believed, should be used to feed the poor. Josette could sympathize with their argument, but not the violence that had followed their protests.

On top of that, the war overseas had already claimed the lives of a generation of young men not only from England, France and Russia. The Germans and their allied countries were suffering greatly as well. Rumors of German spies swirled everywhere. The United States, the world, everything was in turmoil.

At that moment, Josette set her mind to help with efforts to keep America from becoming involved in what was now being called, "The Great War." But what could she, a woman who hadn't quite yet reached the age of majority, hope to do?

Chapter 3

STUDENTS JAMMED the auditorium at Columbia University's Horace Mann Hall, filling it to capacity. Curtis sat on the front portion of the stage between Dr. Taft, the Dean of Columbia's Business Department, and Mr. Frederick Beck, a highly connected official with the German Embassy in Washington, D.C. A half-dozen glaring light bulbs cupped in tin reflectors were situated along the foot of the stage.

Squinting, Curtis raised his hand to block out the brightness. As he scanned the audience, he noticed the outline of a large hat. A woman's hat. "Hmm," he said softly. Straining to see, he noted a group of one, two, three…Curtis counted six young ladies sitting quietly about a third of the way back from the front row of seats. *Most unexpected*, he thought. Columbia, after all, was a men's-only college.

Overshadowed by a group of rowdy boys wearing their white sweaters emblazoned with a large sky-blue letter "C," the young ladies looked as out of place as roses in a field of wild grasses.

At the front of the stage was a chest-high table pushed flush against the lectern. An oddly shaped machine that looked something like a large, open-sided box filled with glass radio tubes sat on top. Curtis had read about these new sound magnifiers but had never seen one. A tangle of wires traveled from the contraption to the side of the stage, disappearing behind a curtain where it was purportedly attached to an electrical outlet. Curtis and Mr. Beck had been instructed to speak directly into the strange machine's big reflector. The device would amplify their voice and send it through a loud speaker so that the audience could hear more easily. An amazing device, Curtis believed, though he had no need for help projecting his voice.

At precisely ten o'clock, Dr. Taft walked to the lectern, decorated on the front panel with Columbia's logo. He leaned close to the voice transmitter, nearly touching his lips to the inverted, dish-shaped gadget. "Please, lads. Seat yourselves," he shouted. There was a loud screech, followed by a crackling noise. A puff of smoke shot out from the equipment and the tubes went dark. All was silent.

Curtis fought back a smile.

"Oh, dear," Dr. Taft said, a shocked look on his face as he stared at the strange equipment. "I suppose this new-fangled contraption has died on us!" This brought about a round of hearty laughter from the boys.

A young man emerged from the darkness just off stage, rushing to peruse the state of the equipment. He moved this and that, bent over and removed a tube, then turned to Dr. Taft with a frown and shook his head.

The dean nodded his understanding, and then cupped his hands around his mouth and yelled out, "Well, there you go, gents. Good riddance to such contrivances, if you ask me."

Carefully removing the transmitting dish from the lectern, the stagehand placed it on the side-table and scurried away.

Curtis was especially thankful he had learned the art of oration at Harvard years ago. Projecting one's voice clear to the back of the room, no matter how large it was, took practice. As a Harvard professor and popular lecturer, Curtis had plenty of experience with public speaking. If anything, this would work to his advantage. Having spoken to Mr. Beck a short time ago, he doubted the German would have the strength of voice he had…not to mention that the man's thick accent would make him difficult to understand, even if he hollered through a megaphone.

Dr. Taft picked up the megaphone resting on a small shelf beneath the lectern and continued. "So. Here we are, then. Without further delay, let us show our guest lecturers our appreciation for their attendance here today." Introducing Curtis and then Mr. Beck, there was hearty applause.

As the auditorium quieted, the dean went on. "Unfortunately," he said, dropping his voice to a less enthusiastic tone, "you are likely aware by now that President Wilson's representative, Mr. Theodore J. Jones, is unable to join us today. I received a letter from his office yesterday, delivering his apologies. He did ask me to read a statement, however."

Dr. Taft set the megaphone down, pulled a neatly folded paper from his coat pocket, smoothing it on top of the lectern with the back of his hand, and then picked up the megaphone again. Looking through the wire-framed glasses resting on the tip of his thin nose, he read:

"Gentlemen of this noble institution, Columbia University. You are among America's finest, best educated young men, and, as such, I had hoped to address you personally today. My apologies to each of you. My duties to our President have kept me in Washington. President Wilson continues in his ever-vigilant campaign to keep our country neutral in the melee occurring at this very moment in the countryside of Europe. Sad, to be sure. And yet, President Wilson has stated repeatedly that the war overseas is just that. It is in Europe. It is not a fight that involves America. To involve the United States in a European war would make no sense whatsoever. Too many of us have cultural ties to the very countries which are fighting each other. Were we to join the Allied troops, our Prussian citizens would feel betrayed. Were we to fight with the Central Powers, we would alienate our close allies in France and Britain. The President has promised that he will not involve this country in a fight that does not involve America's best interests."

Even as Dr. Taft read those words, Curtis felt his jaw clenching. President Wilson was wrong, and it was up to him to counter the comments made by Wilson and his no-show lackey, Theodore Jackass Jones, a name given to him because of his lack-luster performance as an insignificant member of the President's cabinet.

More interesting was that there was little reaction from the members of the audience. No applause, none of the hooting one would normally hear at any kind of political speech delivered at a university of young, opinionated men. Curtis wondered if the men of Columbia were unhappy with President Wilson's policies that had been parroted in Mr. Jones' letter.

"In closing," Taft went on, *"We in Washington, D.C. know that many of you will soon graduate and make your way into the world of business, politics, and other noteworthy professions. The President wishes each of you the best of luck in your chosen fields and wants you to know he has your best interests at heart. God bless you, and God bless America. Thank you."*

An underwhelming applause came from the audience, though the ladies jumped to their feet, seemingly making their best attempt at an affirmative reaction to Mr. Jones's written statements. Laughter erupted from the gents, who obviously found the young women's not-so-thunderous, gloved-hand clapping amusing. The ladies, suddenly aware that all eyes were on them, slid down into their seats again, folding hands in their laps.

Things quickly wound down from a roar to a few coughs interrupting the hush that fell over the auditorium.

It was Curtis' turn to speak. It was up to him to win over the students to his side—an easy task, he surmised, after that half-baked statement sent by Wilson's representative.

Still standing at the lectern, Dr. Taft introduced Curtis as a quintessential expert on the American economy "in its present state." Curtis wished the man had left that last bit out. It wasn't really what he would be discussing. He rose from his chair and shook the department head's hand while the applause died down. He gathered a deep breath, lifted his chin and began.

"Good morning, gentlemen and ladies. First, let me say how honored I am to be here at Columbia University. And most especially, to be in the presence of such prestigious company." He bowed his head in Mr. Beck's direction, an insincere gesture to be sure, since Curtis had every intention of discrediting the German official, as well as President Wilson.

"And to you, sir," Beck responded. The German official was a thick man with a thick neck, dark brown hair, and a full mustache that curled up on the ends. He dipped his head courteously and smiled back at Curtis, displaying an annoying, more-than-obvious air of confidence.

Curtis couldn't understand how anyone could logically defend what the German army was doing in Europe. The latest reports exposed the German's use of chemical warfare to cruelly wipe out both soldiers and civilians. And it was obvious to most people the Germans were already waging secret attacks on U. S. soil. Rumors swirled that German spies had infiltrated even the highest levels of business and U. S. governmental agencies. Plots had been foiled. Germans, even a few born on U. S. soil, had been arrested.

"Thank you, Mr. Beck," Curtis said as sincerely as possible.

Nor would it be difficult to shoot down Mr. Jones's statements. Many people had already challenged the President for his supposed neutrality position, protesting his willingness to sell American weapons and war-related products to the Allied forces.

That was one of the points Mr. Beck would make in defense of Germany and its political allies. Beck would attempt to explain the reasons for Germany perpetuating this heinous war. Hatred for the Germans had already begun all over America. Hell, the New York Police Department had formed task forces to investigate and prevent potential violence from being carried out by men and women loyal to the German Fatherland.Curtis smiled. Oh, yes. Fueling the anti-Germany fire today would be an easy challenge. This would be an interesting, effortless debate, though it had been touted as a discussion rather than a heated argument between men who didn't officially represent their opposing governments. Instead, Curtis and Beck were both learned scholars; experts on the socio-economic history of the countries involved in the fighting.

"I know there are many people in the United States," Curtis began, "and indeed in this very room, who believe we should remain neutral in this, the worst of all wars the world has ever experienced." Curtis spoke in an even tone. "I admit it. I am here today to influence you lads. You are indeed some of the brightest and best New York...nay, the country, has to offer. You are the next generation of businessmen and politicians and lawyers who could make a tremendous difference in the direction the world will take in the future; things like whether or not circumstances warrant going to war. And, it is lads like you who will determine which side our boys will fight for. I am here today to convince you that the United States should change its neutral position and choose a side. The side of right. The side of justice and freedom. The side of Great Britain and its allied nations."

Applause erupted, accompanied by cheers. There were also boos, though those voices were overpowered by the louder boys.

He glanced at the German official again and then turned back to the audience motioning them to quiet down. "Of course, Mr. Beck, here, has the very same intention: to convince those in attendance that the Central powers are fighting a right and just cause. But gentlemen...and you ladies, too," he said, moving his gaze in the women's direction. "I am here to convince you—no, to explain to you—why this would be a mistake of disastrous consequences." This statement brought about a rather noisy stirring in the audience.

One of the tricks Curtis had adopted years ago, whether he was in a classroom or in a large auditorium, was making eye contact with his audience. "Could you please turn on all the lights in the hall?" he instructed.

As the overhead chandeliers lighted the entire room, Curtis smiled broadly, moving his gaze from one side of the room to the other. "That's more like it! Now I can duck if some disgruntled gent decides to throw a tomato at me!"

There was a roar of laughter and even applause.

Curtis looked in the direction of the young ladies. Several who had worn large hats had removed them and placed them on their laps, likely out of courtesy for those sitting behind them. These days, women's hats were often atrociously large, a concoction of fluff, feathers and ribbons. Ridiculous chapeaus, in his opinion. He was glad they had been removed.

Fighting back a smile, he cleared his throat, and continued. "I know, I know," he said. "Proposing that America enter the war is not a popular thing to say, but it's high time you all hear the truth from someone who doesn't have an economic interest in this war. I believe that once I am finished, you will have changed your minds." Curtis turned to face the other two men, still seated. "Even you gentlemen may be surprised at what I have to say. And if I do not convince you of the fact that the best thing for this country would be to enter the war and back the side of the Allied powers of Great Britain and France, I will not only eat my hat, sirs, but I will devour those lovely ladies' chapeaus, as well! Yes, and that includes the feathers!"

While his comments brought about riotous laughter from the young men, the ladies looked put-off.

Curtis had kept his bowler hat on. Removing it, he set it on the lectern. "I'll leave this here for now. I don't know, though," he continued in a casual tone. "I'm told Mr. Beck is quite a convincing speaker. He's likely thinking that I'll have to learn to like the taste of felt and straw, since he's probably pretty sure he can swing you over to his side." Curtis picked up his hat, opened his mouth and put the rim between his teeth.

The audience laughed and clapped again. Curtis turned to see Mr. Beck's look of disapproval. Removing the hat from his mouth, he placed it back on the lectern.

Curtis grinned. "I don't know, fellows. I'll leave it up to you. When we have both spoken, I'll ask your opinion. Agreed?"

Following several loud shout-outs and more laughs, Curtis nodded. "Thank you," he said. "I'll do my best to convince you. So, then, let's get started. I know what I'm going to tell you is the exact opposite of what you've been reading in the newspapers. And I know that some of our politicians, and most especially the president, do not want you to hear what I have to say."

Curtis raised his voice for emphasis, the way his oratory teacher had taught him to do when trying to make an important point. "But hear this you must, or we Americans and our great nation are doomed!" He raised his fist into the air, glancing out at the youthful faces, holding them with his words.

"Gentlemen…and ladies," he said with a wide smile. "We must not forget these lovely ladies. As part of the research for my masters' thesis at Harvard, I studied the events that led to the war in Europe. I believe I understand the events that occurred leading up to the war, as well as their ramifications." He paused for dramatic effect. "I am convinced that Americans need to speak out – nay, to insist that our government declare war on the enemies of our friends."

He began to move about the stage. "Here is the reality, gents." He stopped, making direct eye contact with one, then another, and another young man. "Shipping overseas to our economic markets has nearly ground to a halt. American goods were packed into merchant ships that have been sunk by Germany's military vessels or have mysteriously exploded and wound up…with their cargo and doomed crew…at the bottom of the ocean. Our business leaders are losing hundreds of thousands of dollars in exporting their goods to overseas markets. Receiving imported goods is nearly impossible, as you all may have noticed when you've tried to purchase Guinness or even French wine." He paused. "You are all of drinking age, right?"

There were a few chuckles and shouts from some of the college boys.

"But on a more serious note, lads, this has had a huge effect on Americans. One which will continue to worsen. Workers have been let go, small businesses have closed, and joblessness has grown to huge percentages. Outraged men who can't even feed their families have rebelled by planting bombs and staging all sorts of protests. And that's here in America. In our own backyards!"

He leaned forward placing his balled fist on the lectern. "In England, food rationing is an inevitable reality," he yelled, pounding the top of the lectern as he spoke.

Curtis turned to look at a red-faced Frederick Beck. "Now, I know Mr. Beck, here, is going to tell you that the German people are going hungry, too, but the British live on an island, for heaven's sake! Germany, Austria, and the like are surrounded by farmlands. Curtis stood straight again. "Do they not have more access to food and supplies than the poor British people, who are surrounded by the sea? A sea that is crawling with German submarines sitting in wait to sink any merchant ship they locate?"

Mr. Beck could no longer stay quiet. "The British have blockaded German ports!" he shouted, rising from his chair. "Women and children are starving!"

"Yes, Mr. Beck. You're right. And it's a pity anyone must go hungry because of German aggression. But it was they – you – who started this damned war!"

His statement stirred raw emotions, resulting in both applause and loud boos.

"If products don't get to Britain by ship, they don't get there at all. So, I ask you, gents," Curtis said. "Am I not correct? Are Great Britain and the people of Scotland and England and Ireland the true victims here?"

"Bloody right!" a lad cried out, jumping to his feet and raising his fist into the air. "My family is in the East End. Damned German buggers, I say. They can all starve and go to hell, as far as I'm concerned."

"Now, now. That's pretty extreme," Curtis countered. "Yet, for those of you who do not agree, I simply ask, where would you rather be?" He lifted his arms at his sides in a dramatic gesture, turning his palms face up. "On the continent, like Germany, surrounded by farmland and cities, or on an island, like the Brits?"

"That's not the point," Mr. Beck interjected. "Germany had no choice. We—"

"Please, sir," Curtis interrupted. "You will have your turn to speak in a few minutes."

"Yes, Mr. Beck," Dr. Taft agreed. "This is Mr. Carlson's time. You will have yours."

The German frowned, sat down, and folded his arms across his chest.

"How can we compare the British blockade to the Allied ships that have been pillaged and sunk by German battleships?" Curtis continued. "What about the mines the Germans have anchored in the English Channel, making it dangerous for all vessels, even ships from neutral countries like ours? Oh, and did I mention the mines continually break loose from their anchors in heavy seas?" He glanced over his shoulder at Mr. Beck.

Beck's lips were tightly pursed. His eyes narrowed.

"Unsuspecting neutral ships have been struck by wayward German mines. Good planning, Germany," he said with a laugh, shaking his head in mock disgust.

"That has only happened occasionally," Mr. Beck yelled. "And not intentionally!"

Curtis let out a huge sigh as he said, "Very well, Mr. Beck. I'll give you that one. I know your military didn't intend for their mines to float away willy nilly. And then there's the matter of your U-boats. They are the scourge of the sea. The devils of the deep. They sneak and prowl like invisible serpents, unleashing their torpedoes without warning. How many men have died because of these menaces?" After pausing for affect, he added, "Gentlemen…and ladies. How many more human lives will be lost before this disastrous war ends?"

After the applause settled down, one of the young women stood up and shouted. "So how can all of this be remedied by American boys fighting in a war which has little to do with them?"

Curtis peered out to the center of the auditorium. One of the girls was standing. She was the prettiest of the lot, from what he could see—petite in stature; hair the color of warm butterscotch that caught the light and glimmered here and there with a golden hue. And she wore a small, tasteful hat. She was truly a striking beauty. Not at all the type of girl he would have expected to be interested in such matters as business and war.

"That is a very big question for such a little lady, miss. And I intend to explain the situation, if I may continue."

His comment didn't sit well with her. Even from the stage, Curtis noted her frown. She continued, now shouting. "If you're going to tell these young men they should join the military forces and go off to fight a war in a place that's far away, you are very wrong, sir!" Even then, she was incredibly gorgeous, despite her defiant stance.

"Why don't you introduce yourself, miss?"

She cleared her throat, lifting her chin defiantly. "My name is Josette Rogers."

He held his hand to his ear. "Please speak up so we can all hear you." Truth be told, Curtis hoped this would make her nervous.

"We are all members of Barnard College's chapter of the Jane Addams Club," she said, sweeping her hand in the direction of her female compatriots.

"Ah, yes. Jane Addams. I have read a great deal about her work, and I do approve of her stand on giving women the right to vote. But we're not here to discuss the Suffrage Movement, Miss Rogers. What does that have to do with the issues we're discussing here today?"

"Everything, sir. Miss Addams is speaking out against the possibility of sending young American men into battle. I speak on her behalf."

Curtis rubbed his chin. "I see. The famous Jane Addams has sent you to represent her?"

The young lady shrugged. "Well, not exactly. She didn't send me. Well, not officially. But I convey her thoughts."

"And what exactly are her thoughts, Miss Rogers?"

"She strongly believes that America should remain neutral. Not only does Miss Addams believe if women had the vote, not just in the western states, but across the country; and more importantly, if women held political positions throughout the world, there would be no wars."

"No wars?" Curtis said with a broad grin. Try as he might, he couldn't help himself. "That sounds like a delightful utopian concept, Miss Rogers. Not reality." He chuckled. "My apologies, miss. There have always been wars. I doubt that having women voting would make much of a difference in that regard."

"Have you read about the horrific numbers of young men who have died on all sides in the battlefields of Europe?" She spoke loudly, directing her comments more to the audience than to Curtis. "There are already hundreds of thousands of men dead. God knows how many more were injured. Do you think that women…as mothers… would allow such things to occur? It's a moral issue, Mr. Carlson."

She was taking the topic to another place. He needed to get back on track. "I understand your position Miss Rogers. However, this is not the time nor the place to—"

"Tell me, sir. If you had your way…if Americans were to sign up for the military, why would the United States assist England and her Allies, rather than the Germans? Are we not a nation of immigrants? Are there not tens of thousands of Germans in this very city?"

Curtis cocked his head to one side, amused with her, but trying not to smile again. The girl was good. He'd give her that. "Yes, indeed we are. I believe at last count, one in ten Americans are of German heritage or origin. America represents the nations of the world. But let me, by a show of hands, ask the gentlemen of Columbia University how many of you are of French, English, Irish, Welsh, or Scottish ancestry?"

The majority of the students raised their hands immediately, accompanied by some grumbles. "I'm here from Australia," a fair-haired lad shouted. "We're Canadians," another called, pointing to the clean-shaven youths in his row.

Miss Rogers turned to the audience and yelled, "And how many of you have German or Austrian or Hungarian ancestors? Or, if you were born in Germany, or if your parents were, would you please stand up and identify yourselves?"

About thirty men, who were scattered around the room and seated in small clusters, rose. They looked surprisingly defiant. Backs straight, almost stiff, chins held high. One of them yelled at Curtis, "I agree with the young lady. Why should the United States only support the British and French? How is it fair and unbiased? Why is nothing being done to assist Germany or Austria?"

"He's right, don't you all see?" a young man with light brown hair shouted, looking around the room. "Everyone knows what's going on. Just look at how many confiscated German passenger and cargo ships sit abandoned on the Hudson River. They were seized by the American government. Captured."

"Not really captured," Curtis protested. As he said the words, Mr. Beck was suddenly by his side with the megaphone at his lips.

"Yes! You are correct! Captured! They are not allowed to return to their home ports. German sailors are stranded here, as are German passengers…with no way to get home. And no jobs here, either. Germany believes it's because American bankers and industrialists will make more money by throwing their support behind that damnable nation of tea drinkers."

"Tea drinkers?" a voice erupted from the back of the room. "The British Navy is the most powerful military force in the world!" he said with a thick English accent.

"The German military is far more competent," another light-haired man yelled back as he stood up. "And we drink beer, not tea!" The other German supporters shouted their agreement, fists in the air.

"Please, gentlemen." Curtis hollered, cupping his hands around his mouth to increase his volume. "Please! Be seated."

The German youths ignored Curtis. "We will fight for the Fatherland! America already fights for the British. Declare your war on us. Send money and supplies to Paris and London. We do not care! We will conquer America one way or the other!"

"No, no, my friends. We can support the Fatherland without wanting war against the United States!" Mr. Beck said, trying to calm the crowd. "What we want is financial support! We want horses and mules, like the American ranchers are sending to our enemies! And food! Our people must eat! Rich Americans are getting even richer off spilled German blood!"

"Please!" Curtis shouted. "Please. Let me speak. I will not deny that some industrialists in America are benefiting greatly by producing products for the war, like bullets and military uniforms. But other businesses are suffering. Even my parents' hardware store isn't doing well in these difficult times. Who out there hasn't heard about the protests and bombings by the anarchists? They are worried about people going hungry right here in New York City. We need to bring this heinous war to an end as soon as possible. And the only way to do that is with America's involvement."

"No war! No war!" Miss Rogers and the other ladies began to chant.

"Please, ladies! The British need our help!" Curtis yelled.

He was ignored.

Dr. Taft used the megaphone. "Quiet, please, ladies and most especially, you gentlemen. We are all men of Columbia University, for God's sake!"

The noise died down, just in time for Miss Rogers to yell, "This is directed to both of you gentlemen." She pointed her finger, aiming it at Curtis and then at Mr. Beck. "I want to know exactly what will happen if our nation participates in the war abroad? How will that help Americans? And how many of our own boys will have to die? Who, here...and I don't mean you Germans...is willing to go to France to fight? How many of you are willing to die for a cause that doesn't concern our country?"

"It does concern the United States, young lady," Mr. Beck said in a fit of anger. "It concerns all of you. Have you not listened?"

"Yes. Of course, we have been listening. And reading!" Miss Rogers responded, hands on her hips. And then she yelled, "No war!" The other girls joined in. "No war! No war!"

Dr. Taft bellowed. "Please, ladies. If you don't stop, we'll have to call security,"

"And what about Belgium?" A young man across the aisle on the row where the girls sat called out, jumping to his feet. "The Germans have killed my relatives back home in Antwerp! They have poisoned the water in our wells. America cannot stay neutral, you barbaric German bastards!" His gaze was locked on a mortified Mr. Beck.

"Bastards? You will show your respect, young man," Beck bellowed.

"Gentlemen of Columbia!" Curtis shouted, using the megaphone. "Please calm down."

Ignoring Curtis, the young Belgian leapt across the aisle and grabbed the German lad seated on the end of the row. Balling his fist, he swung hard, connecting with the German's jaw.

"Telephone the Police Department!" Dr. Taft instructed a stage hand.

The other German students were now out of their seats, rushing into the aisle in the direction of the Belgian. Then the students – the supporters of the British lads – joined in the growing skirmish.

Dr. Taft tried again. "Stop this! Gentlemen! This does not happen at Columbia!"

Five of the young ladies pushed their way through the erupting mayhem to escape on the aisle. But not Miss Rogers. Good grief. She was in the middle of the brawl. The foolish girl was standing her ground. Though Curtis couldn't hear her words, he could see her yelling at the boys. The Belgians exchanged punches with the Germans who had been seated on the same row as the young women. Miss Rogers yanked the back of the German's coat, attempting to pull him from the fighting.

Within minutes, the auditorium had erupted into chaos. Curtis could see that Miss Rogers was doing her best to help the Belgian… hitting one of the Germans with her handbag, attempting to squeeze her petite body between them. Long strands of her curls had come loose from their coif, flailing about like shiny ropes each time she took a swing at the German boy with her handbag.

Much to Curtis' amazement, she dropped her handbag and grabbed the German's arm with both hands. "Stop this!" She shouted so loud, he could hear her words. Worried she would be harmed, Curtis dashed towards the stairs leading from the stage to the auditorium floor.

The German stopped his attack on the Belgian and began shaking his arm, trying to free himself from Miss Rogers' clutch. He turned in a circle, swatting at her as if she were an annoying gnat. Then, before Curtis could get to her, the pretty little gal disappeared from view, likely landing in a heap among the seats.

Chapter 4

THE RIDE TO the local precinct office was unbearable. Josette sat crammed side by side on a hard, wooden bench along with ten hooligans, the very same young men she tried to prevent from fighting one another in the auditorium.

Her shoulder throbbed, especially in the area that had struck an arm rest when she tumbled to the floor. She groaned, rubbing the tender area on the upper side of her left arm. Two of the American boys, neither of whom had been arrested, had helped her to her feet, just as a policeman grabbed her roughly by the right arm. Despite her protests, her attempts to explain that she was only trying to stop the fighting, the officer had tugged her outside and pushed her into the back of a police patrol wagon, as if she were some sort of thug.

Josette dared not make eye contact with the student whom she had hit repeatedly with her purse. She glanced at him from the corner of her eye. The right side of his face was the color of strawberries and a thread of blood had dried in the tiny slit on his lower lip. The sandy-haired German lad she had tried to stop glared at her. If he were a gentleman of any sort, he would have apologized for tossing her to the floor.

Closing her eyes, she drew in a deep breath. The windowless police patrol wagon was hot and stuffy, and several of her unwanted companions smelled of sweat mingled with cologne and hair pomade. Josette felt sick. Her nausea was made worse by the thought that her parents would be horribly upset with her for being arrested. Her thoughts swirled. What in the world would she tell them? What would her father do?

Thankfully, the bumpy, cramped, smelly ride ended a few minutes later. A *whoosh* of cool air greeted her face as she stepped down from the back door of the vehicle to the street. Steadying herself, she held her hat in one hand, and her handbag-turned-weapon in the other.

"Move along, missy," an impertinent police officer instructed with a harsh intonation.

Josette shot him an angry glance and *hmphed*. How dare he treat her like a common criminal? She lifted her chin as she walked past him and up the front steps.

The officer laughed. "Lookie at you, pretty lass. Here at police headquarters. That'll teach you to get into brawls, won't it, now?"

Exhaling an angry breath, she refused to let him rile her any further. At least, not visibly.

Things weren't much better when they were herded into the police station's processing area. Josette and the ten Columbia students remained seated while the officer behind the desk called on them, one by one, to fill out forms. And one by one, they were allowed to telephone their families to provide money to bail them out. For those whose families refused to pay the necessary amount due, the young man was led down a hallway where he was put in a jail cell.

"Excuse me," she called to the officer behind the desk. "I don't suppose I could get an ice bag for my injury."

"Not at all, missy," he said in a flat tone. "You'll have your turn to ask for favors and what not. In the meanwhile, stay seated and keep quiet."

She tried to hold back her anger. "I'm not a criminal, sir. You need not be so rude."

"I said to shut up little missy, or I'll take you to a cell right now!" The officer glared at her for a moment then went back to his paperwork.

Josette drew back. "Oh, my goodness," she whispered. She certainly wasn't used to being treated so harshly. She clutched her hat in her lap, leaning her head back on the wall. In the melee, not only had her hat pins loosened, but the curls that that had been piled high on the back of her head had been pulled free. Several large clumps of hair hung to her shoulders in an unkempt mess of tangles. *If only I could visit the ladies' room. If only I had a mirror*, she thought, wishing she could make herself look more presentable. She didn't dare ask if she could go. Not now. Not until there was someone besides that bully of an officer to talk to.

Josette sighed, closed her eyes, and tried to stay composed. To inhale deep, slow breaths. Minutes passed, and she was no more relaxed than she had been an hour ago in the back of the patrol wagon.

"Oh dear," she groaned softly. She never dreamed her beliefs would land her in jail. Her father would be furious. She caught a glimpse of someone to her left. A man. Tall, wide shoulders, dark wavy hair. He stood at the reception desk in the entry hall. "Oh no," she whispered, recognizing Mr. Carlson. *What in the world is he doing here?*

Professor Carlson spoke in a tone too low for her to hear. He turned, made eye contact with Josette, and nodded at her.

She turned her head away from him, drawing in a sharp breath. Was he there to bring more charges against her? Curiosity got the better of her. Josette moved her head the slightest bit to the left, straining to hear him. He was laughing. Actually laughing! She felt her insides twist. How dare he? What did he find so amusing about having her—or even these students—arrested?

"That terrible man has come to gloat," she declared out loud.

The student sitting next to her on the bench, a British lad, whispered, "He's the one I should have punched, miss. The bloke egged us on, he did."

Josette nodded her agreement, casting another glance in Mr. Carlson's direction. He trailed behind the policeman who headed her way.

"All right, Miss Rogers," the policeman said. "You are free to go. Mr. Carlson, here, has brought a letter from Columbia University. They have dropped the charges against you."

Her jaw slackened. "What? But...why?"

Mr. Carlson waited a moment then said, "Because I couldn't bear the thought of you spending even a minute incarcerated. Heaven knows the kind of women you might have been jailed with." He shook his head. "Besides, I owe you an apology. It was probably my fault as much as yours that things got out of hand."

"Ha!" Josette stood up, arms crossed in front of her. "The brawl wasn't my fault at all. You are the one who instigated the boys into a fight, not me."

He drew in a long, thoughtful breath. "Yes, yes. You are, indeed, correct. Not that Mr. Beck doesn't bear at least part of the blame." Mr. Carlson shrugged and headed towards the front door. "Come on, Miss Rogers. Let's get out of here."

He held the door open, smiling down at her as she passed. She didn't say a word as she stepped outside.

"All right," he said with a little chuckle, trailing behind her as she descended the steps. "I know you're angry. You've made that perfectly clear. But let's call it a draw."

She stopped when she reached the sidewalk and turned to face him. He was much taller than she had realized. Over six feet, quite tall compared to her five-feet, two inches without heeled shoes. Not that she minded being on the petite side. Looking up directly into his face, she tried to soften her expression. "Very well, Professor Carlson, though I certainly have not changed my mind about the matter. But I do thank you for stepping in and setting things right."

"Let me make something clear, Miss Rogers. I respect your opinion. And I truly have a great deal of respect for Miss Jane Addams' conviction regarding the war and the vote for women, too. She is a wonderful, intelligent and brave woman. But in matters of this war, there is a great deal you may not understand – ramifications on our economy that could be affected by the war's outcome for generations. I have studied it a great deal, Miss Rogers. I would be happy to meet with you personally to show you my findings."

Josette didn't know what to make of Mr. Carlson or his offer. "As you said, sir, I think it's best we call a truce and simply go our separate ways. But I do thank you for your fairness in this matter. Good day."

He reached up and tugged on the brim of his bowler cap in a show of respect. "Yes, ma'am. Whatever suits your fancy."

"Oh, by the way. I'm quite glad you didn't have to eat your hat, Mr. Carlson. Or mine, for that matter." She flashed him the hint of a smile, stepped over to the curb, and hailed a taxi.

JOSETTE DIDN'T get angry with her sister often, but this time, she was thoroughly annoyed and disappointed with her. She entered Yvette's bedroom without knocking.

"Where in the world were you today, sister?" Josette asked with an accentuated hiss.

Yvette sat at her dressing table poking a hair pin into a pile of curls. She glanced at Josette in the mirror, let out a gasp, and then twisted around. "My heavens!" Yvette's perfectly shaped eyebrows slid into a concerned "V." Standing up, she asked, "What happened to you? You look a frightful mess!"

Stopping beside her sister, hand on her hip, Josette continued. "Never mind! And don't change the subject! You promised to meet me at the university for the lecture. I was counting on you."

Yvette's expression reflected genuine concern. "I am sorry, Josette. I simply couldn't."

"What do you mean, you couldn't? Why not?"

Yvette dropped her gaze. "You know I'm not strong like you. Things like that make me terribly uncomfortable." She looked up. "I don't know how you do it. Why, the very thought of confronting all those men. Weren't you frightened?"

Josette clucked her tongue and shook her head. "Frightened? Good heavens! No." She stepped to the side of sister's bed and flopped down hard. "Besides, I had hoped you would support me in this matter."

"I do! I walked with you in the peace demonstration on Fifth Street last fall. I even helped paint the doves on the white flags we carried. I know it was a march for peace, but I hated the whole situation. Having people shout vile things at us and all. I don't want to do that sort of thing again."

Josette let out a long, slow sigh. "Your life is so, so comfortable, isn't it?" She scooted to the center of the bed, sitting on top of the huge embroidered crimson rose in the center. "You just don't live in the real world." Rubbing her sore shoulder, she let out a moan.

"Are you sure you're all right, Josette?"

"I'm fine," Josette said in a flat tone. She had no intention of sharing the details about the fight at Columbia.

Yvette was her twin, but their taste was as far apart as the sun and the moon. Yvette's bedroom was pink. Not just soft pink, but every imaginable variation of the color, from the boldest shade to the pearly pink hue of her dressing table and headboard. Even Yvette's rosary, draped across her dresser, was made of pink crystals.

"Why don't you take down your doll collection?" Josette said, glancing at the shelves on the wall. "Put them into the attic. We're grown women now, Yvette." Josette shook her head. "It's high time you grew up. You can't continue living in a world filled with such childish things. Just look around, sister. This room hasn't changed since you were a child. It's like you want your life to be… simple. Simple in a world that isn't simple. In a world that is filled with terrible things that need to be fixed. Don't you see? I want to do my part to help fix the broken world. Don't you?"

"My life isn't all that simple. It's just that my life is different from yours. I choose to live each day as if it were my last. I want to be happy. You, on the other hand, worry about everything."

"I do not!" Josette huffed.

"Oh, yes, you do. You worry all the time. It's like you only see the undesirable things in the world. I, on the other hand, choose to only see the good things."

"Oh, my heavens." That was Yvette, all right. She lived in a fairy tale. A romantic one at that. "It must be nice to be you. Life would be so much easier."

41

"You should try it sometime," Yvette said, sarcastically. "Just make up your mind to be happy. Tell yourself that everything will work out. It's very comforting."

Josette sighed in defeat. "You might not be so happy if you had a day like I just experienced." She decided to tell her sister what had happened that morning. The fight. The arrest. Mr. Carlson. It was impossible for her to keep secrets from her sister. She spoke quickly, spilling out the day's events.

"Thank the good Lord you weren't hurt," Yvette commented with a look of concern.

Josette shrugged, letting out a pained *yelp*. "I'm okay. I just hurt my shoulder a little. Actually, my biggest fear is that Father will find out."

"How could he?" Yvette stated firmly. "After all, you did say Mr. Carlson dropped the charges, so there should be no repercussions with the police. Although," she added, her face changing expression, "do you suppose that word could get back to the Dean at Barnard?" Yvette drew back with a gasp. "Oh, my goodness. Do you think they might penalize you in any way?" She stepped to the end of the bed. "Expel you, perhaps?"

"I thought you only saw good things in that fantasy world you live in," Josette grumbled.

"You don't think the newspapers will print a story about the brawl, do you?"

Josette hadn't thought of that. "I certainly hope not. I mean, you would think that Columbia wouldn't want that kind of publicity." She shrugged. "I don't know…unless Mr. Carlson or someone else gave a reporter an interview."

"From what you've said, he doesn't seem like the kind of man who would do that."

Josette pondered for a moment. "No. He doesn't. Or he wouldn't have felt remorseful about my near arrest. She sat up. "I just wish you had showed up."

"I'm truly sorry, Josette." Yvette stepped back to her dressing table. "But if I had gone all the way to Columbia University this morning, I would have missed my music classes. I spent two hours practicing for my lessons." She sat down on the stool and picked up a comb that sparkled with stones that complimented her butter-yellow afternoon gown.

"Oh, yes. We can't miss our piano classes, can we?" Josette said in a sardonic tone.

Yvette's back stiffened. She paused a moment before sliding the comb into a deep wave. "Not if I want to impress Jon with my progress. I'm working on one of Beethoven's most difficult pieces." She added, "It's nearly four o'clock. He will be here shortly." She twisted around. "There. Does my hair look all right, dear?"

Josette simply couldn't stay mad at her sister, a frail butterfly of a girl, and too much like their mother in so many regards.

"Yes, yes. You look lovely, though you might want to smudge a little rouge on those cheeks. They're white as those dolls of yours," Josette said with a snicker.

Yvette didn't respond, though she did let out an incensed groan .

Josette climbed off the bed. "Come to think of it, I'd better tidy up myself before mother gets home from her Bridge club."

"That would be wise." Yvette began to giggle. "You don't want mother to see you looking like that."

"Oh, dear," Josette said, glancing in the mirror.

"See?" Yvette said with a grin. "I told you so. Now, sit down and let me fix your hair."

THE THOUGHT of going back to the office made Curtis' stomach churn. Or was it because lunch time had been hours ago? Whatever in the hell it was, the acids burned, begging him to chew another chalky Diapepsin tablet. Since he had started working at Morgan and Company, he had grown accustomed to carrying a few indigestion tablets in his coat pocket in case of such an emergency. He wouldn't go back to work today. Christ. He needed a breather from it all. Not knowing how his superiors would react to the events that had taken place at Columbia University was too unsettling.

Curtis needed to walk. And he needed to eat. He stopped at Lesser's Deli, bought a pastrami sandwich, and headed to his favorite spot in Central Park. The place he always went when he needed to think. It was a considerable distance away, but on such a glorious afternoon, he preferred a long stroll to taking a taxi. The weather had been warm for the past few days, allowing flowers to blossom in the window boxes decorating the otherwise gloomy brownstone door stoops. As he moved through the streets, briefcase in one hand, lunch bag in the other, it felt as if the heaviness on his shoulders had already begun to ease.

Spring had come early, and the cherry trees clustered in Central Park had burst into bloom, showering pink petals across the ground like a velvet blanket. As a child, the part of the great park where the cherry trees were later planted had been his favorite place to play. His mother would spread out a wool plaid blanket for a picnic lunch. His mind flashed back to the countless times he chased ducks and ran from aggressive geese that squawked at him as if he were an intruder into their world of murky green ponds. Even today, as an adult, he loved this spot, where the tiniest whiff of cherry blossoms made him feel a sense of happiness and peace.

Brushing several wayward petals from the wooden seat, he settled himself onto the well-worn bench, opened the sack and unwrapped the neatly folded white paper containing his sandwich and Kosher pickle. Curtis fished into his vest pocket and retrieved his pearl-handled folding knife. He always carried it with him, a handy tool that had once belonged to his grandfather. He opened the blade and sliced the large dill pickle in half, wiped the juice off on the waxy paper, and then returned it to his pocket.

As he ate, his mind drifted to the incidents of the morning. To the so-called debate. It had all been so carefully planned and contrived, both by him and by his bosses at the office. What no one had counted on was the cheek of the young woman, Josette Rogers, who had deliberately disrupted things. Hammering a nail into her argument and making her look the fool was instinctual on his part. Going for the jugular had been his *modus operandi* while on the debate team at Harvard. His show-no-mercy strategy had worked well against Miss Rogers, too. He did feel a twinge of guilt, though. Young and inexperienced in these matters, she didn't have a chance against him.

Curtis caught a drop of gooey mustard that had wandered to the edge of the sandwich crust, licking it off his index finger. *Hmm. Miss Josette Rogers.* He couldn't help but smile when he thought back on the whole damned encounter. She couldn't have been more than nineteen or twenty. And yet, she had been so brave and bright, speaking out the way she did in a large crowd of men. That took a lot of courage.

With a shake of his head and a small grunt of displeasure, Curtis wished there had been a better way to handle Miss Rogers' comments. One thing was for certain. He wasn't proud of himself. But he had to do it, if he were to fulfill Mr. Morgan's expectations. If he had let her go on with her disrupting diatribe…well, it was over and done with, and the matter was ended. Thank God, she wasn't hurt badly, he thought with a slight bit of relief, a picture of her falling between the hard auditorium seats flashing into his mind.

There was no point of harboring guilt or of even thinking about her. One way or the other, it was finished, and he would never see her again.

Suddenly realizing that his stomach had tightened up, Curtis knew he had to take his mind off the whole damned thing. Drawing in a deep breath of fragrant air, he moved his gaze to the puffy clouds hovering overhead in the lupine blue sky. The gentle breeze seemed to pick up momentum, releasing loose petals from the maze of overhead branches. He smiled with contentment. They reminded him of snowflakes, drifting carelessly on the wind before settling across the paved walkways and bushes like a dusting of pink-tinted confectioners' sugar.

Taking a second calming breath, he crumpled up the sandwich wrapping and the bag, tossing them into the nearby trash barrel. Curtis opened his valise and retrieved a stack of papers. If he didn't go back to the office today, at least he could read through some of his work. One of the assignments he was working on with Mr. Arnold was a loan to a clothing company which had obtained a contract from the British government to supply military uniforms to their soldiers.

He licked his finger and thumbed through the typewritten pages, tilting his head to read his notes scrawled along the borders. There was still so much work to do before things could be finalized.

With a yawn, he stretched his back and neck. The paperwork was boring, though the results of his endeavors would work out well for everyone concerned. At a time when so many people had been jobless, the war overseas was certainly beginning to bolster the local economy.

He read...or tried to read. As the minutes passed, he found himself in a sleepy state of distraction. Nannies passed, pushing buggies with sleeping babies. Children ran and laughed, chasing ducks, geese, and assorted waterfowl the same way he had done as a boy. Curtis hadn't slept well last night. As much as he tried to deny it, even to himself, he had been a little apprehensive about the whole damned debate. It was all the lying that annoyed him.

Another yawn, and he fought to study the first page, reading and re-reading the same paragraph. When several wayward cherry petals settled on the documents, he smiled languidly and flicked the blossoms off with his middle finger and thumb...until his chin hit his chest and he realized he couldn't keep his eyes open. Returning the papers to his valise, he laid it beside him on the seat. Voluntarily letting his eyes close, he quickly dozed off.

Chapter 5

YVETTE ARCHED OVER the grand piano in the Music Room, practicing long runs up and down the keyboard. It was the only time she showed any strength of character, in Josette's opinion. When it came to her music, Yvette was as determined to master Beethoven and Bach as Josette was to finish her college degree. In fact, when Yvette was lost in her music like this, it was all Josette could do to keep from laughing at her sister. She looked positively theatrical, like a dramatic maestro. Her eyes were closed, her chin lifted, and her head bobbed and wagged to the rhythms. Not at all the dainty, soft spoken, all-too-proper young woman that was the usual Yvette.

Playing the same passage near the end of Beethoven's Fifth for what seemed like the hundredth time, Josette had finally had enough. "Please, Yvette. Stop! You've done it perfectly. Over and over again."

"To your untrained ear, perhaps." Yvette's voice bore a mocking tone. And then, she began to play the same passage again.

Sighing, Josette slouched back on the burgundy settee and groaned. "But must you play so loud?" she said, rubbing her temples. "My head still hurts."

"You know this is how I have to warm up," she answered continuing to pummel the keys. Yvette stopped and said with an unexpected firmness, "Please, Josette. Go back to your bedroom and rest. I think Mother has some headache powder in her bathroom cupboard." And then she was back to the keys with a renewed burst of enthusiasm.

"I've already taken it," Josette said, almost yelling. "I'm still waiting for the results. You know I would love to take my leave, but you also know Mother insists I stay here with you and Mr. Franklin lest you be unchaperoned."

Glancing over her shoulder, Yvette said, "That's terribly ridiculous and so old fashioned."

Josette grinned and shifted positions. "I do hope she won't make me take a piano lesson today. I still must study for my European history examination. It's first thing in the morning."

Again, Yvette stopped playing and twisted around to face Josette. "There's no reason for you to have a piano lesson when you're not interested in improving your playing skills beyond a beginning level. I say, go study, sister. Tend to your headache, or whatever else pleases you. And...I did speak with Mother on the matter before you came home. I do believe she may comply and let you stop taking piano lessons altogether."

"Well, well!" Josette leaned forward, resting her elbow on the settee's arm. "Clever girl. I suspect Mr. Franklin would prefer to be alone with you, too," she said in a lowered tone.

"Shush." Yvette turned to look through the open doorway. Then she moved her gaze back to Josette with a worried expression. "Mother might hear you. She can't know...."

"It just seems so silly to have to pretend not to have feelings for each other," Josette remarked. "After all, it's 1915, not 1815! Times have indeed changed. People from different social positions often marry. God knows Mother managed it when she married Father."

"You're absolutely right, sister. Unfortunately, that's the way it has to be for now." Yvette had stopped playing, her voice in a near whisper. "If Mother knew, it might just be the impetus for Father to dismiss Mr. Franklin. Please promise you won't say anything."

"Of course, I won't. Your secret is safe with me." Looking at the ornate Louis XIV clock on the mantle, Josette noted that was ten minutes after four. "It's not like Mr. Franklin to be late."

"It most certainly isn't. I'm sure he has a very good reason for his tardiness." Brows furrowed, Yvette looked at Josette with a worried expression. "I'm fearful Mr. Franklin will be the object of Mother's wrath. You know how she feels about punctuality."

"Stop worrying, silly goose," Josette said. "He will simply make up for the lost time. You'll see."

STARTLED AWAKE by the sound of a child's laughter, Curtis opened his eyes and sat up straight. As the sun had edged its way west, slivers of bright light filtered through the trees, making him feel a little too warm. Peeling off his woolen coat, he glanced at his wristwatch. It was already after four. Damn. He hadn't meant to spend so much time at the park. It was time to go home. Tomorrow would come too soon, and he would face the potential wrath of the senior partners, and possibly Mr. Morgan himself. For now, he would spend the rest of the day in his apartment working on his book.

On a normal day, Curtis walked home to his apartment in Greenwich. The day had already gone on too long, and he was anxious to escape to his own private sanctuary. He hailed a taxi.

Many of the old brownstones throughout Manhattan had been torn down and replaced with buildings that were as high as ten levels, thanks to the elevators that were widely available in the modern structures. That wasn't the case with Curtis' brick building. His apartment was a third-story walk-up with windows facing the Hudson River. It was a small sliver of a view, to be sure. At that, he had to crane his neck to see the greenish water from his big living room window or step onto the fire escape for a less obstructed look-see. Still, it was a view, and he was happy to have it. He had spent countless hours on the Hudson crewing with the Athletic Club's sculling team. When he was stumped for words while writing, when he was tense, when he felt overwhelmed, he had but to go to the window to find solace in watching the boats, both large and small, plying their way along the broad river's expanse.

Last summer, before the war started and the docks along the Hudson had begun to fill with the German ships confiscated by the U. S. government, he had watched several regattas from his fire escape, settling himself on a cushion from his couch and leaning against the brick exterior of the building, glass of wine in hand. Of course, that was then. Now, everything had changed, not just New York, but the world. He doubted there would be any regattas or other such sporting events this summer; not until things had settled down and the German vessels – at least, the passenger-carrying ocean liners – were allowed to sail back to port in Hamburg. For now, though, both the grand ships and German naval vessels had become permanent fixtures at the local docks, snuggly tucked together bow to aft and secured together with huge ropes.

With his binoculars, Curtis often watched pelicans and gulls building nests among the ships' protruding masts and towering smokestacks. Except for occasional government inspectors and policemen, the vessels were completely deserted. They were ghost ships, with fading paint and windows that had been broken by anti-German vandals.

Curtis changed into casual trousers and his faded gray sweater. Closing the dark blue linen drapes to subdue the afternoon glare, he sauntered to the Birchwood sideboard on the opposite end of the living room. He pulled the stopper from the cut-glass decanter and poured Single Malt Scotch whiskey into one of the matching crystal glasses, a gift from his parents last Christmas.

With so many British cargo ships now resting on the bottom of the Atlantic, including those bringing bottles of Scotch to America from distilleries in Great Britain, or, more especially, from the best distiller in the Highlands of Scotland, Curtis had been rationing out the amount he drank. Even then, he only imbibed on rare occasions. Today was one of those days.

It had been years since he had been home this early on a weekday, and it felt a little odd. He strolled back towards the kitchen and set his glass down on the small dining table. Opening his worn leather satchel, still imprinted with a faded Harvard insignia, he pulled out a stack of handwritten pages.

He spread the papers across the table, scanning the words line-by-line, attempting to refresh his memory as to where he had left off. "Ah, yes. Chapter Eight. The Worldwide Credit Shortage," he said with an acknowledging nod. Then he read his neatly printed words aloud: "The governments of the major economic world powers were toppling like gigantic dominos. From Japan in the Far East, to the ancient land of the Pharaohs, to New York City, stock markets crashed and once-profitable businesses crumbled into bankruptcy."

Pleased with his writing, he pulled out a chair and took a seat. He was glad he took the afternoon off work. At least the Panic of 1907 was a more interesting topic than Jonas Prescott's clothing production shops. Uncapping his Sheaffer fountain pen, positioning his tablet, Curtis began to write.

FIVE O'CLOCK came and went, and Mr. Franklin still hadn't arrived. A worried Yvette began to play a softer tune. A lovely one at that. A waltz. Josette found herself swinging her crossed leg in time to the music. From where she sat, she could see out of the music room's double-wide doorway and into the front hall. From the corner of her eye, Josette caught a glimpse of Mr. Herrmann – their sometimes butler, sometimes chauffeur – passing by. A few minutes later, Mr. Franklin was in the hallway. So, unfortunately, was their mother.

Josette quickly rose and scrambled across the room to her sister. Yvette glanced up at her with an inquisitive expression. Josette held her finger to her mouth, indicating that Yvette should stop playing. Then she leaned down and whispered into her sister's ear. "He's here."

When the piano was silent, they could hear their mother's curt tone. "And you do know I will not pay you for the time you have missed. Sixty-five minutes shall be deducted from today's fee."

Josette exchanged a pained look with her sister. Yvette's face contorted into a tortured expression. Eyes narrowed, she bit her lower lip. Josette placed her hand on Yvette's arm in a small effort to comfort her.

"I do apologize, Mrs. Rogers." It was Mr. Franklin's voice. "But I had a meeting with my booking agent that took longer than expected."

"I do not care about your meeting, Mr. Franklin. Just be on time next week."

An anguished look swept across Yvette's face. She covered her mouth with her hand.

Mr. Franklin responded politely. "Yes, Mrs. Rogers. I promise... though I have every intention of spending extra time with Miss Yvette today to make up for the lost time."

"Very well, Mr. Franklin." Their mother's tone remained curt. "But I will still deduct a small sum from your pay to assure this does not happen again."

"Poor Jon," Yvette said softly, shaking her head.

"As you wish, Mrs. Rogers." Jon Franklin's voice was even. Calm.

"You may go in now, Mr. Franklin. My daughters have been waiting. Oh, and Miss Josette won't be having a lesson today. Just Yvette."

"Very well, Mrs. Rogers."

"Thank you, Mother," Josette whispered to herself. It wasn't often that Josette won a battle with her mother, especially when it came to an argument involving studying for school. 'Women do not need to understand the sciences,' she would say. This was, indeed, a victory.

Mr. Franklin walked into the room, peeling off his black leather gloves as he approached. He had removed his hat and coat in the front hall. Jonathan Franklin was of medium height and quite lean, with blue eyes and blonde hair laced with brown strands. He and Yvette were both attractive people, and in Josette's opinion, they made a fine-looking couple. They had known each other for the past two years, as student and teacher. That relationship had certainly changed in the past six months.

"My apologies to you ladies," he said with a rather embarrassed grin. Pausing, he glanced back over his shoulder towards the doorway.

Josette surmised that he was checking to see if Mother had retreated back into her battle trench.

"I have wonderful news!" His mouth slid into a wide grin, tossing his gloves on top of the piano. "I have been booked at Carnegie Hall." His gaze was now fixed firmly on Yvette. "Not in the main hall, mind you, but in one of the smaller venues adjacent to the grand auditorium. I'm told the main hall will be filled with temperance supporters that night. A meeting of some sort." He turned to Josette. "I would imagine you already know all about that, don't you? Are you planning to go?"

Josette shook her head. "No, not temperance. I'm involved with the issue of voting rights for women." She laughed. "Heavens. Father even allows us to enjoy a glass of wine or champagne on special occasions."

"I beg your pardon, Josette," he said, dipping his chin. Jonathan was certainly charming. And good looking, too. Josette understood why her sister had fallen for the young man.

"No offense taken, Jon," Josette replied.

"Tell me more about your Carnegie Hall engagement." Yvette's face looked as bright as a thousand candles. "Just think! You're playing at the Carnegie! The Carnegie, Jon!" She reached out and took his arm. "It's your dream!"

Jon leaned close to her. "Yes, it is, my dear." Under different circumstances, in a different place, they would have embraced. Kissed, most likely.

Smiling, Josette drew in a deep breath. They were so much in love.

"When is the performance, my darling?" Yvette asked.

"It's at the end of the month. April 30th. You must all come! Your parents, too."

"Of course, we will!" Yvette responded, unable to restrain her excitement. Neither of the pair so much as glanced Josette's way.

"Now, it's not exactly a solo performance," he cautioned. "I am to accompany a very well-known singer. An Italian tenor. He's performing several operatic pieces." Lifting his long, split jacket, he settled next to Yvette on the piano bench.

They held each other's gaze for a long moment. Finally, Yvette said, "It won't be long before you'll be performing in the main hall with the Philharmonic orchestra."

"I know, my dear. It's finally happening," he responded in a near whisper, taking one of her hands. Jon had long, slender fingers. Perfect for a concert pianist. Yvette's hand, small and delicate, fit perfectly inside his palm.

Yvette and Jon sat inches apart on the bench before the Steinway, eyes locked in an affectionate gaze.

Josette cleared her throat, breaking the long silence, and glanced to the open doorway. "You'd best begin the lesson, Jon, or our Mother will soon be joining us to see what the delay is."

"Yes, yes. You're absolutely right, sister," Yvette said.

Besides giving rich girls piano lessons in their homes, Jon played in movie houses and at small concerts. Most recently, he had been hired to play the Saturday and Sunday night shows at the Ziegfeld

Follies. Josette knew that Father would never let her and Yvette go to the New Amsterdam Theater to see what he considered a risqué vaudeville show. But now, Jon was to appear in a production at Carnegie Hall, one of the most revered venues in the world. It was… respectable.

Jonathan released Yvette's hand, swung his arms forward and motioned to the keys. "And now, my dearest, let us begin. I have a new piece for you. It's called *Clair de Lune*. I think you'll like it."

Jon's fingers flowed over the keyboard as smoothly as waves on the ocean. A beautiful melody emerged, a tune that took Josette away from her throbbing headache. Away from the pressure of having to study for her examination. Away from her nagging thoughts of the war overseas. She closed her eyes and leaned back on the cushion. For a few minutes, her mind was swept away to a peaceful place. To a pink and tangerine sunrise at the beach on Long Island where she spent happy summers with the Laurent family.

How wonderful it would be if the world could find this sort of tranquility; if this enchanted moment in the Music Room could last forever. Her sister was in love with a man who created magic. And it was wonderful.

Josette's thoughts suddenly turned inward, to her own future. Would there ever be a man in her life? One whom she loved as much as Yvette loved Jon? A man who would understand her ambition and the fact that she wasn't like most other girls? She wanted more in her life than children and a home to keep up. But, then, if she decided to have a child one day, could she have a career and a family? Why not both? Would she have to live her life like Jane Addams and dedicate herself solely to serving others?

Surely not all men were like her old-fashioned father. After all, there was Jon Franklin, sitting a few feet away. He cared nothing about becoming a business tycoon. Jonathan's father was a merchant of some sort. Middle class, from what Josette knew. But Jon was following his own dreams to pursue a music career.

Things were changing, and this was truly a new generation of young people who were being swept towards a more progressive lifestyle. Old-fashioned conventions were disappearing. More women had entered the work force, especially overseas in the countries involved in the war. How ironic that it took a war to make such a drastic change. While the men were off fighting and dying in Europe, women were finally recognized as capable of doing men's work. Women were a necessary commodity, if the war was to be won. And it gave them more power and validity than ever before. Gaining the vote was inevitable. Josette was sure of it.

Chapter 6

SEVERAL HOURS, ten newly written pages, and three half-glasses of single malt Scotch whiskey later, Curtis reclined on his overstuffed brown couch, drifting in and out of sleep. A soft knock on his door roused him. He breathed in deeply and opened his eyes. There was another round of knocks, this time, louder.

"Who is it?" he finally hollered, still groggy.

"Hello, Curtis. It's me," she called out, almost singing her words. "Liliana."

"Oh, crap," he muttered in a low tone. He hated it when she dropped by unannounced…a definite disadvantage of her living across the hall. "I need a minute," he said loudly. His mouth felt dry as ash and his vision was slightly blurred with sleep. As he rose, he felt a little dizzy. After-effects of the whiskey, he knew…and why he rarely imbibed. Liquor dulled the senses and fogged the brain.

"Just a minute, Lil," he called. He rubbed his eyes and raked his fingers through his hair in an effort to look somewhat groomed. Steadying himself, he answered the door. "Ah, yes. Liliana, Liliana," he said, forcing a slight smile. "And how are you this fine day?"

She let out one of her obnoxious laughs. "Oh, Curtis. You're so funny. It's evening! And I'm very well. How's about you?"

Liliana balanced a tray covered with a red-and-white checkered cloth, using her right hand to steady it, and pushing the whole affair into her stomach. She clutched a bottle of wine in her left hand. It was obviously an Italian import, as the bottom was encased in a woven straw covering.

"Good grief, Lil. What's all this?"

"I made you spaghetti and meatballs. It's my Grandma Romano's family recipe."

His neighbor and all-too-frequent visitor, Liliana O'Toole, was a pretty young woman with long legs and voluptuous curves. Dumb as a door knob, though. Curtis smiled. "Smells good, but you didn't need to—"

"Ah, think nothing of it. When I heard you come home early, I figured something was wrong." She scanned him. "You feeling okay? You got the sniffles or something?"

"No, no. I'm doing fine. I just decided to come home early today."

"Well, I figured you'd need to eat something. I had the butcher grind the sausage and pork fresh this afternoon." She blinked up at him. "Aren't you going to invite me in?"

"Oh, God. I'm sorry, Lil. Of course. How could I pass up your Italian grandmother's spaghetti sauce?" He held the door open to let her pass. "Here, let me help you with that," he said, reaching out to take the tray.

She eyed him thoughtfully, brushing through the doorway. "Are you sure you're all right?"

"I've had a stress-filled day," he said, closing the door with his free hand. "And I must admit I had a few drinks and nodded off." The strong aroma of unidentifiable seasonings wafted through the cloth. "Mmmm. I didn't realize how hungry I am. This is very nice of you."

"See. Liliana knows what's best for her Curtis when he's not doing well."

Her Curtis? Oh crap, he thought, swallowing hard. With her living a few steps away, Liliana knew all about his comings and goings. And the difficult situation had been escalating in recent months. With his salary rising at Morgan and Company, he expected to move quite soon into a larger apartment in an even better part of town with an even better view. That is, if he still had a job tomorrow.

"Oh…my…God. Tell Liliana what happened." She sauntered to the kitchen counter, hips swaying with each step, and set the bottle down.

"Let's just say that I had a dreadful morning and let it go at that." He followed her into the kitchen, placing the tray of food beside the wine bottle. Glancing at the label, he said, "Ah. Chianti. I do like Chianti."

"I still have a few bottles hidden under my bed," she said with a wink. "For special friends. I brought you some imported Italian cheese, too. To go with the wine." She removed the cloth from the serving tray. The plate of spaghetti was covered with a large inverted bowl to keep it warm. Beside it was a small saucer piled with thin strips of white cheese.

"I'm honored," was all he could think to say. "Your Chianti, like my Scotch, will soon be impossible to buy, if things keep going like this. The war, I mean." He wondered if she even realized there was a war raging overseas that was affecting imports. Likely not.

"Where's your corkscrew?" she asked, ignoring his comment. Likely, it went over her head. The woman lived in a world of glamour and public adoration. There was no place in her life for unpleasant things like wars, economic downturns, and politics.

He motioned to the drawer beside her. "Thanks, Lil, but I've had my limit of spirits for the day. Save it for a special occasion, why don't you?"

"Nonsense," she said, glancing at him over her shoulder. "This *is* a special occasion, and I want you to help me celebrate."

"Celebrate? Sounds like you had a good day."

"You can say that again!" she said with a coy look. "And the glasses?"

He pointed to one of the cupboards.

Retrieving two stemmed wine glasses, she placed them on the counter. "I had a very good day. Guess what happened!" she said with a hearty laugh, lifting her hands into the air.

"Guess? Why don't you just tell me your news, Lil."

She looked as if she was about to explode with excitement. "Well, I've signed a new contract to model for *Harper's Magazine*." Her very straight, very white teeth beamed a huge smile. "See? Big news, don't you think?"

"Oh, yes. That's…huge news, Lil." He faked interest, an attempt at politeness. "I can see why you're so happy. Congratulations."

"Thanks. I've been dying to tell you." Liliana turned and picked up the corkscrew and drove it into the top of the bottle.

Auburn hair, dark eyes with thick lashes, full lips that she painted red, Liliana had little trouble finding employment as a fashion model for women's attire. Lately, she had appeared in numerous ladies' magazines. O'Toole was her family name. Her manager had changed it to a simple, nonspecific, not-so-Irish sounding, "Lilly May." She was something of an icon and minor celebrity among young ladies intrigued with the latest clothing styles.

"Well, well. *Harpers Magazine*. That's the big time, isn't it?"

She glanced up with a wry grin, twisting the metal coil deep into the cork. "Big time? You betcha! It's the top of Adverist Mountain!"

He cringed. Did she mean, Mount Everest? "Uh-huh. Sounds like you've reached the pinnacle of that mountain...wherever it is." He couldn't stop a chuckle from slipping out.

She frowned. "You know what I mean, Curtis. It's that big mountain over there in India or Vienna or somewhere like that."

"Oh...that mountain. Yes. I see." He had to turn away momentarily to keep her from seeing his smile.

"I'm really quite proud," she continued. "All the best models hope to appear in *Harpers*. And...." She paused for a long moment, extracting the stopper from the bottle. "And, get a load of this. I'm gonna be featured on the cover of the June issue! Can you believe it?"

"The cover. Good for you!" Gathering himself, he turned to her. "That is quite an accomplishment, Lil. Congratulations are definitely in order." He stepped over and took the bottle from her, pouring the wine into the glasses. "Guess we should have a toast."

"Yes. We definitely oughta." Liliana flashed him an alluring half-smile. "But you've gotta eat your pasta before it gets cold."

"Okey-dokey. Let me clear my work off the table." Curtis carried the two glasses, setting them on the sideboard.

"Whatcha you working on?"

"A book." He stepped back to the kitchen, opened a drawer, and grabbed a fork.

"A book? Oh, my goodness gracious, Curtis. You are a wonder. A successful businessman and a writer. So, what's the book about?" She lifted the plate of pasta off the tray and set it on the table.

"Believe me, Lil. You wouldn't be interested," he said as he pulled out a chair.

"No? Try me," she said with furrowed brows. "I do read, you know."

Not much, he thought, settling into the chair. "Very well. It's a history of the economic failures that triggered a panic of major consequences back in ought seven."

She seemed interested. "A panic, you say? In 1907? What happened?"

Well, well. She actually wanted to know something about his work. This was a first. "You see, Lil, I believe President Roosevelt's remarks caused a huge backlash that triggered a financial panic that reverberated across the country." He picked up the fork and stabbed it into the sauce-covered noodles. "There were runs on banks...hence, the use of the word, 'panic.' The New York Stock Market lost fifty percent of its value," he explained, twirling the fork until it held a large bite of spaghetti. "It might have meant the entire American economy would come crashing down if it weren't for the injection of money from our own J. P. Morgan."

"Wait. Isn't that where you work? J. P. Morgan?"

Chewing, he nodded.

"That's who stopped that panic thing that saved the world? Oh my God! Did you have something to do with that, Curtis?"

He paused to swallow, took a few gulps of wine, and responded. "No. I didn't even work for the Morgan Company back in 1907. It was the current Mr. Morgan's father who did the good deed. J. P. Morgan, Senior."

"So, why are you writing a book about it?"

"Because I think it's important that people know what happened." He let out a gentle sigh, sorry he had brought up the subject. Then he took another long drink from the wine glass.

"Why?" She looked confused. As usual. "I mean, that was a long time ago. Anyhow, who cares what happened back then?"

"I do. For one. Believe it or not, a lot of people care. You see, if we don't look back at our past mistakes, we could repeat the same mistakes. That's why people study history."

"Stop! Stop!" she said, laughing. "You're right. That's all well and fine for you, but I'd like it better if you were writing something that was interesting."

"Ah," Curtis said with a nod, not surprised by her comment. It was no use arguing with her. Liliana was hopeless. He stuffed another bite of spaghetti in his mouth. Better to chew than to say something he would regret. As beautiful as she was on the outside, she didn't have much going on inside. And that made her less attractive to Curtis in so many ways.

She rose and went to the kitchen. "I'm sorry, Curtis, I find things such as that book of yours...boring."

Finishing off his wine, he said, "That's what I figured, Lil. But you did ask, after all."

Liliana picked up the Chianti and added more to Curtis' glass. "You haven't said anything about my haircut. Did you even notice?" She walked back to the kitchen as she spoke, returned with a napkin, and took a seat across from him.

"Uh...oh. Sorry, Lil," he said, looking at the cheek-length, turned-under coif. "Actually, I'm still a little dopey and the wine isn't helping. Not to mention the Scotch."

She clucked her tongue, obviously displeased that he hadn't paid more attention. "Naughty boy." She patted the under-turned do. "It's called a bob. It's all the rage, you see. More modern than long hair. The magazine insisted." Liliana lowered her eyes and then looked up at him through her long, dark lashes. "So? Whatcha think, Curtis? Do you like it?"

He wasn't about to say no. He didn't like it at all but thought he had better play it safe. "I certainly understand why the magazine wants you to be in the most up-to-date attire. I'm sure the short hair-dos are what models must wear these days. It makes good business sense. Sells more magazines, I imagine."

"My hair grows fast," she said with a sly grin. "And there's still enough left for you to gather with your fingers," she purred, with a seductive gaze.

She was at it again. "If I didn't know better, I would think you're trying to seduce me, Lil."

Laughing, she rose from the chair. "Would that be so awful? We've known each other for nearly a year and you've never made a pass at me. Don't you find me desirable? Huh? Lots of gents want to know me."

"Of course. You're a lovely gal, but I'm tired and I've had too much to drink and—"

Approaching him, Liliana gathered her silky skirt fabric in her hands, exposing bare legs. Beautifully shaped, long, and lean. "You're not wearing stockings," was all he could muster, sounding more interested than he wanted to.

"And…I'm not wearing nothing under my clothes neither, big boy," she said with a teasing snicker. She continued to inch her dress up to the top of her legs. To the very edge of her most private area.

"Damn." Curtis sighed his defeat. His heart pounded. A stiffness formed between his legs and his breathing became rapid and shallow. "You're really something."

Without another word, she stood beside him, her eyes locked on his. Licking her bottom lip, she let her skirt drop to cover her legs again. She took his hand, her gaze so intense that it felt as if she was undressing him with her stare. "I want you, Curtis."

Swallowing hard, he set his glass down and stood up. The room spun, and he felt woozy. "I don't know, Liliana. We shouldn't."

Giggling, she led him through the open doorway into the bedroom. "Do you want me, too?" she whispered. Dropping his hand, Liliana pulled her blouse over her head, exposing her breasts. She tossed her blouse on the bed, unfastened her skirt, and let it drop to the floor.

She stood there naked in front of him. She had the body of a Venus. Curtis' mind was too foggy to fight his natural urges. It had been a long time since he had enjoyed the pleasure of a woman's body. Too long.

She stepped to him, wrapping her arms around his neck, pressing her naked body to his.

Oh, what the hell.…

EACH MORNING, even most Saturdays, Curtis could hardly wait to get back to 23 Wall Street. Rain, shine, snow. It didn't matter. He had a routine. On the way, he stopped and bought the latest edition of the *New York Times*, had a cup of coffee and pastry at the little diner around the corner from his office; and by eight-fifteen, he was firmly planted in his chair at Morgan and Company.

Today, his routine had gone to hell. He was relieved Liliana had slipped out before dawn. That he didn't have to face her after their night together. He was hungover and had overslept; barely had time to bathe, shave, and get dressed. The booze, the rich food. His temples throbbed and the light stabbing through the windows made his headache almost intolerable. His stomach was queasy, and the thought of eating made things worse.

"Damn," he whispered, closing his eyes as he massaged his forehead. "What in the hell have I done?"

Standing over the wash basin, he stared into the mirror. Dark half-moons ringed under his bottom lashes and red lines marbled the white part of his eyes. His normally lightly tanned complexion looked sallow. God, he looked terrible. And on today of all days. He was nervous about how Mr. Morgan and the senior partners would react to yesterday's fiasco at Columbia. And now, his physical condition wouldn't help matters.

Worse, he was angry with himself. Why did he let things get out of hand? He should have pushed Liliana away before things got so heated. Grunting, he rubbed a dab of taming cream into his hair. Even his cowlick wasn't cooperating. Frustrated, Curtis pressed a wave alongside of his part with the side of his hand and stepped back from the mirror. He could have fussed around for hours and he'd still look like something the cat dragged in.

Damned alcohol did him in. He couldn't let it happen again. Sure. Having sex with Lil was like riding a Fourth of July rocket into the sky. Still, he couldn't think about her. It wouldn't, couldn't happen again.

Curtis took a taxi directly to 23 Wall Street. Instead of his usual stride to his desk, he walked as quietly and inconspicuously as possible. Had his shoes always made that hollow thud with each step on the marble floors? This version of himself was unsure, nervous, headachy and tired as crap.

Before his butt hit the seat of his chair, Rudy Van Camp was standing beside him. "Good morning, Carlson. How are you doing this fine spring day?" His voice thundered in Curtis' head, like a ball bouncing around in his brain.

Curtis cringed. "Keep it down, Rudy."

"Not feeling good this morning, right Carlson? Can't say I'm surprised. Probably didn't sleep much, did you?" Rudy Van Camp was a tall, red-haired man of around thirty. Taller than his father, the younger Van Camp was a thick-necked, thick-headed jerk who relished intimidating people. Everything about Rudy was large, though Curtis didn't believe the man did anything to strengthen his muscles. Strong? Probably not, judging by the flab around his middle.

Yet, with his foul disposition and sardonic vindictiveness, Curtis was sure Rudy was a bully in school. Still was, in fact.

Curtis frowned up at the towering imbecile. "What do you want, Rudy?"

"So… Have you seen this morning's paper?" he said with a satisfied smirk.

"No. Why?" Curtis said, pretending ignorance. "I think you'd better have a look-see, *mister perfect.*"

"Ah, I see." Curtis pushed back in his chair and looked him straight in the eyes. "You've come to gloat, haven't you, Van Camp? he said, forcing a relaxed tone. "If it makes you feel better, go right ahead."

"You botched it, Carlson," he said in a tone loud enough for half the office to hear, despite the clacking of typewriter keys. His mouth curled into a satisfied smile. "I think you'd better read the article yourself." Rudy had the newspaper neatly folded into a compact rectangle. He tapped his finger on the top. "It's right here. On the front page." He tossed it on Curtis' desk, turned and laughed as he walked back to his desk on the other side of a potted palm.

Chapter 7

CLOSING HIS EYES for a moment, Curtis gathered his wits, taking several slow, deep breaths. Rudy's laughter was the last thing he needed right now. He opened his eyes and read.

"*Scuffle Erupts at Columbia. Students arrested in the melee after former Harvard professor preaches his pro-war message to audience of more than 300 students. Six young ladies, representatives of Miss Addams' anti-war group, lit the proverbial fuse igniting Professor Carlson's message that America should enter the war on the side of Britain and her allies. The ruckus began when students of German descent confronted the speaker and students of English and Belgian descent. None of the lady protestors were arrested and no injuries were reported. The scuffle was unprece-*

dented in the history of the fine educational institution (cont. pg. 10).

Curtis unfolded the newspaper to its normal size and turned to page 10, running his finger down the column to find an additional paragraph.

(Cont. from pg. 1) "This reporter, who was present at yesterday's lecture, agrees with Professor Carlson's belief that our country is already involved in this, the greatest war in the history of the world. The American economy will be strengthened by selling much-needed goods to Great Britain and France. If those allies are lost to the German Empire, who knows what the long-lasting effects will be? Mr. Walter Green, President Wilson's representative, was unable to attend. However, we all know the president's message of neutrality. It's doubtful Green could have delivered any new information on this matter. Mr. Beck, representing the German Embassy, was in attendance, though had little of value to plead his case. In my opinion, the professor was victorious in making his point, in spite of the violence that erupted as a result."

Curtis sat back in his chair and let out a laugh. "Hey, Rudy!" he yelled to his insufferable cohort two desks away. "I suggest you finish the article. It's on Page 10."

Mr. Arnold settled into a side chair adjacent to Curtis' desk. "Now, then. That takes care of Rudolph Van Camp." He bent forward, lowering his voice. "Obnoxious bastard. The young Mr. Van Camp is like a fly on manure."

Curtis fought back a laugh. Instead, he nodded and smiled. "Thank you, sir. I couldn't agree more. Unless...," he said in a near whisper, "...I'm the manure in this situation."

Mr. Arnold chuckled. "Perhaps I should have said, 'like an ant on a picnic plate.'"

"That's much better, sir," he said with a chuckle.

Mr. Arnold continued leaning close to Curtis. "I simply do not understand why Jack keeps that buffoon on staff. If his father weren't a partner here, he would have been dismissed long ago."

Curtis glanced in Rudy's direction. Although he was seated at his desk, it was obvious he was straining to hear what Mr. Arnold had to say.

"I couldn't agree more. I certainly didn't expect things to get violent at the lecture. I was worried that the partners here would see it as a loss. Because of the melee, I mean."

Mr. Arnold shook his head. "Not at all, Curtis. I don't see a problem. More importantly," he said with a smile, "neither does Jack Morgan. No one was really hurt too much. Just a few black eyes, from what the police captain said. And, frankly, son, Jack believes the publicity is quite good for his cause. Thanks to you, the public has read the account about how some of the German youth in this country feel about the war overseas. Their patriotism to their country and cultural heritage is quite understandable," Mr. Arnold added. "However, when so many American citizens favor England and France and their allies, an incident like this simply magnifies the fear of the German men in our very midst."

"I suppose, but I never intended..."

"I know, Curtis, but the fact that a fight broke out likely attracted more attention than had it simply been a lecture by you and Mr. Beck. The brawl worked in our favor."

A huge sense of relief swept through Curtis. "I'm sure not everyone will agree a fist fight in a university auditorium is a good thing."

"Perhaps not. But many people will agree that there is a reason for genuine concern about the Germans living in America. We're living with spies in our midst."

"I doubt those lads were spies, sir. In some ways, I can't blame them for their anger at our government. They made several good points." Curtis expelled a slow breath, shaking his head. "But if Mr. Morgan, the partners, and most importantly, you, sir, aren't upset with the lecture's outcome, then I'm very pleased."

"Look, my boy." Mr. Arnold reached out and patted Curtis on the shoulder. "There are still many people in this country who wish to stay neutral. The war abroad is taking a terrible toll; not just the loss of so many lives on both sides, but economically, too. Our Allies need our assistance to end this ugly situation. In the long-run, even

Germany would be better off if the United States puts an end to the fighting."

Curtis nodded. "I just don't understand why President Wilson continues to dig in his heels. What in the world is he waiting for?"

"Something tragic, I fear. And by the time it happens, it may be too late."

TWO WEEKS had passed since the incident at Columbia University, and so far, there had been no repercussions for Josette. At least, none she was aware of. Most importantly, her father hadn't said a word about it. Mr. Carlson had kept his promise to keep her name out of the newspapers. Apparently, no one else had reported her near-arrest to Barnard College's hierarchy. She felt as if the nasty incident was behind her.

The ladies from the Jane Addams' Club at Barnard who had participated in the protest at Columbia decided it was best to lay low for a while. Josette knew it was to keep their families from learning about their political activities, something which she understood completely. Father paid for her college fees. If he became unhappy with her in any way; most especially, if he knew the truth about the rallies she had attended, he would likely make her quit school altogether. What would she do, then?

Indeed, she, too, had to keep up the pretense of acquiescing to her father's wishes. And she was certainly grateful for his financial support and the fact that he had gone against Mother's wishes to allow her to attend Barnard College in the first place.

The school year was drawing to an end, and Josette was overwhelmed with papers to write, examinations to take, and books to read. When Father was gone, she liked to work at his mahogany desk in the library upstairs at the rear of the house. Setting her textbooks and notepad on the end of the desk, Josette settled into Father's chair. The library was Josette's favorite room. Floor to ceiling shelves stuffed with leather-bound books covered three of the four walls. Collections of the great classics that Father had purchased, though she suspected, he hadn't read: Shakespeare, Dickens, Doyle, Browning. Nothing but the finest, and many were antiques at that.

Although the room was a substantial size, there was only one large window. Father had replaced the panel of glass in the arched section at the top with a beautiful stained-glass rendition of a ship at sea. A slight blue glow seemed to dominate the room, not that direct sunlight often shone through. The library looked down over the small patch of formal rose gardens, and huge poplar trees shaded the back of the house.

Despite the library's lack of natural light, the oversized, electrified, twelve-bulb brass chandelier, two free-standing torch lamps, and a small fixture on the desk itself kept the room from feeling dark. Yvette had curled up on the leather settee with a wine-colored lap blanket, her nose buried in one of her ubiquitous romantic novels. Josette sat at their father's desk hunched over her text book. French was one of her best subjects...until it came time to translate a story into English. It was a tedious, laborious task. Elbows on the desk, she glanced over at her sister, sliding her fist under her chin.

"I see you're reading another one of those Jane Austen novels." Josette noted the title in bold gold print on the book's dark burgundy spine. "*Pride and Prejudice*," she said ceremoniously, trying to annoy Yvette. Josette continued with a chuckle. "So, who has the pride? And who is prejudiced?"

Yvette rolled her eyes. "You simply would not understand," she said with a shake of her head. "I fear you do not have a romantic bone in your body."

"Probably not." Josette cocked her head to the side and grinned.

Yvette made no comment, her eyes returning to the page.

"Those stories are so ridiculous." Josette sat up straight, stretching her arms and rolling her head from side to side until it cracked. "Why do you waste your time?"

Her sister looked up with an annoyed expression. "Have you ever read one of Jane Austen's books?"

"No."

"Then I suggest you do so. It might do you good to see how it feels to fall in love." Yvette's gaze lifted, as if she were looking up at the ceiling. "To feel it in your heart." She placed her right hand over her left breast. "To feel a sense of breathlessness when the man you love enters the room or merely smiles at you." Yvette focused squarely on Josette. "You should try it sometime. Why don't you give one of the lads who clamber after you a glimmer of hope, Josette? You never know. One of them might suit your fancy."

"Oh, my heavens," Josette said with a groan. "None of those young men would be of any interest to me. As for your romantic novels, well, they are simply silly. They are a complete waste of time."

"Very well, then. You do what brings you happiness, and I shall do the same." Yvette paused. "Agreed?"

Josette exhaled a sigh. "All right. I agree."

Their arguments were few, most likely because of Yvette's meekness...which irritated Josette endlessly. Yvette rarely spoke her mind or defended herself. But when it came to criticisms of her reading materials or her love of the piano, well, those topics simply crossed over Yvette's line of passivity. Josette rather enjoyed teasing her timid sister into taking a stand on something she felt passionate about.

Minutes of thick silence passed as both went back to their reading...until a delicious smell interrupted Josette's concentration. "What is that wonderful aroma?"

Yvette looked up, wiggled her nose and sniffed the air, looking like a puppy hungry for a treat. "It smells like apples. And cinnamon. You don't suppose Mrs. DuBois is baking something? Apple tarts, perhaps?" she questioned rhetorically. "That would be lovely, wouldn't it?"

"Mrs. DuBois's pastries are far from tantalizing. Still, I need something to eat, and it's hours until dinner." Josette rose and headed for the doorway. "Besides, I rode my bicycle home from school today. It's quite a long trek. It always makes me work up an appetite."

"Wait for me." Yvette followed Josette into the hall and down the curved staircase.

"I don't know if Mrs. DuBois will make us wait until dinner to have a taste of what she's concocted," Josette said, glancing over her shoulder. "But at the very least, I'd love a cup of tea and a snack. Maybe a taste of the pastry, whatever it is."

Entering the kitchen, Yvette stopped at Josette's side. Mrs. DuBois was nowhere to be seen. There weren't any pots boiling on the stove. No apples sliced on the counter or rolled out dough waiting to be filled with fruit. Nothing. And yet, the smell of cinnamon, sugar, and apples still drifted through the room.

Mr. Herrmann, his back to them, sat at the big round table in the breakfast nook. Hearing their footsteps, he turned. "Good afternoon." Quickly scooting out his chair, he rose, as if at attention. "Can I help you?"

"Good afternoon, Mr. Herrmann. Where is Mrs. DuBois?" Josette inquired.

"I am afraid she has stepped out. To the market for fresh fish for tonight's meal."

"I see." Curious, Josette headed to the table, noting a dessert plate containing a pastry dusted with white confectioners' sugar. "What is that pastry? It smells divine."

He glanced at the plate. "Oh, yes, miss. It's apple strudel." He always rolled his tongue and spoke from the back of his throat in a thick accent. "A German pastry. My favorite."

"Did Mrs. DuBois bake it?" Yvette inquired.

"Oh, no, no," he said, waving his hands. A hint of a smile showed beneath his mustache. "Mrs. DuBois complains she has little time to bake these days. My wife made the strudel. You just missed her."

"She made it here?" Yvette asked.

"*Nein*. She prepared it at the bakery in *Kleindeutschland* where she is employed. But she warmed it here in the pie oven."

"We smelled it all the way upstairs," Josette said.

"Mrs. Herrmann stopped by on her way home. We did not wish to disturb you ladies. I hope that you do not mind." He looked concerned.

"Oh, heavens no," Yvette said.

"Of course not," Josette added. "After all the years you have worked here with us, we have never even seen your wife." Josette suddenly realized that she knew very little about the man's personal life. "I wish you would have called us down to meet her."

"Perhaps another time." He dropped his gaze. "But she has only come today because, well, you see, misses," he said with an embarrassed shrug, "today is my birthday."

Josette and Yvette glanced at each other, and then looked back at Mr. Herrmann. Josette said, "Your birthday? Why, that's wonderful. I had no idea. *We* had no idea, did we, Yvette?" Josette corrected, feeling sad that as many years as the dear man had been with the family, they didn't even know the date of his birthday, let alone acknowledge it in any way whatsoever.

"Yes, Mr. Herrmann. Happy birthday," Yvette added.

"*Danke*," he responded with a broad smile. His hazel eyes twinkled with kindness, his wiry brows lifting.

"*Kleindeutschland*? That's Little Germany, isn't it?" Josette asked.

"It is what non-Germans call that part of the city."

For years, Mr. Herrmann had taught Josette a smattering of German words. He had shared stories of his childhood in Bavaria. Talked at length about the castles along the Rhine River, the pine-covered mountains, the beauty of the countryside. One day, she had promised herself, she would visit the places that had become so vivid in her imagination: Heidelberg, the Cathedral at Cologne, the amazing castle at Neuschwanstein. She often wondered what would be left of that region once the war ended.

Mr. Herrmann asked, "Would you like tea? I would be happy to prepare it for you."

Yvette walked to the stove and picked up the kettle. "No, thank you, Mr. Herrmann. We are perfectly capable. Please sit down and enjoy your... oh dear. What was that called again?"

"Strudel," Josette responded.

"Yes, strudel! *Gut!* Your German pronunciation is getting better, Miss Josette," he said, nodding to her as he sat. "Would you ladies care to taste?"

"Tempting, to be sure," Josette responded. "But it *is* your birthday, after all, and it's your favorite treat." She sat beside him at the table. "Thank you for your kind offer, but you should enjoy every last crumb, Mr. Herrmann," she said with a gentle smile. "Besides, I can visit the bakery myself and purchase a piece."

"Oh, no, miss. It's in *Kleindeutschland*."

"Why not? It may take a long time before I get to visit Bavaria or anywhere else in Germany, the way things are going," Josette said with a frustrated sigh. "But I would certainly like to see *Kleindeutschland* here in New York City. Did I pronounce it properly?"

Mr. Herrmann looked pleased. "You did, Miss Josette. Indeed, you did."

"Father purchased my bicycle at a shop in Little Germany a couple of months ago. He said he got the best price there. You know my father and his bargain shopping," she said with a snicker. "Anyway, a young man who works at the bicycle store delivered it to me on campus. He suggested that I purchase a bell for the handlebars. A warning bell when I'm approaching someone in my way, I guess. Do you happen to know the owner? Mr. Decker?"

"I do not know Mr. Decker personally, but the bicycle shop is quite close to the bakery."

"I wouldn't tell Father you're going there alone, sister," Yvette said, removing the kettle of boiling water from the stove. "You know what he would say."

"Yes, yes. I know. He wouldn't permit it. 'You girls shall not go places unaccompanied by a gentleman. Too damnable dangerous,' Josette said, imitating her father's voice; his accent.

Yvette laughed and nodded.

"I would be happy to drive you, miss," Mr. Herrmann said. "I must drop Mr. Rogers at the yacht club first thing in the morning, but I could come back for you after that."

Josette thought for a moment. "Thank you for the offer, but if Father were to find out, it might put you in an awkward position."

"Perhaps you are right," he said with an understanding nod.

Josette leaned forward, her gaze searching his face. "Oh…no. Please don't misunderstand, Mr. Herrmann. Father does not have unkind things to say about the German people, although he was born in England. He's simply overprotective when it comes to Yvette and me. I simply do not want to risk your position here with our family."

"Your father is a wise man. But I could not blame him if he was angry." He paused for a moment and then added, "I feel shame for what is happening."

"Oh, goodness! It's not your fault," Josette said, hoping to reassure him.

The butler's face reflected his sadness. "Most Germans, especially my countrymen who live here in America, are good and honest people. We do not want this war any more than anyone else." His gaze moved between Josette and Yvette as he spoke.

"I'm afraid that not all of the Germans here in the United States share your sentiments," Josette said. "There are stories in the newspapers every day about the spies and bombs they are planting on ships."

"Misguided German youths, I fear." He let out a deep sigh. "They do not understand the ramifications of such a war. America will declare war on Germany one day, and that will be the end of the Fatherland. It will take generations for Germany to recover from the financial losses. And a generation of fine young men will be lost." He shook his head, tears welling in his eyes. "This war, this terrible war. It will not solve problems that began a century ago. In the end, there will be no winners."

Chapter 8

FATHER WASN'T fond of fish, no matter how deliciously it had been prepared. He almost always managed to escape their Friday dinners to attend a meeting at the New York Yacht Club, but tonight was an exception. There was a regatta in New York Harbor tomorrow, and he was to be one of the judges. With piles of paperwork to be completed that evening, Father finally joined the family at the dining room table to eat.

"Saints preserved," Grandmother Murphy commented as Father took his seat at the head of the long table. "Look who's here. And how are you this fine night, Henry?"

"Good evening, ladies…and to you, too, Mother Murphy," Father added in an icy tone. He took his place at the head of the table without making eye contact with the elderly woman. His disrespectful comment brought about one of Mother's nasty glares.

Grandmother Murphy huffed her disapproval at his remark. Her pursed lips accentuated the deep lines around her rouged lips. "I see you're in your usual form tonight, Henry." Despite her sixty-something years, she was a feisty woman with a temper that flared occasionally, especially when Father was involved. Still attractive for a woman of her age, she struck a commanding appearance.

Josette and Yvette exchanged amused glances. If there was one constant thing in their household, it was the fact that their mother's mother and their father were almost always at odds. Their dislike of one another might have been unspoken; but it was an obvious one to be sure.

"I'm glad you could join us tonight, Henry, dear," Mother said, ignoring the friction in the room.

"It's been a while, Henry," Grandmother Murphy said. "And how are things with the Lord of this manor?"

Josette covered her mouth, hoping no one saw her erupting smile.

Father scowled, then drew in a deep breath. Josette knew that look all-too-well. He was trying to calm himself before answering, lest he take his mother-in-law's bait and lose his temper. "I am quite well, thank you," he said in an unruffled tone. He directed his gaze to the maid, who stood beside Josette with a deep platter. "Lucy, may I please have the scalloped potatoes?"

"Right, sir," Lucy responded.

Josette replaced the spoon on the tray so Lucy could move closer to her father.

"And how is your business faring the financial setback caused by the European war?" Grandmother asked. "I spoke with Martha Johnson yesterday," she continued before Father could respond. "She said her husband's retail business has suffered greatly. No shipments arriving from France. Martha's husband imports fine wines and champagne, you know."

"Yes, I am quite aware of Mr. Green's business. He is, after all, a competitor of mine...though on a much smaller scale." Father scooped a large mound of cheese-laden potatoes from the silver serving dish. "It smells of salmon in here, Millie."

"Yes, Henry. It is poached salmon," Mother answered. "I know you're not fond of it, but if you had given Mrs. DuBois more notice that you were joining us for dinner, she could have purchased a lamb chop or something you would have preferred."

Lucy placed the platter of potatoes on the sideboard. "Mrs. DuBois did make a nice 'ollandise sauce especially for you, sir, what with your dislike of the fish and all," Lucy said, picking up another dish. "She thought you might be able to hide the taste a bit with the lemon in the sauce, you see." Lucy carefully lowered the large plate containing several remaining pieces of orange-tinged filets in front of Father.

Father drew in a breath. "Right, then." He reached for the silver spatula and removed a portion. He smiled up at the young maid, which seemed to ease Lucy's apprehension. "Please thank Mrs. DuBois for the effort. I'm sure it will be just fine."

Mrs. DuBois's hollandaise sauce was lumpy with tiny chunks of cooked egg that hadn't mixed in properly. Father's nose crinkled when he took a bite, betraying his reaction to the dish. Yet, he was obviously trying not to make any further fuss about the food.

Grandmother Murphy was Josette and Yvette's only living grandparent. Their mother's father died when they were children, and Father's mother and father had both died of some sort of disease that spread through England before Josette and Yvette were born. The details of their demise, or of Father's childhood, remained a mystery. He simply didn't like to talk about such matters. He did say his only relatives were an uncle – his father's older brother – and a couple of lads who were second cousins. Father called them his branch cousins, referring to them as limbs on the proverbial family tree. He hadn't seen them in decades, though the reason for the lack of visits was as unclear as Father's distant past.

Mother's family, on the other hand, was far less mysterious and certainly not as interesting. Poor Irish Catholic farmers from County Clare who had come to America during the infamous Potato Famine, most had become factory workers in New York or field hands in New Jersey. Two of Mother's three brothers were priests. One of them had returned to Ireland. Their only other living relative was Grandmother Murphy's eldest sister, Mary, who was now in a home for invalids.

"So, is it true, Henry?" Mother asked, a look of deep concern on her face. "Is the import-export business suffering terribly because of the war? I'm told the Germans are sinking cargo ships heading to New York. Winifred Talbert said there's even a shortage of caviar these days. Is it true?"

"Oh, good Lord, Mildred," Grandmother Murphy said with an exaggerated eye roll.

Silence enveloped the large, narrow room, save for the clinking of silverware. Josette and Yvette loved their Grandmother. She never put on airs or pretended to be something she wasn't, like their mother. Grandmother Murphy had spunk, something their mother lacked. Josette couldn't help but wonder why Mother had become such a snob, when she had been raised by such a down-to-earth woman like Grandmother.

What's more, when Josette and Yvette questioned their grandmother about their mother's haughty attitude, she had said, "Having a lot of money all-too-often lifts the noses of the rich so high into the air, you'd think they'd drown in a rain storm. And the newer the money, the higher the nose is lifted, it seems."

"Your concern is for caviar when there's a war going on, Mildred?" their grandmother remarked to Mother, mirroring Josette's thoughts.

"No, of course not," Mother responded in an indignant tone. "With France involved in that mess overseas, Mr. St. John is out of many of those wonderful imported cheeses, too."

"So, now 'tis cheeses you're worried about," was Grandmother Murphy's only response, though her expression reflected her obvious disappointment with her daughter.

Josette was at a loss for words. She merely let out a sigh.

Father pursed his lips for a long moment, then he blurted out, "The Germans have been confiscating cargo from Allied ships since the blasted war started. But that's all changed."

Mother cast Father a cold stare. "Watch your language, Henry," she said flatly.

"I will not apologize, Millie. It's barbaric. All sense of civility is gone. The rules of human decency have been thrown out. Those barbarians are sending the merchant ships to the bottom of the Channel without showing mercy for the crew. Things are likely to get worse, if something doesn't change. The president needs to get off his...well, let's just say, if he doesn't do something to help out our Allies, there will likely be terrible consequences."

"And your business, Henry? Is your business alive and well, or is it time to worry about the future of my granddaughters and their financial legacy?" Grandmother Murphy asked.

Josette had read about the ever-increasing number of ships that had been attacked. "Should we be worried, Father?"

He smiled gently. "Please do not worry your pretty heads, ladies." And then he looked directly at their grandmother. "I have a very large warehouse which still contains plenty of products for me to sell. Naturally," he added with a shrug, "some of my inventory is low. Lace, Scotch whiskey and the like." He picked up the gravy server and poured out additional thick, pale yellow sauce on his fish. "It's just that the war has gone on much longer than anyone expected, so smaller importers do not have enough inventory." He looked up with a reassuring smile. "But I can guarantee you all, Rogers Imports is still doing well."

Mother placed her fork on the plate. "And what if the war continues, Henry? How long can we hold on? Will you please tell us if we must make...adjustments to our life style?"

"Yes, Henry. How long can you continue doing business as usual in the midst of a war of this magnitude?" Grandmother Murphy said with narrowed eyes.

Josette noted her father's face had turned a shade of deep crimson. He swallowed hard, then pulled the napkin from his lap and dabbed his mouth. "If you must know, Mother Murphy, I am anticipating that very scenario. At the present time, I am negotiating a contract with an American company that will be making military uniforms for the British forces."

"Uniforms?" Mother looked puzzled. "And what does that have to do with Rogers Imports?"

"Buttons, Millie. Thousands and thousands of buttons. And cotton fabric from the southern states. We can sell thousands of yards of cotton to the companies who make things, like undergarments for the soldiers to wear in the summer time. There are plenty of button makers and cotton mills right here in America, so I don't need to depend on supplies from overseas." He turned to look at Grandmother Murphy. "So, as you can see, I have things well in hand. If anything changes, or if my accountant needs any assistance in sorting things out, I will be sure you are the first to know, what with your vast amount of business acumen and such."

SATURDAY MORNING was glorious. Puffy white clouds hung over the city like gigantic soft cotton balls. Still, the sun burned bright and intense. By seven-thirty, Lucy had gone through the house, room by room, pulling open the curtains to let in the welcoming warmth of spring.

Up and dressed by eight, Josette bounded down the stairs for breakfast. Today would be a day filled with adventures. She was eager to get out and about; to have new experiences and be in a part of the City she had never seen. Now, however, she would have to manage her way through the gauntlet of obtaining permission from her Father. And that could be difficult. He insisted that she and Yvette go out in public with their mother. Or Mr. Herrmann. Just not on their own. But they were nearly of legal age, and it was quite silly and old-fashioned to provide them with escorts everywhere they went. This was the perfect opportunity for Josette to assert herself and convince Father they didn't need a chaperone.

For the first time since last summer, the morning weather was warm enough for the family to eat breakfast on the screened-in porch overlooking the backyard gardens.

"Good morning, Mrs. DuBois," Josette said, entering the kitchen. The cook didn't bother to turn around to greet Josette. The fragrant smell of freshly brewed coffee permeated the room.

"*Bon jour,*" Mrs. DuBois said in her usual, none-too-happy tone.

Reading aloud softly, Father was already at the table, the newspaper spread before him like the wings of a colossal white bird. "Oh, Josette. It's you."

"Yes, Father. Good morning."

"And what does this fine day hold for you?" he asked, moving his gaze to peek over the small spectacles perched on the tip of his nose.

"Not much, Father," Josette said casually. "Just studying. The usual. Oh, and a trip to the library later to do some research for a paper I must write."

Yvette entered a moment later, sitting beside Josette. Still in her pale pink sleeping attire with matching robe, hair disheveled, Yvette greeted Josette and their father. "Good morning. Sorry I'm not dressed. I didn't sleep well." She clacked her tongue. "And then Lucy came in and woke me up."

"Don't be upset with Lucy. Mother ordered her to open your draperies to wake you. She did the same to me," Josette said.

"And I told your mother to instruct Lucy to do just that. So, don't be angry with your mother, either," Father stated in a firm voice. "No point in laziness, I say."

"Yes, Father," Yvette said in a low tone. Yawning, she pulled a wayward strand of hair from her cheek and tucked it behind her ear.

"Tea or coffee?" Mrs. DuBois called from the doorway.

"Tea for me," Josette chirped.

"I'll have my usual Earl Gray with one lump of sugar, please," said Yvette.

Father moved his gaze to Yvette. "And what do you have planned for the day, dear girl?"

"Me?" Yvette looked as if she faced a judge in a court of law. "Uh, not much."

"Your sister is heading to the library. What's on your agenda?"

Yvette looked as nervous as a new bride. "Well, I, I must practice for my next piano lesson." She stared down into her lap, fidgeting with her napkin. "Mr. Franklin ever so wants me to play in a recital in June."

"A recital? Really? How lovely, Yvette." Father said with a smile. "You should tell your mother the date. Have her mark it down. We must all attend, now mustn't we?" Father went back to reading the newspaper.

Mrs. DuBois approached, sliding a tray laden with a tea pot and two cups and saucers in front of Josette. "More coffee, *monsieur?*" she asked Father.

"Please," he responded without looking up. "And another slice of toast. With plenty of butter and marmalade, this time."

"Just toast for me, please. Mrs. DuBois," Yvette said, "Oh, yes, Father. I forgot to mention that I plan to accompany Josette to the library later."

Josette rolled her eyes. Yvette was such a terrible liar. She searched their father's face to see if he had understood what her sister had said.

He had no reaction whatsoever to Yvette's comment.

Still, Josette thought she should head off possible future problems, should their father realize the oddity of Yvette spending time in a university library, rather than staying at home reading a romantic novel or playing the piano.

"Father? Did you hear?" Josette said. "Yvette is going to the library to read about the lives of some of the great composers. Isn't that right, Yvette?" she said, glancing at her sister.

"What's that?" Father looked up. "Did you say, the library?"

"Yes, Father," Yvette responded. "With Josette."

"Well, well. Jolly good, then. I'll have Franz drop you girls off at Barnard College after he has taken me to the Yacht Club."

"That won't be necessary," Josette quickly chimed in. "I…we would very much like to take the trolley today. It would be quite nice to stop off at the park on the way. For a walk, you see. The flowers are beginning to bloom, with the warm weather we're having."

"Yes, yes. The flowers," said Father in a flat, disinterested tone. "Carry on, ladies," he said, without glancing at either of them again. "Have a swimmingly good time."

Josette and Yvette exchanged relieved glances, though they dared not say another word on the subject. Essentially, their father had given them permission to spend the day unaccompanied. And in a public place. Josette doubted if that fact had truly registered in his distracted mind. Yet, it was his permission they sought, and his permission they now had.

ONCE THEY heard Father closing the door to their parents' bedroom upstairs, Yvette leaned closer to Josette. "Researching the lives of great composers? Good heavens. Wherever did you come up with that one?"

"I had to think of something," Josette retorted. "I added the information about the park just in case someone sees you there with Jon. You could always say you simply bumped into him unexpectedly, could you not?"

Yvette uncrossed her arms and chuckled. "Actually, that's quite imaginative."

Lucy entered the room. "Beggin' your pardon," she said with a small curtsey. "If you please. I wish to speak to Miss Yvette."

"Of course, Lucy," Yvette responded. Puzzled, Josette glanced at her sister.

Mrs. DuBois untied her apron and hung it on a peg on the far wall. "I will not return until four, when I prepare dinner. You will be on your own for lunch today."

"Very well, ma'am," Lucy responded. "I think I can handle slicing up some bread and ham on my own." There was a notable amount of sarcasm in Lucy's tone.

"Clean up after yourself," Mrs. DuBois said, grabbing her handbag from the corner cabinet. "I do not want to come back and do more cleaning. I am too busy as it is. Not enough help in this big house," she grumbled, walking out the door and down the hall.

Lucy's eyes searched the doorway. "Never thought the old cow would leave," she said softly turning back to Yvette. Fishing into her apron pocket, Lucy pulled out a neatly folded piece of paper. "That nice piano teacher left this for you, miss." She handed it to Yvette. "Right good-looking chap, if you ask me," she said, with a wink and a smile.

Chapter 9

"MR. FRANKLIN was here?" Yvette asked, her eyes widening.

"Yes, miss."

A panicked expression washed over Yvette's face. "Oh dear!" She began to fuss with her hair. Yvette glanced at the doorway. "Is he gone? He simply cannot see me like this."

"Oh, no. Sorry miss. He's long gone." Lucy stepped to Yvette and handed her the folded piece of paper. "Mr. Franklin was at the back door 'round twenty minutes ago. He said he didn't want me giving this to you when your Father or Mother was about." She smiled. "So, I waited until the coast was clear, I did."

"Thank you, Lucy," Yvette said, sounding relieved. "I truly appreciate your discretion." Unfolding the note, she read silently. "Oh, dear." Her lips slid into a frown.

"Everything all right, miss?" Lucy asked with a look of concern.

"Yes, Lucy. I shall be all right. Thank you again."

After the maid excused herself and left the room, Josette turned to Yvette. "I assume Jonathan cannot meet you at the park after all."

Yvette nodded. "His booking agent called him. I suppose it's good news. He has a job at a Broadway production this evening. A last minute fill-in for the regular pianist. He must rehearse and cannot meet me."

Josette stood up, reached over and took her sister's hand. "I'm so sorry, Yvette. But don't you see? It's good news, after all. Jonathan is climbing the ladder of success." She smiled. "And since you won't be spending the day with him, you can go to the bakery with me. We shall have a dandy time. Now go upstairs and make yourself presentable!"

THE TROLLEY rattled across the miles to Little Germany on the Lower East Side, grinding to a halt at the bustling intersection at Second Avenue and St. Mark's Place. Mr. Herrmann had drawn a careful map of the area. *Das Bitten Bicycles* was located on Avenue A and was clearly marked with a thick "X."

Negotiating the swarm of humanity along the streets of *Kleindeutschland* was daunting. If Manhattan was busy, these streets were chaotic — more horse-driven carts; more people milling about; more noisy automobiles chugging and coughing their way through the crowds of pedestrians who used the streets and sidewalks in equal proportion.

"I see why Mr. Herrmann preferred to bring us here himself," Yvette commented.

Even Josette felt unnerved by the sweep of humanity that surrounded them at every turn. Mr. Herrmann had explained that over recent decades, many of the wealthier Germans had moved to fancy neighborhoods in Harlem and Yorkville. Yet, they continued to shop and socialize in *Kleindeutschland*. More recently, he said, the Irish had infiltrated the once-predominately German Wards, as had the Eastern Europeans. The result was an over-crowded, thriving region complete with barber shops, oyster saloons, lunch counters, shoemakers, beer halls, cigar makers, tailors, clock stores, and quaint shops displaying traditional clothing from various European countries, though most were still decidedly German. Crowded? Yes, to be sure, Josette assessed. But exciting, nonetheless.

After a quick stop to pick up her bicycle bell, they made their way to Avenue B in search of the bakery. Rounding the corner, the sweet aroma of fresh bread and cinnamon and apples wafted on the afternoon breeze.

"Do you smell that?" Josette said with a sense of anticipation. "Mr. Herrmann said to follow our noses, and we would find Gretchen's Bakery with no trouble at all."

Yvette grinned. "I would say he was definitely right, wouldn't you, sister?"

They snaked their way up the block to the shop with the small green and white striped canopy that Mr. Herrmann had described. Gretchen's Bakery had a charming edifice resembling an old wattle-and-daub, European-style building. The front window displayed plates of pastries arranged on three tiers of shelves, each decorated with doilies and pine bough sprigs.

A tiny bell tinkled overhead as Josette and Yvette walked through the front door. There were several small, round tables on one side of the front area. Four young men occupied the table in the far corner. Empty coffee cups and small plates with bits of crumbs sat in front of them. Huddled, leaning into the center of the table with elbows on the top, they spoke in German; so fast and in such a low tone that Josette could only pick up a word here and there.

Josette and her sister walked to the counter, perusing the assorted pastries.

One of the young Germans, a burly young man with red hair, stood up. "*Auf Wiedersehen*," he said to his friends, as he headed towards the door. He stopped beside Josette.

"Good day, pretty ladies," he said in a strange lilting voice. "My, my. A pair of beauties. Are you two German?" There was no hint of an accent in his voice.

Josette felt uncomfortable. "Does it matter?"

The other young Germans, still seated at the table, had turned around, watching. They began to laugh. "Give it up!" one said, snickering.

Narrowing his eyes, the corpulent man shouted something in German to his friends and stormed out, slamming the door. The bell clanged hard.

"Never mind him," Josette whispered to Yvette.

Nodding, Yvette walked along the glass counter, assessing its contents.

Josette glanced at the Germans. They had begun talking together again. The nice-looking one with blonde hair and blue eyes nodded his agreement to something the other lad had said. "*Ja Gut*," he repeated several times. Josette knew that meant 'yes', and 'good.'

Glancing over at Yvette, she asked, "See anything appealing?"

"Too many to choose from," Yvette said with a laugh.

And then a German phrase caught Josette's attention. One of the young Germans said something about Berlin. Unconsciously, her head twisted around, and she found herself looking at the Germans. Berlin. Why were they talking about Berlin?

Obvious that the young men realized Josette was listening, they abruptly stopped talking. All three turned to look at her and her sister with suspicion. A twinge of discomfort crawled up her spine. Something strange was going on. Swallowing hard, she smiled casually, nodded and greeted them with a charming, "*Guten Tag.*"

Expressionless, they rose in near unison. Ignoring Yvette and Josette, they left the bakery without another word. Without so much as a flirtatious glance or a smile or saying 'hello' back to her, as they strolled past and out the front door.

"That was rather rude, don't you think, sister? Yvette commented.

"Frankly, I've had my fill of ill-mannered college-aged chaps lately." She turned to the glass case filled with delicacies as foreign to her as Mrs. DuBois' French tartlets and Madelene cookies had been to her friends who came to tea. "Now, then, let's see what kinds of sweets the Germans eat!"

A stout woman walked out of the door that presumably led to a back kitchen and stood behind the counter. "May I help you *Fraulein?*" she asked.

"Are you Mrs. Herrmann?" Josette asked.

"*Ja, ja!*" She smiled broadly. "I am." The middle-aged woman wore what Josette supposed was the traditional clothing from her homeland: full dark green skirt, white puffy-sleeved blouse, and a black vest with red trim and lacing in front. Her gray hair was plaited in two braids pinned up in a tight mound on her head. Most of the German women Josette had seen were dressed in American styles. This was likely a costume or uniform that Mrs. Herrmann wore in the bakery to add a cultural touch to the place. Not that it wasn't already quite charming.

"And you must be the Roger girls," the woman said. Her eyes narrowed thoughtfully, moving to Josette and then to Yvette, as she spoke. "My husband said Miss Josette would come in to buy my apple *strudel* today. *Ach du Lieber!*" she said, bringing her hands together in a sort of clap. "I am so sorry, but I do not know which one of you is—"

"It's quite all right, Mrs. Herrmann," Josette said with a laugh. "We're identical twins, to be sure. This is Yvette," she said, motioning in her sister's direction. "And I'm Josette."

"We are quite pleased to meet you, Mrs. Herrmann," Yvette added.

"And I am happy to meet you two lovely girls," Mrs. Herrmann responded. "I saved you a nice big piece of my *strudel*, Miss Josette. But my husband did not say you would both be coming. I'm afraid the last of the apple *strudel* was sold to those *Burschen*...oh, sorry, that's German for lads." Like her husband, Mrs. Herrmann's accent was guttural and a bit difficult to understand. "But I would be most happy to serve you one of our other specialties. *Stollen*? Or perhaps a few *Linzer Auge*?" she said, pointing to the two-layer cookies covered with a thick dusting of confectioner's sugar.

"They all look wonderful," Josette said, assessing the items in the display case. Several types of rolls – presumably sweet, dessert rolls – were stacked pyramid-style on lacy paper doilies. She recognized the marzipan candies – the Laurents had served them at their annual Christmas gatherings. Some were shaped like tiny pigs, while most were fashioned to resemble miniature pieces of fruit.

"I'll have that," Josette said, pointing to what looked like a cake layered with cherries.

"An excellent choice, *Fraulein*." Mrs. Herrmann bent down and opened the door at the back of the case.

"I can't believe we've never met you before now, Mrs. Herrmann," Yvette commented. "Your husband has worked for our family since we were babies, and we've never even seen you. You must come for tea."

"That is very kind," she said, stretching to reach the piece of cake. "My husband has always spoken highly of your family. He is especially fond of you two ladies."

Josette returned the compliment. "Your husband said you are an excellent cook."

"*Ach.*" She gave a little swoosh of her hand in the air. "That's my Franz." Mrs. Herrmann's plump cheeks blushed pink.

The bell on the door jingled again, as a woman entered grasping the hand of a curly haired toddler. Another youngster, a boy maybe eight or nine, walked behind them.

"Can I have a sweet, mommy?" the older child begged.

"Shush, Frederick. You may have a cookie, but we must wait our turn."

"*Guten Tag*," Josette said, smiling at the adorable little boys. They blinked up at her with a confused expression.

"I'm afraid they don't speak German," the woman explained. "My husband – their father – is American. Scots Irish, actually."

"Well, in that case, hello, young gentlemen," Josette corrected, squatting to their level. "And how old are you?" The older boy held up seven fingers. The young one clung timidly to his mother's skirt.

These two little ones were adorable. Half German. Half American. As she stood again, Josette couldn't help but think of the confusion and upset this attractive mother and her husband would experience, should the United States and Germany become sworn enemies. And the boys? Would they be ostracized because of their German blood, even though it was diluted by their father's family heritage?

"Here you are, *Fraulein*." Mrs. Herrmann handed Josette and Yvette the plates of pastries, two forks, and napkins. They walked to the nearest table and settled into their chairs.

From somewhere outside on the street came shouts, the deep bellows of a tuba, and finally, motor vehicle horns.

"What's all that noise?" Yvette asked Josette.

Josette shrugged, turning to look out the front window. "A parade, I think."

"*Nein, nein.* It is about the sailors," Mrs. Herrmann said, shaking her head. "I do not understand why they continue to do this. What good will it do?"

"It only causes trouble," the boys' mother said, lifting the smaller child onto her hip. "We certainly don't need more trouble. Why can they not stop this?"

Puzzled, Josette stood up, walked to the door and opened it. Dozens upon dozens of men – some in what appeared to be military uniforms – marched down the street. "It's a protest," Josette said, stepping back inside the bakery. She peered out the doorway again. Traffic had been stopped. The men merely walked around stranded delivery trucks and motor cars, as the drivers leaned out their vehicles' windows and shouted obscenities in a variety of languages.

Accompanied by a tuba player and a teenaged lad with an accordion, the marchers began to sing in German as they walked.

"*Deutschland uber Alles!*" It sounded more like they were shouting the words rather than singing. Several carried signs painted with the English words: 'Free our Ships,' 'We are not prisoners,' and 'Let us go home.'

While some of the people on the sidewalks cheered as the men passed, others were obviously upset by the procession, turning their backs on the makeshift protest parade.

Josette recognized three of the four young men who had been in the bakery. The fourth, the man with ginger hair, was nowhere to be seen. The handsome blonde with piercing blue eyes was closest. He dipped his head to acknowledge her presence as he passed.

She didn't know why, but she nodded in return. She drew back inside, closing the door. "Oh, my. Is this about the German ships that have been confiscated by the government?"

"You know of such things, miss?" the German mother asked Josette.

"Yes, I do. I recently attended a lecture at Columbia, and the subject, well, let's just say it came up," Josette commented, not wanting to say anything further.

"My parents came here from Heidelberg to visit with us last September. To see their grandsons for the first time," the young woman said. "They were to return to Germany long ago. But when the American government took control of all German ships – even the luxury liners, their crews, and their passengers – they were all stranded here with no way to get home."

"That's terrible," Yvette said, her face reflecting her concern. "It's simply not right. Are your mother and father still with you?"

The woman nodded. "We live in a two-bedroom flat. It is crowded. But we manage."

Josette huffed out a breath. "I don't understand why such a thing has been allowed. We're told repeatedly that America is not involved in this war. Or so our President insists. And yet, we are selling ammunition and other supplies to one side and not to the other. It simply doesn't make sense," she said, shaking her head.

"I'm afraid things will get worse for the Germans before they get better," Mrs. Herrmann said. "Especially those of us here in America."

Josette worried Mrs. Herrmann was right. And yet, she had read about rings of German spies operating in New York and other places in the United States. If those newspaper reports were true, and if the President and the American government continued on this pro-British path, then Mrs. Herrmann was certainly right. Things were bound to get worse for everyone.

FATHER DIDN'T shout often, but when he did, it was like thunder rolling down from the heavens. Today was one of those occasions. Josette and Yvette could hear him clearly as they walked up the front steps of Compton House. And he was furious.

When Josette opened the door, his voice was even louder.

"Hell no!" he roared from his upstairs library. "How could they do that to me?"

"Oh, dear," Yvette said in a low tone, following Josette inside. "Do you think Father and Mother have learned that we lied about going to the library?"

"Surely not. How could they know?" Josette responded in a near whisper.

"Perhaps Mr. Herrmann told Father our plans…though I don't believe he would do that."

"He would never do such a thing," Josette said.

"Be that as it may, something has certainly happened to make Father so upset."

The girls stood frozen in place near the coat rack. Neither of them removed their hats.

"This is not the end of the matter," their father bellowed. "I shall be in touch with my attorney, postehaste." He slammed down the telephone so hard it made a loud thud.

Josette and Yvette looked at each other with puzzled expressions.

"Well…at least we know this isn't about us," Josette murmured.

Mother, apparently in the room with their father, sounded concerned. "*Mon Dieu!* What has happened, Henry? You must calm down and tell me everything."

"Nothing you need to know about, Millie. Just go back to your embroidery and let me—"

"No, Henry. Not this time. Something is wrong, and I want to know what it is. Is the business in trouble?" It wasn't like their mother to be so insistent.

After a short silence, Father finally spoke. "Very well, then. If you must know, luv, I have been counting on a particularly important business deal. It would have been quite lucrative. But it seems as if… well, it's not going through. Not at this time, anyway."

"The one with the cotton fabric and buttons you told Momma about?"

"Yes, Millie. That very one."

"But what happened, Henry? You seemed so certain."

Josette thought back to the night when Father and Grandma Murphy had their little chat over Father's business dealings. She glanced at Yvette, who stood motionless, wide-eyed, looking up the stairs as if she would be able to see through the walls and into Father's office.

"I was sure I had the deal, Millie!" he said in a frustrated tone. "I had all the details worked out. It was some damnable fool over at J. P. Morgan and Company who approved a huge loan for my competitor. Sol Eisenberg, the owner, was able to outbid me for the job. For Christ sakes, Sol Eisenberg!"

Josette could hear Father's heavy footsteps on the floor as he paced.

"He's a small-time manufacturer, who uses young Irish girls for his labor."

"Can't you do something about this? Go to Mr. Morgan and talk to him?" Mother said.

"No, Millie. It's business. I am, however, having my attorney look into the matter."

"Then there's nothing more to be done?" Mother asked.

"At least if I was going to lose the bid, it should have been to Rockefeller or Carnegie. Rich men, they are. But instead, I lost to Sol Eisenberg. The bastard is eliminating the middle man. Buying straight from the producers. Not right, if you ask me. He bought a bunch of sewing machines straight away from Singer, my lawyer told me. Harrods and Selfridges in London also got a couple of hefty contracts with the military. I don't know how they think they're going to manage that, what with the British cargo ships being sunk about as often as President Wilson plays golf! And that's about every day, from what I hear."

"What will you do, Henry? Are we going to be all right?" their mother asked, her voice trembling.

Josette noticed the fear in Yvette's face. She reached over and took her sister's hand. "Things will be okay. You'll see," Josette whispered.

Father's voice was gentler now. "Of course, Millie. I've always taken care of my girls, haven't I?" Then he added, "And please don't worry. I do have a few more coals in the fire, my dear. I am not going to take this lying down. Trust me when I say we will be right as rain."

Josette motioned for her sister to follow her back out the front door. Yvette looked confused but followed her sister. Tiptoeing so their heels didn't make clicking noises on the slate tile floor, Josette carefully opened the door. She and Yvette stepped out to the front porch.

"What are we doing?" Yvette asked.

"Shhh. Pretend we are just now arriving home. I don't think Father would want us to know we heard him and Mother discussing business matters?"

Josette closed the door behind them carefully. A few moments later, she threw it open so hard it hit the inside wall. "Father! Mother! We're home!" she announced.

"Yes...we're home from the library. And the park, too!" Yvette shouted. She looked at Josette with a broad smile.

Chapter 10

THE DIRECTIVE to meet with Mr. Jack Morgan had been sudden. Unexpected. Mr. Van Camp had approached Curtis' desk a few minutes earlier, announcing Mr. Morgan's orders in an abrupt manner. And when Curtis had asked why, Van Camp didn't give any hint of the reason in his voice, nor in his expression.

"Just get yourself up there, Carlson," he had said flatly.

This was the first time Curtis had been inside what was often lightheartedly called the throne room. Indeed, it was everything he had imagined. Palatial. Floor-to-ceiling wood panels. A grand fireplace surrounded by a mantle, which must have come from some historic English manor house. Bronze busts of Mr. Morgan's father and grandfather sat atop marble pillars in the corners on either side of the long row of windows looking out on the bustling financial district. Mr. Morgan's desk was no less impressive. It was quite long with Grecian pillars carved into each corner, and the company logo in the center of the raised molding on the front section.

"Please, Curtis. Have a seat," Morgan instructed, motioning to the burgundy chair facing his desk.

"Yes, sir." Curtis had no idea why Mr. Morgan wanted to see him this afternoon. Had he authorized a loan Mr. Morgan didn't approve of?

Trying to maintain a confident composure, fighting to keep the tycoon from noticing his nervousness, Curtis smiled and settled into the over-sized leather chair.

"I called you up here to discuss something very important."

"Ah. Another debate about the war effort, I presume." Curtis crossed his legs, more relaxed, now that he knew why he was there.

"No...though you did a fine job of holding your own at Columbia, from what I heard."

From the tone of Mr. Morgan's voice, Curtis sensed he wasn't there to receive a scolding for making a mistake or misjudgment. He felt a sense of relief. "I'm very glad you were pleased, considering how it ended."

"This is something far more difficult. It is something you must keep to yourself, my boy."

"A secret of sorts?"

"Indeed," Mr. Morgan said with a brisk nod. "Only a select few will know about your assignment."

Intrigued, Curtis leaned forward, uncrossing his legs. "What kind of assignment?"

"An assignment that will affect the outcome of the war. If we are successful, it will change history."

Morgan's words, his serious expression caused a chill to crawl up Curtis' spine. "You have my attention, Mr. Morgan. What can I do to help?"

Drawing in a deep breath, Morgan leaned back in his seat, his gaze less intimidating now. "The German military is stronger than anyone thought possible. There are rumors their military, or perhaps I should say, the scientists working for the German military, are working feverishly on various new methods of killing that will swing the direction of the war in their favor."

"Christ! What kind of methods?"

"They've developed deadly poisonous gases to unleash on the Allied troops. And we're not just talking about tear gases, but something so toxic, so deadly that the poor chaps exposed to it would die. But not before suffering greatly. Apparently, the fumes burn the flesh and do other unthinkable things. Death is inevitable…and likely, welcomed by the doomed soldiers."

Curtis had to catch his breath. "Good Lord. Do you really think the Germans would sink that low?"

"Yes. I'm afraid so. It has already been produced and tested. I have ears and eyes in Washington, D.C., and I am told there is little the Central Powers wouldn't do to win this war."

Curtis wasn't the least surprised that J. P. Morgan, one of the world's most powerful men, would have covert contacts at the White House. "Shocking, just shocking," he said in a low tone, shaking his head. "And you've found a way to stop them, have you?"

"Stop them? Hell no. We should be so lucky as to have a way to get to Berlin and level the whole damnable city and its laboratories." Reaching in the rosewood humidor on top of the desk, Morgan fished out two large cigars. "I don't know how the bastards can be stopped at this point. Slow them down, perhaps, but not stopped." Morgan unpeeled the fancy band wrapped around each one and used his cigar trimmer, a miniature guillotine of sorts, to lance the tips off the wrapped ends.

"Here you go, my boy. Cuba's finest. Hand rolled," he said, handing one to Curtis.

Thanking Morgan, Curtis reluctantly accepted the long, thick shank. Expensive as hell, no doubt, but, still, a habit he didn't much care for.

Morgan reached for his pearl-encased lighter. "I'm afraid the best we can hope for at this point is to slow down the sons-of-bitches."

"But I don't understand? How in heaven's name can I help?" Curtis asked.

"Patience, lad." He sucked in audibly, rolling the cigar in his mouth until the end glowed. "Did you know the German scientists have developed blimps? I've been told they're being mass produced.

Used to spy at first, but now they're using them to drop bombs." Puffs of gray smoke tumbled from his lips as he spoke.

The suspense was making Curtis edgy. What in the world was Morgan getting at? "Yes, I know. I've read about the German Zeppelins. They're getting pretty good at dropping their bombs, though it seems they often miss their intended targets. Seems like a lot of innocent civilians are getting the worst of it."

"They can cross the Channel just long enough to wreak havoc along the English coast. It's only a matter of time before they can stay in the air longer and make it to London. All hell will break loose when they do," Morgan said. "Here, son. Light up your stogie." He handed Curtis his fancy lighter.

After his father had taken up cigar smoking years ago, Curtis had developed an aversion to the smell. Worse, the smoke made his eyes water and his nose itch. The result was an all-too-frequent bout of sneezing. Putting up with the nasty practice was a necessary evil, especially if he expected to be included at the smoky gatherings of high-ranking, cigar-loving businessmen.

"They seem to have the ability to create new weapons quite efficiently." Curtis put the cigar between his lips, rotated it, and lighted the tip.

"It's a sad truth," Mr. Morgan said. "Just look how fast they got those damnable U-boats into the action." Morgan drew in several puffs on his cigar, releasing a mouthful of pungent smoke. "The idiot Germans are sinking cargo ships, and they're not even confiscating the cargo. Then they whine that they don't have enough food and supplies! Preposterous!"

Curtis pulled the cigar from his lips, holding it to the side. "It certainly is," he agreed, surreptitiously dodging the lingering gray cloud so Morgan didn't notice. His eyes had already begun to burn.

"Wilson is a lily-livered coward," Morgan said, shaking his head. "That's why I've sent another one of my representatives to Washington to meet with Secretary of State Lansing."

The importance of this meeting struck Curtis like a lightning bolt. Remaining calm on the outside, he casually commented. "Oh, I see." Actually, he didn't.

Mr. Morgan fastened his gaze on Curtis' face without so much as a blink. "Listen, Carlson. The Allied countries are running out of capital to continue fighting this war. I've already made them generous loans. But they need more money. Much more to win this war."

Curtis was quite surprised. "I know you've been quite generous with the French and British. You came through with millions for them, when Wilson wouldn't send a dime."

He shrugged. "It was something that had to be done. The president didn't want it to look like the U. S. was siding with the Allies." He placed his cigar in a glass ash tray and continued. "And now, there are meetings going on, both in Washington and in London, to decide how we can further help the Allies...financially speaking, that is, since we can't send troops. Not yet, in any case. In fact, I lunched with one of the president's cabinet members regarding providing Britain and France with a large loan to prop up their governments for the duration of the war."

Curtis was stunned. "I see."

"Your cigar, son." Morgan had noticed Curtis was merely holding the premium stogie. "Take a drag or the fire will go out."

"Oh, right." Curtis glanced at the thickening ash layer on the tip, smiled, and inhaled a shallow drag. Morgan must have sensed Curtis' lack of enthusiasm, for he motioned to the small brass bowl on the edge of the desk. As Curtis expelled the puff, he placed the cigar in the bowl and shrugged, a little embarrassed.

"No worries, my boy. It's an acquired taste." The swivel chair squeaked under Morgan's large frame when he leaned back. He continued, unperturbed. "As an expert in economic matters, I'm sure you're aware that running a war is a costly thing."

"Naturally. But it hasn't even been a year since the war began."

"No one expected the war to last more than a few months. The costs have been gargantuan. Both the British and the French coffers are nearly empty. The Russians aren't doing much better, I'm sorry to say. It won't be long before all of the Allied governments run out of money. And without money, they cannot sustain their soldiers. No food, no ammunition, no medical supplies."

Curtis nodded his understanding. "Of course. And if the Germans are victorious, that could very well lead to a depression here at home. A great deal of the American economy depends on being able to trade with the Allied nations."

"That's right, Curtis." He looked pleased. "The outcome of this war hinges on who runs out of money first."

"Surely the president realizes the economic impact the loss of the Allied countries as trading partners would have on the United States."

"He's finally coming around, though it's been a struggle."

"And you believe this loan will change the outcome of the war?" Curtis asked.

"Absolutely. I've been conferring with numerous financiers and bankers, both here and overseas, who are experts on such matters. We all believe this loan will patch the holes in their declining economies... for now. Until President Wilson gets off his ass and declares war on those damnable German and Austrian bastards."

"So...where do I come in?" Curtis asked, still confused about why one of the world's most powerful men would take him into his confidence on a matter of international secrecy.

"Yes, yes." Morgan's lips curled into a satisfied smile. "No one employed here at my company grasps the situation as well as you do, my boy. That's why you're going to London with Phineas Van Camp. He's been with my company for nearly thirty years, so we know we can trust him. He'll be carrying very important papers with him in which I have made an official offer to loan the British and French governments five hundred million dollars."

Curtis' jaw slackened. "Did you say five hundred million dollars? That's a half billion!"

"Indeed. That's why I need someone I can trust to accompany Mr. Van Camp. I fear the man is becoming...well, let's just say, he's a mite forgetful. You can watch over him and make sure everything goes as it should. You will be provided with all the details, of course, in case you need to explain anything to the British officials you'll be meeting with. So?" He rose. "Do you think you're up to the challenge, son?"

"I...I would be honored."

"Good. You and Van Camp will sail on the *Lusitania* on May 1st. You'll need to get a passport. Pack some formal wear, since you'll be traveling in First Cabin. You will tell everyone Van Camp is your rich uncle. No one can know you two are carrying documents for the world's largest loan. Millions of people's lives depend on the success of this trip."

Chapter 11

APRIL ARRIVED with its usual spring showers. Tuesdays and Thursdays, weather permitting, Josette rode her bicycle the long distance to school at Barnard. This Tuesday morning, however, Josette worried that the on-again, off-again sprinkles would leave her a soggy mess. Instead, Mr. Herrmann had driven her to the college. He was scheduled to pick her up at 12:15 after French class. She scurried through the hallway, dashed down the front steps and hurried to the central courtyard. Mr. Herrmann was already there in the drive, outside the car waiting for her with the motor car's rear door open.

Accepting Mr. Herrmann's hand, she stepped into the Cadillac. "Hello," she said to Yvette in a jovial tone, sliding onto the back seat.

Mr. Herrmann had picked up Yvette from her music school on his way to fetch her. Josette set her handbag and the knapsack carrying her books between them. Leaning closer to her sister, she said, "I'm certainly excited that Father agreed to let us do a bit of shopping at Macy's."

Yvette frowned. "Unfortunately, Mother instructed Mr. Herrmann to take us directly home."

"But Father said—"

"Mr. Herrmann said Father has come home early. Father told him he wants us to come home immediately," Yvette explained.

"How odd. Father never comes home from his office early. I do hope everything is all right."

"IN HERE, ladies," their father called from the parlor. "Please come in."

Josette set her purse beside Yvette's and lifted off her hat. "I don't have a good feeling about this, do you?" she whispered to her sister.

Yvette forced a smile and gave a small nod.

Placing their hats on the hall tree's hooks, Josette and Yvette headed into the parlor. Their parents sat on the satin settee.

"What's going on, Father?" Josette asked. "Is something wrong?"

"No, no," Father waved his hands from side to side. "On the contrary, girls, I have wonderful news. Please sit down." For the first time in weeks, their father looked happy. "No need to worry. Everything is going to work out swimmingly."

Josette and Yvette settled into the matching pair of pale-blue tufted chairs by the big marble fireplace. "What do you mean, Father?" Josette questioned. Had he landed that big contract after all?

Father pulled a folded envelope from inside his jacket pocket. "I received this letter last Tuesday." He proceeded to open it as he spoke. "It was posted three weeks ago in London. With the difficulties getting mail through safely and such...well, then, in any case, it arrived at last. And since then, I've spent the past days working out the arrangements."

"Arrangements?" Mother asked, her eyes wide with anticipation.

"Yes, Millie. I've taken care of most of the details. The passport documents to be filled out and the like," Father said, motioning to a pile of papers on the tea table adjacent to the settee. "I'll explain in a moment, but first things first." He pulled his reading glasses from his vest pocket and slid them on. "Let me read this letter to you ladies. It's best to let the barrister's words explain the situation."

"The barrister?" Josette asked, exchanging puzzled glances with Yvette.

"Yes, yes, Josette. Hush now and listen." Clearing his throat, he began to read:

> "My dear Mr. Rogers. It is with deep sadness I report, herein, the death of your Uncle Silas Pherson Rogers. His will, and the provisions made in the Agreement upon which your grandfather agreed when establishing Rogers and Rogers, Limited, in 1877, was that upon the death of the afore-noted Silas Pherson Rogers, the presidency of said Rogers and Rogers would transfer to Silas' eldest son, Harold, your father's cousin. And in the event of Harold's death, the presidency shall pass to his eldest son, Harold, Jr."

Father bristled. "And...," he drew in a sharp breath and started again.

> "And upon the death of Harold, Jr., the presidency would pass to your brother's second son, George."

Father stopped, eyes closed momentarily before he looked up. "You see, girls, Harold, Sr., my cousin, was actually five years younger than my father," he explained with a pained expression. "My grandfather was a despicable bugger. My father should have been the next in line after his older brother died."

"Why wasn't he, Father?" Josette asked.

"There was bad blood between my father and grandfather. I never understood why. Nor did I understand why my father didn't stand up for himself when his brother, Harold, died in that hunting accident." His jaw hardened. "My father was afraid of Grandfather, I reckon. I always regarded him a coward after that."

Josette's father swallowed hard. She could see the subject was very difficult...which was likely the reason he had been so secretive about all of this in the past.

"That's one of the reasons your father came to New York to establish a small branch of the business," Mother interjected. "He didn't get along with his father and certainly didn't want to work under his grandfather's iron thumb." She leaned into Father, smiling gently as she patted his hand. "We never would have met if things hadn't worked out that way."

"It was for the best in the long run." Father's expression softened, he exhaled a loud breath, and then he began to read again.

"It is with the deepest regret, I must tell you, Mr. Rogers, the unthinkable has occurred. Both of your cousin's sons, Harold and George Rogers, have been killed on the Western Front, and when their proud grandfather, Silas, received word of their demise, he fell dead from heart failure."

"*Mon Dieu*, Henry. That's terrible," Mother said with a gasp.

"Yes, yes. But just wait, Millie. There's more," Father said. "Now, then. Where was I?" He scanned the letter. "Oh yes." He continued.

"Therefore, because your father, Albert N. Rogers, has passed, and because you are the last living relative in the line of succession, you are to assume the presidency of Rogers and Rogers, Limited, my honorable sir. While the business is in good hands with its current manager, Andrew Wilcox, your presence in London is essential. Naturally, your deceased uncle's home in London is part

of your inheritance and will be a suitable residence for you and your family. Please advise me, as soon as possible, with the date of your arrival in the U.K. I look forward to your prompt reply.

Yours sincerely and with deepest sympathy for your losses,
Richard J. Richards, Esq.

Had Josette heard the words correctly? Did he actually say, 'suitable residence for your family?' She felt her stomach twist into a knot.

Josette looked at her sister. Not only was her mouth agape, the color had drained from her face. It was obvious Yvette had the same reaction to Mr. Richards' letter.

Just as Josette opened her mouth to speak, Mother said, "Good Lord! Are you saying you have inherited the entire Rogers estate, Henry?"

"Indeed, I have, my dear," he said, removing his glasses.

Mother's voice trembled with excitement. "Your uncle was a wealthy man, was he not?"

"Indeed, he was, luv. I received a telegram from Mr. Richards this morning listing some of the property and money I am to receive. It is quite a fortune, ladies," he said with a wide grin. "Old man Silas is likely turning over in his grave about now, seeing how I'll be winding up with the whole blooming pot of gold. Sweet justice, if you ask me, though it's certainly sad the boys both died in the war. But I can't help that."

"And the house? Is it wonderful, Henry?" Mother asked, cupping her hands together, a broad smile betraying her utter delight.

"Of course, it has been a long time since I've seen it, but I believe it's very grand, my dear. Near Kensington Palace. I remember going there when I was a young tyke." He chuckled. "I never dreamed it would be mine one day. You will be quite happy living there."

Yvette spoke up. "Wait! You can't mean you're planning to live in England? Permanently?"

"Perhaps not permanently, Yvette," Father replied. "But it will be for quite some time."

"Good heavens, Father," Josette said with a gasp. "Are you serious? You're expected to move to England to take over the business there with this appalling war raging on?"

"Yes, my girl. There's no other choice. However, I wouldn't spend much time worrying about the war. According to the newspapers, the Prime Minister predicts it will end soon."

Josette smirked. "Ha! They've been promising a quick end to the war from the very beginning. Remember the article which came out last fall that promised it would all be over before Christmas? Well, Christmas has come and gone, and things are worse than ever."

"Nevertheless, it will likely be over soon, and with me at the helm of Rogers and Rogers, I'll be able to captain the business into tip-top shape."

"When do you leave, Father?" Josette questioned.

He squinted his eyes, assessing her. "Oh no, my dear. You don't understand. We're all moving to England. We leave on the First of May. I've booked us in first-class staterooms on the *Lusitania*. Nothing but the finest for my three girls." He smiled, as if he hoped that would quiet a possible storm.

"But that's impossible," Josette objected, turning back to her father.

"Yes, Henry. It's too soon to leave." Mother protested. "I need more time to get ready. There's too much to do." She was getting upset. "Why, I shall need a new wardrobe to take. I've been told the *Lusitania* is a very luxurious ship. And I'll need a new fur coat."

Josette was still numb. "And you intend for us – Yvette and me – to go with you?"

"Of course," Father responded.

Yvette stood, her back stiff. "No, Father. I refuse to go to England," she said, stomping her foot, arms folded across her chest.

Their father looked surprised. "Yvette? You're refusing?"

"Yes, Father. I cannot and will not go. I shall stay here in New York."

Their father's face flushed crimson, his features hardened. Josette knew that look. It didn't happen very often, thank God, but her father was about to explode in anger.

He stood. "Look here, young lady. As long as I'm supporting you, you will obey me." His voice grew louder. "I pay for everything you have, every morsel of food you eat, every shred of clothing you wear!"

Yvette's bottom lip began to quiver. Sniffing in pitiful defeat, her eyes welled with tears. "I don't care. I'll find a way. I shall stay here in our home and—"

"No, you will not. You are a member of this family. You will come to England with us!"

Josette spoke up. "Please, Father. I cannot leave, either. I'm almost finished with my schooling. If I leave now, I won't graduate. I'll lose the entire semester. Yvette and I can join you later. This summer, perhaps."

Tears streaming down her cheeks, Yvette shot an angry look at Josette. "No, sister. I won't go at all!"

"We'll find a way, Yvette. Please calm down." Josette was concerned that Yvette would make a slip about her relationship with Jonathan. That would surely guarantee Father would insist on their imminent departure. She lifted her brows and cocked her head to the side. "Just shush for now. Please!"

"Look, my girls," Father said, "I realize this has all happened quite fast, and believe me, I did consider the possibility of leaving you behind in New York." Their father's voice was calmer now. "The fact is, if this war isn't over soon, or if the Germans declare war on America, trans-Atlantic crossings for passenger liners may cease completely. Despite what the Prime Minister is spouting to the newspapers, the reality is that America will enter the war. Some experts think President Wilson will change his mind, what with all these bombs being set off by German spies across the U. S. of A. I've read that Cunard may even suspend the *Lusitania's* sailings between Liverpool and New York if things get worse. Who knows? This might be her last voyage until a peace treaty is signed." He shook his head. "No. We need to get to London as soon as possible. And as a family."

AS WAS THE USUAL routine when Father was home in the evening, Mrs. DuBois had prepared dinner, Lucy served it, and Mr. Herrmann oversaw the entire process. Pale green candles in tall silver stands flickered a soft glow across the starched white tablecloth. The overhead electrified crystal chandelier was turned low, throwing flecks of glittering rainbows across the table and onto the flocked white wall covering. Mr. Herrmann stood at attention like a dutiful soldier beside the fancy mirrored sideboard, a silly ceremonial carryover, Josette supposed, from Father's upbringing in a wealthy British family.

The servants were exceptionally quiet tonight. Even the chatty Lucy didn't utter a word as she ladled potato soup into small bowls and carried them to each diner. They ate in silence, silver spoons clinking against the sides of the chinaware.

Cloistered in her room, Yvette refused to come downstairs to dinner. None of them, not Father, Mother, nor Josette, ate much. How could they, with Yvette's shrieks and all? It was very upsetting. Yvette's sobs could be heard all over the house.

Finally, Father sighed, setting down his empty wine glass. "Do you think you can reason with your sister Josette? After all, this doesn't need to be a permanent move for either of you. As you've so eagerly pointed out, you will both be of age in a short while. With the unforeseen events which have blessed me with a fortune, if you decide to come back to New York, you shall live here in Compton House." He picked up a dinner roll, tore off a piece, and dipped it into his bowl to sop up the last bits of the thick white soup. "What more can I do, my girl?" he asked with a genuine look of concern.

JOSETTE ENTERED Yvette's room without knocking. Her sister laid on her bed, head buried in her pillow. Yvette glanced up. "Oh, it's you. I suppose you've come to talk me into father's demands," she said, her voice quivering.

"Not exactly," Josette said, sitting on the edge of the bed. "I brought you a cup of chamomile tea and soda crackers to settle your nerves."

She rolled over. "That was thoughtful." Yvette's eyes were swollen and as pink as the garish feather boa hanging around her left-front bedpost.

Josette set the tray on the bedside table. "I thought perhaps we could come up with a plan. Something that would make everyone happy."

Yvette forced a faint laugh. "Happy? I would be happy staying here with Jon."

"But that's not going to happen. Not now at least. We have no choice in the matter."

Yvette sat up. "Yes, we do have a choice...or at least I do." Whenever she acted in a stubborn manner, Josette's sister lifted her chin in a very distinct way. "I shall ask Jon to marry me. And he will say 'yes' and that will take care of that!"

"I was afraid you'd say that."

"You're not going to talk me out of it, Josette."

"Can't you see, Yvette? That would be a terrible mistake." Josette reached over and took her sister's hand. "And what of Jon's feelings?"

"He loves me. And he intends to marry me."

"Yes, but would he want to marry you in such haste?"

Silent, Yvette moved her eyes as if searching for the answer in the rows of pink and white striped wallpaper. "I believe so," she finally said. "Especially if he knew I am to move to England."

"Listen to me," Josette reasoned, squeezing her sister's hand. "You must not put that burden on Jon. He is at the true beginning of his music career. His appearance at the Carnegie will likely launch him into a nationwide tour."

"Yes, I realize that. I shall accompany him wherever he goes."

"No, dearest. You cannot. You would only become an anchor to him. A young man, a cellist in my French class, has talked about how the gents in orchestras all share bedrooms when they travel around the country together. That would be impossible for a married man traveling with a wife."

"Well, then we would simply get our own room."

"And what if you were to become—" She searched for a word. "With child, Yvette?" Josette knew that the mere mention of the word, the thought of pregnancy would embarrass her naive sister. Most surprising was that Yvette didn't blush.

"It wouldn't likely happen for a while," Yvette said, pulling her hand away. She slid off the bed. "Jon would first have a chance to earn his fame. Here in New York, there's no absence of orchestras with which he could associate." Yvette picked up her teacup. "We might not even have to leave the city."

"What if you're wrong? What if you have a baby? He would have a wife and a child to support. That can be very expensive. What if he has to go back to accompanying silent films in movie houses or vaudevillian theaters to support his family? Could you live with that?"

"I wouldn't do anything to hurt Jon's career."

"Of course, you wouldn't, sister." Josette hopped up. "If you truly love him, you must consider his life, as well as your own needs. Do you truly think he's ready to get married and take on the responsibility of having a wife? Or do you think you should wait a year or two, until he is established and able to afford to take care of you and, perhaps, a child?"

Yvette's gaze was locked on the floor. Josette craned her neck looking straight into her sister's eyes. "It's all going to work out. You'll see. We'll find a music school for you in England, so you won't get behind with the progress you have made. Maybe Jon can come for a visit in a few months. Or…." Josette had a brilliant idea. "What if he can get a job performing in London? With so many of their young men serving in the military now…or far worse, injured or killed… there are bound to be countless places where he can play."

Yvette looked up at Josette. "Oh my." There was a long pause as she pondered the possibility. "Yes! Yes! That's it!" Yvette put the teacup down. "Jon can come to England. That's brilliant, Josette. Simply brilliant!"

Chapter 12

THE REST OF THE WEEK was a blur of activity: Passport photographs, lists of things to pack and things to stay at home, notes written to friends explaining the family's impending departure from the United States.

Josette's biggest regret had been withdrawing from school so close to graduation. Much to her surprise and delight, Dean Gilbersleeve was more than helpful – she was a blessing. Because Josette was an excellent student with near-perfect grades, and because the school year was so near the end, her teachers agreed to allow her to take final examinations early. There was only one hold-out. Professor Ogden, who taught Social Science, her favorite course.

"You are my brightest and best," the elderly teacher had told Josette when she met with him in his office on Friday. "I expect great things from you, Miss Rogers. You will have a unique perspective of the events unfolding in England during your stay. The effects of the war on the British people you meet. Interviews with soldiers returning from the Western Front and things of that manner. A minimum of, say, fifty pages, and including at least ten interviews with people from various walks of life. Oh, and a list of your sources, too."

"But that will take time, and I won't be able to finish it by the semester's end."

"By the end of summer, then," the professor said with a smile. "I shall enter an expected perfect score on the written test you would have taken, if you had not left my class early. And you, Miss Rogers, will mail me your typewritten paper – double-spaced – by August 31. Do I have your word?"

"Yes. Of course."

"Very good. And once that's completed, I am certain the dean will mail your diploma to you at your new home in England."

"WHAT IS this nonsense I've heard about moving to England, Henry?" Grandmother Murphy said as she stormed into the dining room like a bull charging a red cape.

Father, as always, sat at the head of the table. "Ah, yes. Mother Murphy. It's a pleasure to see you this fine evening."

"The matter is settled," their mother said insistently. "I already explained the situation to you on the telephone."

Grandmother responded with a grunt and said, "If only your father were still alive, Mildred. But then, he's not, and it's up to me to have a say in the matter." She sat in the chair beside Mother, but her glare was firmly planted on Father.

"Cripes, Mother Murphy! Clearly, you do not have any say in this matter," their father demanded. "We are moving to England, and that is final."

"Please, Henry. Hear me out," their grandmother protested.

Cutting off a small piece of roasted lamb chop, he attempted to ignore her.

"Leave Mildred and the girls with me," Grandmother begged. "I will watch over them."

Father didn't say a word, nor did he make eye contact with Grandmother. Instead, he chewed the bite of meat, washing it down with a gulp of wine. "Tell Mrs. DuBois the lamb is like shoe leather again. She should find a new butcher," he said with a dour expression. "Or a new recipe."

"Or a new cook," Josette said softly from the corner of her mouth. Mother scowled.

Grandmother Murphy was relentless. "Please listen to me, Henry. I have plenty of room at my house. Or I can move in here while you're gone. Please. I implore you to do whatever you have to do in London without uprooting your family in the process. Especially, your daughters."

Silent, Father picked up a sharper knife and sawed the hunk of meat.

Their mother spoke up. "I told you, Momma. It's no use. Our minds are made up."

"And what about this appalling war, Mildred? My cousin in Dublin writes that the British people are fearful about being invaded by the Germans. They have those flying balloons dropping bombs on innocent people."

"Blimy, Mother Murphy. They are called Zeppelins," Father said with a roll of his eyes. "Anyway, they can't stay in the air long enough to reach London. And if they ever do, they'll be blasted to bits with artillery fire."

Grandmother Murphy rose, her face reflecting her anger. "You're quite sure of that, are you, Henry? You're positive your wife and children will be as safe in London as they would be here in New York?"

"Quite right. I have spoken to several experts on the topic, and they believe the war will end quite soon. The Germans are going hungry, thanks to the U.K.'s stellar naval blockades. The Royal Navy controls the sea, as we all know, and Mr. Churchill – the First Lord of the Admiralty – is currently directing a battle in the Dardanelles that will lead the Allies to a guaranteed victory. So, I'll thank you to either sit down, be quiet, and eat a peaceful dinner with us, Mother. Or leave."

"EXTRA! EXTRA!" the newsboy shouted. The corner across from 23 Wall Street was his regular spot, come rain or shine. "Turks murder thousands of Armenians. Read all about it!"

"Thanks, Willie," Curtis said, handing the boy a twenty-five-cent piece. "A little extra for you today. And more tomorrow if you promise you'll go to school this morning."

"Gee, thanks, Mr. Carlson," he responded with a toothy grin. Sliding the newspaper from the top of the stack, he handed it to Curtis, headline side up.

Giving the lead article a quick read as he headed for the front door, Curtis shook his head. Turkey had been a hotbed of political upheaval for quite some time, the culmination of which was allying with the German and the Austrian-Hungarian governments in the war. And now, this! Killing countless Armenians.

"Damn," he grumbled, walking as he read. Country after country had become involved in the conflict. Where in God's name would it end? He felt his stomach twist into an all-too-familiar knot. Was there no more humanity? There were so many atrocities committed daily that many people had come to expect it...no, accept it as simply part of the tragedy of war. Heaving a sigh, he folded the paper and tossed it into the trash receptacle near the doorway to Morgan and Company, wondering why he bothered to read the newspapers at all. The news was always horrid these days. Politics. Rather, politicians. The older and more informed Curtis became, the more disgusted he became with the whole topic.

Entering the building, he stopped long enough to look around with a fresh perspective. When he accepted the position at J. P. Morgan's Company, he had imagined he would one day become a rich and exceedingly important banker. He was an economist, for God's sake. How in the world had he become a cog in such an important political wheel? On the surface, Jack Morgan's covert assignment to accompany the loan documents to England was exciting. Amazing. More than Curtis had ever dreamed. He and Van Camp would act on Morgan's behalf in brokering one of the most important loan deals in history. The outcome would likely determine who would win the war. Not that anyone could know. Not anyone outside of the inner circle of bankers and politicians.

Sleep had become nearly impossible for Curtis. He constantly worried he was being followed. Watched by German spies, perhaps. Did they know about the papers he and Van Camp would carry aboard the *Lusitania*?

As he sat at his desk, rolling open the burled cylinder top to expose his papers, his imagination ran wild with "what if's." What if there was a spy within the cloistered halls of Morgan and Company? What if someone who worked on drafting the papers sold the information to the Germans? Surely more people knew about the documents than Jack Morgan had indicated. What if the President didn't support what Mr. Morgan was trying to do? Would there be repercussions that would change Curtis' life? Certainly, the importance of the documents and the money involved would change the course of history. Where all this would take him was merely a guess at this point. He wondered how in the hell he got himself into this.

"Good morning, Curtis," a voice said from behind him.

Curtis had been so deep in thought that he hadn't heard Mr. Arnold approaching. "Oh, sorry, sir. Good morning to you, too."

"Why don't you come to my office for a cup of coffee?"

"I'd prefer a nice cup of tea, if you don't mind. My stomach is a little upset."

Mr. Arnold drew in a breath. "That happens to you a great deal, Curtis. You're such a young man. Perhaps you should speak to a doctor."

Curtis nodded, thanking his mentor for his concern. But Curtis knew the origin of the problem. Stress. Plain and simple, it was too much pressure. If he were to continue working in this high-powered world of Wall Street banking, he would have to come to terms with the fact that nervous tension would be his constant companion.

He followed Mr. Arnold to his office. As they passed his secretary's desk, he instructed her to bring a hot cup of tea to Curtis.

"I wanted to meet privately with you, son," Mr. Arnold said, closing his office door.

"Is everything all right, sir?"

He crossed the room to his desk and sat in his over-sized leather chair. "Yes, Curtis. I'm doing quite well and looking forward to spending more time with my wife and, most especially, my grandchildren."

"I'll certainly miss seeing you here every day," Curtis responded, taking a seat. Mr. Arnold's office was small, though quite nice. "Not that I won't be seeing you as often as possible."

"I wouldn't have it any other way," Mr. Arnold said with a pleasant smile. "In fact, just as soon as you get back from London, my wife and I would like you to come to dinner at our home. She makes a mean pot roast."

Shocked, Curtis drew back, suddenly aware that the so-called secret trip wasn't so secret at all. "You know about London?"

"Of course," he said.

"Morgan said no one else knew about the assignment."

Mr. Arnold rose, stepping to the sideboard set with several cups and saucers. Steam escaped from the spout of a plain white coffee pot. He poured a cup for himself.

"Jack approached me about having you accompany Van Camp to England before he talked to you about it. I asked Jack to leave you out of this. To send someone else, like Rudy."

"Rudy Van Camp? He's a dolt!"

Mr. Arnold laughed, setting his coffee on his desk. "He is certainly that!" He sat down, looking at Curtis with a gentle smile. "It's just that I've grown quite fond of you, my boy. The Atlantic Ocean can be a dangerous place, especially when one approaches the British Isles."

"So, you do think the Germans could sabotage the *Lusitania*?"

Mr. Arnold shrugged. "Who knows? So far, they've targeted non-civilian vessels."

"I've read that the Kaiser doesn't want to do anything to make the president change his neutral position. Don't you think attacking a passenger liner would push him over the edge?"

"Yes, Curtis. But there's a war going on, and stranger things have happened."

There was a gentle tap on the office door. "May I come in, sir?"

"Enter, Miss Baxter," Mr. Arnold said in a loud tone.

The secretary opened the door, carrying a steaming cup. "I have your tea, Mr. Carlson," she said, sounding more like a maid than a typist. "I thought you might like Oolong for a change. No sugar, just cream." She handed it to Curtis, looking at him with a coquettish glance.

"That will be fine, Miss Baxter," Curtis said, accepting the cup. "Thank you."

She curtsied, then left.

Mr. Arnold chuckled. "That one has a crush on you, I'd say. Too bad she's a good ten years older than you are."

Curtis cleared his throat. Never mind Miss Baxter wasn't attractive, he thought, but kept to himself. "She's also typing up my notes for my book. She's very efficient."

Placing the tea cup on the desk, Curtis continued. "So, you don't think I should have accepted Mr. Morgan's request to accompany Van Camp on this mission?"

Mr. Arnold drew in a deep breath. "I don't know, Curtis. It's just that I…well, I will worry about you. I wouldn't want anything to happen to you."

"I appreciate your concern, but I'm sure Mr. Morgan wouldn't send me, or Van Camp, or those important papers to England, if he thought something was going to happen to that ship."

Mr. Arnold took a sip of his coffee. "Well, he did book your staterooms on one of the upper-most decks. I wouldn't be surprised if he did it so you could make a quick escape, should the unthinkable happen."

"To get to the lifeboats fast, you mean?" Curtis questioned.

"To get to the lifeboats with the documents," Mr. Arnold said flatly. "There's talk this will be the *Lusitania's* last trip to England. If anything should happen, it could mean Great Britain will be cut off even more than it already is. No ship – neither British nor American – would likely want to make the journey, if the Germans do something foolhardy."

"Then we'll be safe," Curtis commented.

"You'll be safe if the Germans don't get wind of those documents. Or if the *Lusitania* isn't carrying American-made weapons for the British troops."

Curtis shifted uncomfortably in his seat. "Surely the president wouldn't allow weapons to go on the same ship that will be carrying a bunch of civilians. And some of them are Americans, I understand."

Mr. Arnold leaned forward, elbows on his desk. "One can only hope, my boy. One can only hope…and pray." Sitting erect again, Mr. Arnold's expression softened. "Well, then, on a happier note, will you be coming alone to my retirement dinner Friday evening? Or is there a young lady in your life by now?"

Curtis shook his head and grinned. "Well, there's a young lady who would certainly like to be in my life. But, no, I'll be coming alone."

Mr. Arnold chuckled, rubbing his chin. "And the young lady? I take it you're not too keen on her, but that she has other intentions?"

"That would be the case, I'm afraid. She's, well, she's not the type of woman I want to settle down with."

"And what type of woman are you looking for, Curtis?"

"Uh-oh. Are you trying to set me up with someone, Mr. Arnold?"

He shrugged innocently. "Not me. But my wife does have a friend with a beautiful daughter who is just about the right age for you. We could bring her to the restaurant with us."

Curtis wagged his hands. "Nope. I'm happy being a bachelor at the moment."

Mr. Arnold looked serious. "It would be wise for you to settle down, Curtis. Especially if you are on the path to a senior partnership." He leaned forward. "A wife and children are good for one's career. A wife can manage the home and hearth, so you can further your ambitions. I would love to think of you sitting here at my desk one day."

"Thank you, sir, but—I"

"The young lady Mrs. Arnold has in mind for you is quite accomplished with the cello. Her voice is tenable, though not the best I've heard. Still, she speaks French fluently and, I'm told she is an excellent horsewoman. I assume you'll want to move out of the city when you have children. Fresh air and sunshine is good for family life. You can buy a home on Long Island or somewhere you can own a small piece of land."

"Sounds like you have my future all laid out, Mr. Arnold," Curtis joked.

"Of course not, Curtis. Just trying to help you out. You work long hours here, and that leaves little time for finding a wife. Or resting."

Curtis shrugged. "Thanks for the offer, but I'm not sure that's the kind of woman I'm looking for. She sounds a bit…old fashioned, I suppose. Oh, not that I'm criticizing her," he quickly added, hoping not to offend. Unsure what else to say, Curtis tried to lighten the moment. "Perhaps someone like Mrs. Arnold," he said tactfully. "I admire your wife's intellect, her determination to accomplish things."

"You mean, her charitable work? Yes, Dorothy is as hard working as any man I know."

"So is my mother. Mom did my father's accounting for many years, even after she had my sister and brother and me. We all pitched in at the hardware store. Anything that needed to be done, well, we all worked together as a family. My mother never learned to play the piano or how to host parties. But now that they have opened additional stores, there's enough money for her to do whatever she wishes. Still," he said, lifting his shoulders, "Mom is involved in the business, as well as working with her church to help the needy in Queens."

"Yes, my boy. I can see your point." Mr. Arnold stood up and walked around the side of the desk. "And yet, if you are to become a Wall Street banker of high standing, you will indeed need to present the proper image. Having a wife who is of gentle birth, from one of Manhattan's most upstanding families, would help you rise in your profession." He patted Curtis on the shoulder. "Just remember, son. It's all about presenting a successful image."

Curtis drew in a deep breath, fighting the urge to tell his mentor he didn't agree. That he wanted a more modern woman than the past generations had considered a proper wife for a proper gentleman. Times were changing. Women's rights, or lack of them, were under scrutiny. Mr. Arnold and his generation held on to their old Edwardian ideals. And Curtis intended to be part of the new way of thinking, especially when it came to finding a wife. Pretty, yes. Womanly, yes. But confidence and ambition were something he wanted in a woman. She was out there somewhere, just waiting to meet an open-minded man like him.

Chapter 13

ON THURSDAY afternoon, Mr. Herrmann drove Mother, Yvette and Josette to the Passport Office in Lower Manhattan. Prompted by the war overseas, passports were required for anyone and everyone traveling abroad. Germans weren't allowed to leave the United States. Citizens or not, they were not issued passports. In Josette's opinion, it was an ironic turn of events, considering America wasn't part of the Allied coalition. Distrust of Germans in America seemed to be gaining momentum every day, prompted by newspaper accounts of heinous war crimes they had committed in Europe, and fueled by reports of German spies running amuck all over the country; most especially, in New York City.

Most surprising to Josette was the large number of young men lined up in a queue that ran well beyond the front door and down the sidewalk.

"What do you suppose this is about?" Yvette commented. Exiting the automobile, she and Josette followed their mother in the direction of the Passport Office's front entrance.

"I wonder if they're all signing up to go to the Front?" Josette said. "I still don't understand why our own boys are signing up," Josette responded, looking directly into the light-brown eyes of a lad of seventeen or eighteen who stood in the open doorway. He wore a large hat of some type, and his wavy hair hung to his shoulders. Obviously, he wasn't a New Yorker.

Filing past him, half-pushing her way into the crowded doorway, she decided to ask. "Excuse me," she said, Mother and Yvette disappearing inside. "Are you heading to France?"

The youth smiled. "Oh, yes, ma'am," he said, with the hint of a drawl.

The fact that he had called her "ma'am" set Josette back. "It's miss, young man," she insisted. "I'm not much older than you are."

"Oh, sorry, miss," he corrected, tugging on the edge of his wide-brimmed hat. "Reckon where I come from, it's politer to call all the ladies 'ma'am.' That's how my momma taught me."

"I see," she said with an amused smile, realizing he was a likely from a southern state. "I hope you don't mind my asking, but I can't help wondering why you would want to join in the melee overseas. Americans haven't been called to serve in the military. We're not part of this war. Do you have family abroad?"

"No, ma'am...miss. But what's going on over there right now, what with them Huns killing babies and such...well, Lord knows it's just wrong. Some of these boys is here with me," he said, motioning to the other young men wearing the same type of hats. "And well, we all prayed about the matter, and the Lord said we're needed over there to help whip those Germans' bee-hinds, if you'll pardon my language, miss. I mean, ma'am." Shaking his head, his cheeks took on a tinge of pink.

She smiled. "Very well. You may call me, ma'am. I promise I will not be offended."

When he grinned, dimples appeared on either side of his mouth. "And where are you boys from?"

"Texas, ma'am. Moody, Texas." That explained his over-sized hat. He was some sort of a cowboy. They were likely all from ranches or farms.

"We heard tell they need us ranch hands over there in France to handle the horses. The ranchers are rounding up their herds, even wild horses from the plains. They're selling them to the U. S. Army. Someone's got to go there to train them horses, so they'll be fit for service."

"The good Lord is on our side. We're Methodists, one and all," his friend said, his chest puffed out proudly. "We all grew up going to the same church. There's sixteen of us in all."

"My, goodness. Sixteen?" Josette said. "That's quite a sacrifice for your town, I'm sure." Scanning the rosy-cheeked innocents, some barely old enough to shave, she couldn't help but wonder how many of them would die.

"Oh, yes, ma'am," a third Texan added. "We intend to make our families...and our pastor, right proud. We're sure the good Lord will protect us."

The logic escaped Josette. She reached out her gloved hand and squeezed his shoulder. "Then may the Lord keep all of you safe," she whispered, fighting the urge to say more.

"Thank you, ma'am. Sorry. I reckon I mean miss." He dipped his chin in respect.

Josette forced a smile. "Good luck to you all, then." There was nothing more she could say. "If you'll excuse me," she said, pushing past him.

Inside the lobby, a man with blonde hair caught her eye. He stood in the line and was about ten people from the front. Josette stopped, straining to see his face. He was so familiar. He must have felt her gaze boring into him, as he twisted his head in her direction. Lips parting, his jaw slackened when he saw her.

Josette was taken aback. It was one of the Germans from Gretchen's Bakery.

The lad's expression changed. His dazzling azure eyes moved rapidly between Josette and the clerk at the check-in counter. *Good heavens,* she thought. *He looks frightened.* Josette drew back, blinking rapidly.

"Josette Marie!" Father called. She turned to see he was already seated at an employee's desk behind a waist-high wooden room divider that separated the employees from the general lobby area. Mother and Yvette sat in chairs to Father's right.

"Hurry up, girl! We're waiting for you," Father shouted over the droning racket of countless conversations echoing through the lobby.

"Yes, Father! I'm coming." And when she turned back to glance at the German, he was gone. The nicely dressed chap in front of him was also missing. She strained to view the entry door and noted the two men unapologetically shoving and pushing their way past the queue – including the cowboys. The pair disappeared outside.

"How strange," she muttered, strolling through the swinging doors towards her family. And then it struck her. Why were the Germans at the Passport Office? Weren't they aware of the travel restrictions for German people? Puzzled by the incident, Josette walked to the vacant chair and sat, placing her handbag on her lap.

Seated at the desk, the heavy-set, balding passport agent looked down, shuffling through the pile of documents that Father had brought: applications for their passports, birth certificates, recently taken photographs, proof of Father's British citizenship, and the like. Josette leaned over to speak to her father. "Germans aren't allowed to obtain passports, right?"

Surprised, Father drew back with a questioning expression. "Yes. Why?"

Her comment caught the attention of the clerk. He looked up through thick glasses with a look of concern. "That's right, Miss Rogers. They are not." Like Father, he asked, "Why?"

Exhaling a puff of breath from the corner of her mouth, Josette responded. "I just saw a German young man. I believe he was here to obtain a passport. I mean, why else would he be standing in that long line?"

The passport agent glanced around the lobby. "Where is he, and how do you know he's German?"

Oh dear. Josette bit her bottom lip. She had really put her foot in her mouth. Father and Mother still didn't know Yvette and Josette had visited Little Germany. If she answered honestly and said she had seen the young German in the bakery and marching in a protest parade, their parents would be furious. If she lied, the handsome young German, and possibly his friend, might return to obtain passports after Josette and her family were gone. On the other hand, what if the man had legal documents that would somehow allow him to obtain a passport? Perhaps she had let her imagination get the better of her.

"Josette? Did you see a German here or not?" Father probed.

"Yes, young lady. Speak up," the clerk said in an impatient, irritated tone.

"Oh, no. My apologies, sir." Josette directed her comments to the passport agent. "I was mistaken. I just realized that the man I saw on a visit to Macy's had much darker blonde hair. He was at the perfume counter and spoke German to his female companion. The man I saw here in line had hair that was much lighter. Sorry to trouble you," she said, shrugging with feigned embarrassment.

The clerk smirked at Josette in a dismissive manner, as if to say, 'silly girl,' and went back to the pile of documents.

Josette drew in a deep breath, hoping she had made the right decision. That nothing was amiss with the two Germans who left the building when they saw her.

Yvette leaned close to Josette's ear. "You're speaking about the boys we saw at the bakery, are you not?"

Josette swallowed, hoping Father, or the inquisitive clerk, hadn't heard. She reached up to her nose, as if she had an itch on the tip, and managed to quickly place her index finger over her lips. It was her signal to her sister to be quiet. Yvette gave a deliberately nonchalant nod and returned her gaze to the clerk.

For the next forty-five minutes, the passport agent examined each piece of paper, questioning, reviewing every detail. Josette crossed her legs, nervously kicking her foot. Thinking about the incident with the German lads over and over in her mind, hoping she hadn't made a mistake by holding back information, she glanced up at the wall clock. Her stomach rumbled with hunger, and she needed to find the ladies' powder room.

She rose, excusing herself, headed to the rear of the room to the sign that read *Ladies and Gents*. As she reached for the door handle, the sudden screech of motorcar tires came from the street outside. It was followed by loud shouts. Josette spun around to see what had happened. An instant later, she heard a loud crash and the sound of shattering glass, as one of the front windows crumbled into shards. A brick wrapped in what looked like a piece of paper tied with a string sailed into the room, smashing down with a hard *thud*. An edge of the projectile had grazed the passport agent's head on its inward trajectory. It landed a few feet from her parents, who had quickly huddled together on the floor.

Screams erupted throughout the entire complex. The organized line had broken into pandemonium, as people scattered in hysteria. Many had dived to the floor seeking protection. Paralyzed with fear, Josette half-expected a bomb to explode or something more to happen.

It didn't. The car carrying the men who had thrown the brick apparently sped off with a loud rev of the engine, blaring the claxon horn to frighten people out of their vehicle's path.

One by one, dazed men and women, climbed to their feet.

Josette dashed to her family. "Are you all okay?"

"Right as rain, Josette," Father said, helping Mother to her feet.

"Thank heavens," she said softly, hugging Yvette, then Mother and Father.

Not surprising, Mother was shaking, tears streaming down her cheeks. "What has happened, Henry?" she said through shuddering sobs. "Is no one safe?"

"Damnable blokes," Father muttered.

Several employees had gathered around the clerk, still lying on the floor. One woman placed her lace-rimmed handkerchief on his head wound, soaking up a rivulet of blood. "I'm all right," he mumbled as he sat up. He was obviously dazed.

The clerks at the two other desks closest to the broken window hadn't fared as well. Josette could see they had been cut by glass fragments. Thankfully, their injuries didn't appear to be serious, although the older man, whose hair was slicked straight back with pomade, had a glittery dusting of tiny glass shards all over his dark suit jacket. Both he and the other agent had multiple small cuts on their faces, heads and necks.

"It could have been so much worse," Father pointed out, "if one of the large slivers had found its way to the chap. They're sharp as knives."

His comment only upset Mother more. "Please don't, Henry. Please."

"There, there, Millie." As usual, Mother melted into Father's protective arms.

A young man had picked up the brick and untied the attached message. "Germans!" he yelled.

"Are you sure?" Josette questioned.

He nodded, his hands shaking so much, the tattered note shook, too. "It says Germans should be allowed to return to their homeland, and they should not be treated like prisoners, trapped here in America."

"Oh dear," Josette whispered.

Yvette stepped a few feet away, motioning to Josette to come. "Do you think it was him? The German we saw at the bakery?" Yvette asked in a low tone.

"I would like to think it wasn't. But I fear it was," Josette said, tears welling in her eyes. "I should have spoken up. If I had, maybe this wouldn't have happened."

Yvette placed her hands on Josette's shoulders. "It's not your fault, sister. There was no way of knowing he would do something like this."

"Perhaps it wasn't him. That note could have been written by—"

"Unlikely that it was written by anyone else," Josette said, wiping her nose on her sleeve. He left here upset when I saw him. I saw it in his face. He knew I could identify him. I believe he was trying to scare me."

Yvette sighed, looking straight into Josette's eyes. "Then we must do the right thing, Josette. We must tell the police about the boys we saw in Little Germany. Mother and Father don't need to be present when we tell the police our story."

Drawing in a deep breath, Josette nodded her agreement.

"Now, then," Yvette said, dropping her arms to her side. "Fetch your handkerchief from your handbag. Sleeves are not hankies! We'll talk to the police and tell them what we know."

"WE MIGHT be able to help," Josette explained when Father insisted that they leave.

He eyed both of them with a confused look. "So, Josette. You believe the German chap you saw in the lobby might have been the same man you saw at Macy's after all."

"Yes, Father," Josette said, once again having to lie.

"Very well, then. You may stay a while longer to speak to the police," Father said, placing his felt bowler hat back on his head. "Do what you can to help. I'll send Mr. Herrmann back for you when we get home. He'll come for you straight away, so don't be long."

"Father. Maybe that's not a good idea to send Mr. Hermann," Josette said. "I don't think Germans are very popular around here today."

Father paused. "Yes. You may be spot on, my girl." Fishing in his pocket, he retrieved his wallet and pulled out a bill. "Then take a taxi home as soon as you can. We'll keep Mr. Herrmann out of harm's way, just in case things get out of hand."

With their parents' departure, Josette and Yvette returned to the chairs in front of the passport agent's desk. Two policemen had arrived, interviewing the injured employees. They were to be next.

"Excuse me, ma'am." The Texan approached. "Are y'all okay? I saw that your family was close to the line of fire. From the brick, I mean."

"Why, yes. Well, my sister and parents were close to the brick when it struck. But we're all fine. Thank you for your concern." Josette managed a smile.

Removing his hat, the young man squatted beside Josette's chair. "Are you sure you ain't hurt?" he asked with a worried expression.

"Actually, I may have seen something that could help the police identify the culprit," Josette said.

"You mean, the German what done this?"

Josette nodded, swallowing hard.

"I figure I saw him, too. Nearly knocked me over when he tore out of here like a bull at a rodeo. I would have punched him, seeing how

117

he was pushing folks around, if I wouldn't have lost my place in line. Figured he wasn't worth the effort. If I'd known he was a German, I reckon I would have gone after him anyhow."

"Then you should also talk to the police and tell them what you saw."

"Reckon so," he said with a nod. He stood up again. "Is there anything I can do for you ladies? A glass of water, maybe?"

Looking up at the broad-shouldered boy, Josette fought back her tears. "Just one thing."

"Anything, ma'am."

Drawing in a breath, she said, "Promise me you and your friends will go back to Texas. Promise me that you won't join the military and go over to France to fight." Josette rose, her eyes locked on his.

The Texan drew back, surprised. "I'm afraid I can't promise you that, especially now. After all of this." He glanced around the room, gazing at the broken window. At the man sweeping the shards into a pile. "Someone has to go and stop them Germans before things get real bad."

Josette shook her head. "It's already terrible. Haven't you been reading the newspapers? Hundreds of thousands of young men have already been killed. The Germans are now using poison gases to massacre the Allied troops. Do you want to be in the middle of that?"

He stood there, obviously surprised by Josette's rant.

Tried as she might, Josette couldn't hold back her tears. "Go home. Go to your families. Get married and have children," she pleaded. "Leave the fighting to the men living in Europe. They don't have a choice in the matter. And if the war continues and the United States becomes involved, then you may have to fight. But for now, you do not have to go over there." She reached out and took his hand. "Why put yourselves at so much risk? Would your Lord and Savior want that? Or would he want you safe and sound in Moody, Texas?"

With a somber expression, the boy seemed to be considering her words. "Well, ma'am. You've got a point. I'll talk to my friends. I reckon we should pray hard on the matter before signing up." He turned to leave then paused, twisting back to Josette and Yvette. "But I can guarantee that if them Huns ever plan to step foot in Texas, they'll die trying."

Chapter 14

WITH THE DAYS quickly slipping by before the family's departure, Father had asked Mr. Herrmann and Lucy to meet him and Mother in the parlor after dinner. Mrs. DuBois left early to visit her ailing sister, which was fine with Father. He said he would deliver the news of their move to the cook in the morning.

Josette asked to be present, but Yvette was still far too emotional for good-byes – any good-byes – and opted to continue her self-imposed isolation inside her bedroom.

Better, Josette concluded, that her sister not have to witness something as difficult as dismissing Lucy and Mr. Herrmann. Especially, Mr. Herrmann, who had been like a member of the family for a long time.

Father said he had met with the two Irish cleaning women at his office earlier in the day. They were both full-time employees of Rogers & Rogers in Manhattan, and would not, therefore, be losing their jobs. Instead, Father had explained he would simply increase the number of hours they cleaned at his office and warehouse. And because he would not be selling Compton House, they would come to dust and keep things up every two weeks. "No problem there," he had said.

The situation would be quite different for the butler and maid. Josette dreaded the conversation that would quickly change their lives; that would force the two servants to seek new employment. They had both served the family well and deserved nothing but the best from a future employer.

Father settled into one of the large chairs in the parlor, looking a bit like a king gracing a throne. Mother and Josette sat on the settee. None of them spoke a word. In fact, the only sound in the room was the loud ticking of the gold-leafed mantle clock.

At eight o'clock, the usual time Mr. Herrmann and Lucy finished their duties and left each evening, the two servants entered, somber expressions reflecting their worry.

Josette was certain they had realized something was amiss before now. Surely, they had overheard a conversation between her parents or her father speaking on the telephone to make the arrangements for the move abroad. How could they not know they were leaving?

"Please come in and have a seat," Father instructed the pair.

"Thank you, sir," Mr. Herrmann stated, walking to one of the smaller side chairs that faced the more regal high-backed seating where Father chose to conduct the gathering.

Lucy trailed behind Mr. Herrmann, arranging her black skirt and apron as she lowered herself in the other chair. Scooting to the front of the seat, she looked at Father. "Is everything all right, Mr. Rogers?" The maid cast him a dreary stare. "Please, sir. Have I done something wrong, 'cause if I have—"

He cut her off. "No, no, Lucy. You've done nothing wrong. Mrs. Rogers and I have asked you both here, because it's high time we shared our future plans with you." Father straightened, exhaling loudly. "Now then, as you know, the war has gone on far longer than anyone believed it would."

Both nodded.

Lucy clasped her hands in her lap. "It surely has been a terrible time for everyone back home, what with the lads heading off to the war and all. They say the boys are dying off faster than flowers in the fall. If you ask me, it's wrong, and the Americans need to get on the band wagon before it's too late."

Josette squirmed, holding back her own opinions on the matter of the war. This certainly wouldn't be the right time to voice her feelings about Americans going to the Front.

"To be sure, Lucy," Father agreed. "Sad, but true." His legs were wide in a "V" configuration. He leaned forward, planting his arms on the tops of each leg. "Let me be frank with you both. I trust you know that my business has been affected by the loss of merchandise I've ordered from overseas. Products I purchased on cargo ships that are now sitting on the bottom of the sea, thanks to the Kaiser's navy."

"Oh, blimey, Mr. Rogers. I've been expecting this." Lucy sounded as if she was about to burst into tears. "I said to me friend, Helene, Mr. Rogers' business is going to be hard-hit by this 'orrible war, it is. He might need to give me the sack, if things don't get better soon, I said."

Father and Mother exchanged glances. "No, no, Lucy," he said. "That's not it. Well, not exactly." Father loosened his tie as he continued. "I'll not be giving you the sack."

"Upon my soul, sir. You had me quite worried." Lucy heaved a loud sigh, appearing quite relieved. Dragging the back of her hand across her forehead she let out a chuckle. "Jolly good, sir. 'Cause I don't know what I'd do without me position here. People aren't hiring maids and such right now, from what Helene says."

"And me, Mr. Rogers?" Mr. Herrmann asked in a concerned tone.

Father shook his head. "No, no, Franz. Neither of you will be losing your jobs."

Mr. Herrmann sniffed, a hint of a smile visible beneath his mustache. "Thank you, sir."

Lucy nervously fingered her starched apron, her gaze locked on Father, likely anticipating why he had called them both to the parlor.

"So, you see, Lucy...Mr. Herrmann," he addressed them, moving his gaze from one to the other. "What I'm having to do is make... adjustments." His brows furrowed. "Changes that affect all of us." Father expelled an audible breath. "Here's the thing. I am moving my family to England for a time. I must take over as the head of my company's main office in London."

"Blimey, sir," Lucy spoke up. "If I might say so, you're going in the wrong direction. I hear that the Americans are coming back from England. Getting out of the line of fire, they are."

"It's all quite complicated, I fear," Father said.

"My father's relatives – the young men who would have taken over the company – were both killed in France," Josette interjected, feeling as if they deserved further explanation. "Father must step in and do his duty. It was all quite sudden, you see."

"Oh, cripes. That's terrible, sir!" Lucy said. "Seems we've all lost someone, thanks to the evil Huns." She glanced at Mr. Herrmann with a sudden realization. "Sorry, Mr. Herrmann." Her gaze moved to the floor.

"I, too, grieve. And I am sorry for your losses. But many of my German nephews have died in this ridiculous war, as well. Mothers have lost their sons on both sides. We are all victims of the Kaiser's selfish need to take over foreign territories."

"Quite right." Father cleared his throat and changed the subject. "Nevertheless, my family must leave for England on the First of May. But not to worry. I have found you both positions at my office," Father reassured. "Franz, you learned to drive a motorcar and have been an excellent chauffeur. You are quite experienced in negotiating the traffic jams of New York City, as it were. So, you will be driving a truck to make deliveries for my company. And at a substantial raise in salary, I might add."

Relief swept across Mr. Herrmann's face. "Thank you, sir. That is a wonderful opportunity."

Lucy spoke up. "And what about me, sir? I can't drive a motor, and I'm not good for much more than polishing silver or sweeping the floor. You already have cleaning ladies at your place of business. What can I do there?"

"Don't sell yourself short, Lucille." Father smiled gently. "I have made arrangements for you to attend secretarial school here in town. You are still quite young, and I believe you can do more with your life than performing menial tasks as a servant."

She looked stunned. "Secretarial school, sir? You mean, typing and such?"

This was the first that Josette had heard of this. She was delighted. "That's wonderful, Father." She turned her gaze to the maid. "What do you think, Lucy?"

"Why, I don't know quite what to say, Miss. Typing? I don't know that I'm capable of working one of those machines."

"Nonsense," Mother chimed in. "I learned to type when I was a girl. You'll do fine."

"Go on now. You were a typist, Mrs. Rogers? You're pulling me leg."

"No, no. I was an executive secretary at my husband's office," Mother said with a nod.

A grin crept across Lucy's lips. "An executive secretary," she said softly. "Blimey O'Reilly! The likes of me? Clacking away on a typing machine?" Still smiling, she looked as if she could cry. "I don't know quite what to say, sir."

Father beamed. "A thank you will suffice, Lucy."

CHATEAU LE BLANC was one of Manhattan's finest restaurants. The interior of the main dining room was decorated with heavy, navy-blue brocade draperies, a carpet patterned with gigantic burgundy roses, and wood wall paneling, giving the place an old Victorian charm.

The electric wall sconces were few and far between, allowing the large candelabras adorning the sideboards and small candles inside shallow crystal bowls in the center of each table to cast flickering yellow light and shadowy shapes throughout the room.

Squinting in an attempt to have her eyes adjust to the dim light, Josette followed Father, Mother, and Yvette, as the *maître de* guided them through a doorway adjacent to the main entrance and into a small, much plainer meeting hall. A round of applause erupted.

"Jolly good, gents. Thank you all for coming," Father said, as he made his entrance. "Have a seat, ladies," he instructed, motioning to them to take their places beside him at a table near the podium. Looking around the room, Josette noted that they were the only women attending the event, something which shouldn't have surprised her.

Father had been a member of the New York Yacht Club, a long-time bastion of the city's most rich and powerful yachtsmen, for twenty-two years. It must have been painful for him to sell his beloved sailboat last week. "I can always buy another boat one day," he had said, trying to sound chipper. "Maybe even a larger sailing craft." His sloop had been a mere thirty-six feet, while most of the other members had yachts that were forty-, fifty-feet or more.

With their impending move to England, Father had to terminate his membership in the yacht club. He had judged regattas, served on the Board of Directors with the likes of both Mr. J. P. Morgan, Senior, and his son, Jack, and had donated money to the Club's building funds. And yet, his farewell dinner couldn't be held at NYYC's main location on 44th Street. Women simply weren't allowed through those hallowed doors.

In the past, Father hadn't exactly been an advocate of the suffrage movement. "Women belong in the home, not in the office," he had voiced. And whenever he delivered that same edict, Josette reminded him that Mother had once worked in his downtown office.

As the speeches began, the waiters brought chilled bottles of champagne to the tables, filling the long-stemmed glasses, including Josette and Yvette's. Father nodded his permission for the girls to partake, something they were allowed to do on special occasions. Toasts were made to Father, compliments and kudos about his abilities as a sailor.

Josette felt a sense of pride, knowing he had stood his ground on the issue of having his "three ladies" with him tonight; not just his male friends and fellow-officers from the elite organization. "The Yacht Club be damned," he had said. And then he booked the meeting room at Chateau Le Blanc, inviting the Club's entire membership and all the officers to join him at his own farewell dinner. Judging by the large turnout – at least one hundred men – no one seemed to mind that the event wasn't held at their sacrosanct Manhattan location.

The five-course dinner was delicious – caviar and small toasts, lobster bisque, oysters on the half-shell, Cornish game hens in an orange sauce served with grilled potato slices, and last, a salad with chopped carrots and tomatoes laden with sweet Thousand Island dressing.

The organization's commodore, president of the club, stepped to the podium to make announcements about upcoming club events, while the waiters delivered dessert trays to the tables. Josette helped herself to several treats, wanting to take small tastes of each.

Yvette, still upset about moving to England, had picked at her food, refusing to even look at the dessert selection. For days, Yvette hadn't eaten much. As a result, Josette could see that her sister was getting too thin. Tonight, her sparrow-like appetite was even worse than usual.

"You should try the lemon tart, Yvette," Josette said softly.

Frowning, Yvette shook her head and crossed her arms.

At 8:30, Mr. St. James, the evening's final speaker, went to the podium. "We have gathered here to present our own Mr. Henry Rogers with a plaque commemorating his twenty-two years of membership and service to our noble organization." He motioned to Father to join him.

Mr. St. James began to tell a story about a sailing journey he and Father had taken together a few years ago. How they had gone out to sea and were caught in a fog bank that suddenly rolled in. And how Father had gone to the bow sprit to watch for nearby vessels. The boat had listed on a swell very suddenly, and Father's leg had become entangled in the anchor chain. "Henry slid off the deck and was left hanging over the port side, thrashing about like a huge a Seabass!" The men roared with laughter.

Poor Father blushed with embarrassment. "Jolly good, St. James," he said, wagging a finger at the speaker.

Mr. St. James went on. "Wait, wait! There's more. The anchor was well secured in the deck, so Henry was stuck. The buttons on his trousers were snagged in the chain links, and our refined British lad, here, continued to slide head-first towards the water. Of course, he was rescued by another crewman, but not before he had nearly lost his trousers and under-drawers." St. James began to laugh. "I'm telling you, gents, I never saw a pair of buttocks that white. Like a couple of full moons!"

Laughter filled the large room.

"Oh, good heavens," Mother whispered, placing her hand over her open mouth, as she glanced around the room with a mortified look.

Father's face was crimson. "Sounds like a rather *cheeky* fable, if you ask me," he responded in a good-natured tone, bringing about another round of laughter.

In Josette's opinion, the story wasn't amusing at all. In fact, it was rather scary. As many times as she had been out sailing, no one had ever fallen overboard.

"I'll be in the powder room," Yvette whispered to Josette, as she got to her feet.

"But the plaque!" Josette said.

Her sister didn't turn to look back, negotiating her way through scores of tables.

Once the presentation was over, Josette leaned to her mother. "I'll be back in a few minutes." And then she left the room in search of her sister.

THE DOWNSTAIRS meeting hall at Chateau Le Blanc was a perfect place for occasions like retirement dinners. There was plenty of space to seat and feed more than two hundred people and, tonight, every table was filled with New York City's most important business leaders. They had all come to honor Curtis' mentor and friend, Mr. Ernest Arnold.

After dinner, Curtis and the rest of Mr. Arnold's associates settled into the usual evening of drinking Scotch and cigar smoking. As always, there was plenty of talk about the latest battle, the startling number of presumed dead, and if President Wilson should take action. Whether or not America would get involved in the war overseas was always a favorite topic.

Mr. Morgan announced that another three American cargo ships sailing from New York Harbor had experienced explosions in the past couple of weeks. Surely German saboteurs were to blame, weren't they? But how were they sneaking bombs aboard the merchant ships? The stevedores? The crew? And why wasn't Captain Thomas Tunney and his large force of New York City officers able to find the culprits? Everyone had a theory. No one had the answer.

As the evening wore on, the wives of the attendees had gone upstairs into the main dining room at Chateau La Blanc for an aperitif or a cup of tea. The gents remained in the meeting hall downstairs, passing boxes of expensive Cuban cigars around the tables. In a matter of minutes, the air inside had become as thick as a foggy morning on Long Island.

Curtis refused a cigar but stayed put as long as he possibly could. Bending his head down, he rubbed his eyes, hoping no one would notice his physical reaction to the cigar fumes and billows of smoke. It was useless. Not only did his eyes hurt like a son-of-a-bitch, they began to water from the irritation. Curtis excused himself and exited through the door into the back hall for a breath of air. Closing the door, he spun around, nearly bumping into a fair-haired young woman who had come down the stairs from upstairs where the restaurant was located.

His vision was still slightly blurred. "Oh…excuse me, miss."

She turned to fully face him, looked up and smiled. "You are excused, sir."

Letting out a breathy gasp, he stepped closer. "Miss Rogers! How good to see you, again."

She paused, tilting her head to the side as she assessed him. "I beg your pardon?" A puzzled look spread across her face. "Do I know you?"

That took Curtis by surprise. He blinked several times, making sure his eyesight was back to normal. "Know me? Of course, you know me. Good grief! It hasn't been that long."

Her brows furrowed. "I'm sorry, but I'm sure we haven't—"

"Well, I must say," he said, raking his fingers through his hair. "I didn't think you would miss me or anything like that. But I never expected you would forget me this easily." He shook his head and let out a small chuckle. "Bruises a man's ego, you see!"

"Yvette?" A woman's voice came from behind her in the direction of the staircase.

Curtis turned, glancing to the stairs. Another young lady—a replica of the one standing beside him—approached. His jaw dropped open. His gaze darted back and forth between them. "Good grief! There are two of you!"

Chapter 15

"HELLO AGAIN, Mr. Carlson," Josette said with an amused expression. "Allow me to introduce my twin sister, Miss Yvette Rogers."

"How do you do, Mr. Carlson," Yvette said with a polite nod.

"Mr. Carlson and I met a number of weeks ago when he was—"

"Ah, yes," Yvette interrupted, her gaze locked on him. "If memory serves, you were the speaker at Columbia my sister told me about." Her lips curled into a sly smile. "She did talk about your rather unusual encounter."

"No doubt your sister had a lot of wonderful things to say about me," Curtis kidded. "How good-looking I am. How fabulously intelligent she found me."

"Uh, let's just say…no. Those were definitely not the words I used when I discussed our disagreement at Columbia, although I wasn't terribly unkind," Josette stated. "Right, sister?"

"I don't think those were exactly complimentary descriptions of Mr. Carlson that you used," Yvette said with a little smile.

"But they could have been worse," Josette quipped. "Don't you think so, Yvette?"

"Yes, I suppose. Much worse."

Curtis felt like he was at a tennis match, turning his head from side to side as each twin spoke. Thankfully, they were dressed differently. One was in pale pink and the other one, Josette, in a more modern black dress that was well above her ankles. Other than that, they could easily be mistaken for one another. Their hair color, green eyes, and facial expressions were very similar. Yvette was soft-spoken, while Josette had a much more sarcastic tone to her voice.

"I must say, you look lovely tonight," he said to Josette. "Much better than the last time I saw you," he added with a smile.

Josette smiled, her cheeks flushing. "I would certainly hope so."

"If you'll excuse me, Mr. Carlson, I'll leave you two alone to sort things out." Yvette snickered, turned and disappeared up the stairs.

After a long, awkward silence between Curtis and Josette, she finally asked, "What are you doing here, Mr. Carlson? Enjoying dinner with…a wife, perhaps?" She glanced down at his ring finger. Surreptitiously…or so she apparently thought.

Interesting…. She hadn't said anything curt this time. Obviously, she was trying to find out if he was married. He willingly took the bait. "I'm a bachelor. I'm here for a retirement party for a friend. And you?"

"Yvette and I are here for our father's farewell dinner from the New York Yacht Club."

"Farewell dinner? He's leaving the Yacht Club?"

"Yes. He's been a member for years."

When it came to matters of the Yacht Club and anything else that related to his love of the sea, Curtis couldn't contain his enthusiasm. "Sorry. I didn't mean to cut you off like that. Why is he leaving? No difficulties with the organization, I hope."

"No. It's not that." She drew in a long breath. "You see, we're moving away soon."

"Moving?" he interrupted again. "Where are you going?"

"To England. London, actually."

"Really?" Curtis felt an unexpected sense of let-down. "When?"

"We depart on the First of May."

Curtis drew back. "Well, well. Isn't this a coincidence, Miss Rogers? I, too, am leaving here on May 1st! There's only one ship sailing on the first. The *Lusitania*."

Josette's mouth fell open. "Yes. We are indeed sailing on the *Lusitania*, Mr. Carlson."

"It seems fate has brought us together once again. I'm sure we'll have time to get to know each other better on board. Maybe we can have that debate we talked about."

Looking a little embarrassed, she said, "I rather doubt we'll be seeing much of each other on the ship. I'm afraid my father has booked us into First Cabin. I believe we won't be allowed onto the lower decks with the second-class — or is it third-class passengers?" She shot him a questioning look.

"I suppose I could take that as…. Hmm What's the opposite of a compliment?"

"Oh, dear. I truly didn't mean that as an insult. I merely meant…. I assumed…. I do apologize. Which class will you be traveling in?"

It was time to begin the ruse, Curtis realized, even though he didn't enjoy the prospect of lying to the pretty young woman. "I'll be traveling with my uncle. Like your Father, Uncle Phineas has booked each of us in first-class staterooms."

"Oh? How lovely for you."

Curtis tried to read her reaction. Was she happy they would be traveling together? He couldn't tell. Her words had been expressed in a flat tone.

Josette added, "They say making the crossing on the *Lusitania* is a divine experience, especially if one is fortunate enough to travel in the first-class accommodations. So…how are you able to take so much time away from your teaching this late into the term, Mr. Carlson?"

"My classes? Oh, yes. I have teaching assistants who can finish up with my students," Nervous, he shifted his weight from one foot to the other. He wondered if she believed him.

"And why is your uncle going to England?"

"For business purposes. He has important affairs to attend to, and since he's an older gentleman, he asked me to accompany him. Investment matters, you see, and he trusts my judgment in these affairs."

"How very kind of you to take time out of your busy schedule for your uncle."

Curtis shrugged. "I do have a small, self-serving reason for going," he said. "You see, I'm writing a couple of books, and the research I'll be doing about the economic impact of the war on the British and French will be invaluable." Curtis was telling a half-truth now…which made him feel a little better. He truly intended to write more books when he had finished the one he was currently working on.

"So, you're a writer, as well as a professor. Very admirable."

"And your family? I know it's not my concern, and I don't mean to pry, but why is your father taking you and your family into a war zone? It could be very dangerous, you know."

"Yes, I know, Mr. Carlson. Believe me. But Father's import business here in New York...well, let's just say he has been struggling because of the events overseas. He has a sterling opportunity awaiting him in England. He's to take over his family's business there."

"And your father's company here in New York? I mean, if he was a member of the New York Yacht Club, then surely he..." Curtis stopped short of asking more questions. He didn't want to meddle too much. Yet it was very expensive to belong to such a prestigious organization.

She seemed to understand what he was going to ask. "I'm certain that you, as an economist, understand the problems with bringing articles like Belgian chocolate, hand-made lace and other such products to America from Europe in the midst of a war. Father said with the blockades and merchant ships being sunk, many of his shipments never arrived."

"Ah. I see. What a pity the war has had a negative effect for your father, especially when so many businessmen have profited."

Josette nodded, her mouth reflecting her displeasure. "I suppose if he were exporting ammunition to the British, like some of his competitors, instead of importing fine foods and products, it would be an entirely different matter."

"That's the terrible truth. The war is rapidly becoming good for the American economy."

"That's what I've read," she said sarcastically. "Father did intend to export some war-related products. Something happened, however, and those plans never materialized."

With that comment, it struck Curtis. Rogers. Henry Rogers. "What is the name of your father's import business?"

"Rogers and Rogers in the U. K. Rogers Imports and Exports in New York. Why?"

"Oh, no reason," he said casually, trying to keep his facial expression locked in a smile. "I thought I might have heard of his company, but I guess not." *Holy crap!* That was the company he denied the loan for. Instead he had approved a massive loan to Mr. Eisenberg, a competitor of Rogers' company. Something about buttons and fabric to be used to make uniforms for the British. He had reviewed

Henry Rogers' applications, recommending against lending him the substantial amount of money he had requested. The only equity he had was his New York mansion, not nearly enough to cover the equity required by Morgan. Curtis swallowed hard. He simply didn't have a choice in the matter. Securing a loan for Mr. Rogers without ample equity would have been an unwise move on his part.

"I'm glad to hear that things have turned around for your father, Miss Rogers. It sounds as if providence had another plan for your family. Will you stay in England for an extended time?"

She looked at him with an anxious expression. "I'm sorry, Mr. Carlson, but it's a very long story, and I must go. I'm sure my parents wonder what's keeping me."

He bowed in a princely manner. "Then I bid you a good evening, Miss Rogers. I look forward to seeing you on board the *Lusitania* and continuing our conversation."

WITH ONLY a few days left before his departure for England, Curtis doubled-up on his workload at the office. The last thing he needed was a visit from Rudy, who meandered nonchalantly over to Curtis' desk.

"I suppose you're pleased with yourself," Rudy said with a smug expression.

Curtis, who had pretended not to notice Rudy for a long moment, looked up. "Oh? Whatever do you mean, my red-haired annoyance?"

Rudy leaned his hip against the desk. "You know perfectly well what I'm talking about. You've managed to worm your way into this business by accompanying my father to England."

"I did no such thing. It was Jack Morgan's decision. I didn't even know about the trip until I was called into Jack's office…by your father, I might add. And, I also might add that your father seemed supportive of my going with him instead of you. So, you might have to talk to your dear old dad and ask him why."

Rudy drew in a sharp breath. "Look, you conceited beast—" He looked around the room, most likely to see if anyone was listening. Then he leaned so close that Curtis could smell the coffee on his breath. "If anything happens to you and my father, I want you to remember. It'll be me sitting at my father's desk, not you. And the papers…well, you'll be blamed for their loss," he chortled, his lips curled into a wide grin.

Curtis pulled back. "Papers? What are you talking about?"

"Surprised I know about the big secret, Carlson?" Rudy whispered. "I know a lot more about what's going on in this company than you'll ever know."

"Look, Rudy. We won't ever be friends, but we do have to work together. So, why don't you pull in your claws and go back to your lair. This isn't grade school, and you're bullying tactics don't work on me. So, let's act like professionals and let this matter rest."

Stepping back, Rudy seemed to gather himself. "I look forward to the day I see your ass permanently heading out the door." With that, he sauntered back to his desk.

Curtis rolled his eyes, shaking his head. He hadn't done a damn thing to Rudy, not when he first started working for the Morgans, and not since. According to Mr. Arnold, Rudy Van Camp was simply jealous of Curtis. Rudy wasn't as educated as Curtis. Not to mention the fact that Curtis was landing the biggest accounts. And then there was the crew team that Morgan used in his yachting races. Rudy had tried out, failing miserably. Plus, the jackass had been snubbed as the man chosen for the debate at Columbia.

Perhaps even worse was the fact that Rudy and his father were often heard arguing through the elder Van Camp's office door. It was obvious there was no love lost between the pair. Their words were heated and usually involved strong cursing; so loud that Mr. Morgan had cautioned Phineas Van Camp that their personal disputes should be saved for times when they were in the privacy of their own home.

Drawing in a deep, calming breath, Curtis decided he wouldn't hate Rudy Van Camp. If their lots in life had been reversed, he might have resented someone as gifted as himself, too.

The workday was ending, and the rest of the employees packed their belongings and headed for the front door. More often than not, Curtis stayed late. But not today. He needed to stop off at the tailor's shop to pick up his new tweed suit and the formal evening long tailcoat he'd had made for his trip on the *Lusitania*.

He rose and closed his roll-top desk, picked up his briefcase, then called to Rudy. "See you tomorrow, Rudy, my boy. No hard feelings, eh?"

Rudy returned Curtis' comment with a scowl.

APRIL 30th had arrived dreadfully fast. The past days had been filled with tearful good-byes at Barnard and at Josette's last meeting with the ladies of the Jane Addams Club. The family's trunks were packed and ready to go, except for the clothes they would wear to the ship in the morning, and the evening dresses Josette and Yvette would wear to Jon Franklin's performance at Carnegie Hall that night.

Mr. Herrmann had purchased what seemed like acres of heavy white cloth, draping everything that might gather too many layers of dust and cobwebs while they were abroad. Of course, the maids from Father's office would clean Compton House to keep things as tidy as possible in their absence.

With Father's Cadillac comfortably nested inside the former carriage house-turned-auto garage at the end of the driveway, the Ford had to suffice for their last days in Manhattan. After Mr. Herrmann dropped them off at the Cunard pier in the morning, he would drive the utilitarian motorcar back to Compton House and park it on the side of the driveway.

Everything was ready. Everything except Yvette's heart. It was broken, and despite Josette's assurances to her sister that she would see Jon sooner than later, she had cried for days agonizing over her imminent separation from the man she planned to marry.

And now, there was nothing more to do. It was their last night in New York, and somehow attending Jon's performance with Enrico Garavelli, the famous Italian operatic tenor, seemed like an appropriate farewell to the city that had been the girls' home their entire lives.

As promised, their Father drove them to Carnegie Hall, dropping them at the front entry on Seventh Avenue. Jon had sent special passes for Josette and Yvette, and their seats were in the front row of the recital hall, a long, narrow room that seated around two hundred. It was a beautiful venue, to be sure, with its white paneled walls trimmed with gold leaf designs, crystal wall sconces, and an enormous crystal chandelier that dangled from the high ceiling.

Entering to a polite applause, Jon took his seat on the piano bench. Yvette's eyes shone like stars when she looked at him. "Doesn't he look divine, sister?"

"He's very handsome," Josette said with a smile. His unruly curls had been tamed with cream and combed straight back from his forehead. He smiled and nodded a thank you to the audience.

Tossing his long split tails behind him, Jon settled on the bench and immediately began to play Mozart's *Rondo Alla Turca*, an extremely difficult piece that was one of Josette's favorites. She found herself drifting off, likely because she hadn't slept a wink in days. Her eyelids slid closed.

"Josette," Yvette whispered harshly, jabbing her in the arm with her elbow.

"Hmm?" Josette blinked several times, trying to wake up. "Sorry."

When the song ended, the crowd rose, clapping loudly. Yvette wore a proud-as-punch smile.

Jon sat again, lifted his hands, and played the liveliest of songs. *The Entertainer.*

"He's playing Ragtime!" Josette whispered.

Yvette looked worried. She was certainly thinking the same thoughts as Josette.

It was a Scott Joplin melody Josette had heard him play for her sister countless times. But here, at the Carnegie? She glanced around, wondering if the well-heeled crowd found the music acceptable.

Long, rousing minutes later, the melody ended, and the theater was quiet. Then came a thunderous applause and even cheers.

"He's certainly a sensation!" Josette shouted in Yvette's ear.

"Isn't he marvelous?"

And then the real star of the evening entered. Enrico Garavelli, a stout man with a short black beard, was an internationally renowned singer. Jon was his accompanist on this night of wonderful nights. Wonderful, and yet Josette fought back her own sense of loss. Her heart was broken. She loved New York. It would always be home. But she would continue to hold her head high and support Father's decision. At least on the outside, Josette would stay strong…until she could come back to Manhattan.

Chapter16

SPIRITS HIGH and feeling a sense of excitement about leaving for England in the morning, Curtis negotiated the stairs up to his apartment, two at a time. Nearly finished packing his trunk, he had decided to grab a quick bite of dinner at the Italian restaurant around the corner. It was just past nine o'clock, and there was still plenty of time to go through the last bits of his handwritten research notes to determine how much paperwork he would take with him.

The ship would be a perfect place for him to get some writing done. His book, which he had decided to simply call, *Crisis in America: 1907*, was well underway. There was nothing like a visit to the ocean to bring him a calming sense of peace. That's what had drawn him to water-related sports when he was at Harvard. His parents were always too busy working in their hardware store for such frivolities as boating, but they did manage an occasional trip to the beach during the summer months. He had learned to swim and body surf when he was thirteen. That's when his love affair with the ocean had begun, and it had never ended.

As he reached the hallway and headed for his apartment, Liliana's door swung open. Curtis felt his stomach drop. Not again. Had the woman really been listening for him to come home? *Goddamn....*

"Hey, there! Good evening, Curtis," she said. She was wearing an overcoat, small hat with a wispy black feather on top, and carrying a handbag.

He forced a smile "Hello, Lil. I see you're back home."

"I just got in a few minutes ago and decided that I'm hungry. I'm off to have dinner," she said. "Care to join me?"

"No, thanks. Just finished," he said. "And where were you this time? Chicago again?"

"Florida, actually. *Harper's Magazine* wanted photographs of me on the beach wearing the latest in modern swimming attire. And you should have seen me, Curtis," she said coyly. "I was a knock-out, if I don't say so. The new designs leave little to the imagination. My bosoms were busting out all over, if you get my drift," she said with a wink and a chuckle.

"Ah. Yes. I'm sure you looked terrific."

Tilting her head seductively, she asked, "Do you want me to come over for a drink later?"

"Thanks, but I've got to get up early. I'm heading out of town tomorrow."

"Oh? You're off on a trip?"

"Yep. On business. I'm leaving for England," he said. What he didn't say was that he would be looking for a new apartment as soon as he returned. A larger place where Liliana wasn't his neighbor.

"What's that old saying?" Liliana wasn't exactly a deep thinker. But now, Curtis could almost see the wheels churning in her head. "It's something about boats going past each other in the night, or something like that. Oh, I don't know. No matter. Anyways, that's what we've been lately, Curtis. Like those ships."

He didn't know how to respond. "Uh-huh."

She stepped closer. "If I didn't know better, I'd think you were avoiding me, Curtis Carlson. Are you trying to avoid me, hmm?" Her voice was already annoying enough, but when she said things in that sing-song tone, it drove him nuts.

"I've been pretty busy, Lil. Working a lot getting ready for this trip abroad. We'll see each other when I get home in a few weeks." That was for sure. This had to end.

Liliana rose to her toes and kissed him on the cheek. "I'll be looking forward to it. Safe passage, Curtis."

THE ITALIAN tenor's performance lasted for more than an hour. After a standing ovation, Garavelli and Jon strolled down the center aisle and exited. Josette and Yvette made their way to the lobby and then to a side door, where they would meet with Jon, a pre-arranged rendezvous to give the lovers one last chance to say good-bye.

Jon rushed to Yvette the moment he saw her. Enclosing her in his arms, he scooped her up, her legs dangling like a rag doll. "I did it!" he said, swinging her in a circle.

"Yes, Jon. And you did it beautifully," Yvette said in a gleeful voice.

He lowered her to the floor. They didn't let go of each other, their faces so close they surely could feel each other's breath. Josette suddenly felt like she belonged somewhere else. Somewhere far enough away so Yvette and Jon could be alone.

But then, Josette realized that Father would be there to pick them up in a few minutes.

"I'm so, so sorry, Yvette, but we must go."

"You go. Please. I'll meet you in the lobby near the entry. I'll follow shortly."

A few minutes turned out to be twenty. The lobby was empty, with the exception of Josette. Glancing out the window, she saw Father's Ford parked in front, lights still burning, engine running.

At last, Yvette and Jon appeared. Dear Yvette. She was crying again. His arm was around her shoulders in an effort to comfort her.

"I have spoken to my agent," Josette heard him say to Yvette. "He has promised to find me work in London, my love. I will come to you as soon as I can."

"Promise," she responded through sobs, looking up into his eyes.

"Yes, my darling. I promise you the sun and the moon and the stars. We will be together again soon."

"Each night we're apart, I will look up at the sky and think that you, too, are looking at the same moon."

Josette fought back a smile. Her sister was such a romantic.

With that, the couple embraced, their lips touching in a loving, gentle kiss.

Josette turned away, as if it would give them a little more privacy. Through the glass in the front doors, she noticed a man was approaching. "Oh, no! It's Father!" she said in a raised tone.

Yvette and Jon immediately stepped apart. "Head him off!" Yvette said.

Nodding, Josette opened the entry door, as their father reached for the door's handle. "Father!" She couldn't think of anything else to say, stepping outside beside him.

"Where is your sister? What's taking you two so long? The show has been over for nearly thirty minutes."

"She's saying her good-byes, Father. To Mr. Franklin."

Father cupped his hands around his eyes to peer through the glass. "Is she in there?"

"Please, Father. Just a few more minutes. It means the world to her."

"Oh. I see." Father seemed to truly understand. "I didn't realize…" He stepped back from the door. "Very well, then. We shall wait a few more minutes."

AT LAST, Father knew why Yvette was so upset about leaving New York. On their way home, he didn't say anything for the first few minutes. Josette and Yvette exchanged worried glances but were also silent. Suddenly speaking loudly so they could hear him in the back seat of the Ford, he said, "I'm sorry to have caused you such sorrow with this move overseas, Yvette. I didn't know you and Mr. Franklin were romantically inclined."

"Would that have made any difference? Would we have ever had your blessing?" Yvette shouted over the engine noise.

"To be honest, my dear girl, there's no way under the sun your mother would have let you become serious about him. She has high hopes for you girls. In truth, your Mother expects you both to marry well."

"And what did your own family have to say when you married Mother?" Yvette asked in an uncharacteristically blunt tone.

"I'm certain they would have had the same feelings about your mother." Obviously uncomfortable, he added in a blunt tone, "Besides, I am a man, and I have more choices in these matters than young ladies have."

"That is so hypocritical! Mother certainly wasn't in your social class, was she, Father? She was a secretary! And a Catholic one at that." Yvette sounded very hostile, which surprised Josette.

"Let's not dilly-dally about the matter," Father said. "What I did has no bearing on you, Yvette. The reality is that you and your sister are from a wealthy household. You must be careful that some chap doesn't come along and marry you to get to your money. You will inherit substantially one day when I am gone."

Father stopped at an intersection where pedestrians were crossing. Twisting around, he said firmly, "You must realize that if you marry a man who already has his own fortune...or will have a fortune through his family estate...you will be certain he is genuine about marrying you for love."

Yvette thrust her back against the seat, her jaw set hard. Josette had never seen her sister so angry. And when Father pulled into the driveway at their home, she quickly exited the car, scampered to the front door and entered before Josette had even climbed out of the Ford.

"I suppose I've broken her heart," Father said to Josette, as they walked up the steps. "And you, my girl. Are there any Mr. Franklins hidden away in your life?"

"No. Not at all."

PART TWO

Chapter 17

SATURDAY MORNING, the taxi driver stacked Mr. Van Camp's large trunks on top of Curtis' more modestly sized suitcases on the back rack of the cab, securing them with leather straps. Under normal circumstances, Mr. Morgan would have sent a chauffeured limousine, most likely his fancy black Cadillac, to pick up Curtis and Van Camp at the Wall Street office. Since they were traveling incognito, however, and because it was possible that German spies were watching the Morgan and Company location to see if anyone was picked up the morning of the *Lusitania*'s sailing, they worried they could be followed to Pier 54.

That's how Mr. Williamson, Jack Morgan's personal assistant, had explained it to Curtis. And that much, Curtis understood. Where the reasoning left him was why the Germans would think a Morgan representative would be heading to England in the first place. No one had explained that logic to Curtis, a fact that made him uneasy. What weren't they telling him?

"Good morning, Carlson," Van Camp said, stepping into the vehicle.

"Morning, sir. A little damp, though."

Mr. Van Camp wore formal attire, including a top hat, a fashion trend that was about as modern as the horse and buggy. Except for very formal occasions when etiquette called for white ties and tailcoats, it was mostly older gentlemen who donned the stove-pipe chapeaus. Van Camp placed a saddle-brown leather valise between him and Curtis and settled his portly body on the seat. Curtis noted the shiny brass lock on the front flap of the case was securely attached.

"Hard to believe so much is resting on those papers in there," Curtis commented in a soft tone, so the driver wouldn't overhear. Not that it was likely he could listen, considering the loud, pulsating thumps of the engine, the grinding of the gears with each shift, and brakes that screeched like a banshee whenever the driver so much as tapped on the pedal.

Still, Van Camp frowned, sliding closed the glass window between them and the driver. He turned to face Curtis with an annoyed look. "We must guard these with our lives, Carlson. The very outcome of the war depends on us."

Curtis let out an annoyed *hmph*. "Did you *not* see the ad the German government ran in the newspaper this morning?" Before Mr. Van Camp answered, Curtis added, "My father telephoned me. He and my mother are very concerned. Everyone taking this vessel will likely be as nervous as a cat sitting by a rocking chair."

"I saw it," he responded, showing no emotion. He removed his hat and placed it on his lap.

"And you still think we should go?" Curtis asked, trying not to sound too concerned.

Mr. Van Camp clucked his tongue. "It's a ploy. An empty threat."

Curtis lowered his voice. "So, you're not worried that someone… say, a spy…has learned about the papers we're carrying to England? Do you think the Germans know what we're doing? I mean, why else would they post a warning that anyone traveling on the *Lusitania* is risking their very lives?"

"Shush!" Mr. Van Camp's eyes narrowed. "You can't speak of these things, Carlson. No one knows about our mission, except for the two of us and Jack Morgan."

"That's horseshit! What about all the others who worked on the negotiations? And the clerk who typed up the loan agreement documents? And the banks who are participating in this grand plan? And your son?"

Mr. Van Camp shot him a piercing look. "Are you implying that my Rudolph would deliberately leak a secret to our enemies? That my own son would betray his father…and his employer and friend? Preposterous!"

Curtis immediately regretted saying such a thing. "I'm sorry, sir. My point is that the more people who know about this, the more chance there is that the information will accidently slip out in an innuendo or… pillow talk. Or that someone may have overheard."

Mr. Van Camp's eyes narrowed. "I know Rudolph hasn't said anything to anyone. Nor have I. Even the secretaries have been sworn to secrecy, under penalty of treason by the U. S. government." His face contorted into a sinister expression. "The only person who might have let out such a guarded secret could have been you." He tipped his head, scrutinizing Curtis' face.

Curtis fought back the words he wanted to say. If he was going to keep climbing up the ladder of success with Morgan's company, he had to keep his personal feelings locked inside. "Believe me, I'm not saying that your son would say anything; it's just that he was quite upset he wasn't chosen for this undertaking."

Mr. Van Camp's lips tugged at the corners, as if fighting a smile. "This may come as a shock to you, but I told Jack that Rudy didn't want to accompany me to England this time."

Puzzled and surprised, Curtis didn't know how to respond. This was likely the most important assignment Mr. Morgan had asked anyone working for him to complete. "Really? Why in God's name would Rudy turn down this opportunity?"

"Rudolph and I decided he should not be put into any danger. He's my only child. My wife lost a baby, a son, when he was only two months old. She never got over it, and she would have worried herself to death if Rudolph and I both were making this trip together. It's too damned dangerous."

That almost knocked the wind out of Curtis. "So, you *are* worried about the *Lusitania* being attacked?"

Mr. Van Camp remained stoic. "Only slightly, or I would not have agreed to go myself. There is, however, a chance—"

Curtis was stunned. "Oh, I see. You're saying you didn't want Rudy to go because it's possible we could die on the voyage." He shook his head, still trying to sort out Van Camp's comments. "Correct me if I'm wrong, but basically, you and Jack Morgan belive I'm expendable!" Curtis let out an indignant laugh.

"No, no. We don't think you're expendable. And do not forget that I, too, will be on the same ship as you." His tone was rather indignant. "Neither Jack nor I truly believe the German government is stupid enough to target a ship filled with passengers. So, it's most likely we are both perfectly safe."

"Why in heaven's name would the German Embassy publish an advertisement in New York's top newspaper advising people not to sail on the *Lusitania* today if they don't intend to back up their threats?" Curtis felt his stomach burning. He'd need to get his stomach medicine out of his suitcase once they were on board the ship.

"Don't you see, Curtis? The Germans understand the human psyche. After all the war crimes they have already committed, all they need to do is simply rattle the cage. Ever heard of Pavlov's dogs?"

Curtis thought for a moment. "That was the Russian scientist who experimented with making dogs salivate when he rang a bell, right?"

"Yes. Pavlov rang a bell and then fed his laboratory dogs. Eventually, all he had to do was ring the bell to make the animals slobber, anticipating they would soon be eating. That's what the Germans are doing with this nonsensical warning. They know that mere threats will scare some people out of their skins. It's just like making the dogs react to something they expect by mere suggestion. It's like ringing the bell."

It made sense.

"As an economist, surely you know that Cunard and the other ocean liner companies have suffered major financial losses since the war began. The Kaiser would love to see Cunard lose passengers... even go bankrupt. That would be sweet revenge for the American military confiscating the German ships stacked up along the quays, wouldn't it?"

Nodding his agreement, Curtis noted a small smile through the thick mustache hairs that curled clear down to Van Camp's lower lip.

"It's a brilliant ruse, if you ask me," Mr. Van Camp said with a smirk. "Something that our firm might have thought up in a similar situation."

"I do hope you're right, sir. On all levels."

Mr. Van Camp shrugged. "In any case, someone has to take the official documents to London to be signed before the money can be transferred to the British and French governments. It's a righteous mission we're on, Curtis. Without Mr. Morgan's loans to those governments, there would be even more bloodshed for the Allies." He sniffed. "If you ask me, they would all be speaking German before year's end."

"Still. With all of this espionage business going on, I'll be glad when we're back home with the signed papers."

"I'm keeping the valise locked in my stateroom." Van Camp patted the leather bag. "Should anything happen, God forbid, we simply must risk everything to keep these papers out of harm's way." Pausing, his brows furrowed, his face taking on a melancholy expression he then said, "And if I should die…" He lifted his head gallantly. "I trust you will get this valise to Mr. Morgan's associates in the London office. They will take them to the proper authorities for signing. Then you must take them back to New York as soon as possible. Understand?"

"Of course." He definitely knew how important this mission was. Still, his ego had been bruised. Rudy would have had the assignment if it hadn't been so dangerous. Damn. And he thought Jack Morgan chose him because of his competence. Sighing, Curtis sat back in the seat and stared out the window.

"You should begin calling me Uncle Phineas. And I will call you by your given name, as well. I know it will be difficult, but it's crucial that people believe we're related."

Curtis nodded. Relatives? The Van Camp men had dark red hair and strawberry flushed cheeks. They were both rotund, though Rudy was taller and had a thicker body. Would anyone believe Curtis was Van Camp's nephew? He would do his best…but…ridiculous.

The driver dropped them in front of the Cunard's building at Pier 54. Two porters loaded their luggage onto carts and accompanied them into the first-class waiting area inside the huge green building.

Mr. Van Camp glanced around. "The check-in line isn't very long."

"I'm not surprised, what with the warning of impending death issued by the Germans this morning." That came out a little more sarcastically than Curtis had intended.

Van Camp huffed, something the surly man did far too often. "I was assured by Cunard they are checking each and every passenger's passport and identification documents very carefully. No one with a German name will be found on board this ship." He sounded quite self-assured. "That's why the line is moving slowly. Paperwork and all that."

Curtis stepped out of line and glanced at the registration desk about fifteen feet and twenty passengers in front of him. A small-framed young lady with an unusual shade of blondish, butterscotch-colored tresses stood in profile with her family. When she turned to look around, he saw Josette Rogers. Or, was it her twin sister? He strained forward, trying to get a better look. Her gaze locked on him. He smiled and nodded at her.

She smiled back and then turned to her twin to say something. Both girls waved to him. One of them mouthed something.

Oh, damn. He wasn't exactly sure which was which. Curtis grinned, tugging on the tip of his hat brim.

"What are you doing there?" Mr. Van Camp craned his neck to see what he was looking at. "Quite the ladies' man, aren't you?"

Curtis knew it wasn't a compliment.

"We've only been here five minutes and you're already flirting with those attractive young ladies." He leaned close to Curtis, speaking softly from the corner of his mouth. "Don't you forget that you're on a business trip. Keep your hands to yourself and your trousers buttoned. Got it?"

"I'm not flirting, Mr. Van Camp. I mean, Uncle Phineas. I know those girls."

Mr. Van Camp's gaze moved back to Curtis. "Even more reason to keep your distance. Do they know who you work for?"

"Of course not."

"Good. Be careful, Carlson. No one can know who you truly are."

Another knot twisted in his gut. God, he'd be glad when this trip was over; when he didn't have to spend more than a minimal amount of time with this bastard at the office. "The girls think I'm still teaching at Harvard. All they know is that I'm sailing on the *Lusitania* with you. My uncle."

THE *LUSITANIA* had been scheduled to leave at ten o'clock, but according to the purser, there was a delay because dozens of passengers were to be transferred from another ship. There was also a rumor about a delayed train that had numerous passengers on board.

Standing in the first class check-in line at Cunard's embarkation hall, Josette overheard her father and another passenger discussing the possibility that German saboteurs had attempted to derail or otherwise damage the late train. It had, after all, happened to rail lines several other times. Had it happened again?

"The Germans are certainly afoot," Father said, sounding like Sherlock Holmes, his favorite fictional character. "It's quite possible there was a bomb planted on the tracks."

The middle-aged gentleman, dressed in semi-formal wear and a top-hat, nodded his head vigorously. His expression was quite serious. "Quite right, my good man. We must remain diligent, in light of these events. Perhaps my wife and I should reconsider if we want to make this crossing," he said, glancing at the well-dressed women standing beside him. She looked to be at least fifty-years old, with deep lines around her eyes and down-turned lips. Josette could tell by the lady's facial expression that she was worried. "Please, Mac. Let's go," she said to her husband, looping her hand around his arm.

"Now, now, Mary. Just ignore us. Mr. Rogers, here, and I are simply speculating. I do believe he's correct in saying that the Germans are only trying to frighten all of us. We will not give in to their terror tactics."

"But, my darling—" she protested.

"No, dearest. We will not alter our plans because of a war of words. In our thirty years of marriage, have I ever let you down?"

She shook her head, a look of defeat sweeping across her face. "Of course not."

He gave his wife a reassuring smile and turned back to her father. "And will you change your plans, sir?"

"Henry?" Mother sounded quite serious. "We simply must go to England."

"Quite right, Millie," he said to her and then turned back to the gentleman.

"Alas, my good man. I cannot. Commitments in London, you see." Father straightened and continued. "Besides, old chap, we're British. We cannot let those German devils dictate what we will or will not do." He stood stoic, his chin, his eyes, set with a determined bearing.

Josette wondered if anyone was leaving the check-in line. Curious, she twisted around to assess the situation. A tall man dressed in dark trousers, a tweed jacket and wool cap looked in her direction.

"Look, Yvette. It's Mr. Carlson," Josette whispered to her sister.

Mr. Carlson beamed, seemingly happy to see her.

Josette smiled and gave an acknowledging nod and a half-hearterd wave. Yvette spun around, mouthing a "Hello," as she made a silly waving gesture.

Somehow, seeing Mr. Carlson made Josette feel safer. If Mr. Carlson, an educated man who was well-versed in the matters of the war, was making the voyage, surely, they were all safe. Of course, she would never let him know she respected his point of view or his level of education.

"He looks quite pleased to see you, Josette," Yvette said in a teasing tone.

"Oh? I hadn't noticed."

Yvette giggled. "I do believe this will be a very interesting week."

Josette shot her sister a glare. "Well, at least you seem to be in a better humor now. I suppose you're welcome to taunt me, as long as it makes you feel happy."

The girls turned to face forward again, moving closer to the front counter where the clerks were checking passports and tickets.

Then Josette saw a young, couple with their two small children leave the queue. She watched them guide their two little boys to the desk marked "Information" to speak with a Cunard representative.

Were they canceling their tickets? Were they taking the Germans' threat seriously?

The clerk pointed them in the direction of another desk, presumably to ask for their luggage to be retrieved. The number of people canceling their passage on the *Lusitania* had grown quickly. Josette hadn't noticed before now. With that realization, her short-lived feeling of relief disappeared in a flash.

Chapter 18

FATHER LED Josette, Yvette, and Mother up the first-class gangway and into the ship's main reception area where the Purser's counter was located. Three uniformed clerks greeted the boarding guests and directed them to their staterooms. Because Father had traveled on the *Lusitania* once before to conduct business abroad, he was familiar with the ship's layout.

"We aren't able to go to our staterooms until the trunks have been unpacked by the stewards," Father announced. "Meanwhile, we shall wait in the Lounge. It will be warm in there."

Like ducklings, they followed Father as he wound through the crowd of immaculately appointed gentlemen and ladies. They climbed up the stairs to the next level and entered the massive room. Josette stopped just inside, admiring the beautiful décor. The pastel green walls created a perfect balance with the dark wood panels. Most impressive were the dozen or so overhead stained-glass skylights. The way they were back-lighted, one would have sworn they opened to the outside. Impossible, Josette realized. That would have been much too dangerous for a ship at sea.

Overstuffed chairs and couches, each one embroidered with baskets of pink roses, had been positioned around the large room. Fires burned in the two fireplaces located on opposite ends of the lounge. Making their way to the far end of the room where several empty chairs awaited their arrival, Josette noted a lovely piano in the corner.

Yvette, who had returned to her melancholy mood once on board, sprang to life. She let out a little squeal and clapped her hands, her gaze set firmly on the beautifully appointed piano. "I can't believe it!"

"What?" Josette asked, puzzled by her sister's sudden mood change.

"It's a Broadwood piano, Josette. Don't you know anything?"

"Not about pianos."

"Well, my dear sister. Let me explain. The tone of the Broadwood is simply... indescribable. Superb. They're very expensive instruments. I've never even touched one."

"I know where you'll be spending time, Yvette," Josette teased.

Father let out a hearty laugh and settled in an armchair. "I would imagine you're correct."

Following his lead, Mother and Yvette chose their own seats in the grouping. Both girls removed their coats. Mother did not. Josette wasn't at all surprised. As she settled into a chair adjacent to Father's, she fought the urge to roll her eyes. Her mother was, indeed, a beautiful woman. But her need for attention...to have men ogle at her when she entered a room and other women envy her...drove Josette crazy.

Dressed to the nines, Mother wore a lavender dress with lace inlays in the bodice, collar, and sleeves. A small matching hat perched on top of her upswept curls. Even though they were inside and out of the cold, Mother continued to wear her white woolen coat trimmed with mink that ran from the neck clear down the front edges to her ankles. Her grandest diamond rings and bracelets sparkled over her lavender gloves.

As the room continued to fill, uniformed waiters carried trays with glasses of cold lemonade for the ladies and spirits for the gentlemen.

"What in the blazes is causing the delay for our departure?" Father asked one of them.

The waiter, a tall string-bean of a lad, responded politely, despite their father's cursing. "It's all right, ma'am. I do have a message for everyone. Captain Turner says to tell folks he hopes to leave by noon. Captain says he's received word that the last of the passengers are finally headed to the pier by motor bus. Shouldn't be much longer now, he says."

Josette spoke up. "Excuse me. Where can I get something to eat?"

"Sorry, miss," he said. "The cooks are preparin' lunch in the galley right now." He couldn't have been more than sixteen, and his accent, Josette believed, was from one of the poorer areas of London…like Lucy, who almost always dropped the letter 'h' from the beginning of a word. In fact, she had noticed several of the Cunard employees were quite young, likely, she thought, because the older boys were fighting at the Front.

"We'll be serving lunch soon as we're underway, miss." The waiter excused himself and stepped to the next group.

"Heavens!" Josette slumped in her seat. "I knew I should have packed a sandwich."

"Rubbish! I told you to eat breakfast, young lady," Father scolded. "Now, you'll have to wait for luncheon like the rest of us."

She didn't tell him she hadn't slept a wink last night. Apprehension? Excitement? No matter. Josette hadn't touched her eggs and toast. Now, she was famished. "Very well, Father." Finishing the last sips of her lemonade, she rose and stretched her back.

"May we look around the ship, Father?" Josette asked.

"Yes, yes. Go on. But be sure to listen for the announcement that will signal our departure. Your mother and I plan to go outside on this

148

deck to watch us leave port. We'll try to find a spot near the bow on the starboard side. Be sure to come out and join us."

"Yes, Father," both girls said.

"I know why you want to explore," Yvette taunted. They walked out the doorway onto the side deck, dodging the people entering the lounge. "You hope to see Mr. Carlson, right?"

"What? No. I have no interest in him." Josette picked up her pace.

Trailing behind, Yvette kept talking. "I don't believe you. I saw the way you two looked at each other at the restaurant. And then down in the terminal. I could tell there was something going on between you. Flames! Flames of romance are locked in the kindling of your hearts, just waiting to be ignited."

Josette hated it when her sister sounded like one of her novels. "Oh, my goodness." Josette stopped, turned and placed her hand on her hip. "Don't you understand? Mr. Carlson, well, he...he annoys me. We seem to disagree on everything."

"Oh, sister. That was not annoyance. I recall that you blushed when he paid you a compliment the night of Father's retirement dinner. And you never, ever blush."

"Nonsense!" Josette turned on her heel and headed to the stairs leading down to the Promenade Deck.

While the lounge had been fairly staid, the Promenade was quite a different story. The air was simply charged with excitement. Anticipating their imminent departure, rows of people had already lined up along the railing facing the Cunard dock. Raucous laughter mingled with shouts between those on board and their families, their friends, and hundreds of curious onlookers on the quay. Moving picture cameras had been set up in several places along the pier, raised on high platforms to photograph the spectacle. John Phillip Sousa's famous Grand Concert Band had played "March King," several times upon their arrival. Now, they performed other, familiar marching tunes. It was lively and uplifting, adding the feeling that something memorable, a celebration of sorts, was taking place.

This wasn't the *Lusitania's* maiden voyage. In fact, Father said this would be her one-hundred-and-first crossing from New York to England. Why, then, was there so much fanfare? It truly seemed odd.

"Excuse me, sir," Josette said, stopping one of the men dressed in a Cunard uniform. He was likely an officer, since his white shirt had epaulets and gold braid on the shoulders. "My sister and I are quite hungry. Is there somewhere we can find a bite to eat?"

His eyes narrowed in thought for a moment. "Right, miss. Try the Verandah Café. They're likely able to find some cheese and bread for you," he said. "It's at the back of the Boat Deck, up one level. We can't have such lovely ladies such as yourselves going hungry, now can we? Tell them First Mate Bronson sent you." He tugged on the rim of his cap.

THE VERANDAH Café was a large, beautifully decorated room filled with wicker chairs, at least a dozen potted palms, and numerous small tables. What made it particularly unique was that the outside wall opened, allowing guests to enjoy views of the sea. Wooden doors were hinged in panels and could be folded closed, accordion-style, in stormy weather, Josette supposed. For now, the café's movable wall was open; the chairs, however, were all occupied. And from what Josette could see, the waiters were only serving the same liquid faire as they had in the lounge: lemonade and spirits. No pastries, no sandwiches. Nothing solid.

Josette groaned. "This is ridiculous. It looks as if we're to be starved for a while longer."

Yvette simply shrugged. "Indeed."

Giving up on her quest for a snack, Josette led her sister forward to an empty spot where they could watch the third-class passengers walking up the long gangway a several levels below.

"There are so many young families boarding," Josette commented. "Look at all of the children." She smiled. "Have you ever seen so many little boys in sailor suits?"

Yvette leaned her elbows on the wooden railing and scanned the newly arriving passengers still on the ramp. "Adorable," she said with a laugh.

Josette's gaze focused on the assemblage of third-class passengers at the foot of the gangway. Women and men and children from various social levels made their way up the ramp. The quality and style of their clothing gave their status away. Sadly, some of the children were shoeless. And there were quite a few nurses, women – both old and young – wearing sky-blue dresses and nun-like white veil head coverings.

Several young men dressed in well-worn suits and trousers flirtatiously assessed the nurses, ogling and hooting at the pretty ones as they passed on their way to the long ramp. They laughed, obviously making jokes among themselves about the large breasted nurse who strolled past. An older woman paused at the foot of the gangplank. She must have made a disparaging remark to the men, for whatever she said, they all looked ashamed.

"Good for you!" Josette said in a booming voice...although she realized the woman couldn't hear her, with all the noise and confusion on the dock.

Yvette, who hadn't been watching, turned and looked over the railing. "What?"

"Oh, nothing. I've been watching those folks who have been relegated to the depths of the ship." Josette sighed. "The *Lusitania* is beautiful where we're staying, but I wonder what it's like for them down there."

Josette's gaze moved to a capless man with light brown hair, who stepped onto the inclined gangway, chatting with two friends. He nonchalantly lifted his gaze, scanning the ship. Even from three decks up where Josette and Yvette stood, she noticed his vivid blue eyes.

Josette had a sudden flash of recognition. Her heart caught in her throat. "Yvette! Look! It's the Germans from the bakery." She glanced down again.

Yvette looked over the railing. "Where, sister?"

"There!" Josette said, pointing.

It was as if the German had some sort of innate sense, as if he knew someone was watching. He glanced up. His eyes seemed to focus directly on Josette and her sister.

"Oh, crackers!" Josette pulled Yvette away from the rail. They ducked down. "I think he saw us. I think he's dyed his hair a darker shade, but I do believe it's him."

Yvette's eyes were round as teacup saucers.

"Come on!" Josette said, as she spun around. "We must tell the captain there are Germans on board."

"Perhaps we should tell Father first. The captain would listen to him."

Yvette and Josette made their way back to the lounge. The aroma of baking bread and roast beef drifted up through the cracks and crevices from the kitchen on one of the lower decks. The serving waiters had disappeared, replaced by a cabin boy sounding a three-toned xylophone. "All ashore who's going ashore," he shouted.

Many of the passengers, including their mother and father, had already left the lounge, apparently going outside to watch the casting off activities.

Josette cried out to her sister. "We can't sail until the captain knows about the Germans."

A glamorous woman wearing a great deal of face paint spun around so fast, the glass beads on her hemline rattled. "*Pardone*." Her dark, perfectly penciled brows arched in surprise, nearly meeting in the middle. "Did you say you saw Germans on this ship?" She spoke with a thick French inflection, not unlike their mother's adopted imitation Parisian accent.

The woman's pretty face was quite familiar, though Josette couldn't place where she had seen her. "No, *mademoiselle*. We didn't see any Germans," Josette said to the woman. "You must have misunderstood."

Grabbing Yvette by the arm, Josette leaned close. "Let's get out of here."

"Wait, *s'il vous plaît!*" the French woman called, following them. "I distinctly heard you say you saw Germans on this ship."

"No, *madame*. No Germans," Josette said without looking back.

AS INSTRUCTED, their parents stood between the fourth and fifth lifeboats on the starboard side. Father was speaking to a handsome, beautifully dressed gentleman. Josette raced to his side. "Father! Father! I saw them!" she interrupted, almost out of breath.

He stopped talking and turned, frowning. "Please, Josette. Can't you see I'm busy?"

"Yes. Sorry," she said. "My apologies, sir," she added, turning to the dashing gent beside her Father. "But it's urgent."

The man dipped his head. "Go ahead, young lady. I am sure you must have a piece of vital information."

Father sighed. "Yes, Josette Marie. What is it?"

Josette leaned close to her father, trying to keep too many others from hearing, though by now, there was so much commotion on the ship that it was highly unlikely she would be overheard. "I just saw the Germans from the Passport Office. They're on board! They're traveling in third-class! Yvette and I saw them!"

Father drew back, drawing in a contemplative breath. "Did you hear that, Mr. Vanderbilt? My daughters believe they saw German spies boarding the ship."

"Mr. Vanderbilt?" Josette sputtered. "*The* Mr. Vanderbilt? Good heavens!" Vanderbilt was one of the world's richest men. She had seen his photograph in the newspapers on many occasions. He was famous. One of the country's most important people. And if he was on the *Lusitania*, there was no possible way that Germany would attack the ship.

"Indeed! Alfred Gwynne Vanderbilt. At your service, young lady." He dipped his chin in a polite gesture. His back was rigid, his legs slightly apart in a rather regal stance. "Now, then, what's this about German spies, ladies? How can you be sure?"

Josette placed her hand on her hip and looked the millionaire straight on. "Well, for one thing, we heard them speaking German." *Oh, my. That came out more cynical than I intended.*

"Here on board?" Father asked, a shocked look on his face. "Why would they speak German while boarding the ship? If they are indeed spies, they'd have to be daft to do that."

Yvette shook her head. "No, Father. It was another time, when we were in Little Germany. At a bakery where Mrs. Herrmann works."

Josette's eyes fluttered closed for a moment, and she let out a small sigh. Leave it to Yvette to spill the beans under pressure.

Father took on an angry appearance, his lips and mustache drooping. "When were you girls in Little Germany?"

It was too important to keep these details secret now. "It was a while before we went to the Passport Office. We were merely picking up a bell for my bicycle," Josette explained.

Father's eyes narrowed. "And...the bakery?"

Yvette answered. "We wanted to try a piece of apple strudel, and—"

He cut her off. "We'll discuss this later, young ladies. For now, we need to figure out if those men you saw were truly the Germans from the Passport Office…and the bakery."

Mr. Vanderbilt let out a hearty laugh. "Let me interject here, sir. I'm sure your girls are mistaken. It's not possible for Germans to board the *Lusitania*. The president personally assured me that everyone, from first- to third-class, would be evaluated before being issued a passport."

Nodding his agreement, Father added, "You girls certainly remember the rigmarole we went through when we applied for our own passports. Photos, birth certificates, and the like. Every stone is turned over, so no spies could have possibly slipped through the cracks."

"I'll tell you what. Why don't you young ladies keep a sharp eye out for these so-called German lads?" Mr. Vanderbilt spoke with a mocking smile that made his thin black mustache curl up on the ends. "I know! Pretend you are Pinkerton investigators." He fished in his coat pocket and pulled out a pocket watch, popping open the ornately etched front. "Then report back to your father if you see them again."

Josette wasn't happy with the millionaire's tone. He was a nice-looking gentleman, to be sure. His clothes were made of fine-cut cloth and were perfectly fitted. He might be Mr. Alfred Vanderbilt, but Josette resented his comments. "Thank you, sir, but you are mistaken."

Mother gasped. "Josette! How dare you speak to Mr. Vanderbilt in such a tone?

Josette ignored her mother, turning to her father. "Please, Father. You must believe us."

He shook his head, narrowing his eyes. "There are so many people on board. Might have very well been someone else who merely resembled him. They were, after all, some distance from you." Father gave a dismissive wave. "I'm certain you girls are mistaken."

The bugle sounded, announcing their departure.

"But Father—" Yvette pleaded.

"Surely you can't expect Captain Turner to delay us once again while they search the entire ship for your…your supposed German spies," Mr. Vanderbilt said, striking a match on the painted metal of one of the lifeboat's davit brackets to light his cigar.

"Please forgive me, Mr. Vanderbilt. They are not my *supposed* Germans. There are at least two of them. Perhaps more. And I intend to find them."

Chapter 19

DISCOURAGED and utterly furious her father hadn't believed her, Josette turned away. *Good heavens!* Father had experienced the terrible event at the Passport Office likely caused by the young German she had just seen for the third time. Why was he being so dismissive? Balling her fists at her sides, Josette set her angry glare over the starboard railing where her father wouldn't see her face.

Father said something to Mr. Vanderbilt about the type of wine he would have with dinner. His voice was suddenly obliterated by a blast from the ocean liner's deep-throated horn. A warning, Josette surmised, that the *Lusitania* was about to depart.

The engines rumbled to life, vibrating the teak decks beneath her feet. After the gangways had been withdrawn, burly dock workers removed the gigantic ropes from their over-sized cleats and tossed them into the murky water. Josette felt the sudden need to get off the ship. Perhaps she was being paranoid. Everything was going to be all right, she reassured herself. Besides, it was too late. And Father would never allow her to leave, anyway. She leaned out to watch Cunard's on board crewmen pull the lines up the steep sides of the ship, spiraling them into perfect, progressively larger circles on the bow deck.

Overhead, ridiculous amounts of inky, black smoke billowed from the towering stacks, unusual in that there were four, one of the *Lusitania*'s most distinctive features. 'Most ships only have three,' Father had explained a few days ago, though Josette was never sure what difference that would make. More speed, perhaps? The air smelled of coal from the furnaces but, thankfully, a breeze carried the sooty cloud away from the ship. Still, over time, traces of the powder-fine coal dust had stained the white lifeboat covers, tinging them to a light-gray color.

"If you'll excuse me, I shall take my leave now," Josette heard the millionaire say in a polite tone. "My valet should have my stateroom ship-shape by now…if you will excuse my little witticism."

Josette twisted around and dipped her chin, though she didn't smile at him. How could she?

Smiling politely, Mr. Vanderbilt tipped his hat and poked his cigar back into his mouth.

Mother stepped forward, extending her gloved hand, as if she expected the millionaire to give it a polite kiss. He did not.

Mother withdrew her hand, pretending to ignore his snub. "*Enchanté*, Monsieur Vanderbilt. Ever so charmed to meet you," she said with a curtsy.

Mr. Vanderbilt looked at Mother quizzically, removing his cigar. "*Mais oui. Et vous, aussi*, Madame Rogers. I didn't realize you're French. And where were you born? Paris, perhaps?"

Mother's smile melted into a panicked expression. That was the question too many asked when she put on her asinine French airs. Mother was silent, as if trying to sort out how to answer.

A twinge of pity washed over Josette. *My heavens. Could Mother look more ridiculous?* She was speaking with one of the most successful men in the world. Would she lie, or would she tell him she was born in New York? That she was a Scots-Irish American?

Father came to her rescue, as usual. "You see, my good man, Mrs. Rogers has spent a great deal of time in Quebec, as well as in Paris. We honeymooned in Paris, and my wife fell in love with the city. She picked up the language rather well, if you ask me."

"Ah. I see." With a dismissive nod, Mr. Vanderbilt looked at Josette and Yvette. "Good day, ladies," he said, heading for the stairwell.

Waiting for Vanderbilt to be out of earshot, Father said at last, "His cabin is on the Promenade Deck. The old boy has one of those big Regal Suites complete with a room for his personal butler." He chuckled, shaking his head. "I don't suppose our butler would have been welcomed on the *Lusitania*. Franz would have likely caused a panic of sorts, being a German."

"Oh, Henry…." Mother scowled.

"I wonder where Mr. Carlson is," Yvette said in Josette's ear. "We haven't seen hide nor hair of him since we left the Cunard building. I wonder if he's down on the Promenade Deck?"

"I'm certain we shall see plenty of him in the next seven days. There aren't too many places to hide, after all."

Yvette's gaze searched the faces in the crowd and then moved to the hundreds of horse-drawn buggies and wagons and the dozens of private motor cars and taxi cabs parked in the areas adjoining the overcrowded pier. "If only Jonathan could have come to see me off."

"I'm sure he would have come if he hadn't had to rehearse for tonight's performance."

"I know. Still…." Yvette sighed.

Josette turned to face her sister, placing her hand on Yvette's arm. "Listen to me. After his performance at Carnegie last night, I'm certain employment offers will continue to flood in. You must be patient. It will all work out. I promise. This is an amazing opportunity for Jonathan."

Three startling, ear-throbbing blasts of the ship's horn announced their departure from New York. From America. The *Lusitania* began to move, pushed and prodded by several tugboats assisting the mammoth ship away from the dock. As the liner's slender bow was eased into the center of the Hudson River, a flurry of powder bursts exploded in at least a half-dozen news photographers' flash trays. The moving picture photographers furiously cranked their awkward cameras, following the ship's progress.

A flurry of white handkerchiefs and small American flags fluttered like hundreds of butterflies, matched by cries of "good-bye," and, "bon voyage!" emanating both from the *Lusitania's* decks and from the myriad of well-wishers on the quayside.

Father and Mother excused themselves to head to their stateroom in the forward section of the Boat deck. Josette and Yvette decided to watch as the vessel moved away from the dock and headed down river. Josette felt a strange, hollow sensation in the area between her breasts. One of mourning. Of emptiness. Her life, her plans had been interrupted by forces she couldn't control. She and Yvette didn't speak for quite some time. If she was feeling this sense of loss, Josette could only imagine how her twin sister felt.

Minutes later, Josette noticed three small gray ships patrolling the Jersey shoreline, where rows of German ships rose and fell on the river's swells. She recalled Mr. Carlson's lecture and the fact that American military vessels had confiscated dozens and dozens of the Kaiser's ships – both cargo carriers and passenger liners. It was one thing to hear the German students complain that seizing their country's ships in America was against maritime law. It was quite another to see it with one's own eyes.

Josette commented to Yvette, "How can President Wilson justify what seems like an act of war against the Germans, while maintaining America's neutrality? Just look at how many of their ships have already been seized, and the war began only a matter of months ago? Why don't they have as much right to sail to and from America as the British and French ships?"

Yvette merely shrugged.

Josette knew what her sister was thinking about. Jonathan. Yvette stood silently watching the tall buildings of Manhattan shrink into dollhouse-sized miniatures. She began to cry again, retrieving a handkerchief from her purse.

The pilot got off the ship near Sandy Hook, the last spit of land before the *Lusitania* would head to the open sea. After the mighty Lady Liberty had faded from view and the coast of New York was merely a sliver on the horizon, a steward passed by sounding his three-note xylophone.

"Finally," Josette said, heaving a sigh. "Dry your eyes, and let's see what this famous ship is serving us for lunch."

JOSETTE AND Yvette negotiated their way down the Grand Stairway, descending level after level, on their way to the dining room. The *Lusitania* had begun to pitch on the swells, making walking in high-heeled shoes a bit precarious. Not that they couldn't have taken one of the two elevators to make the trip between the upper decks and the dining saloon easier. But with Yvette's irrational fear of enclosed spaces—or whatever it was that kept her off Mr. Otis' wondrous invention, it was much easier to take the stairs than to argue with her sister about the convenience of taking an elevator.

The two-tiered, first-class dining room, if one could even call it that, was a cavernous affair. Calling it a dining room or saloon seemed far too ordinary for the massive amount of gold gilt, Grecian columns, thick carpeting and ornate swiveling chairs. There were lavish wall sconces, swirls atop the columns and carved cherubs peering down from the high ceiling. Silky rose-colored upholstery covered the chairs. And as if that weren't enough ostentation, it was all topped by a massive dome, which was back-lit by electric bulbs.

Josette paused, assessing the sumptuous surroundings. "This place looks like something out of Buckingham Palace. I'm sure Mother is in Georgian-motif heaven," Josette commented, as she and her sister were escorted to their pre-assigned table, where they would join their parents.

"And the colors...they're perfect for you, Yvette." Josette grabbed the back of an empty chair to steady herself when the ship suddenly rocked. "Lots of pink in here. I'll just bet you're feeling right at home."

Yvette glanced back over her shoulder. "It's rose, Josette. Dark rose. Not pink. And I believe it's quite lovely."

"Of course, you do!"

Though their parents were already seated and eating lunch, many of the tables were still empty. The waiter explained that a buffet had been served upstairs in the Verandah Café, while other first-class passengers chose to have sandwiches delivered to their cabins. Soup, sandwiches, fresh fruit, cakes and tarts were brought to their table on a rolling silver cart.

Josette was famished, and everything she ate was quite delicious. Yvette, on the other hand, only had a few spoonfuls of beef consommé.

"Are you all right, my girl?" Father scanned Yvette's face with a look of concern. "You don't look well."

"Your pallor is quite terrible," Mother commented. "A bit gray, perhaps. No," she corrected, scanning Yvette more closely. "A tinge of green, I believe."

"May I please be excused," Yvette said. She placed her spoon on the table and leaned forward. "It's my stomach."

"Crikey! We're barely underway, and you already think you're seasick."

"It's not my imagination, Father," Yvette said with a groan.

"You've always gotten sick the moment you step foot on a boat. Or the pier where the boat is tied up. The *Lusitania* is designed to cut through the waves, to give a smoother ride, child." His impatience with Yvette's condition was evident in his tone.

"Let her go to the stateroom, Henry," Mother said softly.

"Nonsense! The Cunarders are world-class luxury liners. I can assure you the greatest care was taken by the designers to assure she would provide her passengers with the smoothest ride possible. The last thing they want is a bunch of people upchucking into buckets. Makes the company look substandard."

"Must you be so graphic, Henry?" Mother said, rolling her eyes. "Surely you realize some of us are born with sea legs, and some of us are not."

"Sorry, Father. I really feel awful," Yvette said. "Please. May I go?"

Poor Yvette was prone to seasickness, an unfortunate fact they realized years ago when she attempted to accompany Josette on their father's sailboat. Josette and their father were the sailors in the family. Yvette and Mother were the shoppers. Father never accepted that fact. Now, it was time for Josette to intervene.

Josette stood up, grabbing half of a ham and cheese sandwich. "I'll take her to our room. We wouldn't want her to…well, it would be most humiliating if things were to happen in here. At least there's a WC in the stateroom."

Father's gaze darted around. "Just go," he said with a wave of his hand. "This is your key. Enter the corridor at the top of the stairs on the Promenade Deck. Your room adjoins ours."

"And Josette, make sure your sister gets out of her tea dress immediately," Mother called as they exited. "It was very expensive. I wouldn't want any stains."

THEIR ROOM was as pretty as any Josette had seen when staying at even the finest hotels on family vacations to Canada, Connecticut, and Massachusetts. Two beds with brass headboards had been pushed against opposite walls. A small marble-topped night stand with an attached lamp was situated beside each headboard. Neatly arranged throughout their quarters were a matching armoire, four-drawer dresser, high-back chair, and a vanity table with a cushioned stool. The stewardess had neatly laid out their two brushes, combs, hand mirrors and hair accessories.

Yvette groaned, flopping face-down on top of the silky tan bedspread. "I hate the ocean," she muttered into the pillow.

Josette opened the armoire's door and found an empty hanger sandwiched between two beaded formal dresses. "Why don't you change into something more comfortable? Your night clothes, perhaps?" Josette said. She crossed to Yvette's bed. "Let's get you out of that outfit."

Yvette simply moaned. "Please. Just leave me alone."

"Poor dear. I'll tell you what. I'll go find the doctor's office to see if there's some sort of remedy to help you feel better. A powder of some sort."

It was a half-truth. She also intended to locate the Purser's Office and ask for a diagram of the ship. Third-class, she believed, was in the forward section, in the bowels of the ship. Were there connecting stairs or passageways between the first- and third-cabin areas? Surely there would be some sort of map that would help her figure out how she could explore that part of the vessel. She was determined to find the Germans. Had the blue-eyed one recognized her?

Laying the hanger on the end of Yvette's bed, Josette felt a sudden, horrifying thought sweep over her. What if he indeed recognized her? What if he knew she could identify him and his friends as spies? And what if…if he was going to come after her? She felt a sense of panic. Her breathing was shallow, her heart pounded in her chest. For the moment, however, she kept her worries to herself.

REACHING THE PURSER'S DESK, she was directed to the doctor's office down one level on the C Deck, where a half-dozen men, women, and children waited for medical assistance. Several held paper bags, anticipating the worst. A young boy sat on the floor leaning against the wall, while his mother squatted next to him in an attempt to comfort the seasickness away.

When it was Josette's turn, Doctor Webster gave her a bag of pulverized ginger powder. "Take your sister up to the port-side Promenade for some fresh air. I'll send a steward with a pot of tea and honey and digestive crackers. She should be better by dinner time."

Standing up to leave, Josette had a thought, a way to speed things up. She turned back to the doctor. "By the way, I hate to trouble you, but I have a dear friend traveling in third-class. Do you happen to know how I can go down there to see her?"

SETTLING YVETTE into a deck chair, Josette covered her sister's legs with a soft, white blanket emblazoned with a blue Cunard symbol and tucked in the edges. A steward had also provided a small pillow, which she slid under Yvette's head.

Josette removed the package of ginger powder from her handbag. "When the steward brings you up your tea, mix in a teaspoon of this with each cup," she explained. "And try to watch the horizon and not the deck."

Yvette's brows lifted in surprise. "Why? Are you leaving?"

"Just for a short time. I want to do a little more exploring."

"Very well. Have you seen Mr. Carlson yet?"

"I expect he's busy getting his uncle settled in. I'm sure we'll see him soon." Josette smiled. "Now then, you just rest."

THE DOCTOR had drawn a diagram of where Josette could enter a stairwell that led to the third-class decks. Those exits had been gated and locked on the *Titanic*, resulting in the death of hundreds of people trapped on the lower decks. While that wasn't the case on the *Lusitania*, there were deck hands stationed to guard the cordoned off areas, an effort to keep the lower-class guests from making their way up to the domain of the rich, where they might be inclined to steal jewelry, cash, and other valuables from their staterooms. Such utter nonsense, Josette had thought when the doctor made that comment. This was a common myth about people of lesser means. Her sociology teacher had discussed the topic at length last semester. It was a prejudice that needed to be overcome.

As expected, a young crewman, one of the boys who ran errands and carried messages for the first-class passengers, stood at the top of stairs. "You see, I would like to visit friends from my school, who are making the crossing to England in the third-cabin class," she lied. Smiling, she casually pulled a coin from her pocketbook and handed it to him.

He glanced around, likely to make sure none of his superiors was near, and then accepted the twenty-five-cent piece. "Thanks, miss," he said, opening the rope.

"That was easy," she whispered to herself, descending the stairwell. It was much narrower, steeper and had less light than the stairs in the upper-class section. Josette was quite alone now, listening to the groaning of wood and steel straining against the power of the sea. The roar of the massive engines rumbled throughout the lower decks, as they worked their magic, producing as much power as hundreds of galloping horses. Steam hissed in the distance. A leak perhaps? Or a valve of some sort?

In what seemed like a labyrinth of stairs and step-downs and corridors, Josette finally heard the sound of laughter coming from an open area down the hall. She gathered her courage and walked in that direction, stopping at the edge of the doorway to peek inside. Josette scanned the room with a slow, evaluating gaze. It was a dining hall—nearly as large as the gymnasium at Barnard College, it seemed. Filled with long rows of plain wooden tables, the ceiling was low, though well-lit with dozens of utilitarian electric lights. Most of the people had finished eating, though a few children were sitting on their mothers' laps as they were fed bites from bowls.

The Germans weren't there. At least, not the ones she had recognized. Where else could they be? In their rooms, most likely, since it was well after two o'clock. Maybe there was a smoking room for the men in third-class. Or a card room? Or maybe the men she sought were out on the deck smoking cigarettes, a popular past-time among men from all levels of society.

"Oh dear." How in the world would she ever find them? She needed a map. A real map to conduct a real search. She would make another attempt to find them tomorrow, when Yvette could go with her. For now, she needed to familiarize herself with as much in third-class as she could, and then find her way back to the Promenade Deck before Father discovered her absence.

Chapter 20

"AND HOW are you feeling?" Josette sat beside her sister in an empty deck chair.

"I think I may live." Yvette let out a faint laugh. "I'm still not sure if I'll be able to eat dinner, however." She straightened her blanket. "And where have you been, sister?"

Glancing around, Josette leaned closer. "I've been down to the third-class section."

Yvette drew back. "What? How in the world?"

"Don't ask. Let's just say…this isn't going to be as easy as I thought. There are hundreds of people down there, and they tend to move around. I shall return tomorrow to do some more searching… in case you would like to come along."

Yvette frowned. "Silly goose. Of course, people tend to move from place to place." She clucked her tongue. "And what will you do if you see the Germans? What if the blue-eyed one sees you looking for him? Wouldn't he simply run away and hide? Or worse…what if he realizes you can identify him and—" Yvette's face changed. "Oh, my Lord in heaven, Josette. What if he tries to hurt you? You cannot go back there alone. Father must come with you."

"No! He didn't believe me a while ago, and he won't believe me tomorrow either." Josette stiffened. "I have to find the Germans first. To make sure. Then I'll get Father's help."

MOST EVERYONE in the impressive dining room was dressed in the same clothing they had worn all day. Except Mother. She looked lovely in a scarlet beaded gown, long white gloves and two ostrich feather plumes stuffed into the curled coif which a ship's lady maid had styled for her. Mother's grand entrance was all but ignored by just about everyone. In fact, Josette imagined that most of the other women viewing Mother's attempt to be noticed could cause her to be snubbed by them.

The Rogers' table accommodated eight people. They had been alone for lunch, but at tonight's dinner, an elegant older woman and her adorable West Highland terrier took up two of the seats.

After the waiter made the formal introductions, Josette sat beside the Westie. "Pleased to meet you, Mrs. Donaldson. And you, too." She bent over and patted the dog's head.

"The pleasure is mine, lass. And this is Mr. Duns." She spoke with a charming Scottish inflection. Lifting the dog, she cradled him in her arms, so that he faced Josette.

Smiling, Josette noted the black bow tie on his neck. "Hello, Mr. Duns. My goodness! Such an interesting name for a pup."

The dog's ears lifted. He cocked his head from side to side, as if to understand her words.

"Aye. He's named for the town where I was born in Scotland."

"I do like dogs," Father commented. "Just not at my dinner table, if you'll beg my pardon, Mrs. Donaldson."

The elderly woman smiled pleasantly. "Please do not concern yourself, Mr. Rogers. Mr. Duns is quite the gentleman. He promises he won't leap across the table and steal your dinner. In fact, he's getting a bit too old to do anything of that sort. Like me," she said with a warm chuckle. "I'm afraid my bounding days are behind me, too."

Father merely grunted and took a drink of water from his crystal goblet.

"And you say you're from Duns?" Josette commented rather rhetorically.

"My late husband and I moved to New York a few years after we were married, but we kept a home in Duns. It's a lovely country house. In the summer, the hydrangeas along the lane grow as big as melons." She had a melancholy expression on her face as she spoke. "Oh, aye. Such a lovely place. We visited as often as we could."

"I've been to Duns. A charming area, that," Father said. "I had business to conduct there years ago."

While Father went on to explain his dealings with Scottish wool dealers, Josette bent closer to the dog. "And how are you this lovely evening?" The Westie opened his mouth. A pink tongue slid out, curling as he panted. Expressive brown eyes peered out from behind a fluff of fur.

"You look quite happy to be here, boy." Josette scratched behind his ears. While the longer hairs around his face felt wiry, the underlayer of fur was soft. Josette glanced up. "I'm utterly delighted to be seated beside you, Mrs. Donaldson. And your precious pet."

"Are you going to Scotland for another visit?" Mother asked, ignoring the dog.

Mrs. Donaldson gave Mother a thoughtful smile. "A permanent visit, Mrs. Rogers. Before my husband died last October, he asked me to return his ashes to Scotland. No one dreamed this war would continue so many months. That buffoon of a British Prime Minister promised it would be over before last Christmas. I should have made the trip sooner."

"We're sorry for the loss of your husband, Mrs. Donaldson," Father said.

"Thank you." Drawing in a breath of composure, Mrs. Donaldson moved her wine glass closer to the table's edge, so the waiter could pour from the bottle of Chateau Margaux without missing his target. "Lord help us. We humans cannot keep from killing each other for one cause or another, can we, now?"

"Quite right, I fear," Father said with a concurring nod.

"I don't believe this will end well for anyone, do you?" Josette glanced around the table.

While the waiter filled their wine glasses, there was a long silence. After he walked away, Father cleared his throat, something he did when he was uncomfortable. "I trust you can find a more appropriate topic of conversation for dinner, Josette Marie."

"Of course, Father. But it's true."

Father drew in a sharp breath and shook his head in defeat.

"May I propose a toast?" Mrs. Donaldson said, setting the dog back on the seat.

"Jolly well, my good woman." A look of relief melted across Father's face.

They all picked up their glasses half-filled with the expensive Bordeaux.

"*Slainte*. To future peace and a safe voyage," the Scottish woman said.

Taking a sip, Josette noticed Mr. Carlson approaching. His lips were curled into a wide smile. The *maître d'*, an Indian man, judging by the look of him, guided Mr. Carlson to their table, stopping beside Yvette. Josette suppressed a gasp, nearly choking on her wine.

After introducing Mr. Carlson as one of their dining companions, the *maître d'* excused himself and headed back to the entry.

Mr. Carlson gazed down at Yvette. "Good evening, Miss Rogers. It's good to see you again. Can you believe this coincidence, sitting at the same table?" Before Yvette could say anything, he turned to Father. "You see, I am an acquaintance of your daughter's."

Father's eyes took on a suspicious expression. "Is that so. Which one?"

"Miss Josette," he said, motioning to Yvette...who began to giggle.

"Good heavens. That's my sister, Mr. Carlson. I'm Josette."

Moving his gaze to Josette, Mr. Carlson's cheeks flushed. "Oh. Yes. My apologies, ladies."

Without responding, Josette turned to her father. "As you can see, Mr. Carlson and I are barely acquainted."

"And where did you meet Mr. Carlson, Josette?"

"I fear it's a rather long story, Father." She narrowed her eyes and glared at Mr. Carlson, giving him a don't-you-dare-say-anything look.

"Uh…yes, sir. Long story." Mr. Carlson rotated the swiveling chair on the opposite end of the table into position and slid onto the seat.

Father introduced Mother, who whispered her usual, 'Enchante'; and then Mrs. Donaldson. Even Mr. Duns. The terrier looked at Mr. Carlson, wagging his tail as if to say hello.

Mr. Carlson chuckled at the dog. "And he's dressed in formal black tie, I see. He's quite the dandy."

"I suspect he's a little overdressed this evening." Mrs. Donaldson shot back with a grin.

"Yes, yes. Jolly, good." Father went on. "It would seem you've already met my girls."

Mr. Carlson, obviously embarrassed, shrugged. "Please forgive me, ladies, but you do look a lot alike."

"Oui, Monsieur," Mother said with a dainty laugh. "When the girls were children, they fooled their teachers by exchanging places in their classes."

"Only when Yvette needed me to take a mathematics examination for her," Josette said.

Smiling, Mr. Carlson nodded. "I can see where that would have come in handy."

Josette smiled. "Aren't you here with your uncle?"

"Correct. Mr. Phineas Van Camp. He's a bit under the weather and preferred eating in his stateroom tonight."

"You should have him try some ginger tea," Yvette said. "It's not a cure for mal de mer, but it does help. If the doctor's office is closed, I would be happy to share some of the powder the doctor provided for me."

"That's kind of you, Miss Rogers," he responded. "But my uncle will be fine."

A moment later, the waiter was there taking their orders. The menu was sumptuous, as amazing as the faire offered by the Palace

Hotel in Manhattan when Father had taken her and Yvette to lunch for their birthday last year. As soon as the waiter left, a boy of around sixteen rolled a cart filled with shelves loaded with hors d'oeuvres to their table: French snails drenched in butter and garlic; fruit cocktails in parfait glasses; boiled shrimps in red sauce; rolls of sliced ham. The smells wafted, especially the garlic and the shrimp.

The color suddenly drained from Yvette's face. "Oh, my." She addressed the young server standing beside the wheeled cart. "Can you please bring me a bowl of consumme and a few crackers? Soon."

Nodding his understanding, the boy quickly retreated towards the Galley.

Father frowned his disapproval. "Still sick, my girl? It's all in your head." Then he turned to Curtis. "You never said where you met my daughter."

"Actually, I happened to meet your daughter …Josette," he said, making eye contact with Josette this time, "It was at *Chateau Le Blanc* the night of your retirement from the Yacht Club. I mentioned that I would be accompanying my aging uncle on a business trip to London. Your daughters and I thought it was quite a coincidence we would all be sailing on the *Lusitania*."

Relieved that Mr. Carlson hadn't brought up their encounter at Columbia University, Josette nonchalantly reached to the cart, selecting a glass bowl filled with shrimp in red sauce. One of her favorites.

Mr. Carlson continued talking. "We will be staying in London for a short time. Just long enough for Uncle Phineas to take care of some of his investments."

"You see, Father," Josette interjected. "Mr. Carlson is an expert on economic issues. He teaches at Harvard University."

Father's questioning gaze moved from Josette to Mr. Carlson and back again. "You must have had quite a lengthy discussion at *Chateau Le Blanc* Restaurant that night."

Mr. Carlson jumped in. "Uh, I did a speaking engagement at Barnard College several months ago."

"Yes, Father. I didn't meet Mr. Carlson at his lecture, but I did attend. So, um, when I saw him at the restaurant, I said hello. I told him how much I enjoyed his lecture, didn't I, Mr. Carlson? And we had a small discussion about the, the—"

"About the effect of the war on the American economy," Mr. Carlson chimed in.

Mrs. Donaldson seemed interested in Mr. Carlson's financial expertise. "Are you advising your uncle regarding his portfolio, young man?"

"As much as possible, ma'am. Uncle Phineas is a quite stubborn man, though please don't tell him I said so," he added with a grin. "He does get a bit confused at times, and my aunt requested that I make the journey with him, just to be on the safe side."

"And your aunt? She decided not to make the journey on the *Lusitania*, no?" Mother asked in a surprised manner.

"Most people would give their eye-teeth to travel on this vessel," Father sniffed. "Not to mention that they would be meeting the likes of Mr. Vanderbilt and Charles Frohman, the most famous theatrical producer in the world, I imagine." He motioned in the direction of a large table located closer to the center of the room.

"Mr. Frohman?" Yvette inquired, glancing over her shoulder. "Oh my gosh!"

"Quite so, my girl. At the captain's table."

Josette twisted from her waist to see. Sitting on Captain Turner's left was Mr. Vanderbilt, who appeared to be deep in a conversation with a round faced, middle-aged man.

"Is that truly Mr. Charles Frohman, Father?" Yvette said, her eyes wide. Josette knew her sister's expressions very well. Yvette was actually excited. This was the most animated her sister had been in weeks.

"You've heard of him, have you, Yvette?" Father asked.

"Of course! Jonathan...uh, Mr. Franklin...recently auditioned as an accompanist for one of Mr. Frohman's plays. Do you think he's a friendly sort of man...I mean, with his fame and all?"

"Oh, aye," Mrs. Donaldson said. "I've spoken with him on many occasions. Play openings and the like."

"What is it you have in mind, Yvette?" Father's eyes squinted with suspicion, an all-too-familiar look.

"I would imagine with the loss of so many men's lives at the Front, there is a shortage of professional musicians to fill the orchestras' seats these days. Especially in the London Theater District," Yvette commented.

"I reckon you're correct, since it's mostly men who make up the orchestras," Father said between bites.

"Sadly, bullets do not discriminate between the soldiers' social classes nor their special abilities." Mrs. Donaldson broke off a chunk of buttered roll, feeding it to Mr. Duns. The dog swallowed the piece with barely a chew, wagging his tail to request another bite. "I cannot even imagine the number of talented men who have been killed or permanently maimed. It's as if an entire generation of fine lads will have been planted under the earth before this misery has ended."

"Well said, Mrs. Donaldson," Mr. Carlson agreed. "That's why I believe America needs to step up and support the Allies. The sooner the better."

Feeling as if her hackles had been raised by that remark, Josette dabbed her lips with her napkin. "You see, Mr. Carlson is what you would call a warmonger."

Mr. Carlson opened his mouth to object when Yvette spoke up. "Please! We're getting off the point here."

"Which is what, lass?" Mrs. Donaldson inquired.

"I just so happen to know an extremely talented American pianist who would be most happy to come to England to take over one of those job vacancies." There was a mischievous glint in Yvette's eyes. "And I intend to speak with Mr. Charles Frohman about the matter as soon as possible."

AT NINE o'clock, the orchestra stopped playing and left the balcony, presumably to move to the Lounge to continue the evening's entertainment.

Dinner and dessert were finished. So, when Mrs. Rogers, the twin daughters, and Mrs. Donaldson got to their feet, Curtis and Mr. Rogers politely rose. Curtis noticed Josette's gaze had abruptly locked on something in back of him. The expression on her face was one of worry. Or was it fear? Curious, he turned around to have a look. The captain's table was about ten feet away, partially blocked from view by a pillar. All six men and women, Captain Turner's dinner companions, were standing, chatting.

Captain Turner was the epitome of what Curtis imagined a ship's captain should look like: weathered face, crisp uniform, graying hair, all of which said he was a man of great experience and competency.

When Josette let out the words, "Oh, heavens! It's her," Curtis twisted around and looked at Josette.

Mrs. Donaldson chuckled. "I see you recognized Rita Jolivet, Miss Rogers."

"Who?" Curtis had never heard the name Rita Jolivet.

"Rita Jolivet is the lassie talking with the captain." Mrs. Donaldson attached Mr. Duns' leash as she spoke. "Do you no' recognize the famous actress?"

Curtis glanced over his shoulder again to view the woman who seemed to be causing quite a stir.

"She's quite bonnie. And, she isn't married, if memory serves." The Scottish woman smiled coyly.

"Mmm. Not my type," he said with a shrug.

"Quite right," Mr. Rogers said with a chuckle, taking his wife's arm. "Too much face paint for my taste."

Still standing beside the table, Josette and Yvette exchanged nervous glances. They whispered secrets Curtis couldn't hear. "Is everything all right?"

Josette glanced at Curtis. "Yes. Fine." Her voice was curt. Her expression said things were not at all fine. "If you will all excuse us." Josette and Yvette headed for the door, continuing their conversation without even saying goodnight.

"RITA JOLIVET," Yvette said with a discouraged sigh, exiting the dining saloon. "I knew she looked familiar. I've seen her in a few moving pictures."

"Wouldn't you know it would be someone famous – someone other people might listen to – who overheard us talking about—" Josette glanced around to make sure no one was close enough to overhear. "About you know who." They headed for the grand staircase.

"Stop, girls!" Father's voice bellowed as he drew near. "You two certainly made a quick exit."

The girls paused and turned.

171

Mother had her arm looped through his. "I'm heading for the Smoking Room to imbibe in a glass of brandy," Father explained. "Please see to it your mother gets back to the stateroom." Their parents proceeded to the elevators.

"We're taking the stairs, Father," Yvette called.

"When will you get over that ridiculous fear of elevators," Mother said loudly.

"Never, Mother," Yvette sang out. This bolder version of Josette's timid sister stopped and looked at their mother: her eyes narrowed, lips pursed, hands on her hips. "Just think about it. There's nothing beneath your feet except a plank of flooring. What if the lines pulling the car up snap? Or what if the door jams and you cannot get out?" Yvette began to climb the stairs, unaware of the number of concerned-looking passengers who had overheard. "I much prefer not to take my chances with those contraptions."

Stepping beside her sister, Josette laughed. "That's telling them, Yvette."

"Your mother will be waiting for you on the Boat Deck. Please hurry it along." Father led mother into one of the side-by-side lifts.

"Miss Rogers! Josette! Wait!"

Josette recognized Mr. Carlson's voice. Most surprising was that he bounded up the stairs like some sort of pole vaulter. They paused to let him catch up. "Mr. Carlson. Please do not call me by my familiar name," Josette said, trying not to sound too snippy. "Not yet."

"Yes. Of course. So sorry, Miss Rogers. You ladies left before I could ask if you would like to accompany me to the Music Room. Or, perhaps, take a stroll on the deck."

"No, thank you. My sister is still a little queasy and I'm quite tired." Josette took the handrail again and climbed to the next step. Then she paused and turned to him. "By the way, I wanted to thank you for not telling my father about Columbia University." Embarrassed, she dropped her gaze. "You see, he doesn't know I participated in that ruckus or about my, my…." She glanced up to make sure no one else could hear and lowered her voice to a whisper. "My near-arrest. He would be understandably upset."

"That's what I figured." Curtis chuckled. "You should have seen the look on your face."

Yvette laughed as she continued up the stairs. "You did look like a frightened mouse, Josie!"

THE THREESOME chatted as they climbed to the next deck and the next. Mother waited near the entrance to the interior corridor leading to their stateroom.

"Goodnight, Mr. Carlson," Josette said. "Perhaps we shall see you tomorrow."

"Most likely, ladies. My uncle and I are in the suites on the port side of this deck. And since we're all sharing a table in the dining saloon…"

"Yes, Mr. Carlson," Mother said. "I suppose there's no way to avoid you."

NOT YET recovered from Mrs. Rogers curt, insulting remark, Curtis knocked on Van Camp's cabin door. "It's me, uh, uncle."

Footsteps approached, the lock clicked, and the door opened. Mr. Van Camp wore a black velvet lounging jacket with red satin trim on the collar. "Come in, Curtis." He turned and walked across the small parlor towards the large easy chair. "Lock the door behind you."

"Of course. I take it you're worried someone might pay you an unwanted visit."

Sitting in the chair, Van Camp placed his feet on the matching ottoman and picked up a piece of paper from the side table.

"You should have come to dinner. I had to make excuses to the other guests at our table."

Van Camp's wire-rimmed reading glasses sat low on his nose. He peered down at the single sheet. It was abundantly clear he didn't give a damn about the opinion of his dining companions. He didn't look up.

"Was your stomach causing you so much grief that you couldn't have a cup of bisque or consommé?" Still, no response.

Van Camp rose from the chair, walked past Curtis, and went to the desk where the satchel had been opened and the papers spread out. "I wonder if we should keep these with us…or if they would be more secure down in the Purser's Office." He spoke in a low tone, grumbling his words to himself.

"What are you talking about?" Curtis was shocked by the question. He stepped to Van Camp's side. "Jack Morgan gave us specific instructions that we shouldn't let them out of our sight."

"Yes, yes. You do not need to remind me." Removing his spectacles, he glanced up at Curtis, rubbing his forehead with his forefinger and thumb. "But what are we to do about things like going to the dining room? Carrying a locked case such as this would be a dead give-away that there's something very important inside. Something secret. Wouldn't that merely call more attention to the situation?"

Curtis sensed his worry. "Good point, sir. But no one paid attention to the satchel when you carried it on board."

"That's because I did a splendid job concealing it under the coat I hung across my arm."

"I suppose. But you can't carry it around everywhere you go on the ship." Curtis crossed the room to the sideboard where a selection of American brandies, a crystal decanter of Scotch, and a quart-sized bottle of sweet port invited an after-dinner drink. "I don't believe Mr. Morgan expected you to stay here in the stateroom, like a bird sitting on her eggs to guard them from hawks."

"Precisely. I believe we should take the files to the Chief Purser for safekeeping."

"But if we take the valise to the Pursers' Office, as you propose, and a German spy has somehow managed to infiltrate the crew, he would likely know the combination to the ship's safe." Curtis wiggled loose the top of the Scotch decanter and poured the caramel-colored liquor into an aperitif glass. "A Cunard spy could read the loan documents at his leisure, whenever he's alone." Curtis replaced the fancy stopper, turning back to Van Camp.

"A Cunard crewman spying for Germany? Impossible!" Van Camp protested. "He would have to be in cahoots with one of the wireless operators to send the information to Berlin. How many Cunarders would get themselves involved in such a scheme?"

"Unlikely scenario, I agree. The British government has a heavy hand in what happens on this and every other British-owned ship. My guess is the last thing they would want is for the Germans to worm their way into the staff on board." Curtis took a tiny sip of Scotch, letting its warmth travel down his throat and into his stomach. "From what our London office said, it's very doubtful the crew has been infiltrated."

"And yet…." Van Camp glanced up. "Earlier today, I overheard a French woman saying that someone on board recognized some German men traveling in third-class."

"German passengers?" Curtis sat in a chair adjacent to Van Camp. "How is that even possible? All of the passengers were to be carefully screened for proof of American birth and citizenship. Passport photographs and all sorts of identification were required, as you well know." Curtis gulped down another mouthful. "Was this woman – the one who said there were Germans on the *Lusitania* – reputable?"

"I'm not certain, but we need to look into the matter tomorrow," Van Camp said in a somber voice. "And if there's even the slightest possibility there are German spies on the *Lusitania*, we could be in big trouble."

Curtis nodded slowly, as he thought about the situation. If the Germans somehow knew about the loan documents, then that could very well mean there was a leak in either Morgan's London or New York offices. It would have to be someone who knew the documents were on board the *Lusitania*. But who? He drew in a deep, thoughtful breath. "Let's not jump to conclusions. We need to find out if the rumor is true. In the meantime, let's keep the documents in here. We'll find a place where no one would think to look for them." Exactly where that was, Curtis wasn't sure, but he would figure something out tomorrow.

Chapter 21

Day 2 - Sunday

BY SEVEN-THIRTY, Josette was dressed and ready to go. Most of the first-class passengers, including Yvette, were most likely still asleep. She preferred to rise early, a habit acquired from years of commuting to classes at Barnard College. She favored living at home over the noisy, cramped dormitories on campus. Dressing as quietly as possible so she wouldn't wake her sister, she tiptoed out the stateroom door, down the carpeted hallway, and then to the outside deck.

A blanket of fog hung low, partially obscuring the top of the smokestacks and leaving large beads of moisture on the teak deck and shellacked handrails. The morning air was cold and damp and invigorating. Buttoning her coat's top buttons, Josette paused and gazed out at the never-ending expanse of ocean. There was something peaceful about the dark sea – the playful dolphins racing along the ship's wake. She could hear the hiss of the salty water, seven levels down, breaking against the hull as the ship sliced through the waves.

The *Lusitania* rose and fell rhythmically like a teeter-totter in Central Park, scattering a fan of spray a good ten feet into the air. The salty mist lifted on the breeze and was carried up to the Boat Deck. To Josette's face. Wiping the moisture from her cheeks, she steadied herself with the side railing and made her way aft to the Verandah Café, where she would be sheltered from the chilly draft. Settling into a wicker chair inside the open-sided cafe, she ordered tea and toast from the waiter.

She placed her book on the glass-topped table, opened it to the page marked by a piece of black ribbon that sufficed as a place marker, and searched for the paragraph she had last read.

"Well, well. If it isn't Miss Rogers," a man's voice interrupted.

Josette looked up. Mr. Carlson stood at the opposite side of the table. "Oh. Good morning. I see you're up and about quite early." He was dressed casually in a high-necked molasses-colored sweater, dark brown loose-fitting pants, and a brown tweed cap.

He squinted at her, cocking his head to one side. "Hmm. Let me see. Which one are you? Miss Josette or Miss Yvette?"

Closing her book, she looked up at him, crossing her arms, leaning back in her chair. "Guess," she said, smiling coyly.

"Very well, then." He leaned forward, as if to analyze her features, her hair, more closely. "Well…" He tapped his cheek with a finger. "What book is that you're reading?"

She quickly covered the title with her hand. "What do you think I'm reading?"

"Let me think. Ah, yes," he said, glancing up momentarily, as if deep in thought. "Poetry, I'll bet. 'My love is like a red, red rose.' Right?" His gaze moved back to her face. "You're reading Elizabeth

Barrett Browning, right? And you love poetry. The more romantic, the better."

"Oh, good heavens," she grumbled. "You're not even close to knowing my taste in books." Annoyed, she fought a frown. "Besides, I'm allergic to roses...and, for your information, I'm reading *David Copperfield*. And it's my sister who is the hopeless romantic."

"Ah-ha! I tricked you, don't you see? So, you are indeed *my* Miss Rogers. Josette. The serious one. Am I correct?"

She let out an incensed laugh. "*Your* Miss Rogers!? Heavens!"

"Good morning, Miss Josette. And are you truly allergic to roses?"

"Yes. I'm allergic to the very flowers most women love. I know that's unheard of, but they make me sneeze. I tried and tried to help my mother tend to her rose garden. But my eyes itched and my nose tingled and, well, the doctor advised me to stay as far away from those thorny beasts as possible. Poor mother could no longer bring them into the house. She was most perturbed." Josette realized she was talking too much. Her reaction to roses was none of his business.

"Allergic to roses. Hmm. Then I'll bring you another flower when I come to call on you. Carnations, perhaps? Or, something more down to earth. Daisies. Yes, daisies. White with yellow centers." He tipped his head to the side, as if examining her. Again. "Daisies do seem to suit you. They're strong, very resilient and at the same time, they're quite pretty."

Chuckling, Josette shook her head. "You're going to call on me with daisies in hand? Well now. That would certainly be a trick, Mr. Carlson, what with you residing in Manhattan, and me in England."

He shrugged and looked at her with a rueful grin. "You could say I'm full of surprises, Miss Rogers."

"Not only that, you are certainly presumptuous, Mr. Carlson. And far too flirtatious."

"That I am, Miss Rogers. Mind if I join you?" he said, pulling out a chair on the opposite side of the very small round-topped table.

She laughed again. "It would seem I have no say in the matter."

"Of course, if you object." He made motions as if to push his chair back into place.

"No. It's fine. Sit down. Please." Josette gave him a quick smile. "Of course, I'm not sure why you want to have morning tea with me, Mr. Carlson. It's obvious we don't agree on many things. As a matter of fact, we've done nothing but disagree on everything from the moment we met. Even before we met," she corrected.

"That's not true," he said with a boyish grin. "Look. You're reading one of my favorite books. And we both rise early. That's two things we agree on, and we've only just started."

The waiter arrived with her tea and toast, interrupting the awkward moment.

"Thank you," she said.

The waiter nodded. "And you, sir?"

"I'll have coffee. With a little cream, please."

Reaching for the pot, Josette poured the tea into the cup, adding a lump of sugar with the silver tongs. As she stirred, she stared into the cup as if she were watching the crystals dissolve. Unsure as to what she should say, nervous about what Curtis Carlson would say next, she lifted the cup to her lips. The temperature was still too hot, slightly burning her top lip. "Ouch!"

"And an impatient young woman, I see. Anxious to get on with things. There's yet another thing we have in common." He leaned back, cupping his hands behind his head and smiled.

With an annoyed shrug, she set the cup back on the saucer and then folded her hands in her lap searching for something to say. "Do you truly read Dickens?"

"Indeed. He's one of my favorite authors…and please do call me Curtis."

Josette inhaled a deep breath. "I don't know, Mr. Carlson. It may be too soon to be on a first-name basis."

"Really? After all we've been through together?" He dropped his hands and shrugged. "I humbly disagree. And we'll be seeing a lot of each other on this journey – as your mother pointed out so nicely. So, I believe we might as well be friends, right?"

"Oh yes. About my mother." Josette didn't make eye contact. "Please pay her no heed. She has always been overly protective when it comes to my sister and me being courted by a young man."

"And now we're courting." Curtis let out a chuckle. "Then we must be on a first-name basis now?"

She let out a defeated sigh. "Very well. You may call me by my given name."

"Very good, Josette. And please call me Curtis."

"I shall…Curtis." Unsure what else to say, she smiled, picked up the tea cup and blew on the steaming liquid. "Tell me what you like about *David Copperfield*."

"Let me think. It's been years since I read it." He sat back in his chair, seemingly pondering the question. Again, he slid his hands together in back of his head, his brows furrowed.

Josette doubted the man had actually read more than the title on the book's spine. Perhaps on a library shelf. But not the text itself. Until he said, "Generally speaking I admire Mr. Dickens. I believe David Copperfield is more a story about the author's own life rather than a fictional novel. Both Dickens and Copperfield, his book's hero, were self-made men. They were hard-working and intelligent. Like my father. And yours, I believe."

Surprised, Josette placed the cup back on the saucer. "Oh, I see. Is your father a businessman?"

"Yes and no. When my grandparents came to America, my father was a boy. He went to work in a mercantile store in Queens when he was fourteen. By the time he was thirty, he bought out the man who owned it and introduced more things to sell, like tools and nails and the like. The store did quite well. We were never rich, mind you…not like your family, but we lived comfortably."

"I can see how you identify with Mr. Dickens and his Copperfield story. I, too, admire both the man and the fictional character for the same reasons." She paused. "And was your father happy with your decision to become a professor of economics? Or did he expect you to work in his store?"

"Very astute, Josette. I worked in the store from the time I could count out nails and screws. My sister dusted the merchandise, while my mother helped with the bookkeeping. It was a real family operation."

"And now? Does your family still have the store?"

"Yes. In fact, there are two of them. The original hardware store in Queens and a second one on Long Island, though dad's health has been poor for the past year. I used to help Mom and Dad when I was young. Frankly, that's how I became interested in business. And economic issues. Hands-on education, I guess."

So, the man she imagined was a cold-hearted war supporter and a hopeless flirt was human, after all. "Sounds like you're close to your family."

"I am. Much like you and your sister."

That was far from the truth. Her father was hardly a self-made man, and mother was as cold as frost. In some ways, she envied Curtis Carlson. He was handsome, educated, and interesting. And yet, there was his pro-war stance.

She rose, glancing at the pendulum clock ticking loudly on the stationary wall to her left. "Speaking of family, I really must go. Mother and Yvette will be attending church services in the Music Room, and Father asked me to join him for breakfast."

Mr. Carlson stood. "It's been very nice talking with you, Josette. I wish you could stay longer. I would have liked to continue our discussion."

"I'm certain I shall see you later. Like Mother said, there aren't too many places to go around here." She gave him a teasing wink... to which, he laughed. Ah, yes. The college professor had a sense of humor, in spite of her mother's acerbic tongue.

"And where will you be later?"

"It depends on how my sister is feeling." Josette wasn't about to tell him about her plan to find her way into the third-class section to find the Germans. That was first and foremost in her mind. She hadn't imagined seeing them yesterday, and by gosh and by golly, she would keep looking until she located them.

BY TWO o'clock, the sun blazed in a clear sky, warming the air and drying the morning dampness. Most of the Promenade Deck was sheltered by the walkway on the Boat Deck one level up. In the shaded areas, Curtis noted dozens of passengers in two parallel rows of wooden lounge chairs enjoying the good weather. Some read. Others appeared to be napping.

How nice to have so much leisure time. For him, there would be little time for relaxing on this voyage. He was a man of action and accomplishment. Driven, he was determined to get a few more chapters of his book written. At noon, he had grabbed a ham and cheese sandwich and coffee in the Verandah Café. That gave him more time to tend to his writing…and to escape the formalities and wasted time he would have spent in the fancy dining room.

Even though he didn't mind acting the role of a refined gentleman, he was certainly more comfortable in his casual clothes enjoying the outdoors than fraternizing with the rich. Besides, this evening he would wear his stiff-collared tuxedo and keep up appearances at dinner. Van Camp had pulled a few golden strings, securing two seats at the highly coveted captain's table, where he would meet Mr. Vanderbilt and several other dignitaries. Always good to socialize with the world's most powerful men, he rationalized. In truth, he dreaded having to make polite conversation; yet, it was part and parcel to the life he had chosen as a New York investment banker. If he were to realize his goal of making a million dollars by the age of forty, he would need to make as many connections with these men as possible.

Of course, there was the matter of Miss Josette Rogers. She was a distraction, to be sure. He was too damned attracted to the feisty young beauty, constantly reminding himself not to be too sidetracked by her. Yet, sitting beside her in a deck chair while they both read. What harm could there be in that?

Curtis strolled along on the starboard side, searching for Josette among the lounging passengers. Many people simply slept, heads leaning back on small pillows provided by the stewards, blankets covering their legs and torsos. Others read, their books open, pages flapping in the breeze that constantly plagued the fast-moving ship.

He spotted one of the Rogers twins sitting in a shady area against the bulkhead. Was it Josette or Yvette?

"Hello, Miss Rogers," he greeted as he approached. "And how are you feeling this fine afternoon?"

She looked up from her book with a faint smile. "You do know I'm Yvette, do you not?"

"Yes. I know," he said with a grin, glancing down at her book. *Pride and Prejudice*. By Jane Austen. Probably not something that the seemingly pragmatic Josette would read.

"I'm feeling better, thank you."

"I'm very glad to hear that." He looked around then returned his gaze to Yvette. "And may I ask where your sister is?"

Yvette's lips slid into a coquettish smile. "She said she was going to the Purser's Office and then to the Library to write or something. That was a while ago."

A sudden gust of wind rustled the book's pages and lifted the front of Curtis' soft felt cap. He grabbed it to keep it from flying off and pulled it snug again. "The Library? Guess I'd better do the same. I thought I might work out here in the fresh air, but I fear my papers might blow overboard." He lifted the small satchel he carried in his right hand to show her.

Yvette smiled. "Oh, my goodness. I see you brought work with you. So, did my sister."

"I'm in the middle of writing a book." He didn't mean it to sound apologetic.

"Oh, yes. Josette mentioned that."

"I thought I could get some serious work done while I'm on board. Not many distractions when you're at sea." Of course, the fact that he had given a great deal of thought to Josette was certainly a diversion. Still....

Yvette grinned. "I must say, Mr. Carlson, you and my sister seem to be cut from the same cloth. She's determined to spend time writing a lengthy paper for one of her professors. I told her she should rest for a few days, but, well, that's my sister."

"I fear we're cut from opposite ends of the same cloth, Miss Rogers," he said with a chuckle. "But we are both extremely determined and stubborn. I'll give you that."

"Perhaps you two can meet in the middle. Or somewhere near."

It was a nice thought. "We shall see." He turned to leave, bidding her a good afternoon, when she called to him.

"Oh, by the way, Mr. Carlson. If you find my sister, would you please ask her to wait to do that thing she wants to do, until I can join her? In an hour or two, perhaps. She'll understand."

Chapter 22

AFTER BREAKFAST, Curtis had explored the second-class section of the ship. He hadn't noticed anyone who acted suspicious, though he didn't know how or when or if he would find someone acting German, whatever that meant. But he was determined to find out if there was any validity to the rumor that several Germans were on board. On the other hand, if they had come this far without being caught...hell, if they had managed to pass through the government's gauntlet of tests and paperwork to get on board in the first place, then locating them would be like finding a needle in a haystack.

While passengers from the second and third-class cabins weren't allowed into the first-class sections, Curtis had no problem convincing the young stewards guarding the stairwells to let him pass. Slipping them a few coins helped, too.

The second-class areas were actually much nicer than he had expected. Swanky, in fact, by most people's standards. In reality, he would have been perfectly happy traveling in the median-class section. Later today, he would look around the third-class public rooms. For now, he would see if he could get some writing done and pay a visit to Josette in the Library.

Entering the room, he immediately spotted her at one of the numerous writing desks. Crouched over and deep in thought, she had a large piece of paper spread out before her. She adjusted the table lamp, squinting as if to get a closer look. "Good afternoon," he said, causing her to jump.

"Mr. Carlson! Oh, my goodness. You startled me."

"I beg your pardon. I can see I've broken your concentration." He stepped forward to see what she was examining. "Hmm." Puzzled, he moved his gaze to her. "Those look like plans of the ship. Why?"

Josette folded the pages closed without making eye contact. "I was just curious. That's all."

He narrowed his eyes at her, noting she wore the same guilty expression that she had when she lied to her father about how they had met. "You're curious about the third-class cabin layout, are you?"

She shrugged.

He threw her a smile. "I suppose you think there might be slaves down there rowing the ship, right?"

Josette rolled her eyes. "I'm interested in the socially acceptable mores placed upon the classes. I thought I might include that in a paper I'm writing for one of my college courses."

"Ah, yes. Your sister mentioned you're working on a project for your school. And yet, you're moving to England?"

"My professor has generously allowed me to mail her a sociology exposition in lieu of taking my final examination in a few weeks," she explained matter-of-factly. "That way, I will receive full credit for the course, in spite of not completing the class."

"I see. Well, if it's of any consequence, I plan to snoop around down in third-class myself for a project I'm working on. Want to tag along?"

Josette pondered his invitation briefly. "Tag along, you say?" she said with a scoffing sound. "I'll have you know I'm perfectly capable of going alone. Besides, I'm the one who has studied the ship's interior plans, am I not?"

Curtis fought back a laugh. Oh, yes indeed. Feisty was the exact word he would use to describe Josette Rogers. And that was one of the things he liked about her. "How about if I tag along with you, then?"

"Very well. I think that would be fine."

"Oh, and by the way, your sister asked me to tell you to wait for a couple more hours before you do…what it is you wanted her to do with you. Whatever that means!"

JOSETTE WAS TRULY happy Mr. Carlson wanted to explore the third-class accommodations with her. Yvette had been terribly nervous about going. Besides, she rationalized, her timid sister wouldn't have added any security if they happened across the German men. At least Curtis Carlson was tall and broad-shouldered. He could protect her, should things get physical…not that it was likely to happen.

After an hour of working on their respective projects in the library, Josette and Curtis returned their pages and writing supplies to their staterooms on the Boat Deck. Then Josette followed Curtis across the main deck to a well-lighted staircase in the bow section leading down to depths of the ship. He paid the teenaged Cunard employee, the so-called guard at the top of the stairs, several coins. This was a much easier way to get down into the third-class area, rather than the crew's staircase where Josette had ventured yesterday.

There was far more activity in the common rooms today. Josette guessed that many of the passengers had adjusted to the ship's movement by now. Or perhaps they had simply opted to get out of the tiny cabins shown in the diagrams and into more open spaces.

"Good grief!" Curtis commented. "It's like a labyrinth down here. I keep expecting to bump into the Minotaur every time we round a corner."

Josette laughed. "My sister doesn't like small spaces. I do believe she would have gone mad if she had to travel through these narrow, dimly lit hallways."

"Ah, yes. I suppose that's why she has a fear of elevators."

"Exactly. Any enclosed space," Josette answered. "But most especially, elevators. She's always been like that. I've never understood why."

"It could make anyone a bit claustrophobic down here, especially if one happens to be over six-feet tall," he said, ducking his head as they stepped into the dining hall.

Curtis walked behind Josette as they wandered among the tables. They smiled and greeted the passengers. In return, they received questioning looks and a few muttered comments. Josette realized that her expensive lace-trimmed dress, as well as Curtis' tailored suit were a dead giveaway as to their social standing. They were both about as welcome in this part of the *Lusitania* as a worm in an apple.

Sitting at a small table in the far corner, a mother held a sleeping baby to her chest, humming an unfamiliar, but lovely tune. On the bare wooden floor in front of the woman, a curly-haired blonde child played with a homemade ragdoll. Nearby, two older men were playing chess.

Strangely, there were no young men in the stuffy room.

Josette motioned for Curtis to follow her into the hallway. "Where do you suppose everyone else is?"

"Outside smoking or playing games on the deck where they can get some fresh air, I'd say. Or in their rooms, maybe?" He shrugged. "Let's check out the next deck."

She nodded, moving in the direction of the bow. Then they descended the stairs another level. Surely, this was the lowest passenger deck. It had to be, because the engine noise and vibration was much louder. And the rooms… Compared to the first-class accommodations, the third-class cabins were extremely small, judging by how close together the cabin doors were. And yet, entire families slept in those tiny spaces.

Josette felt a twinge of guilt. Her life had been extremely privileged compared to so many people. Seeing these dramatic differences in the way people traveled – especially on this luxury liner – truly affirmed her commitment to helping the disadvantaged and poor through social work.

Josette's thoughts were interrupted when she heard men's voices coming from around the corner at the end of the hallway. She paused.

"What is it?" Curtis asked quietly.

"Shhh." Listening again, she tiptoed forward. Curtis was directly behind her.

Stopping, she let out a gasp.

His eyes were wide with surprise. Curtis opened his mouth to speak, but she touched her index finger to her lips, straining to hear more.

"They're speaking German," she whispered.

Curtis drew back with a shocked expression. "You speak German?"

Josette nodded and lifted her hand to indicate 'a little' with a space between her thumb and forefinger.

"I'll explain later," she said quietly, swiveling around.

"*Ich bin hungrig.*" The voice sounded…youthful.

"I think he said he's hungry," she said softly.

"Mmm. *Wurst,* the German said.

"Speak English, Heinrich," one of them scolded.

"Idiot! They don't have *Wurst* on a British ship!" another man's deep voice growled.

"*Ach*! I am not the idiot, Frederick. You are!" The younger-sounding man snickered. "You should use my American name until we get to Berlin. Isn't that right, Joseph?"

"Yes, of course. And unless you want to wind up in prison, speak no more German!"

Looking squarely at Curtis, trying to make herself breathe, Josette finally managed to choke out, "It's them, Curtis! I'm sure of it. It's them." Josette felt her knees weaken.

"Them? Who are they?" Curtis muttered in a barely audible tone.

"Spies!"

Curtis' jaw dropped open, a look of surprise widening his eyes.

"Do you think they're still serving lunch, Joseph? I could use a bite, too." It sounded like the third man's voice again.

"Of course. They serve until two." Presumably, Joseph answered. "Let's go, gents. Make sure the cabin door is locked."

"Maybe they'll have some *stollen* for dessert," the younger one teased, laughing.

When she heard what sounded like the click of a lock, Josette panicked. "We need to go. They mustn't see me!"

She turned, sprinted in the opposite direction when the ship suddenly heaved. Tripping on her long skirt, she reached for the wall railing. Curtis had tried to stop her fall, but she landed on her knees, letting out a little cry.

"Wait, Joseph! I heard something."

Josette and Curtis froze in place, exchanging troubled glances.

Rapid footsteps moved in their direction.

Curtis helped Josette to her feet, then pushed her against the adjacent cabin door. The knob dug hard into her back.

"What are you doing?" she said as faintly as she could manage, grimacing from the pain.

"Just kiss me!" he ordered in a whisper, sliding his hands around her shoulders. "Now!"

She understood. He was trying to create a diversion. To make them look like lovers, rather than eavesdroppers.

She rose on her toes, slipped her arms around him, lifting her chin. He bent down, pulled her against him and touched his lips to hers.

The Germans were suddenly there. They stopped beside her and Curtis. She could feel their eyes upon them.

One of them giggled like a twelve-year-old, then said, "Good for you, pal!"

Curtis and Josette didn't break their kiss. In fact, Curtis made their embrace even more passionate, pressing his mouth harder on her lips and letting out a groan for good measure. She fought a smile.

"You two should find an empty cabin," the juvenile-sounding young man chortled.

Apparently, the three Germans had bought the ruse.

"Leave them alone, Peter. Let's eat," the man with the deepest voice said insistently.

Josette listened carefully. They walked again, moving away and towards the stairwell. The men laughed, muttering slurs about girls who let gents have their way with them in public places. And then, they were up the steps.

Yet, Curtis didn't pull back. Instead, his lips lingered on her mouth. She didn't break their embrace either. In fact, it was rather pleasant, now that the danger had passed.

Slowly, he lifted his head a few inches away. Breathing hard, he held her gaze for a long moment. "My apologies, Josie. I…I couldn't think of anything else to do."

"It's quite all right," she reassured. "After all, who knows what they might have done if they realized we overheard their conversation."

"Why would they have wanted to harm you?"

"I'll tell you everything when we're in a safe place."

BACK IN the first-class section, they found a quiet corner in the Lounge and settled into comfortable chairs. Josette told Curtis the whole story. About the bakery, the passport office, and seeing the same men walking up the gangway to board the *Lusitania*.

"The question is, what should we do now?"

Hunched over, Curtis sat perched on the edge of his seat, legs apart. He reached out and took Josette's hand. "We have to tell the captain. He'll know what to do."

Josette nodded. "And my father. I must tell him. He will believe me now, since you – a man – were there to hear them speaking German." As much as it hurt her to say that, she knew it was true. Neither her Father nor Mr. Vanderbilt had taken her seriously when she saw the Germans boarding. How would she handle it when they apologized? Would she gloat? Would she be able to act humble? Following Curtis Carlson to the door, she felt a sense of satisfaction. Either way, she would triumph.

CAPTAIN TURNER and several crewmen, including one of the two detectives employed by Cunard to travel incognito on the ship, brought Josette, Curtis, and Father to a private office just off the ship's Bridge.

"Please, Captain Turner. I...I...." Wringing her hands, she fought to get the words out.

The last thing Josette wanted to do was to return to the third-class section to identify the Germans.

Captain Turner paused. He must have sensed she was shaken by the incident, for his features softened. "Don't worry yourself, Miss Rogers. You need not go downstairs to identify the Germans. It shouldn't be too difficult for us to find them, thanks to you and Mr. Carlson." The captain gave them a pleased smile.

Josette exhaled a sigh of relief. "Thank you, sir."

The captain moved to face Curtis, his wiry gray brows lifting. "You can point them out to the ship's officers, can you not?"

"I'm afraid I didn't see their faces. My back was to them as they passed," Curtis said.

Turner let out a disheartened sigh. "Yes, yes. I know that's what you said, but did you not see anything?"

"I only heard them speak, sir."

"Look, Captain Turner," Detective Pederson said. "We now know the section they were talking in, which side of the ship, which deck and so on. So, that's where they have a cabin. And we have Miss Rogers' physical description of at least one of the men. Staff Captain Anderson is working with the Purser and Detective Pullman at this very moment, going through the passenger lists to find cabins in that area assigned to three young male passengers. It's just a matter of time until we can track them down."

Turner shifted his gaze to Josette's father. "Of course, when we find them, your daughter will have to see these men one more time for a final identification before we arrest them."

"We'll bring them up to the crew's dining hall before locking them away for the duration of the voyage, until we reach Liverpool," said the detective, a handsome, rosy-cheeked gentleman. He traveled on the ship anonymously in the guise of a well-to-do passenger. To look at him and his fine clothes, one would have guessed he was a tycoon of some distinction. "They'll be turned over to British authorities for further action."

The captain turned to Curtis. "And you're positively certain you didn't actually see their faces, even though they walked directly past you? Is that correct, Mr. Carlson?"

A smile tugged at the corners of his mouth as he shot a quick glance at Josette. Her breath caught in her throat. She hoped and prayed Curtis wouldn't mention the kiss.

Curtis turned his attention back to the captain "That's right, sir."

"Very well." Captain Turner motioned to several crewmen indicating they should begin the search. "For now, Mr. Rogers, until we have the spies in custody, I would recommend that your daughter not be left alone. You should all retire to your quarters. We shall send for you when we have the men in custody."

"Right, then. Come, Josette," Father instructed.

"Oh yes, and do bring your other daughter with you when you return, Mr. Rogers. I understand she can help with the identification process," Turner added.

"Jolly, good." Father slid his arm around Josette's shoulders. He seemed to understand how difficult the situation was for her.

"There's one more thing, and this applies to all of you," Captain Turner said, moving his gaze between Josette, Father and Curtis. "No one else is to know about this. No one! There's already enough fear and trepidation on this ship. Having spies on this ship would only raise the passengers' concerns. I won't have a riot on my hands. Is that clear?"

Chapter 23

WELL OVER an hour had passed since Josette and her father returned to the stateroom. Mother was still napping in the master suite bedroom adjacent to the parlor. Father wanted it that way. He insisted she be only partially advised of what had occurred. "Best to keep her out of this situation, or she'll likely have an attack of the vapors."

"Good heavens, Father! I'm the one with a reason to be apprehensive."

Father let out a defeated sigh. "You girls know your mother cannot handle upsetting occurrences well."

Mother's feigned fainting spells were merely a tool she used to get her way. Even Yvette had figured out their mother's manipulative games. Josette let it go. Disagreeing with their father never served any purpose.

Thankfully, a steward had delivered a tray of tea and sweets. Careful not to clink the spoons against the sides of the cups when stirring in the sugar cubes and milk, Josette and Yvette carried their tea and a few molasses cookies into their adjoining bedroom.

"I feel terrible about all of this," Josette said, setting her cup and saucer on the small table at one end of the room. "I hope I'm doing the right thing."

"Why would you say that, Josette? Who knows what those Germans intended to do."

"But what if all they wanted was to go to Germany? Maybe to their relatives?"

"You mustn't worry about that, sister. That's up to the authorities to figure out."

Father poked his head through the doorway. "Time to go. Detective Adams has come to fetch us."

THEY FOLLOWED the detective to the Officers' Mess Hall, an unpretentious eating room on the starboard side of C Deck. Curtis was already there. The three Germans were led inside, wrists tied with heavy twine. The one with the cornflower-colored eyes locked his stare on Josette with such a hardness, it was all she could do to keep from running away.

"So, it was you," he said in perfect English. "I thought I saw you when we sailed."

Josette drew back, a prickling feeling crawling up her neck and on her arms.

"Be quiet, Hun!" the detective ordered in a startling tone that snapped Josette to attention.

Turning to Josette, Detective Adams' eyes glowered. "He goes by the name Joseph Redmond, Miss Rogers. Do you know his German name?"

"Of course not. How would I?" Josette wondered why it was she who was being treated like a criminal.

"You said you heard them speaking German, did you not?" Adams said.

"What? No. Only a little. Our butler back home is German."

The second detective walked toward Josette. He seemed to be assessing her. "Then you did understand some of what they were saying, did you not?"

Curtis intervened. "Miss Rogers only recognized a few German words. Why?"

Mr. Adams, the harsher of the two detectives, paced, his hands locked behind his back. "So, you young ladies are sure these are the same men you saw in the German bakery in New York. Correct?"

"Yes. They were there," Yvette said softly.

Fists clenched, Josette spoke up. "As I explained earlier, two of these men were also at the Passport Office in New York City." She pointed to the one identified as Joseph, and the young man with a receding hairline. "They were obviously attempting to get passports. And I believe they were responsible for throwing a brick through the Passport Office window."

Joseph shot a troubling, angry glare at Josette. "You have no proof."

Mr. Adams ignored Joseph's comment. "So, you saw these men twice before meeting them again on the *Lusitania*. What are the odds of that, young ladies?"

Josette snapped back. "What are you saying, sir?"

"Did you plan to meet them on the ship?" Detective Lewis' gaze moved to Joseph and back to Josette. "Some sort of tryst?"

Father, who had been uncharacteristically quiet, interjected. "Enough of this! My daughters are trying to help. How dare you make these accusations."

"Mr. Rogers is right." Curtis had an impatient expression on his face. "You're grilling the wrong person. These men chased us. Miss Rogers and I *both* heard them speaking German, as well as the mention of the name 'Heinrich.' So, I'm guessing one of them is named Heinrich! And both Yvette and Josette have identified two of the three as German speakers they saw at a German bakery. Now, then, are these men under arrest, or are they not?"

First Officer Anderson, a tall, nice-looking lad spoke up. "Our difficulty is that it's impossible for someone to fake all of those passport documents."

"Hardly," the detective said, redirecting his gaze to the Germans. "There's an entire network of German agents in New York City, Washington, D.C., and various cities around America. They've created forged documents and falsified identification papers brilliantly."

Josette noticed a look of pride slipping onto Joseph's face. She frowned at him, bravely returning his glare.

"Dozens of Germans have been caught on Allied ships in recent months," the detective explained. "They smuggle incendiary devices on board to sink the vessels. These Huns, here, are likely part of the international espionage ring that has connections in New York. Possibly all the way to the German Embassy in Washington."

"Ridiculous! We are Americans. And stop calling us Huns!" the youngest German, no more than seventeen or eighteen, cried out.

"Quiet, you!" Adams hollered, "Or I will be forced to gag your mouth." The German immediately stopped talking, his shoulders slumped in defeat.

"Do you believe these men brought explosives on board the *Lusitania*?" Captain Turner said to the detective with raised brows and a noticeable look of concern.

"Quite possible," Detective Adams responded.

"If you smuggled any explosives on the *Lusitania*, we will find them," the captain said in a controlled tone. "Thanks to this brave young woman, your plan has been thwarted."

Josette swallowed and forced a small smile. None of this felt as good as she had anticipated. "And thanks to Mr. Carlson, too."

Captain Turner almost smiled. "Of course, Mr. Carlson. Thanks to both of you, these spies will be punished appropriately."

"We are not spies!" the German, presumably Heinrich, shouted with desperation.

"Is that so?" the detective said with a smirk.

Joseph looked directly at Josette...again. "Just because we were eating *strudel* in a German bakery and marching in a protest parade does not make us spies. I was born in Brooklyn and went to university at Columbia." He nearly spat his words.

Josette stepped closer to the three young men. "If you truly are not spies, and if you are American citizens, the British authorities will clear you and send you back to New York."

"We can't go back to America," Joseph yelled, twisting his head in Josette's direction.

First Officer Anderson and Detective Adams led the three Germans toward the door. Joseph struggled against the detective's prodding. "I studied to be an electrical engineer and graduated with honors. It didn't matter. After I graduated, I couldn't find work. None of us could because of our German heritage. There's no longer a place for us in America."

I'm sorry, she thought, but didn't say the words out loud. She was beginning to believe they weren't guilty of anything besides leaving America. It was too late to undo what had already been done. It was now up to the experts...and, perhaps, to God, to determine their fate.

"Those men are to be guarded twenty-four hours a day," the captain ordered. "Take them chamber pots. Meals are to be delivered with an armed officer. They're not to leave their room for any reason. Do you understand?"

Mr. Anderson nodded. "Aye, captain."

The sound of shoes thudded on the outer deck as the Germans were led away. Inside the crews' dining hall, everyone was silent. Once the footsteps had faded, Father spoke.

"Are you quite finished with my girls?"

"Yes, Mr. Rogers. You may all go." Captain Turner turned to Josette and Yvette and nodded. "And my apologies for any discomfort you have been caused."

Josette looked the captain directly in the eyes. "What if they aren't spies? I can't blame them for wanting to go to Germany, seeing how poorly they were being treated in America. I've read about Americans breaking windows in German-owned businesses...and worse. The way some people are treating innocent German citizens is appalling."

Detective Adams' features softened. "Even if they are not spies, we must find out how they managed to board the *Lusitania*. Someone in New York helped them obtain the forged documents. And, this is the most important thing – there must be a network in England that would have assisted them to board a vessel bound for Germany or France. The authorities will need to find out if and where they were to be picked up by a submarine or a fishing boat or some other type of vessel. It's crucial that we know, and you have provided the Allied countries with a highly valuable source of information."

"What you did, coming forward like that, was very important," Father added.

Josette nodded and forced a smile. She just didn't want to know how that information would be forced from the three young Germans.

The captain cast a firm glare at Josette, Yvette and even Curtis. "And, please. No mention of this incident to anyone. As far as we're all concerned, the matter is closed. No one else need to know about this. Am I clear?"

FATHER AND Curtis walked behind Yvette and Josette, continuing up the stairs to the Boat Deck. Not a single word had been uttered since leaving the crews' eating quarters. What could be said that hadn't already been said?

Yvette broke the silence. "If you don't mind, I'd like to rest before dinner."

"Not quite yet. Please, follow me. I have a few questions on my mind." Father headed towards a group of empty chairs lined up against the bulkhead wall.

Curtis shot a confused glance at both Josette and her sister. Josette shrugged in response, then turned and went after Father. Curtis and Yvette trailed behind.

"I'm certainly curious, Father," Josette said. "What is it you wish to talk about?"

"Actually, I'll address this to Mr. Carlson and you." He leaned forward, his eyes focused on Curtis. "What were you two doing romping around in the third-class section? My daughter was unchaperoned, Mr. Carlson, and she's under legal age. Care to explain?"

"I'm afraid I coaxed Josette into accompanying me into the third-class area, sir."

"My Josette doesn't do anything she doesn't want to do, son," Father said.

"You see, Father," Josette interjected, "We bumped into one another in the Library. We both have projects we're working on. Coincidentally, we were both interested in evaluating how the third-class passengers were treated. I intended to go alone, but Mr. Carlson volunteered."

Father squinted at Curtis and then at Josette, as if to evaluate whether or not they were telling him the truth. His features began to relax. "Right, then. I suppose it was a good thing Mr. Carlson was there to protect you from the culprits, Josette."

He turned to Curtis. "If she had happened upon them while she was alone…well, there's no telling what would have happened."

Father stood. "Just one more thing, Carlson. I'm still trying to understand why you didn't see the Germans as they passed by you and my daughter. You said your back was to them. And Josette said she didn't want them to see her face. So, what happened?"

Josette noted Curtis's eyes were wide, his brows lifted. Since she had met Curtis Carlson, he had never been at a loss for words. Until now. "He shielded me from them, Father."

"Shielded you? How so?"

Curtis glanced at her, as if to say, 'What now?'

"He…he pretended to kiss me, Father."

"It all happened so fast, sir," Curtis blurted. "I didn't know what else to do."

"That's right, Father. It was the only thing we could have done to keep from being discovered. They believed someone was spying on them. When they saw us in an embrace – I mean, a make-believe embrace – they went by and left us alone."

After an excruciatingly long silence, Father let out a sigh. "Well, done, Mr. Carlson." Unbuttoning his suit jacket, he added, "But if you and my daughter decide to go mucking around this ship again, there will be hell to pay. Am I clear on that?"

JOSETTE WAS exhausted. If her father hadn't insisted that she join him and Mother for dinner, she would have preferred a tray to be brought to the room. Try as she might, she couldn't put the day's incident out of her mind. The German lads were human beings, after all. And they were angry. Were they truly going to Germany, a place where they would be welcomed, not ridiculed because of their heritage? Were they planning to sign up as soldiers? Josette couldn't imagine why they would want to fight in a ghastly war where so many men on all sides had been killed. Like Julian Laurent.

She reminded herself the three Germans weren't completely innocent. They were on board illegally, for heaven's sake. And there was the brick incident at the Passport Office. On the other hand, when Father had gone back to the Bridge to speak with the captain an hour ago, he was told that no incendiary devices had been found in the threesome's possessions.

In her heart, Josette knew she had done the right thing. The authorities would have to sort things out. She simply couldn't let the incident continue to haunt her. There was nothing she could do now, except hope and pray that Joseph and his friends would be treated justly; that there would be no rush to judgment without evidence that these lads were indeed guilty of more than wanting to leave America.

After taking a short rest, Josette and Yvette dressed in the silky evening gowns Mother had bought for them – one lavender and one pink in similar styles. Both had a long row of annoying tiny buttons running up the back from the waist to the high neck. Worse, there was barely enough silky fabric to breathe. Yvette still wore corsets. Josette had given up on the ridiculous contraptions over a year ago. Women with eighteen-inch waists were so nineteenth century, for heaven's sake.

If there was any hope of squeezing into the expensive clothes that Mother had paid a seamstress to sew, Josette had to temporarily set her prejudices about corsets aside and have Yvette lace her up. Never mind she wouldn't be able to eat more than a mouse-sized meal while wearing the torturous device, something that should have been banned as a health risk for women long ago.

Tonight's dinner was quite formal. The gold-embossed menus reflected the regal atmosphere. Hors d'oeuvres included oysters on the half shell and the saltiest caviar Josette had ever tasted. Most surprising was that neither Curtis nor his uncle had arrived for dinner, leaving two empty places at their table.

Even Mr. Duns was missing. Mrs. Donaldson had decided to leave the Westie inside her suite. "He dinna feel like wearing his white tie tonight," she joked, sounding more Scottish than usual. "Perhaps he'll wear his wee Clan plaid jacket another time."

"If you think she's jesting," Father said with a laugh, "I saw the pup wearing his McDonald Clan's plaid jacket this morning. Young Thomas had him on a leash taking him up to the poop deck to do his business. I reckon you should have given the dog a kilt, Mrs. Donaldson. He was, after all, going regimental."

Mrs. Donaldson burst into laughter. "Aye, that he was."

Yvette and Josette chuckled. Father could have an amusing sense of humor. Mother, on the other hand, was mortified. Her mouth hung open, her penciled brows arched high.

She fanned herself with her hand. "Poop deck? Really, Henry?" Mother gave their father one of her classic evil-eyed glares.

"Oh, don't be such a stick in the mud, Millie. It's just a pup we're talking about here."

From the corner of her eye, Josette noticed Curtis entering the dining room. His uncle trailed a few steps behind. Curtis was every bit a modern gent, dressed in a fashionable tuxedo. On the other hand, his uncle, Mr. Van Camp, donned a top hat and a split-tailed jacket straight out of the Victorian era.

Yvette had also noticed Curtis' arrival. She leaned close. "I'm telling you, sister. He's the living, breathing embodiment of Mr. Darcy."

"Who?"

"Mr. Darcy!" Yvette pulled back, making a scoffing sound. "Oh, good heavens, Josette. He's only the most intriguing, romantic gentleman in all of Miss Austen's novels." She unfurled her freshly starched napkin. "Honestly. You really must read more fiction."

Mrs. Donaldson's dangling diamond earrings swayed when she shook her head. "Oh, my, lass. Even I know who Mr. Darcy is, though my taste in romantic literature has always leaned in the direction of William Shakespeare's *Romeo and Juliet*."

Moments later, Curtis stood beside Father. "Good evening, everyone. My apologies, but I'm afraid I won't be dining with you this evening." Curtis didn't smile. In fact, he didn't appear happy at all.

"Oh?" Josette was surprised. And disappointed, though she wasn't sure why.

"Yes. My uncle requested that we sit at the captain's table. As you know, he's been under the weather, but now he's decided to come down for dinner, so we won't be dining with you this evening. So sorry." He glanced at Josette with a boyish smile and a shrug.

Father didn't get up. Instead he simply said, "I understand, Carlson. Who wouldn't prefer dining with the likes of Alfred Vanderbilt?"

"You must do as your uncle wishes," Mother said in a typical Mother-like way.

Josette thought she knew Curtis well enough by now to believe he wasn't one to be ordered about like a child. There must be more to the story. "Yes, Mr. Carlson. You should do as your uncle wishes." She lifted her hand and covered her mouth, suppressing a giggle.

He eyed her, his smile fading. "If you'll excuse me." Curtis turned and maneuvered his way to the largest table, where another four distinguished-looking men, millionaires, Josette imagined, sat chatting.

Mrs. Donaldson took a sip of water and set the carved crystal goblet back on the table. "I wouldn't be so impressed with the likes of Mr. Alfred Vanderbilt." She addressed Father. "I'm not one to gossip, mind you, but he's quite the source of scandal."

"Truly?" Mother said. That certainly grabbed her attention.

"Oh, aye. He spends his fortune on frivolous things, like race horses, fancy automobiles, and wives – he's had more than one, you know. My husband liked the spoiled lad about as much as an empty bottle of Scotch."

Letting out a belly laugh, Father said, "I understand that the man's spending is so uncontrollable, he even had solid gold nameplates placed on each of his horses' stalls."

Mrs. Donaldson took a sip of wine. "My husband, God rest his soul, said Alfred Vanderbilt inherited his wealth from his father. If he'd had to work for it, he might be more frugal. He's certainly not like Mr. Andrew Carnegie and my dear husband. They worked hard to make their fortunes, and they were both great philanthropists."

Father didn't say a word. He picked up his glass of wine and cleared his throat. He, too, had been born into wealth, though not on the same level as the Vanderbilt family. Yet, Josette knew that he had worked hard to keep his business in America flourishing. She hoped her father would use some of his newfound wealth to help the needy – she would certainly encourage him to do so.

Chapter 24

AFTER THE dessert plates were cleared and coffee had been served, Curtis led Mr. Frohman over to the Rogers' table. They stopped directly behind Yvette.

Father smiled, looking over at the two men. "Jolly good, Mr. Carlson. I see you brought us a visitor."

"Yes, sir," Curtis said. "May I introduce Mr. Charles Frohman? He's come to meet your daughter, Yvette."

Yvette swiveled her chair around so fast, the layers of beads on her dress rattled. Beaming, she stood up. "I'm so pleased to meet you, Mr. Frohman."

"And you, my dear." Frohman dipped his chin regally.

Father rose, reaching out to shake Frohman's hand. "Pleased to make your acquaintance, Mr. Frohman. My wife and I took our girls to see your *Peter Pan* play years ago. Brilliant production, if I might say so."

"A Brit, I see," Frohman said. "Mostly Brits on this ship. Going home are you, Rogers?"

"That I am, sir," Father answered. Then he turned to Mother. "May I introduce my lovely wife."

"*Je suis enchanté*," Mother said, with dramatic flair. "I've heard a great deal about you, *Monsieur* Frohman." She stretched her gloved hand in his direction. "We simply adored your J. M. Barry production."

"It's a pleasure, Mrs. Rogers." He took her hand and feigned a kiss on the back of it. "Peter Pan will always be one of my favorite productions."

"And who is this?" Frohman asked, looking at Josette.

Charles Frohman wasn't what Josette would call a handsome man. He was a bit stocky, had thinning hair, and he wasn't very tall. The middle-aged producer walked with a decided limp, assisted by a shiny, black cane topped with a brass bird's head. And yet, there was something likeable and interesting about him.

"I'm Josette Rogers," she said with a grin. "I'm the eldest twin. But Yvette is the most talented."

"Is that so?" Mr. Frohman's gaze lingered on Josette's face, then moved to Yvette, as if assessing the two of them. "And what beautiful twins you are. Have you ladies ever thought about going into show business? I would certainly be happy to have you audition for a play I will be producing." His head leaned to one side. "Yes, yes. I can see it now. Identical twins. That would be a perfect plot for a story I have in mind."

"Heavens no!" Mother shook her finger at the producer. "My daughters could never be…actresses. They are cultured, young ladies. Educated in the social graces."

Frohman's eyes narrowed. "Some of my dearest friends are actresses, Mrs. Rogers. Rita Jolivet and Maude Adams are two of the finest human beings I've ever known, madam."

"Henry?" Mother said, peering at Father with a questioning glare, something she did when she wanted him to step into a conversation.

Josette answered before Father had a chance to respond. "Thank you kindly, Mr. Frohman. But no thank you."

"I don't think I would like acting, but I do have plans to continue with my musical training," Yvette added.

"Very well, ladies, but if you should ever change your mind…." The producer's gaze moved across the table. "Ah, my good lady," he said to Mrs. Donaldson. "I heard you were on this voyage. I was so sorry to hear about your husband's passing." Frohman dipped his chin in reverence. "You have both been loyal patrons of my theaters."

The Scottish woman smiled gently. "Mr. Donaldson and I were always fans of your productions."

"I shall be eternally grateful to your husband for introducing me to Mr. Carnegie. Another great and generous Scot, I might add," Mr. Frohman said.

Mrs. Donaldson nodded. "That he is."

"Well, ladies and gentlemen. I shall make my exit, with your permission. I bid you *adieu*." The producer turned to make his exit.

"Wait, Mr. Frohman. May I ask a favor?" Yvette said.

He twisted around. "Certainly, Miss Rogers."

Yvette straightened, making direct eye contact. And yet, both hands fumbled nervously with the silky skirt fabric. "You see, my friend, Jonathan Franklin, is a brilliant pianist. Much better than I shall ever be."

"That's not true, Yvette," Josette protested. "She's quite good, Mr. Frohman. You should hear her play."

Yvette's brows arched. She sent Josette a quick 'be quiet' glance. A moment later, she continued, seemingly gathering her courage, her confidence. "Jonathan has performed with numerous orchestras in New York. Even at Carnegie Hall. I know he wants to come to London and play on the theater circuit. I would be happy to give you the name of his agent."

Mr. Frohman took a few steps towards Yvette and smiled. "Say no more, my dear. I'll be quite occupied until my new production is launched this coming Saturday. However, I would be most happy to send a wire to my business manager in New York. If your Jonathan is as good as you say he is, Mr. Goldberg will invite him to come to London."

"Oh, thank you ever so much!" Yvette said with a little clap of her hands.

"My pleasure, dear girl."

The ship suddenly rolled from side to side. Frohman grabbed the back of a chair for stability. "Drat! I hate these ocean voyages. One never knows what kind of conditions one will encounter when on the 'Rolling *Lusy*.'"

"Oh, Mr. Frohman," Josette said. "Would you have time to come to the Music Room in the morning to hear my sister play?"

"Yes! Please. I would love to play for you, Mr. Frohman," Yvette said in an unexpected, very animated tone. "Do you like Ragtime?"

Josette was pleasantly surprised with her sister's response. Her sister was generally shy, especially when it came to performing in public.

"That would be marvelous, ladies," Frohman responded. "Now, if you'll excuse me, I must be off to my cabin. My knee is acting up again. Dampness doesn't help the situation, you see. I would very much like to take you up on your kind offer tomorrow at, say…10:30…if you promise no waltzes. If I have to hear one more Tchaikovsky or Strauss piece," he muttered, "I think I'll go batty!"

Mr. Frohman certainly had a point. As much as Josette loved classical music and, most especially, waltzes, the *Lusitania's* small orchestra seemed to play nothing else. They performed during each and every meal, broken up occasionally with a soloist singing opera.

"I find it disturbing that the British musicians are playing Austrian and German tunes when their soldiers are being killed by men from those same countries at the Front," Mrs. Donaldson said.

"Here, here! Yet another reason to play something else. Show tunes, perhaps," Mr. Frohman said with a chuckle. "A few Irving Berlin songs would do nicely." He steadied himself and bid them good evening.

"See you in the morning, Mr. Frohman," Yvette almost sang as he shuffled away.

"May I escort you to your stateroom, Mrs. Donaldson?" Curtis asked.

"Thank you, lad. That would be lovely."

Yvette turned to Curtis. "Thank you ever so much for the introduction."

"My pleasure," Curtis said with a wink.

BACK IN their room, Josette unfastened the long row of pearl buttons on the back of her sister's ankle-length gown. Already undressed clear down to her undergarments, including the dreadful corset the dress required her to wear, Josette sat at the vanity, unpinning her curls. She picked up the silver-backed brush and ran it through her hair. "Did you notice how quiet Father and Mother were when we left the dining room?"

"Of course, I did." Yvette carefully slid her dress to the floor, stepping over the pooled fabric. "Do you think it was because they realized that Jonathan will be coming to London?"

"I wouldn't be surprised," Josette said.

Yvette walked to the closet and grabbed a velvet hanger, inserting it into the top of the dress. "Mr. Frohman seems like the kind of man who isn't affected by things like social status. After all, he has produced plays with grand love stories about star-crossed lovers." She positioned the hanger on the wooden bar between two day-dresses and spun around. "Do you think he could speak with Father?"

"What could he possibly say to change Father's mind?" Josette spoke to her sister while looking in the mirror. "I honestly don't think it would be right to discuss such personal matters with Mr. Frohman, sister."

"Mr. Frohman is an artist. He lives in a world where people believe in true love. Artists believe that keeping lovers apart is wrong. If anyone would understand about Jon and me, it would surely be a man whose life is grounded in the world of theater."

Chapter 25

AFTER EATING a quick breakfast in their stateroom – rolls with butter and strawberry jam and tepid tea – Josette and Yvette had gone directly to the Lounge, which, technically, was also the Music Room, depending on the time of the day. Yvette wanted to practice a while before Mr. Frohman's arrival.

While Yvette played, Josette settled into a large upholstered chair with her book, placing her feet on the matching ottoman. Her mind drifted back to Compton House, to their own music room and the nights when Yvette practiced. Had it only been a few days since they had left for England? She inhaled a lingering breath. Oh, how she longed to return to that time. And to New York.

The theater producer arrived, as promised, at precisely ten-thirty. After greeting Yvette and Josette, as any gentlemen would, Mr. Frohman maneuvered into a comfortable chair, leaning his cane against the side table. "Let's begin with *Alexander's Ragtime Band,*" Frohman instructed Yvette between puffs on his hand-rolled cigar. A waiter provided him with a pot of coffee and sweet rolls arranged neatly on a silver tray, placing it on the table beside him.

Yvette's face lit up. "Of course, Mr. Frohman!" She scooted around to the keyboard, arranged her pink crepe flounced skirt, raised her arms, placed her fingers, and began.

There were only a few people in the room when she began. The lively Ragtime music drew in passengers who were strolling on the deck just outside the open windows, like moths to the flame. Including Curtis. He smiled at Josette and tapped the rim of his cap to greet Mr. Frohman. He walked to the side of the room, settling on a long settee.

Josette smiled in acknowledgement to Curtis, and leaned over to Mr. Frohman, nearly shouting over the raucous piano music. "My sister is very good, isn't she?" More a statement than a question.

Smiling, nodding, Mr. Frohman poured out a serving of coffee, used the tongs to add two lumps of sugar, and stirred.

At that moment, Yvette finished the spirited Irving Berlin piece. The listeners, now numbering maybe three dozen, applauded.

Mr. Frohman said in a loud voice, "Here, here, my girl. Bravo!"

Josette was filled with joy at her sister's success. This was, after all, her first public performance, and she had played beautifully.

CURTIS SPOTTED Josette on the Promenade deck. He hurried his pace to catch up with her. "Good afternoon, Josette. I see you've decided to join me in my afternoon walk."

Glancing at him over her shoulder, she said, "I'm hardly joining you, Curtis. There are dozens of people out here." She turned her head forward again, keeping up her gait. "However, I did take your suggestion that taking a brisk walk while many of the passengers are at afternoon tea or are napping was quite a good idea. Too many people in the way does impede one's progress."

Josette moved forward at a surprising pace.

He found himself taking long strides to keep up with the petite creature. "I couldn't help but notice that you're not wearing a skirt."

"They're called pantaloons. They're becoming quite the rage among women who move their bodies to exercise, you see. Skirts are far too cumbersome."

"And what else do you do to…exercise your body. Tennis? Golf?"

"I often ride a bicycle." She sounded out of breath. "I've learned to play tennis, though I have little time for it. And I adore sailing, though."

Bright, beautiful and she shared his passion for sailboats. A rare combination, indeed. "That seals it. You have to go sailing with me when you come back home."

Stopping at the railing, Josette breathed heavily. "We shall see, Mr. Carlson."

"I shall count on it, Miss Rogers," he said with a chuckle.

She stepped away from the railing and moved forward again. Rounding the corner, she headed down the port side. Curtis caught up with her.

The blare of a bugle startled both Curtis and Josette. They stopped abruptly and stepped aside when one of the crewmen rushed towards them. They exchanged confused glances.

"Excuse me," Curtis yelled at the sailor. "Why is the bugler signaling? Is everything all right?"

The crewman paused, peering over his shoulder. "No worries. It's only a drill for the crew." He continued on his way.

"That's certainly a necessity, especially considering the fact there's a war going on," Curtis said to Josette. "It's high time they had a drill. We've already been at sea a few days."

Josette nodded her agreement. They strolled side by side at a slower pace.

Heading aft and just past the third funnel, about a dozen crewmen stood beside one of the lifeboats. A group of curious passengers had begun to gather.

Curtis and Josette stopped to watch the training exercise. The men were dressed in crisp dark-blue uniforms with wide, sky-blue collars. The word "*Lusitania*" was embroidered in gold letters on their caps. Except one. He wore an officer's garb.

"Cunarders! Attention!" he hollered. "Ready! Begin!"

Two crewmen scrambled up the arched metal davits and into the lifeboat. The canvas covering had been pulled back to expose the barebones inside the rescue craft. The heavy chain securing the boat to the side of the *Lusitania* rattled as they climbed in, and then strained to keep the boat from swinging out too far from the weight of the men. Once inside, the pair scrambled around, placing the two long oars into their locks. Sitting side-by-side on the center-most seat, they stopped, motionless. "Oars readied, sir," they shouted in soldierly unison.

The officer then yelled. "Very good, gents. This drill is successfully concluded."

With that, the Cunard crewmen climbed back onto the deck.

"Wait a minute. What was that?" one man, a father who had been walking with his three young children, said with a gasp. "That's what you people call a drill?"

Another passenger – Curtis recognized him as the American publisher from New York City whom he had met playing poker after dinner last night – shouted in an angry tone. "That's the poorest excuse for an evacuation drill I could possibly imagine. Where is the rest of the crew? They should all have participated, not merely two men. Preposterous!"

Curtis joined in. "And what about the passengers? When are we to have a lifeboat drill, sir?" He looked squarely into the now-reddened face of the officer. "We should all be prepared!"

The Cunard officer drew back. "And who are you?"

"Curtis Carlson."

"The passengers do not need lifeboat drills. We have everything under control. It's the crew who needs to understand the process of evacuation. Not that it will ever be necessary. It is, however, a requirement by Cunard that the crew be fully aware of—"

"It is my understanding we will soon be entering a very dangerous region of the sea," Josette countered. "Do you really think that climbing into a lifeboat constitutes the best way for your crew to be trained to save the passengers on board this ship?"

The officer turned away from the unwelcomed observers. "Reckon you will all have to discuss this with the captain. I'm just following orders."

Curtis drew in a sharp breath, turning to the other onlookers. "How about it, gentlemen. And ladies. Shall we take up this lackluster display of incompetence with the captain?"

ON THE one hand, Curtis and Mr. Van Camp were supposed to merely take the voyage as ordinary passengers. No calling attention to themselves. No raising a ruckus. But right was right, and Curtis said he would join the other witnesses to the so-called drill when they confronted Captain Turner.

Curtis hadn't told Van Camp about his involvement in the apprehension of the three Germans. His superior would be furious. Now, if he knew Curtis was joining what amounted to a revolt against the captain for not instructing the crew and the passengers in how to escape the ship in the event of an emergency, he would certainly lose his temper. Yet, Curtis wasn't one to keep quiet and behave. Right was right.

Even Josette's father insisted on coming along. Mr. Vanderbilt added his support at the last minute.

Captain Turner was in his day cabin just off the Bridge when the dozen men and five women, including Josette, made their way to the Navigation Deck.

The first mate announced their visit in a loud voice through the closed door. "There are passengers here, captain. They insist on speaking with you, *post haste*, sir."

Several minutes passed before the captain opened the door. By the look of his rumpled hair and pink-tinged eyes, he had been napping. "How can I be of service, gentlemen? And ladies." Captain Turner tugged on his hat, scanning the group.

"We saw what was supposed to be a drill for your crew earlier today," Mr. Rogers said. A half-truth, since several of the group hadn't witnessed the fiasco.

Turner's wiry, graying brows slid into a puzzled 'V.' "Supposed to be a drill, you say?"

"Not much of a drill, Turner," one of the men in the group yelled. Several others expressed their agreement.

"For God's sake," Mr. Rogers said. "Why wasn't a lifeboat lowered as a part of the drill?"

Mr. Vanderbilt spoke up before Captain Turner responded. "And what of the passengers, my good sir? How would anyone know what to do in the event of an emergency? A torpedo, for instance. Are we not under the possible threat of torpedo attack?"

Turner shook his head. "If that were true, we would have received official word from London."

"But instructing your passengers in how to survive any type of disaster would be smart," Curtis said.

Captain Turner appeared to be losing his patience. "Cunard's directors considered holding drills that would include the passengers, but their conclusion was that it would frighten the ladies."

"That's utterly ridiculous!" Josette protested in a loud voice.

"Miss Rogers," the captain said, his eyes boring into her. "I'm afraid I have no choice in the matter. I'm following orders from my superiors." He moved his gaze from Josette to the rest of the group. "If you all wish to take this issue up with Cunard, please contact their London office when we get to England."

"What good will that do?" Mr. Vanderbilt said. "Please send a wire to Cunard's headquarters and tell them I insist on this. The directors of Cunard Lines must take the threat of attacks on their ship seriously. Above all, the matter of passenger safety should be forefront in their minds."

Mr. and Mrs. Green had stood silently. Mrs. Green stepped forward, a defiant expression on her face. "As for the women on board, knowing how to properly secure the life jackets and what to do in an emergency would give the ladies a little peace of mind. It certainly would be a wise move on your part, sir."

Turner stiffened. "I believe I know what's best for my ship, gentleman…and ladies. As for the life vests, there are instructions on their proper use posted around the ship."

"That's not enough! Have the blasted drills!" Josette's father said, his face red with anger.

"As I've said repeatedly, if the *Lusitania* comes under attack from a U-boat or any other German vessel, I assure you I shall take the appropriate evasive actions. And, God forbid, if she's struck by a torpedo, the water-tight doors will keep her afloat. Additionally, the *Lusitania* has enough lifeboats for everyone." He turned and looked directly at Curtis with a fierce glare. "There'll be no repeat of the *Titanic* fiasco on my ship."

Mr. Vanderbilt, a man who was used to having his orders obeyed, spoke in a fierce tone. "Do you realize many of your most prominent passengers received telegrams shortly before our departure from New York warning us that we would die if we boarded this vessel?"

"No, sir, I was not," Captain Turner said with a surprised expression. "How very odd."

Curtis glanced at Josette. She looked frightened.

"Crikey!" Mr. Rogers said. "Is that right?"

"I can assure you it's true. I, too, received such a telegram." Mr. Vanderbilt's exasperation was obvious.

"And yet you all came," Captain Turner said. "You must have reached the same conclusion that I have about these sorts of things. It was merely another scare tactic perpetrated by the Huns hoping to bankrupt Cunard. Imagine the amount of money that would have been lost to the company if you and the others had heeded their threats."

Curtis asked, "And what about the newspaper warning from the German Embassy. Did anyone actually cancel?"

The First Officer, who had joined the group at the captain's door, let out a laugh. "As a matter of fact, an additional ten first-cabin passengers booked at the last minute. There were very few cancelations, even after that ridiculous advertisement in the newspapers telling people that the *Lusitania* would likely be attacked."

Captain Turner looked upset. "You have my word nothing will happen to this vessel. Additionally, by the time we reach the Irish Coast, a contingent of British ships will escort us all the way to Liverpool. I repeat...I guarantee you are all safe and sound. So, please, ladies and gentlemen, sleep peacefully and enjoy the rest of the journey."

Chapter 26

AFTER LEAVING the captain's quarters, Josette and Curtis intended to take a stroll. "Do you believe Captain Turner's explanation?" she asked.

"I can only hope he follows up with his promise to send a wire to Cunard's head office about holding some sort of drill for the passengers."

"At the very least, we should all be shown how to put on and secure our life vests," Josette said insistently.

"Of course. In the meantime, please practice putting yours on," he insisted. "It can be complicated, so you do need to prepare."

"Very well. I shall practice with my sister."

"Good," he said. Stepping to the railing, he leaned forward, breathing in the fresh air. A sudden wind gust blew a fine mist of sea water into his face. "Whoa!" he said, grabbing his wool cap as he jumped back.

Josette couldn't keep herself from laughing. "Oh, my goodness!"

"Amused, huh?" Grinning, Curtis reached in his coat pocket and pulled out a white handkerchief, dabbing droplets of moisture from his cheeks.

"Sorry," she said, still chuckling.

"Looks like the breeze is getting stronger," he said. How about a cup of tea in the lounge?"

"I truly don't mind getting a little damp. I love the ocean air ever so much." Just then another wave struck the side of the ship, sending a large surge of spray upwards to precisely where they stood. With Curtis standing slightly back and more out of the way, Josette was the water's main recipient.

"Oh, no!" she yelled. Josette's hat and coat were soaked. Brushing the water beads from her clothes, she laughed. "On the other hand, a cup of hot tea does sound quite good."

ONCE INSIDE the lounge, they made their way to a couch close to one of the fireplaces where they could warm up. Removing her straw hat, she laid it on the side table and turned to him. "I've given a lot of thought to the conversation we had when you insisted we have a lot in common. Now, then," she said, peeling off her wet gloves. "Tell me how you reached that conclusion."

"All right. How about our love of sailing? And the sea…though at this moment, I'm not so sure!"

"True," Josette responded, smiling. "There is that. What else?"

"I love New York."

"Me, too," she said, grinning.

"I love to read."

"As do I."

"I'm planning to write quite a few more books."

"Very well. You have made your point, Curtis. But I still don't know much about you. How about discussing silly topics, such as what your favorite color is?"

"Very well, then." He tipped his head to one side, as if in thought. "Hmm. Favorite color. I guess it would be – now don't laugh. Pink."

"Oh, my heavens! You must be joking! Pink? That's my sister's favorite color."

"See. I knew you'd react that way. Pink isn't considered very masculine."

"Yes, indeed," she said. "Pink? Good heavens. I must say I'm a little surprised. You don't seem like the pink type. Orange, maybe, but—"

"Hear me out, Josie. I love the various shades of pink the cherry blossoms turn in the spring. They change from the palest of pale, to a most vivid pink that almost glows against the green leaves of the cherry trees."

"Why, Mr. Carlson. You almost sound like a romantic."

Lifting his chin, he laughed. "Perhaps, so. There are many things you don't know about me," he said with a slight grin. "For instance, I love to go to Central Park and sit on a bench under the cherry trees. I've been doing it since they were brought to New York a few years ago. For some reason, I find that I can think better there. I eat lunch and even write in the shade of those trees whenever I can...even after the blossoms are gone." He leaned his elbow on the armrest. "Someday, we'll meet under my cherry trees in Central Park. Deal?"

"We shall see," she said with a deliberate coy tone and tiny smile.

Curtis sat back, threading his fingers together and sliding his locked hands around the back of his neck. "I'll count on it. So, what about you? What's your favorite color?"

"Blue. But not the same hue my mother uses in our home in Manhattan. That's a traditional French blue. No, my blue is more like the color of cornflowers. More of a royal blue, I suppose."

"I'll have to remember that in the future." He smiled and looked at her for an uncomfortably long moment. "And do you know what my second favorite color is?"

She laughed. "Lavender?"

"You think you're quite amusing, don't you?"

She shrugged.

"No, not lavender. Butterscotch."

"Butterscotch?" she said in a mocking tone. That's not a color. That's a flavor."

"Yes. But it's also the color of your hair. And when the sun hits you just right, I can see strands that seem like they're made of twenty-four carat gold." He squinted, assessing her damp curls more closely. "Or, maybe, it's more like honey."

"Oh, my goodness, Curtis. You're embarrassing me!" Josette laughed, flipping her hair off her shoulder. "You are such a flirt." Before Curtis could retort, Yvette approached.

"There you are, Josette. I've been looking all over for you." Yvette smiled and nodded at Curtis. "I might have known you'd be together again."

"Yvette. Yes. Mr. Carlson and I have been having a conversation. And I'm trying to dry out from the sea spray that targeted me."

"I see." Yvette looked at her, then at Curtis with a knowing expression. "Well, then. I came to tell you that Mr. Frohman has invited me to his stateroom for a light snack and to listen to music on his phonograph machine. He asked me to include you two."

JOSETTE INSISTED that she change out of her damp clothes into an afternoon tea gown and straighten-up her hair. She and Yvette met Curtis on the Promenade deck thirty minutes later and proceeded to Mr. Frohman's suite. It wasn't as large as a Regal Suite, like the one occupied by Mr. Vanderbilt and his butler, but it had ample space to accommodate the twenty-something people who had crowded inside for a pre-dinner soiree.

The theater producer sat in an overstuffed floral-print chair in the corner. His right leg elevated on a small leather ottoman, he looked like a king observing, watching, listening. Yvette wondered if he was concocting ideas for his next play.

Glancing around the room, she recognized several theatrical people Mr. Frohman had introduced her to at tea yesterday – a group of friends traveling with him to England which included playwrights, actors and directors. *Such fascinating people*, Yvette thought, feeling privileged to have been included at a party with men and women whom she admired. Artists, one and all. If only Jonathan could have been with her. He would have fit into the group beautifully. They were his kind of people. Hers, too.

A DINING TABLE stood at the end of the parlor, where the stewards had placed trays of cheese and crackers, sliced fruit, and assorted cookies and pastries, together with pots of tea and coffee. Bottles of champagne and wine were in ice-filled silver buckets. Music from the phonograph's large flower-petal-shaped, sound-amplifying horn could barely be heard over the raucous laughter and loud talking.

Walking with Curtis and Josette to the food table, Yvette noticed Mr. Frohman rubbing his knee, a pained look covering his face.

"I'll be back in a few minutes," she said to Josette, as her sister leaned to pick up a gold-rimmed plate. "I want to speak to Mr. Frohman."

"Of course," Josette said, stabbing a square of cheese with a serving fork.

Yvette pushed past two rather glamorous women, who chattered noisily between sips of champagne. "Excuse me, ladies," she said, stepping closer to the producer.

"Ah. Miss Yvette. So glad you could come."

"I wanted to thank you for including my sister and Mr. Carlson here today. It was very kind of you."

"Think nothing of it, my dear. Truthfully, I invited you today because I want to speak with you about your career. You seem to think your boyfriend—"

"My fiancé, really," she corrected with a mild chuckle.

"Ah, yes. Your fiancé." He cleared his throat. "Truth be told, I would like to employ *you* as an accompanist for one of my plays in London."

"Heavens! Me? But Jonathan—"

"Your Jonathan is still in America. I need someone sooner rather than later. Too many musicians are serving at the Front. Damned waste, if you ask me. Putting these talented gents in trenches with guns is ridiculous. Getting their heads blown off. It's, it's obscene."

Yvette drew back at the visual image.

"Oh, apologies, my dear." His features softened. "I just get so upset when it comes to this war. We can only hope the Kaiser realizes he doesn't have a chance against Great Britain. Who can stand up to His Majesty's Navy, I ask you?"

"Father says it will all be over soon."

"Let's hope so." Shifting in his chair, he asked in an impatient tone, "And what is your answer, Yvette? Will you play at my theater in Golden Square? It's quite nice. And you'd be doing it for the people of England."

She laughed. "My goodness! For the people of England! That's quite a responsibility."

"It's true. Theaters cannot survive without musicians. And the British thrive on their cultural experiences. It's a fine way to keep up their spirits, you see."

Yvette drew in a long, slow breath as she regarded Mr. Frohman's words. "Thank you for the wonderful offer, Mr. Frohman. I will certainly take it under consideration." What she didn't add was that her father would likely forbid it. Now the question was whether or not she would go against Father's wishes.

"Very well. But I need your answer soon." He shifted again, readjusting the position of his troubled leg. "In the meantime, there's a copy of the sheet music to *It's a Long Way to Tipperary* over by the phonograph. I would like you to learn to play that piece as soon as possible."

She must have had a questioning look, for he continued to explain.

"Ever since the war began last August, that lively song has become a sort of anthem for the British. It's quite rousing and makes people feel a sense of joy, something that's sorely needed during these dire days. I believe it would lift everyone's spirits here on the ship, especially since we will soon be in the danger zone."

"Of course. I would be most happy to perform it."

"Good. Now, then, my dear. Would you be an angel and get me a plate of pastries? I do like my sweets, you see."

As she turned to leave, the French actress, Rita Jolivet, approached her.

"So." She placed her hand on her hip. "You are the girl who saw the German spies, n'cest-ce pas?"

"Oh. Well. You see, my sister and I—"

"Is that true, Miss Yvette?" Mr. Frohman asked, leaning forward, his face crumpled with a questioning expression.

Yvette and Josette and all the others who were involved in the arrest of the three German youths had been sworn to secrecy. She thought for a long moment, hating to lie, but knew she had no choice.

"As a matter of fact, it was all a big mistake," Yvette said, trying to look, to sound nonchalant. "We're quite sorry if we caused you distress, Miss Jolivet."

The actress shot her an annoyed look. "Distress is hardly the word, *mademoiselle*. You and your sister caused a near panic. I lost a great deal of beauty sleep because of you girls."

"Now, now, Rita," Mr. Frohman said. "I doubt there would have been a near panic if you hadn't spread the rumor in the first place." He let out a soft grunt when he lowered his raised leg and sat up in the chair. "I'm quite sure the sisters didn't mean to cause you any upset."

Looking at Frohman, the French woman's expression softened. Her cherry red lips pouted like a child. "But, *mon cheri*— "

"But nothing, Rita. Leave the girl alone. She already apologized."

Uncomfortable, Yvette felt the need to escape. "If you'll excuse me, I must fetch snacks for our host," she said to the actress. Yvette took a step backwards. Scowling, Miss Jolivet glanced at her with narrowed eyes and a frown.

Yvette spun around and edged herself between a slender, blonde-haired woman wearing an ankle-length black fringed dress, and a baby-faced young man with curly brown hair that had been amply greased with pomade and parted in the middle. "Pardon me," she said.

Josette and Curtis hadn't moved very far away from the food-strewn table.

"I need to talk to you, Josette," Yvette said. Grabbing a plate, she inched closer to the tray of boiled shrimp.

"Now?" Josette said, sounding puzzled. "What's happened, sister?"

"Apparently, we caused a panic of sorts among the passengers!"

"Are you serious?" Josette said, her eyes wide. "How?"

"I'll tell you later. But let's get the heck out of here."

Chapter 27

WHILE MOST of the millionaire passengers who were privy to dine at the captain's table were rotated nightly, Curtis' uppity uncle had managed to hang on to their seats. This was night number three, and the only other dignitary who had sat there as many times was Mr. Vanderbilt. Which was understandable. But a college professor and his snippety uncle...well, that didn't make much sense.

Every time Josette glanced at Curtis from the corner of her eye, she noted that he looked miserable. For some reason, that made her smile...perhaps a guilty pleasure.

"Josette, dear," Mother said in an uncharacteristically mellifluous tone, bringing Josette's attention back to their table. "You haven't eaten a bite of your pork roast. It's *tres jolie.*"

"Hmm? Oh, sorry. I'm simply not hungry," Josette said. As tempting as it was to snip back at their mother, Josette didn't want to say that she and Yvette had attended a soiree in Mr. Frohman's stateroom; that they had listened to phonograph music and snacked with his theatrical friends that afternoon. Mother would not approve. Actors and musicians were, in Mother's opinion, some sort of insignificant beings; people with whom upper-crust ladies shouldn't associate.

"Are you enjoying the voyage, Mrs. Donaldson?" Father asked.

The Scottish woman had missed several meals. "I fear my stomach isn't resilient as it used to be," she said with a hearty chuckle. "I must say I shall be happy to see dry land again."

"How is Mr. Duns fairing the voyage?" Yvette inquired.

"Quite well, actually. He's with our bellboy again this evening. I believe Tommy has grown fond of wee Dunsy. And the feeling seems to be quite mutual."

"I would love to walk Mr. Duns for you sometime," Josette said. "We used to have a dog – a terrier – but she passed away two years ago. I do miss having a furry friend these days." She shot a look in her father's direction.

"You should look into getting yourselves a Westie. Smart dogs, they are. And as loyal as a MacDonald clansman," Mrs. Donaldson said, picking up her glass of wine.

"Yes, yes. Right then." Father straightened, clearing his throat. "Loud and clear, Josette Marie. Perhaps your mother and I will buy a dog once we're settled into our home in London."

"Then we have several things to look forward to in London, don't we, sister?" Josette teased, wondering when Yvette would work up the courage to tell their parents about Mr. Frohman's offer.

AFTER DINNER, the Welsh Choir performed upstairs in the combination Lounge and Music Room. The ship's social director, who Josette believed was a hypocrite, had coaxed the troupe into an impromptu performance for the first-class passengers. Members of the choir were all booked into the second-class cabins and hadn't been invited to perform for the guests there.

Their choir's reputation as an excellent musical group had preceded them and, thusly, the room was packed to capacity. Many passengers – even some of the ladies – had to stand around the periphery, since the chairs and settees were all occupied.

Josette and Yvette stood near the doorway, poking and bobbing their heads to see. Impossible. They were both five-foot-two inches tall, and the men in front of them were blocking their view.

"Chivalry is dead," Yvette commented under her breath.

Still, it was a choir, not a stage play, so watching wasn't necessary.

Yvette managed to scoot forward between two men, standing in front of the low planter box filled with an assortment of yellow, red, and white flowers. Josette wasn't much for big crowds and opted to go out onto the portside Promenade, where she could hear the choir's lovely harmonies without enduring the shroud of tobacco smoke and the elbow-to-elbow throng.

The evening air was balmy, even warm, as if a wayward tropical wind had decided to make its way to the North Atlantic. Josette wiggled her fingers out of her lamb's wool-lined gloves, placing them on the ledge under a large, rectangular window. She gazed out at the vastness of the inky sea. Overhead, the moon and stars spread out like crystals on a black velvet background.

Living in New York City, where there were street lights, head lamps on automobiles, and electric fixtures illuminating light from windows, the night sky was decidedly less spectacular. Even though the moon wasn't full, in this uninterrupted stretch of blackness, it let out enough of a glow to throw a silver stripe across the water and diamond-like glints off the tips of the waves.

Unbuttoning her coat, Josette drew in a breath of fresh air, feeling the breeze on her cheeks. She watched the frothy white water sprayed up from under the ship's bow. A sense of peace came over her. For the moment, she felt no fear about German spies, had no worries about what might happen tomorrow or the next day or the next. There were no submarines, no battlefields. Nothing but the night sky and the ocean.

"Beautiful, isn't it?"

She turned to see Curtis leaning his shoulder on the bulkhead next to the window.

"Are you following me, Mr. Carlson?" Josette grinned.

"As a matter of fact, yes." He let out a chuckle. "I saw you leave and wondered how you're doing."

"I'm all right," she said, sighing.

Curtis turned to look out at the vast emptiness. "I've been thinking a lot about the Germans we caught. If they are on the *Lusitania* to spy – or even if they're not spies for that matter but have made arrangements with authorities in Berlin to get them to the war front, that means someone—a German sympathizer—must know they're here. Attacking a ship carrying their own young men wouldn't make any sense. Right?"

"I suppose not."

Curtis faced Josette. "In fact, the Germans would have a great deal to lose if they were to do something as stupid as attacking a passenger vessel, particularly a luxury liner carrying Americans. That would likely make President Wilson change his mind and declare war on Germany and their allies."

"Thank you, Curtis. I needed to hear that."

A sudden gust lifted her gloves from the ledge where she had placed them, blowing them to the deck. Josette let out a yelp, running to recover the wayward gloves as they bounced along their way, like children escaping their parents' grasp.

Curtis leaped, trying to catch them, just as one, then the other sailed overboard.

"Oh…crackers!" Josette said with a groan. "Those are my only warm gloves."

"Sorry, Josie, but they belong to Poseidon now." He laughed as he straightened.

"Mother will surely have a fit when she realizes I've lost them. They were quite expensive, you see."

"Ah, yes. Your mother. Madame Rogers," he said with a snicker. "What's up with that French affectation of hers… n'cest-ce pas?" He exaggerated the Frenchness. "From what you and Yvette have said, your mother was born in New York. Is her family French?"

"In truth, she's more Irish than anything. I believe our hair color comes from our Scottish blood, however. Father is an Englishman, tried and true."

Laughing, Curtis retorted, "He seems like a jolly good bloke, he does. Quite down to earth for a Brit, especially a wealthy one."

"Actually, he is, though Mother gets really annoyed with his East End slang," Josette said with a small chuckle. "Of course, he's much too old fashioned and over-protective. But underneath it all, he loves us and does his best to take care of us. And he puts up with my mother's French nonsense." Josette rolled her eyes. "I just wish he was more understanding when it came to my beliefs about things like women's rights and all."

"Did I mention my mother has marched in more than one suffrage parade? She even went to jail once for blocking the entrance to a courthouse, protesting against the fact that women can't sit on juries."

"Truly? I must meet her one day," Josette said, delighted with the thought that Curtis' own mother shared her ideals. "And how do you feel about such matters, Curtis?"

"I grew up in a household with parents who believe in rights for women. I believe women will get the right to vote sooner than later."

"I couldn't agree more! That's certainly refreshing, Curtis. The young men with whom I have associated didn't share your opinion." The breeze had turned cold. Shivering, Josette pulled her jacket closed, fastened a button, and tucked her hands into her coat pockets.

"Should we go back inside?" Curtis offered. "Or to the Verandah for a cup of coffee and dessert?"

"Thank you, but I'm still quite full from dinner," she said, listening to the applause coming from the Music Room. "Another time, perhaps?"

"Of course," he said, nodding. He paused. "Do I need to ask your Father's permission to write to you?"

"Of course not. I'll be of age soon."

"Just promise me you'll come back to New York as soon as you can."

"I can't promise, Curtis. It depends on a lot of things."

"I do hope I'm on that list of things," he said in a gentle tone.

"Perhaps." Josette felt herself blushing, thankful the light was too dim for him to see. "And you must promise to come to England to visit me."

"Definitely."

And then a sudden, jarring thought struck her. "Oh, Curtis. What if the United States enters the war? What if you have to go to France to fight?"

"If the President institutes a mandatory draft, I suppose I'll have to go fight with the other young men."

"And yet?" she said in a questioning way. "Do you still believe America should enter a war half-way around the world between countries that have all been our allies and trade partners at one time or another. Are you willing to risk your life for it?"

Before Curtis said anything, a swarm of passengers streamed out of the Lounge, chatting loudly as they passed by.

Josette hadn't realized the singing had stopped. "Oh, dear. I guess the entertainment is over." That meant her parents would soon be passing by on their way back to their stateroom. "I should go now. Mother and Father will wonder where I am."

"May I walk you back to your cabin?"

"Of course."

"And did I mention how utterly breathtaking you look tonight, Josie?"

She dropped her gaze. "Thank you."

Walking, Josette looked up at Curtis. "I've been meaning to ask you about your Uncle Phineas. He doesn't resemble you in anyway whatsoever. He has dark red hair, for instance. You're a brunette, and your eyes are light brown. His eyes are pale blue."

Curtis uncomfortable with the question. He simply looked down at the deck as they strolled, as if thinking about how to respond. "He's actually my mother's half-brother. His own mother died and..." Curtis' voice trailed off.

Grabbing her by the elbow, Curtis stopped suddenly and looked at her with great intensity as he urged her into the shadows between the dangling lifeboats. "Look, Josette. I can't keep up this pretense. You must promise you won't share what I'm about to tell you with anyone. Not your parents, and not even your sister. Do I have your word?"

"Of course, Curtis. What is it?"

"I haven't been truthful with you, Josie. Van Camp and I are here because—"

"Curtis! There you are! I have been trying to catch your attention. Did you not hear me calling you?" Mr. Van Camp said in an agitated tone. "I must speak to you. Follow me to my stateroom immediately."

AFTER BIDDING Josette goodnight at her stateroom door, Curtis joined Mr. Van Camp in his private parlor. "What in the world is going on?" he said, closing the door behind him.

The senior partner headed to the sideboard covered with a lace-trimmed napery and a selection of liquor bottles. Still facing the small mahogany cabinet, Van Camp poured Scotch into two small glasses. "Shortly after I left the dining room, a bellboy delivered a wireless message to me from Jack Morgan."

"Jack Morgan sent us a Marconigram?"

Replacing the decanter's lid, Van Camp nodded and walked to Curtis, handing him one of the glasses. "Have a seat, Carlson. We have a major problem."

"Sounds serious, sir." Accepting the Scotch, Curtis placed the drink on a side table, settled into the adjacent chair, and leaned forward, resting his elbows on his knees. "What's happened?"

Before answering, Van Camp gulped down the entire contents of his tiny crystal tumbler. His shoulders lifted and dropped with a heavy sigh. "Morgan, as you know, has far-reaching tentacles. He not only has the ear of President Wilson, he has connections with the British War Department. According to Jack, three German spies were captured right here on the *Lusitania*, if you can imagine that."

Curtis didn't know what to say. "Really? That's terrible." He feigned a confused look with a quick shrug. Turner had obviously notified the British Admiralty regarding the arrest of the three young Germans. "Well, at least they've been put out of commission." The less Van Camp knew about his involvement in the Germans' capture, the better. He sat back and reached for his drink.

"Well, thank goodness for the Cunarders." *Did that come off as acerbic?* He hoped not. "So, that's settled, then."

"Yes and no. Impossible as it seems, Jack believes there may be more Germans on board."

Curtis straightened. "Why would he think that? Does he think the Germans know about the documents?"

Van Camp lifted his shoulders in a troubled shrug. "All I know is that Jack asked us to remain alert. And to be cognizant of the fact that our identity and our secret mission may have been compromised."

Chapter 28

A LOUD *thump* and the sound of something heavy scraping against the hull jarred Curtis awake. "What in the world?" he muttered, propping up on his elbow. Men's voices and grunts and rattling chains came from the deck outside his window.

The air in his stateroom was chilly, so he climbed out of bed and grabbed the robe he had draped over the back of a chair. Sliding his feet into his slippers, he crossed the room and threw open the draperies.

Curtis could see that two Cunard crewmen had climbed up the crane-like davits that held the lifeboat closest to his room.

"My God!" he said, his heart pounding. There must have been a submarine sighting. Swallowing hard, he unscrewed the window's bolts, pushed it open, and poked his head outside. An officer stood beside the lifesaving craft.

"Hey! What's happening?" Curtis called, gathering his robe closed at the neck. "Are we under attack?"

The officer turned. Curtis recognized him as one of the senior officers. "No, sir. The captain ordered us to ready the lifeboats as a precautionary measure. No need to worry, sir. Just go back to bed."

Christ. No need to worry? Curtis thought with a disgruntled smirk. Everyone was already nervous about entering the War Zone off the coast of Ireland. This precaution would cause more upset than peace of mind, if that was what Turner was going for.

"I doubt anyone is still asleep what with all this ruckus."

"Begging your pardon, sir. Just following orders, here," he said, tugging on the brim of his white cap.

Curtis shut the hinged window and tightened the screws. Closing the draperies, he crossed the room, turned on the lights, and plopped down on the edge of the bed. He hadn't slept well last night. For hours, he had lain awake thinking about the possible repercussions he might face upon returning to New York in a couple of weeks. Would there be reporters waiting for him and Mr. Van Camp?

Although he believed in Mr. Morgan and in the whole concept of helping the Allied countries, he knew that making this massive loan to the British government would be terribly unpopular with many American citizens. The President had promised neutrality for America. His popularity, the reason he had won the election was because of that stance. Eventually, every American, every European, everyone, would know despite the secrecy surrounding the agreement between Morgan and his banking cohorts and the heads of government in both Britain and France.

As the late Mr. Morgan Senior, and more recently, Jack Morgan, had explained to Curtis, the family fortune was to be used to support their beliefs, both in business and in what was best for the United States. For years, the Morgans had made loans to the American government. Even New York City had been bailed out from its financial troubles. The three generations of Morgans had bought and built railroads and ships and steel mills. And yet, the Morgan name had often been marked with controversies. Words like robber barons and monopolies had flawed their reputation until their philanthropic works became public knowledge. If Curtis was to work for this amazing giant of finance, he would need to snuff out any personal doubts about Morgan's motives and judgments. Still, he had a nagging feeling that most Americans would be outraged by a half-billion-dollar loan to prop up a war they didn't support. The repercussions worried him.

Stretching his back, neck and arms, he rose and headed to the washroom. Thirty minutes later, after shaving and combing his hair, Curtis dressed in a warm pair of trousers, coordinating woolen sports jacket, and casual shoes, and stepped out his cabin door and into the indoor hallway. Poor timing. Mr. Van Camp emerged from his stateroom just as Curtis passed.

"Carlson," Van Camp said in a demanding tone.

He stopped, drew in a steadying breath, pasted on a smile, and pivoted around. "Yes, sir. Good morning."

"I was just coming to fetch you."

"I'm sorry, but I have an appointment."

Van Camp lifted a suspicious brow. "With that pretty little Rogers girl?"

"Yes, but—"

"But nothing, Carlson. This can't wait. We must head up to the Bridge to have a talk with Captain Turner. I intend to find out the true reason he's had the lifeboats readied. Surely, he's heard something from London that has caused him to take this extreme action. We have to make him understand the importance of getting us to England safely."

Curtis followed him down the hall. "You're talking about the papers?"

"Precisely!" Mr. Van Camp pushed open the hallway door, stepped over the raised sill and took a few steps before opening the door leading onto the outside deck.

Curtis was baffled. Once they were out of the range of hearing by several other passengers strolling on deck, he placed his hand on Van Camp's shoulder to stop him. "But no one can know about them," he said in a strained whisper. "That was Mr. Morgan's direct order."

"I don't give a damn about Jack Morgan's order to keep our mission secret. He isn't here. He's likely at his desk in the Manhattan office sipping tea." Van Camp continued, stepping up his pace. "He's not a goddamned sitting duck like we are."

Van Camp reached the bottom of the external stairs leading to the Bridge and began to climb up. "Look, son, it's obvious Turner has slowed this ship when he should have been adding speed. The faster we get through the damned War Zone, the better chance we have of avoiding a catastrophe," he grumbled, out of breath. "If he knows about Morgan's loan documents, perhaps it will convince him to speed up this floating palace."

Mr. Van Camp didn't knock on the door leading to the Bridge but burst through like a bull charging a red cape. "I need to speak to Captain Turner. Immediately."

A little embarrassed, Curtis followed. Damn. This was his third trip up to see the captain.

Captain Turner stooped over a high table assessing a navigation chart. He straightened and turned to answer. "Carlson! Not you again! What in the hell is it this time?"

Mr. Van Camp stepped over to the captain. "We're here because I'm goddamned angry. Angry that this ship isn't traveling at nearly the speed she should be."

One of the high-ranking officers, Mr. Braswell, dashed to the captain's side. His cheeks were flushed like two red apples. "I don't care if you're here representing the King of England. You cannot simply barge onto the Bridge. Passengers are only allowed here by appointment or invitation. Shall I eject them, sir?"

The captain held up his arm, his hand bent up in a flat position to expose his palm. "No, no. They're all right, Mr. Braswell. At ease."

Officer Braswell saluted, turned and walked back to his position at the helm.

The captain, usually staid in his demeanor, looked annoyed. "Now, then. What can I do for you gentlemen?"

"Captain Turner," Van Camp said dryly. "We represent J. P. Morgan and Company. We are traveling to Great Britain on official government business, and I demand that you speed up this ship!"

Turner reached for a coffee cup situated on a table beside a cushionless chair. He narrowed his eyes, moving his gaze between Curtis and Mr. Van Camp. "I am the captain of this vessel, gentlemen. I am under strict orders by the British Admiralty to conserve coal. And that is the end of this conversation."

Van Camp stood his ground, placing a fisted hand on his hip. "You know perfectly well that you cannot guarantee this ship can outrun a torpedo if you don't give the *Lusitania* more speed!"

"The British government will notify me of any danger should an enemy submarine or armed ship be spotted anywhere along our current course. And there will be a Royal Navy escort to accompany the *Lusitania* on the last leg of her voyage in the more perilous areas. It's an armed flotilla that has accompanied us on former crossings."

"When will we see this flotilla, Captain Turner?" Curtis asked, moving closer.

"Very soon." Turner's voice had a distinctly dismissive tone.

"Listen to me, gentlemen." Turner took a casual sip of coffee. "I can assure you we will not be attacked. Now, if you will excuse me, I must get back to my duties."

"No, sir. We will not excuse you," Van Camp said. "Not until we've explained our purpose."

Captain Turner stepped backwards, as if riled that anyone would dare disobey his orders. "Well, I—"

Curtis interrupted. "May we please talk in a more...private place, sir?"

The captain looked puzzled. And disgruntled. "I can assure you that anything you have to say to me can be heard by my officers."

The edges of Mr. Van Camp's lips drooped, accentuating the bulge of his double chin. "I'm afraid we must insist. You'll understand why once we have explained our assignment." He turned to Curtis. "And you...I'm ordering you to take care of the papers. Get them into the Purser's safe, immediately," he roared. "No arguments! Just do it now!"

AFTER LUNCH, Josette strolled down the corridor toward the Library. Like so many other passengers, she and Yvette had been awakened by the commotion outside their stateroom that morning. Father had gone outside to see why the lifeboats were being moved, if there was some sort of emergency. There had been no warning signals for evacuating, no stewards rapping on passenger's doors to wake them, to tell them to put on their life vests and to make their way out to the decks. Nor had the evacuation drills the passengers asked for ever occurred.

When Father had been awakened by the noise, he'd gone out on the deck. The crewmen had assured him that the lifeboats were set into position as a required safety measure. It was Thursday. Six days after the *Lusitania* had left New York. Six days closer to Great Britain. And from what everyone said, they would soon enter the ghastly War Zone, where German submarines lay in wait to sink ships. But the *Lusitania* wasn't a war ship, nor was she a merchant vessel. Why in the world would they target a bunch of innocent men, women and children who had nothing whatsoever to do with their dreadful war? Curtis was right. It didn't make sense.

Reaching the Library, Josette maneuvered her pile of papers and pen, opened the door with her free hand, and entered.

As usual, no one else was in the long room. Most of the first-class travelers were finishing lunch or had headed out to play in the afternoon shuffleboard tournament. Curtis would meet her at one o'clock. He'd had some sort of commitment with his uncle earlier that morning and needed to take care of some business, he had said.

The Library was utterly quiet, except for the ever-present rumble of the engines purring from deep below the deck. Between the constant motion and gentle vibration, she found her surroundings quite relaxing. Indeed, the Library was a perfect place for her to work on her school paper.

Josette unscrewed the lid from her ink pen and began to write. During the past days, she had recorded her observations about the passengers she had encountered, from Mr. Frohman to Mr. Vanderbilt, to Lady Allen and her two naughty little daughters. Lady Allen was married to a well-known Canadian shipping magnate, though he hadn't made the trip abroad with his family. Exactly why she was traveling without her husband on the *Lusitania* was unclear to Josette, but it must have been for a good reason, she imagined, considering there was a war going on. No one in their right mind would have taken such a chance traveling through a war zone, unless it was absolutely necessary.

Glancing at the wall clock, Josette realized Curtis would be arriving soon. She sat up straight, screwing the lid back on her fountain pen. She turned when she heard the door open and approaching footsteps. "Curtis?"

Mr. Elbert Hubbard, the world-famous author and philosopher approached. He smiled as he moved in her direction, gazing down at her with intense eyes.

"Good afternoon, sir."

"And a good afternoon to you, too, miss," Mr. Hubbard said as he sauntered past. He dipped his chin to her in respect. Josette knew a few free-spirited college boys attending Columbia University who sported a long mane, but Mr. Hubbard looked around fifty and had long, brown hair that curled under at his collar. That wasn't his only rebellious trait. The man was positively a non-conformist in his attire, wearing baggy brown trousers and a loose-fitting tan shirt with puffy sleeves rolled up to his elbows.

From the corner of her eye, Josette watched him sit at a desk a few feet away. She fought her enthusiasm, her urge to approach him and engage in a conversation. She had met a few of Mr. Frohman's famous writer-friends at his soiree, including a renowned playwright. But she hadn't engaged in a tête-à-tête with any one as interesting as Mr. Hubbard.

The man had the inexplicable bearing of a serious writer, the kind of individual who wrote about significant issues, like the horrors of war. And yet, his appearance was that of one of those creative beings who lived in Paris among the likes of Monet or Cezanne.

She had seen him a number of times, including one night at dinner when he sat with the captain. Father had met him in the smoking room and said Mr. Hubbard was heading to France to report on the war. And to do an actual interview with the German Kaiser, of all things.

At tea, Mother and several other upper-crust women gossiped about Mr. and Mrs. Hubbard. Mother had voiced her opinion. "*Mon Dieu.* No respectable man would bring his wife to the Western Front. Where will they stay? In a trench with the soldiers?"

From the corner of her eye, Josette watched as Mr. Hubbard removed his wide-brimmed hat—more appropriate for a cowboy than a writer—and placed it on the end of the writing desk. He opened his canvas satchel and retrieved several loose papers. Settling back, he lifted a copy of the *Cunard Daily Bulletin*, the little newspaper that relayed information about everything from the day's planned events, to stories about the most important passengers, to the latest happenings at the Front.

"Excuse me, Mr. Hubbard," Josette called, unable to resist the urge to converse with the man. "I'm Josette Rogers. I understand you're a writer."

He looked up with a casual smile. "I am, among other things. And you? You seem to be doing some writing of your own."

"Yes. Well, not exactly. I'm recording my thoughts about the trip for a school paper."

"I see. A college girl. Very good! I should introduce you to my wife. She's a very progressive woman. And how is it that you're here on the *Lusitania*?" he asked.

"We're moving to England for my father's import/export business."

The man's smile faded. "Import/export? I do hope he's not one of those rich Americans making a fortune by shipping bullets and bombs to help with this heinous war."

Josette straightened, feeling very uncomfortable. "Why, no. He's planning to have things like cotton and buttons shipped to the Allied forces to be made into uniforms. Food items, too. Oh, and he's British, by the way." She didn't mean to sound so defensive.

Mr. Hubbard rose and stepped toward her. "Does your father realize how dire things are for everyone – French, British, as well as the Germans and Austrians? They all need supplies."

"I'm quite sure he keeps up on the latest reports, Mr. Hubbard."

"According to today's *Cunard Bulletin*, things are improving for the Allied troops. But it's an out and out lie." Intensity grew in his eyes. "I have my own sources keeping me informed, you see. Thank goodness for Marconigrams. Naturally, they have to be worded carefully. Encoded messages, you see." His lips curled into a smile. "That way, the information isn't shared with the wireless operators."

"I don't understand, Mr. Hubbard. Why in the world would Cunard print lies?"

He chuckled as he shook his head. "To keep us all happy and free from worry. You see, we are likely a ship of fools, young lady."

"But the captain assured us that the *Lusitania* can outrun a torpedo. She's the fastest ship in the world, correct? That's how she earned her name, 'Greyhound of the Sea.'"

"That's a bucket full of...well, let's just say if a German submarine fires a torpedo at this ship, we'll likely be in trouble." Mr. Hubbard leaned closer. "Ask one of the officers why the speed has been reduced."

She felt her heart pounding. Curtis had made her feel better about the German threat. And now this. "Why would the captain do that? It doesn't make any sense at all."

"The captain spouts things like having to save coal for the military ships. Such utter nonsense. Believe me, my girl. Just keep your life vest handy and your eyes on the water. Heed my words. The closer we get to Britain, the more danger we'll be in." He leaned on the edge of her desk. "War is a terrible thing, you see. For all concerned. I plan to publish the story of everyone's plight, including that of the German people. We are all human beings. We must all take responsibility for this war, including we Americans, since it's the Americans who are supplying the Allies with bullets and bombs to kill German soldiers. There will be no winners, no matter what happens. It's a terrible loss on all accounts."

"Here you are, Josette!" Curtis said, approaching. "And I see you've met Mr. Hubbard."

She looked up at Curtis, feeling a huge sense of relief.

"You've forgotten. It's time for our walk," Curtis said, tucking his satchel of work behind his back. "If you'll excuse us, Mr. Hubbard."

"Of course, Carlson. Miss Rogers," the writer said. He turned and walked back to his chair.

"But Curtis," she said softly. "Aren't we going to work?"

He shook his head and motioned to the door.

Understanding that he wanted to leave, Josette scooted the chair backwards and picked up her notebook and pen. Rising, Curtis put his hand on her shoulder and guided her toward the entrance.

Mr. Hubbard added in a loud voice, "Stay diligent, young lady. Stay diligent."

Chapter 29

"JUST IGNORE HIM," Curtis cautioned, leading Josette onto the deck. "Hubbard may be a brilliant man, but he has no right to cause you to worry."

Finding a pair of vacant deck chairs, Josette placed her things on the small table between them. "Mr. Hubbard said the war isn't going well for the Allies, Curtis. Do you think it's true? Apparently, the ship's daily paper said things have improved for the Allies at the Western Front."

Sitting in the deck chair beside her, Curtis swung his feet up and leaned back. He turned his head to make sure no one was close enough to hear. Then he faced her. "Please listen to me, Josette. Don't pay attention to Mr. Hubbard or anyone else. Believe me.

Everything will work out. Even if the troops are losing ground at the moment, things will soon get better. The soldiers have been running out of ammunition, and that will change shortly. They will receive new shipments. Large shipments. And that will make a tremendous difference."

Her eyes narrowed, Josette tilted her head. "How is it you know about these things?"

"Sorry, Josie. I can't say. I can only assure you that once Van Camp and I finish our business in London, things are going to improve."

Lifting her skirt a little, she moved her feet up onto the chair and rested against the back. "Well, then, let me ask you about something else Mr. Hubbard said. He believes the *Lusitania cannot* outrun a German submarine. He believes the ship is moving slower than it should be. Have you heard any such reports?"

"Yes, as a matter of fact I have, though it's hardly a secret now. The matter came up a couple of nights ago among some of the gents who had a gambling pool running. They have been betting on the distance the ship would travel the following day. By Tuesday, it was obvious the *Lusitania* wasn't traveling at full speed, which should have been something around twenty-five knots, if memory serves. But she's only moving at around twenty-one knots."

"Did they confront Captain Turner about it?"

"I don't think so. But I hope the captain listened to what Van Camp and I had to say. We're hoping he'll send a Marconigram to the Admiralty and get permission to get back up to speed. Time will tell."

"Quite frankly, I've lost my confidence in the captain," Josette grumbled. "He makes promises, but nothing seems to change. I wonder if he has any intention of contacting the Cunard offices or anyone else about our demands."

THE SUN'S warming rays and the ship's gentle rolling motion made it difficult for Josette to focus on her work. She rested her notebook on her stomach, still holding the pencil.

"How is your composition paper coming along?" Curtis asked.

"Hmm?" Josette sat up. "Oh, sorry. I suppose I haven't written as much as I had hoped. How about you? Are you making progress on your book?"

"Yep. I've written another chapter. I find I can concentrate when—"

A small black rubber ball bounced, then rolled in their direction. A freckle-faced, curly-haired boy wearing a miniature sailor's uniform chased it. He looked to be around eight or nine.

Curtis reached out to stop the ball from rolling under his deck chair. "Is this yours?"

The lad nodded.

"What's your name, son?" Curtis asked.

"George." He stepped closer, standing with a straight back, like a tiny soldier called to attention. "George Updike Taylor the Third, sir!"

Curtis glanced at Josette and chuckled. "That's quite a mouthful, Mr. George Updike something or other the third. Uh, sorry, kid, I forget the rest."

"Taylor," Josette added with a laugh.

"Go back a little and I'll throw the ball to you," Curtis instructed.

With a smile, the boy turned and ran about five feet away. Pivoting to face Curtis, getting into position, he held out his arms, spread his legs wide to counter the ship's rolling motion, and prepared to catch it.

As Curtis took aim, a woman's voice called, "Georgie! Get back here!"

"Rats!" The boy said with a groan. "That's Nanny Louise." He twisted around and shouted, "Just a minute!" Then he turned to face Curtis and held out his hands. "Ready, sir."

"Here you go!" Curtis lobbed the ball at the child, who caught it, spot on. "Excellent, Georgie!"

The boy grinned. "Thanks, mister." Then he scampered towards the area where other children were playing games.

Curtis moved his gaze to Josette. "Come on. What do you say? Let's go see the kids."

"But what about our writing? Perhaps Mr. Hubbard has left the library by now."

"Look, Josie. We're nearing the end of our trip. Let's enjoy ourselves and have a few laughs," Curtis said, climbing out of the deck chair.

Josette thought for a moment, only a moment and grinned. "You're right. We've earned a day off." She pulled her legs over the edge of the chair. "I must say, you never struck me as the type who would want to play with children."

He looked puzzled by her comment. "Really? I have a ten-year-old cousin. We play catch whenever I see him." He paused for a moment, as if to think about the boy. "I need to spend more time with Wil."

"You are certainly filled with surprises," she said.

Chapter 30

May 6, 1915

FOR DAYS, Josette had heard passengers discussing the fact that the ocean liner was steaming ever closer to what everyone called "the danger zone." And now, it was Thursday night and the *Lusitania* neared the south coast of Ireland where, rumor had it, merchant ships had been torpedoed and sunk.

Although Friday would be another full day at sea, this was the last formal dinner. Considering the widespread nervousness among the passengers that had been exacerbated by the captain's order to lower and uncover the lifeboats that morning, Josette presumed many people would order dinner in their cabins.

She was wrong. The dining room buzzed with life, with chatter, with laughter. Spirits seemed to be surprisingly high, considering the possibility that a torpedo could strike the ship at any moment. Champagne flowed, caviar and hors d'oeuvres were served, and dinner was nothing less than fabulous.

At lunch, Curtis had announced that he and Mr. Van Camp would be joining Mrs. Donaldson and the Rogers family at dinner tonight. The captain had finally requested Curtis and Mr. Van Camp vacate the head table so other privileged passengers could take their turn in the rotation. That pleased Curtis, but he said Van Camp had fumed. And since Mr. Van Camp always ate breakfast and lunch at the Verandah Café or in his cabin, this was the first time they would all have to converse directly with the unpleasant man.

Curtis had promised Josette he would do his best to buffer any rude statements his 'Uncle Phineas' might make that evening.

Josette hoped that Mr. Duns would be kept in Mrs. Donaldson's cabin tonight. Otherwise, most likely Mr. Van Camp would have a great deal to say about sharing a table with a canine. And yet, when Josette and Yvette entered the dining room, they saw the Westie sitting proudly in the seat next to his owner, wearing his dog-sized plaid jacket and miniature bowtie.

Arriving a few minutes late, Curtis and Van Camp took their seats at the Rogers' table. By the disgruntled look on Van Camp's face, Josette knew things were about to turn sour.

"Madam," he said, his stern glare set hard on Mrs. Donaldson. "You do know you are the only person in this entire dining hall with a dog at the table."

"I paid for a seat for my Dunsy. Is that bothersome for you?" she snipped back.

"It's simply not appropriate, Mrs. Donaldson. Dogs are filthy creatures." He sat back in his chair, moving his gaze around, as if to seek the agreement of each of the Rogers' family.

"Mr. Duns has far better manners than some humans, I'd say," Josette commented.

"Good God," he grumbled with an angry glare. "They belong in a kennel or, at best, locked up in one's stateroom. Wouldn't you say so, Mr. Rogers?" he said, his eyes flashing at Father.

"No. I don't agree, old chap. Dunsy is a delightful pup and quite well mannered. He'll not be a problem, I can assure you."

Mr. Van Camp's jaw hardened. He crossed his arms, leaning back in his seat. "It should be outlawed," he groused.

Clearing his throat, Curtis changed the topic. "I'm sure we'll all be glad to be on dry land on Saturday...though I'll certainly miss the fine food on this ship."

"Me, too," Yvette agreed. "And the good company. For the most part." A smile nudged at the corners of her lips. She quickly covered her mouth with her hand, glancing at Josette.

Josette could barely contain herself. She fought a grin, then asked Mr. Van Camp, "Were you and Mr. Carlson able to take care of your business issues earlier today?"

"Yes, miss. We did," Van Camp said. He unfolded his arms and picked up a menu.

"We had some paperwork to go over before we arrive in London. Last minute ideas, you see," Curtis said, as if to enhance the explanation.

"And what type of business are you in, sir?" Father asked, picking up his goblet of water.

Mr. Van Camp seemed uncomfortable with the question, squirming, rearranging himself in his chair. "Financial matters," he said. "Investments and banking."

"Were you acquainted with my husband? Or, perhaps with Mr. Carnegie?" Mrs. Donaldson asked.

"Not directly, madam." Van Camp didn't make eye contact.

Knowing that Mr. Carnegie and the senior Mr. Morgan had been sworn enemies, Curtis was relieved Van Camp didn't speak about his affiliation with the House of Morgan. He changed the subject. "My uncle has many investments. With my background in economics, I have been one of his advisors."

"And what do you think of the war, Mr. Van Camp?" Father asked. "As an American, do you agree with President Wilson's stance on neutrality, or do you support the Allied efforts to defeat the Germans and Austrians?"

"Why don't we save the military conversations for the Smoking Room, Mr. Rogers," Curtis said. "I'm sure some of the ladies don't want to hear a debate about such an upsetting topic." He turned to Josette with a tiny wink, knowing she would have been happy to participate in a political discussion.

"Yes, please," Yvette said. "It's all quite disturbing. Can we please eat in peace?"

DINNER SEEMED to go on forever, so when the gong was sounded, and they headed upstairs for the nine o'clock performances in the Lounge and Music Room, Josette was quite relieved. Settling on a small couch near the front of the room, she was wedged between Curtis and Yvette.

At that moment, the War Zone seemed as far away as Neverland. The music, the laughter seemed to have calmed most everyone's nerves. Numerous passengers performed, including a quartet of handsome young Canadian men heading to London to sign up for the military. Accompanied by the band as they sang *Moonlight Bay, In the Good Old Summer Time,* and *Shine on Harvest Moon,* the audience – young and old – joined in the singing.

At last it was Yvette's turn to perform. If the four Canadians had impressed with their singing, Yvette's rendition of *Till the Boys Come Home* would truly light up the room. It was an important song that supported the Allied war effort. The lyrics and rhythmic music would, at the least, make even the sullen Mr. Van Camp tap his feet.

Yvette lovingly placed her fingers on the Broadwood's ivory keyboard and played the opening chords.

Without warning, Captain Turner and First Staff Captain Anderson, dressed in their finest white uniforms and looking quite regal, entered the room, followed by several other officers. Yvette played on, oblivious to the unexpected visit by the Cunard's officers, until one of them walked to her and tapped her shoulder. Startled, she stopped and looked up at the young man. He bent and whispered to her, turned and, stiff-backed, walked to First Staff Captain Anderson's side.

Raising his hand, Captain Turner scanned the room in a silent demand for everyone's attention. Yvette swiveled around to view the captain. She positioned her hands in her lap. The waiters paused in place. And the room fell into a strange silence.

"Ladies and gentlemen," Staff Captain Anderson said. "We apologize for interrupting your evening of merriment. The captain has received a wire from the British Admiralty." He shifted his weight from his left foot to his right, as he drew in an audible breath. "The Admiralty reports there is increased submarine activity off the coast of Ireland," he said haltingly.

There was a collective gasp. Unintelligible chatter erupted throughout the room.

Josette and Curtis exchanged a glance. He took her hand and squeezed it, as if to reassure her that she would be safe with him.

"Now, now, folks," Captain Turner said, stepping forward. "Settle down."

A heavy-set, red-faced man rose suddenly and hollered, "Are you saying a German U-boat has been sighted?"

"No, sir. The *Lusitania* crew hasn't seen a submarine," Staff Captain Anderson explained.

"How close are we to the place where the submarines were seen?" Mr. Van Camp asked without rising from his chair. His voice betrayed his fear.

"Please remain calm," Anderson instructed. "Everything is under control. We are taking the necessary safety precautions."

"Such as?" Mr. Van Camp asked loudly.

"Well, sir, there are many things we can all do to ensure this ship cannot be seen by the enemy. Firstly, we have asked our stewards to close all draperies. Please do not open them in your own quarters, nor in other rooms under any circumstance. Portholes must remain closed at all times." He shifted his weight again, a sign of nervousness to be sure. "Secondly, we have turned off all deck lights, so please mind your step when returning to your cabins. Thirdly, we ask you gents not to smoke outside tonight or tomorrow night. Even striking a single match could give our position away to a lurking submarine."

Four waiters entered at that point, moving around the room's windows to pull the heavy draperies closed. No one spoke. It seemed everyone was mesmerized as they watched the Music Room, a joyful respite from the reality that waited somewhere under the sea, be changed into a sheltered place where they hid from the view of the enemy U-boats.

Curtis leaned over, smiling gently at Josette and her sister, "Don't worry. We'll be okay."

"In addition, we are taking many precautions," the Staff Captain went on. "Since receiving the wire, the captain doubled the number of men on watch, straight away."

"Why, then, are you not increasing speed?" someone yelled. "Many of us have discussed the fact that you have slowed this vessel, and that one of the boilers has been shut down. I direct the question to the captain."

Other men in the room rose, mumbling their agreement.

Captain Turner spoke up. "Please, gentlemen. Please. We're still moving faster than any submarine can travel, despite our coal-saving measures – as ordered by the Admiralty. At my insistence, I have received permission from Cunard to increase speed as we pass by harbors and inlets. Those are the most common places for submarines to lie in wait. I assure you, we will keep you all safe and sound."

"Horse feathers!" Father roared. "And if anything happens to this ship, you'll have the governments of the Allies *and* the United States on Cunard's backside."

Captain Turner didn't respond to Father's remarks. "Let me remind you all. The crew will pick up most of the luggage from the passengers' staterooms after tomorrow night's dinner and ready it for off-loading once we're in Liverpool. You are advised to retire early tomorrow night so you may rise at dawn, dress, and have a light breakfast before disembarking. The last-minute, smaller pieces of luggage are to be placed outside stateroom doors by six a.m. Saturday morning.

"Sandwiches and light snacks will be served for dinner Friday night, so please eat a hearty lunch," Staff Captain Anderson added.

AFTER THE captain and his officers had gone, the disheartened audience began to disperse, leaving poor Yvette sitting at the piano wearing a bewildered look. Josette knew her sister didn't know whether she should resume playing.

Josette glanced around the room. She could tell by everyone's stunned expressions, their spirits were low. She looked at Yvette. "Play the new song," she called out.

Yvette understood. She spun around and began to pound the keys. Enthusiastically.

"Come on, my friends!" Josette shouted. "Join in!" She clapped to the music.

Smiling, glancing at Josette, Curtis did, too.

One by one, people who had been walking toward the exit turned around to face Yvette and began to sing along. "*It's a long way to Tipperary. It's a long way to go!*"

"It's one of the songs written for the war effort," Josette said loudly. "A good way to get spirits up."

Curtis grinned and nodded.

Looking around the room brought a smile to Josette. She was proud of her sister; happy that in some small way Yvette had been able to lighten the mood, if even for a short time.

And when Yvette began to play the song for a second time, Curtis said to Josette, "Follow me. I have something I want to talk to you about."

THE DECK was dark. The exterior wall lanterns had been turned off. Even the ever-present running lights – red port and green starboard – had been extinguished.

"This whole situation…being on the *Lusitania* surrounded by the nothingness and the immenseness of the sea. It, it feels so strange," Josette said. They walked slowly, side-by-side. "It makes one feel so helpless." She stepped to the railing and gazed out at the inky water. "Do you think they're out there?"

"German submarines?" Curtis expelled a sigh. "I imagine they are. But, again, they would have no reason to attack a passenger ship. Please don't worry, Josie. I won't let anything happen to you." His voice took on an air of thoughtful assurance.

"I've always believed God created this wonderful universe, but now I don't know. If there is a God, why does he allow all of this killing; all of this evil?" Josette said, not really expecting an answer.

"That's one of life's great mysteries," he said. "One that people have contemplated for centuries. I certainly don't have the answer, but I do know this. Our paths have crossed for a reason. I'm not a religious man, but I'm sure we were meant to meet. Was that some sort of divine plan?" He lifted his shoulders in a shrug. "All I know is I'm sure that no matter what happens, we'll be together one day."

She fought back tears. "Is this what you've been trying to tell me for the past few days?"

"Frankly, there are quite a few things I need to tell you, Josie." He took her hand and drew her closer. "First of all, I care deeply for you. And I promise to come to England as often as I can to see you."

Josette laughed nervously. Could he hear her heart pounding in her chest? "I care about you, too, Curtis." She moved her gaze to the deck. "I don't know how you'll manage to make very many trips to England when there seems to be so much danger on the crossings, but I hope you can find a way." She looked up at him.

"Don't worry. I already have a plan." He gave her hand a squeeze. "I'll request a transfer or, at the very least, to shuttle information between my employer's New York and London offices."

"Wait, Curtis. I thought your employer was Harvard University."

"That's what I've been trying to tell you. I'm no longer a college professor. I'm traveling to London on official, very important business.

Chapter 31

FRIDAY MORNING, Josette met Curtis for a bite of breakfast at the less formal, open-air café, where they could have more privacy and talk about matters Mother wouldn't approve of. In the days they had spent together on the ship, they had become quite close. Josette found herself wishing they would never reach England; that they could sail on forever to some magical place where there was no war, no fear; nothing but joy and peace of mind.

Though Curtis hadn't provided her with the exact details of the business affairs he and Mr. Van Camp would conduct in London, she knew it had something to do with a large loan they were dealing with. He wouldn't...couldn't say more.

Most surprising was his admission that he worked for J. P. Morgan, Junior, at the House of Morgan as some sort of investment banker. Curtis had promised to provide her with more details when he could. But for now, the fact he and Mr. Van Camp were on some sort of covert government project that would affect the outcome of the war, and that he had serious feelings about her gave Josette all the information she needed. And she was delighted. If only she could tell her father about Curtis' true employment. He would most certainly be impressed.

Even though this was their final day at sea – and likely, the last time they would see each other for quite some time – Josette and Curtis kept their conversation in the Verandah Café light. They talked about their lives, from their earliest memories until now. Likes and dislikes. They didn't speak about the war, politics or any sort of danger they might be in.

Josette dreaded tomorrow morning when they would have to part for the last time. She would do her best to maintain her decorum, but she had never felt this way about any young man.

At noon, Josette was back in her stateroom changing into her pale blue tea gown. The sun had finally made its appearance, chasing away the fog and dampness with its warming rays. And Ireland could be seen in the distance, still a small, dark outline on the edge of the sea.

Yvette entered, giddier than she had been since the voyage began. "Hello, sister!" she said, closing the door. "You'll never guess what?" She skittered towards Josette.

"What's happened?" Josette asked. "You must have had good news."

"Yes! Indeed! I've just come from having tea with Mr. Frohman. He received a wire from his business manager in London, and both Jon and I are guaranteed employment playing for his theatrical productions." Yvette picked up their silver-trimmed comb. "You see, this means Jon can come to England as soon as possible."

"That's wonderful, sister. Simply wonderful." Sitting at the dressing table, Josette turned back to the mirror, inserting a final hairpin to secure a curl. "Now, my dear, all you must do is break the news to Father and Mother."

"AND WHERE ARE our two tablemates?" Father asked. Unfurling his napkin, he spread it on his lap. "Will they be joining us for luncheon?"

"Curtis and Mr. Van Camp are having a quick bite in the Verandah Café," Josette said. "Curtis said they would join us for dinner tonight."

"Frankly," Mother said, "I'm rather relieved we won't be seeing that unpleasant Mr. Van Camp for a while."

"He is a rather ill-tempered bloke," Father commented, cutting a bite from his slice of roast beef. "Mr. Carlson, on the other hand... well, he seems a pleasant chap." He paused before putting the bite into his mouth and looked directly at Josette. "It would seem you have grown quite fond of him, my girl."

"Aye. That it would," Mrs. Donaldson said with a pleasant chuckle before Josette could answer. "You've spent a goodly amount of time with the lad, I must say." The elderly woman winked at Josette...which surprised her. But, then, that was Mrs. Donaldson. Feisty and full of life for a woman her age. "Of course, my Dunsy is quite happy you and Mr. Carlson have taken such a liking to him." Frail, thin fingers with red polished nails stroked Mr. Duns' fuzzy back. He rested contentedly in her lap, his large brown eyes blinking up lovingly at his owner.

Josette leaned over and stroked the Westie. "As a matter of fact, Curtis and I...we thought Mr. Duns would appreciate one last visit to the doggie poop deck, as Father has so appropriately named the cordoned off space. All right?" She directed her question to Mr. Duns.

"I must say, Josette Marie, we have seen far less of you on this voyage than Mr. Carlson or this dog has." Mother's tone was curt. "So you do have a girlish affection for him, do you not?"

Josette folded her napkin. "Who? The dog or Curtis?"

"You know very well what I'm talking about, young lady," Mother said, clucking her tongue.

"Don't worry, Millie. It's nothing more than a shipboard romance," Father said. "Quite common, and rightly so. I remember well when I was a lad..." His mind seemed to momentarily drift off. "Well, never mind that, my dear. It meant nothing."

Mother glanced at him with an unhappy frown.

Father added, "They never seem to last. Once one's feet are on dry land...it's over straight away. It's the romance of the sea, from what they say."

"This is not a shipboard romance," Josette protested. "I believe it's...more."

Yvette wore a mischievous expression. "It was fate that brought you together."

"Fate or not, the lad seems like a good catch," Mrs. Donaldson said in a pleasant tone.

Josette didn't know what to say.

"In my opinion, Curtis has a good job and a fine future, too," Yvette commented without looking up from her fruit plate.

Josette nudged Yvette's foot with hers and shot her sister a decisive 'stop-it' glare when she glanced up.

"A fine job, you say? As a teacher?" Father said with a smirk. "College professors don't make a large salary, luv. You best continue searching for a husband who can provide for you."

Expelling a sigh, Josette sat up, placed her elbow on the table and plunked her chin on her bent hand. It was all she could do to keep Curtis' secret. But she couldn't.

"Teaching at Harvard is a noble profession," Yvette said softly. Setting her knife and fork down, she lifted her gaze. "He's also an author. From what Josette tells me, his master's thesis was so exceptional, it is soon to be published. Right, sister?" Yvette turned to Josette, as if for protection from any negative response to her comments from their parents.

"Yes, that's correct. He has a second book in the works, as well." Josette was suddenly unable to hold back her enthusiasm. "Curtis has studied the Panic of 1907. He's done a great deal of analysis that even President Wilson will be interested in."

Father sat back thoughtfully, fingering the edges of his mustache. "Well, then. Splendid. The chap might become involved in politics one day. Perhaps, as an economist for the president or some large banking firm."

Fighting a smile, Josette stood, tossing her napkin on the table. Leaning over to pat the dog on his head, she said, "We'll be out on the Boat Deck if you need Mr. Duns or me."

As she stepped back, a waiter approached with her white woolen coat that had been hung on a nearby rack. With the waiter's assistance, Josette slid her arms into the coat. Thanking him, she tied it closed with the narrow sash.

"It's still quite chilly outside, Josette," Mother said brusquely. "Where are your gloves?"

Josette hadn't told her mother they had blown overboard. She opened her mouth to speak when Yvette came to her aide.

"Don't trouble yourself making a special trip to our cabin to fetch your gloves, sister. You may wear mine. I won't be needing them for a while." Yvette handed Josette her new monogramed pair. "They're the ones I purchased at Macy's."

Josette gave Yvette a grateful smile. "I'll take good care of them."

Yvette nodded, returning Josette's smile. Then she turned to their parents. "If you will all excuse me, I, too, have a few things to take care of," she said, carefully folding her starched napkin along its creases and replacing it on the table. "I have a wire to send to a friend."

"Don't be long. You girls must get cracking. The cabin boys will be picking up your trunks in a few hours."

"Of course, Father," Josette and Yvette said in near unison.

Josette turned to Mr. Duns, still perched on the Scottish woman's lap. The dog had stretched his head over to sniff Josette's abandoned bowl of chicken soup. "Ready, Dunsy?" When he heard his name, his ears lifted, his shaggy tail wagging.

"That he is, lassie. I'm certain he'd love a breath of fresh air." She glanced over at their mother. "It's become a wee bit stuffy in here."

Josette fought back a laugh, wriggling her fingers into Yvette's gloves.

By the time she attached the dog's leash to his collar, her sister was gone. Josette smiled and said, "Please excuse me. I shall see you all later."

Father looked up from his bowl of chocolate pudding. "Yes, luv. We shall see you soon."

JOSETTE GUIDED Mr. Duns up the stairs to the Boat Deck's starboard side, forward to the place where the passengers' dogs wandered free in a small fenced-off area. The Westie was always thrilled to be outside, pulling her forward faster than she could walk.

"Whoa, boy!" she said with a laugh. Ignoring her command, he lifted his head, sniffing the cool wind that ruffled his fur. Josette detached his leash, and he pranced into the enclosure. Two other dogs – a large shaggy gray one, and a tiny, white Pomeranian – were already scouting around the pen, sniffing, peeing, wagging their tails. By now, they had all become friends.

Josette stood nearby, chatting with the woman who owned the Pomeranian, Mrs. Michael O'Reilly. She said she was traveling in second class with her husband and daughter...and little Sassy, a fluff of white fur who looked more like a hand muff than a dog. Mrs. O'Reilly had to come up to the first-class promenade to let her dog do its business.

"Have you looked out upon Ireland yet?" she asked, her brogue so thick she was a little hard to understand.

"Oh, yes. We were on the port side for a few minutes. It's a splendid site."

"'Tis a fine comfort to be back home, it 'tis. We'll be back in Kilkenny in a few days. Such a shame the captain cannot simply let us off in Queenstown," she said with a hearty chuckle and a shake of her head. "We could take the train home from there." The pretty woman had a flawless complexion and the rosiest cheeks. Her auburn curls peeked out from under her snuggly tied hat, framing her round face.

"I hope to spend some time in Ireland before returning to New York."

"You're but a visitor in Great Britain, are you now?" Mrs. O'Reilly asked rhetorically. "How long will you be stayin'?"

Before Josette responded, she spotted Curtis heading her way. "If you'll please excuse me," Josette said to the Irish woman.

Mrs. O'Reilly chuckled. "Don't be giving it another thought, Miss. I'll keep an eye on your pup for you."

Thanking the woman, Josette hurried to meet Curtis. He wore a warm coat over his brown tweed suit and vest, and a coordinated wool cap covered his wavy hair. "Hello!" she called, weaving around a strolling couple. She smiled, thinking he looked even more handsome than usual.

"Here you are," he said with a big grin. "I passed Mrs. Donaldson on her way to her stateroom." He stopped, then chuckled. "She said she left the dining room because your father was having a heated discussion with an officer about the military vessels that are supposed to escort the *Lusitania* through the War Zone today."

Josette stood in front of Curtis, letting out a laugh. "Well, I'm not surprised. Father was quite upset that the naval ships were nowhere to be seen this morning."

"Mrs. Donaldson said he's going to organize a group of gents to pay another call on Captain Turner to complain," Curtis said. "It is quite odd this so-called armada isn't already here. Mr. Van Camp is quite upset, too."

"Should we join in the protest, Curtis, or—"

"Let's leave that up to someone else this time. We've spent too much time with the captain on the Bridge. I want to spend our last day together...alone. Well," he snickered, "As alone as possible on a ship with two thousand people!"

Josette smiled. "Me, too."

Curtis' gaze moved to the dog pen near the front of the deck. "I see Mr. Duns is saying his farewells to his new-found buddies."

"I wanted to spend some time with *wee* Dunsy. I hate to say goodbye to him. I have grown quite fond of the pup, you know."

"Me, too." Curtis turned to her. "Say. I have an idea. What if we head up to Scotland on one of my visits to England. We'll go see Mrs. Donaldson and Dunsy."

Josette was surprised by his suggestion. "Take a trip together? Father would have you hunted down and shot!" she said with an embarrassed giggle. Even the thought of traveling with him all the way to Scotland – without a chaperone – brought a surge of heat to her cheeks. "Why, Mr. Carlson, I'm a lady. There will be no trips taken with you."

Staring into her eyes, he smiled gently. "Perhaps you'll change your mind one day. He took her hand and stepped closer, his eyes filled with a warmness that bored clear to her soul. "You see," he said, looking more like a school boy than a grown man. "I think I'm falling in love with you."

It felt as if a thousand butterflies fluttered in her stomach. She stood silent, her mouth agape, trying to find the right words to say. "I...I—" She could barely breathe. "We've only known each other for six days."

"Six terrific days of getting to know you. The real you. And I like everything about you. Even that stubborn streak that makes you so determined to change the world. Especially that," he said with a little laugh.

She looked at him with a teasing smile. "Even though I caused a near riot during your debate at Columbia? And even though you had to bail me out of jail and I was almost arrested? Would you have liked me if I had a police record?" Josette joked.

"Yep. Especially then. I love that you have so much spunk. That you stand up for your beliefs...even if they're wrong."

"Wrong?" She drew back, lifting her eyebrows to pretend she was shocked. "I wasn't wrong, Mr. Carlson!"

"That remains to be seen, Miss Rogers. Nevertheless, I think I fell under your spell when I saw you take a swing at that lad who was harassing you."

Josette laughed. "Truly?"

"Uh-huh." Curtis leaned in closer.

"Curtis! No! There are too many people who can see us!"

"I don't care. This may be our last chance."

Her heart pounding, Josette raised on her toes and closed her eyes. At the very moment their lips touched, a man screamed from somewhere overhead.

"Torpedo! Starboard side!"

Instantly breaking their embrace, Josette opened her eyes. She and Curtis glanced at each other, then up to the Bridge wing. Seaman Morton hollered into a megaphone painted with Cunard's gold logo. "Torpedo coming this way!"

Chapter 32

"MY GOD," Josette gasped. "They did it! They really did it!"

Seaman Morton glanced down at her and Curtis with a terrified expression. "Run for it!" He dropped the megaphone and disappeared inside the Bridge doorway.

Without a word, Curtis grabbed her arm. Together, they sprinted aft, in the direction of the stairwell. The thunderous sound of shattering metal followed a loud *thud*. An instant later, an explosion emanated from the heart of the liner, violently shaking the deck beneath their feet.

"This can't be happening!" Her knees went weak, buckling beneath her. She grabbed the handrail on the bulkhead wall. Screams and shouts came from everywhere. Footsteps pounded on the deck.

"The dogs!" Josette turned around just in time to see a terrified-looking Mrs. O'Reilly, the three dogs, and several other passengers running in their direction. A thick column of water and steam spewed up from the area where the torpedo struck. Everything – the forward deck, the passengers, the dogs – were wet from the heavy spray and shaft of steam that had blown over the front section of the ship.

"Get your vests on!" a terrified Mrs. O'Reilly yelled, as she bolted past, heading for the stairwell. "We're all doomed!"

"Wait!" Curtis yelled. "Are you all right?"

Mrs. O'Reilly didn't answer, didn't look back, and disappeared around the end of the bulkhead. Little Sassy followed her owner, her leash dragging behind her.

As Mr. Duns sprinted past, Curtis tried to grab him. Panicked, the Westie wasn't having any of it. He zipped through Curtis' grip and kept running.

"We need to go after poor Dunsy," Josette yelled, feeling the urge to cry.

"No. We can't. We need to get our life jackets."

"No! I have to save him." She stepped out to run.

He grabbed her arm. "Wait, Josie. Go get your life jacket. My room is near Mrs. Donaldson's. I'll check to make sure the dog—"

A deafening sound, an explosion far greater than the first one, shook the ship with such force that both Curtis and Josette were knocked to the deck. The ship shuddered, its bow lifting, then dropping hard. Horrible sounds – things crashing, breaking glass, shattering windows – could all be heard over the screams. The *Lusitania* rolled from side to side, finally settling itself.

Her ears ringing, Josette raised her head and glanced in the direction of the blast. The plume of steam was laced with fiery orange and black fragments, rising hundreds of feet into the air. Josette gasped, covering her mouth with her gloved hands. It looked like a volcanic eruption.

Strangely, the wreckage which had shot skyward seemed to hover in the air. As the ocean liner continued to move forward, burning chunks of debris began to rain down – wood shards, pieces of metal, and bits of glowing black matter – bounced and plinked as it hit the smokestacks, the Bridge, and the deck close to them.

"Get down!" Curtis said, pushing her to the deck and closer to the bulkhead wall. He laid on Josette to shield her, yanked at his coat, and pulled it up to cover the back of their heads. "Don't move," he whispered in her ear.

Josette laid face down, her cheek against the deck. Trembling, she closed her eyes. Where was her sister? Her parents? Though Curtis had braced himself to keep from having his entire body weight on her, she could feel his rapid breathing, his heart pounding in his chest. And it was hard for her to breathe.

After what seemed like an eternity, he raised his head and looked around. "It's stopped." He rolled off her. "Are you okay?" he asked.

She wasn't. Not really. But she nodded 'yes,' moving into a sitting position.

Curtis scrambled to his feet, removed his coat, blackened with dust and ash, and tossed it to the deck.

Josette was shaking. She tried to stand, but her knees felt like melted butter. Curtis helped her to her feet. The air smelled of smoke, of coal, and pungent oils. "Was that another torpedo?" she managed.

"I'm not sure. It could have been a boiler exploding inside the ship." He turned to look at the billowing smoke coming from a large gaping hole where the deck had been. "We've got to get out of here." He moved his gaze back to her. She could tell that he was as frightened as she was. "Christ, Josie. The ship is already listing. That means she's filling with water."

The *Lusitania* suddenly dropped several degrees on the right side and towards the front, like a table losing one leg. Curtis grasped her arm, his legs spread apart to steady himself.

A Cunard officer ran by. "Go back to your rooms and get into your flotation devices," he shouted.

"Stupid bastards!" Curtis muttered with an angry glare. "There's no time for that. They've got to get everyone off this ship or they'll have another *Titanic* on their hands."

"But our life jackets," she protested.

"Listen to me. The ship is already on fire." Curtis locked his eyes on hers. "We've got to get out of here." He craned his neck, looking around. "We have to head further aft."

She nodded her agreement, glancing at the damaged forward lifeboats. One of them had been completely blown off, together with a large chunk of the deck. A strange numbness crept up her spine, as the reality of what was happening swept over her. "You're right. Go aft."

Holding her hand, Curtis guided her through the onslaught of humanity. Frantic passengers flooded from the stairwell, pushing, pushing in their fight to escape the sinking vessel. They gathered in desperate clumps around the boat stations, waiting for the order to board. Room stewards, bellboys, a cook wearing a soiled white apron smeared with gravy from the luncheon meal – so many of the crew who had no idea how to conduct an evacuation – wrestled with chains and ropes to free the lifesaving crafts from their confinements.

With a sudden jolt, the wounded ship dropped several more degrees to the starboard side. Screams rang out as passengers lost their footing. Growing hysterical, people from both first- and second-class could no longer wait for permission to board the lifeboats. They climbed up davit poles, even as others yanked them back down in an effort to get themselves, their children into the boats.

The *Lusitania* was already leaning precariously, causing the newly released starboard lifeboats to swing out several feet from the deck.

Like a swarm of ants, of mindless creatures fleeing probable death, men and even a few women climbed on the railing, securing themselves with a hand, a leg, which they wrapped around the metal davit arms. It was a losing battle. One by one, they lost their footing, toppling down the side of the *Lusitania*.

Josette screamed when she saw Mrs. O'Reilly make the climb. "No. Please don't," she yelled. But it was too late. The pretty Irish woman jumped for a lifeboat, a good three feet out from the side of the ship. She hung, bare feet dangling from beneath her skirt, clinging to the thick rope which was laced through eye bolts around the boat's perimeter.

Mrs. O'Reilly let out an agonizing shriek when she lost her grip and dropped into the icy sea. It was too much. Josette muffled a scream, pushing harder against Curtis.

Curtis gently urged Josette back and scanned her face. "Please, Josie. We need to go further aft," Curtis said with a tender expression. "Maybe it's better there."

Wiping her tears with her gloved hands, she nodded, sniffing several times.

Threading their way through the crowd, tears streaming down her cheeks, Josette managed to say, "That poor woman. I wonder where her daughter and husband are. And what about her sweet dog?"

Josette wasn't sure Curtis could hear her in that terrible cacophony of noise. "Everyone said the Germans wouldn't dare attack a passenger liner. I'll bet Father is really angry. He'll soon give the captain a piece of his mind. That's for sure!"

And then it occurred to her. Josette stopped. "Wait! Please. Curtis, I must go back. I must find my family."

"No!" Curtis ordered. "There's no time for that. We need to get you into a boat."

"But I have to help them. Yvette isn't capable—"

"Please listen to me. Judging by the rate the ship is filling with water, well, it's going down fast. I'm not going to let you drown, Josie."

"Don't worry about me, Curtis. I'm an excellent swimmer. But Mrs. Donaldson. She won't survive. Please. You must help her. I'll go find my parents and Yvette."

"I'm sure they're already in a lifeboat. There's no more time," he said in a heated tone.

The *Lusitania* dropped several more degrees. Twisting metal let out a groan that sounded like a wounded animal. Objects that hadn't been well-secured to the bulkhead or a wall or the floor, slid down the sloping deck, banging against the railing before falling overboard. Potted plants, deck chairs, pedestal ash trays, small outdoor tables – everything was in motion.

Dodging the obstacles, maneuvering around people who had fallen; rolling liquor bottles, shards of chinaware and glasses from the Verandah Café, Josette and Curtis pushed their way to the end of the Boat Deck, to the next-to-the last lifeboat on the starboard side.

When she saw how far it had swung away from the ship, Josette let out a loud gasp. It was at least a four-foot gap. Though the large lifesaving craft could hold around 60 people, it was only half-full. For most passengers, it would be nearly impossible to make that leap safely. The men and women who had hoped to board this, their last hope to escape, stood silent, watching helplessly.

Josette swallowed, her body trembling. She was physically stronger than most women, thanks to the hilly areas she had to climb on her bicycle to get to and from school. And yet....

"This is it, Josie," Curtis said, turning to look at her. "Let's get you on this one."

Before she could protest, she saw the young waiter who had helped her put on her coat after lunch standing at the rail. "Where is your life jacket, miss?" he asked her.

"There wasn't time."

"Then you must take mine," he said, untying the straps.

"No. Please. Keep it for yourself."

"I insist, miss. I'll get another from the crews' cabinet as soon as we get you launched."

Josette turned to Curtis. He nodded, thanking the young man as he accepted the life vest.

"Promise me you'll get yourself another one right away," Josette said to the lad.

"No worries, miss," the waiter said.

She smiled at him, sniffing. "Thank you," she said softly.

Curtis helped her into the bulky life vest, securing the ties. He glanced out at the craft, swaying as it dangled over the water. "Think you can make it?"

"My legs are quite strong." Her voice quivered, giving away her lack of confidence.

"That's my girl. Now you need to take off your shoes."

Nodding, she bent down, unlaced and removed each one and threw it aside. As she stood up, Curtis slid his hands around her waist. Josette paused, looking into his eyes. Would this be the last time she would see him? "You need a life jacket, too. Please, Curtis. I can't lose you."

He smiled. "You won't lose me." He leaned in and kissed Josette. She kissed him frantically, sliding her hands around his neck.

He pulled her back. "I love you, Josie. Now, go!" He turned her around, lifting her so her feet were on the railing and steadied her as she got her balance.

"I don't want to leave without you, Curtis." Her voice cracked into a whimper.

He smiled. "I'll see you soon. I promise I'll find you. Jump on the count of three."

She glanced at him over her shoulder. "I love you, too."

He grinned. "One...two...three!"

Drawing in a breath of courage, she jumped off with a thrust that sent her out several feet and in near perfect alignment with the lifeboat. She landed inside with a *thump* that sent a shock through her feet and rocked the craft violently. Thankfully, two men helped her, keeping the boat from tipping.

One of the men, still wearing his heavy woolen coat, maneuvered her into a space beside him. No words were spoken.

Looking up at Curtis, he shot her a wide smile and a nod, as if to say, 'That's my girl.' She smiled back and nodded. And then he was gone.

"Keep 'er steady," one of the sailors instructed. Josette glanced around, recognizing the faces of several of her new companions. Most were first-class passengers, though two men were obviously from the second-class section. The cellist from the ship's orchestra, still dressed in his tuxedo, gazed down with a blank stare. Seated beside him was one of the violinists, clutching a black case in which, presumably, he had saved his instrument. Ironic, she thought, he saved that, instead of a child. In fact, there were no other women and no children on the craft. If they had tried to make the leap, they weren't successful.

Above, a crewman on the deck shouted at the Cunarders who were operating the ropes attached to their lifeboat. "Ready gents! Lower away!" he shouted.

As the men cranked and the boat went down, the ship's top deck slowly disappeared. Though the *Lusitania* was low in the water, she rolled with the passing waves, causing the lifeboat to swing in towards the hull, and then out again. Upper portholes were closed. The lower ones had already disappeared underwater.

The chaos, the horrors of the life and death struggle for those left on the *Lusitania* was too much for Josette. She closed her eyes. Josette drew in deep breaths, an attempt to calm herself, and opened her eyes. Forcing herself to look up, she could see the crewman fighting the tension put on the ropes as the ship rocked.

The two rowers inside the lifeboat called up to the men working the ropes on the ship. "Take it down slow, lads. Keep 'er steady."

Josette looked down at the ocean's churning, debris laden surface. Scores of men, some still wearing their hats; women with as many coif styles as there were colors of hair; all bobbing on the swell of waves.

Why are they jumping? And then she saw chunks of floating lifeboats, apparently dashed into pieces when they swung back and hit the side of the ship. One had simply overturned. She watched as an almost empty one – halfway-down the side – swung out, then bashed back into the *Lusitania*. When the ship rolled, passengers were spilled into the sea.

"Oh, dear God," she said, her heart breaking at the sight.

As her boat jerked its way down the thick ropes, she glanced up and saw one of the first-class gentlemen, Mr. Thomas Kendall, had climbed up on the railing. He was rotund, easily well over two hundred fifty pounds. He teetered, preparing to leap off in their direction.

The downward drop, by now, was easily eight feet. If Mr. Kendall didn't time his leap when the lifeboat had swung towards the ship, it would surely be disastrous. "Please don't jump!" Josette hollered with her hands cupped around her mouth. The two crewmen inside the boat had also seen him. One called up. "You can't make it, sir. Do not try!"

The second rower, an officer of some sort, also yelled to Mr. Kendall. "Please, sir! The boat is too low now! You'll never make it."

Ignoring their commands, obviously panicked and not in his right mind, he sprang from the railing. He didn't scream or make a sound as he fell, feet first, as if he were entering a swimming pool.

Realizing he was about to hit the side of their craft, Josette screamed. Mr. Kendall cried out, bouncing sideways when his head struck the boat. Then he plunged into the water. The force of his impact caused the heavy lifeboat to shift and sway. Josette grabbed for the edge of the wooden plank upon which she sat, gripping it with all her strength. Ropes that held the lifeboat to the tackle block on the boat deck had snagged and twisted on one side. The two Cunarders who handled the ropes fought and tugged, but something snapped. The thick shaft of rope unfurled, loosely falling from its restraints on the davit. The left side of the lifeboat suddenly dropped out from beneath her. She screamed, grabbing for anything to hang onto. There was nothing.

She felt herself tumbling, her body striking other people. As she hit the water, the painful burn of icy cold enveloped her body. The man who had helped her when she landed in the boat was suddenly on top of her, kicking, struggling to survive. His shoe pushed against her chest, as he attempted to propel himself to the surface. A final thrust of his foot drove her deeper, despite of the buoyancy of her life vest. Her coat had soaked up so much water that it became a weight of sorts.

Eyes burning in the salty water, she looked up. Above her, she saw the churning mass of thrashing people and debris and bubbles rising in the clouded water. And then she saw streams of sunlight poking through the murky green and knew the surface – and survival – were close. Out of breath, she felt herself drawing in water as if it was air. Finally, she began to rise, as the life vest began to do its job. Kicking her feet wildly, using her arms and hands to thrust herself upwards,

Josette finally surfaced. Coughing out a mouthful of water, she drew in a huge breath of fresh air.

"Help!" she called as best she could. In the distance, she saw a lifeboat moving in the opposite direction. "Help! she cried out again.

A large object – a chair, perhaps – bobbed a few feet away. Trying to gather strength, she swam in that direction, pushing debris aside. Arriving, she saw it wasn't a chair at all. It was woman dressed in a flower-print dress. She held a child to her chest. They were both motionless, eyes closed as if they were sleeping.

"No! God no!" she sobbed, pushing the bodies away. Treading water, grasping her life jacket, Josette turned in a circle. She suddenly realized she was surrounded by a floating graveyard. The frigid water had quickly taken its toll. Men, women, babies; even the two teenage daughters of the Canadian timber millionaire. All dead. Her body began to shiver, and she was losing feeling in her feet and hands. How long before she, too would succumb?

Desperate, sobbing again, she tried to swim away. It wasn't working. She was pulled backwards. Managing to glance over her shoulder, she realized suction had been created by the sinking vessel. Her teeth chattering, growing weaker by the minute, the force pulled her to the *Lusitania*. Pieces of debris fell around her. An oar splashed to her left, followed immediately by a piece of wood.

Screams overhead. More passengers tumbling into the water, landing, splashing all around her. More explosions inside the disappearing ship. Something falling straight at her. With her last bit of strength, Josette raised her hand to protect herself. The end of a deck chair struck her on the right side of her head with a dull thud. It felt as if her body had disappeared. All that was left was her throbbing temple. A floating sensation. And then, darkness.

Chapter 33

CURTIS CAUGHT his breath, paused, and scanned the chaotic scene. Pandemonium. Utter madness. Sheer panic had taken over otherwise civilized people. Ladies from all social classes ripped off their outer garments and lifted stockingless legs to the railing; pulling themselves over the awkward angle, they let go and plunged into the sea. Except for Mrs. Grant. Decades younger than her husband, as pretty as a Gibson girl's picture, she wore her ankle-length brown mink coat and an enormous diamond necklace.

Mr. Grant, a distant relative of President Ulysses Grant, begged his wife to take it off. "It will weigh you down like an anchor," he cried out. She refused, pushing the elderly man backwards. He stumbled and fell to the deck. Before he got to his feet, she disappeared over the railing in a final act of desperation.

"Sarah!" Sobbing, Mr. Grant got to his knees, his feeble body shuddering.

Children were carried or dragged along by their frantic parents in search of a place for them in a lifeboat, sobbing out their desperation when they discovered there were no more boats that could be launched. Babies wrapped in blankets and held tightly by their mothers obviously sensed the terror, bawling among the shouting and screaming. "Get into the collapsible boats!" he shouted at them.

Curtis swallowed hard, steadying himself against the bulkhead corridor wall that led to the port side. He had to hold it together. Drawing in a breath, he made his way up the steep incline to the doorway leading to the first-class rooms.

And then it struck him. The loan documents. Had Mr. Van Camp gone to the Purser's office to retrieve them? "Oh, crap," he whispered, shaking his head. The *Lusitania* was sinking fast, too fast to save both Mrs. Donaldson and the papers. Surely Van Camp had taken care of Mr. Morgan's precious documents. In an instant, he decided. He headed down the hallway to the elderly woman's stateroom.

Something deep inside coursed through him, taking over his thoughts, his body. He negotiated down the tilting interior passage, now empty of passengers. Reaching Mrs. Donaldson's cabin, he pounded on the door. "Mrs. Donaldson?" he shouted.

No answer.

The ship's angle had become more severe with each passing minute. Pushing hard against gravity to open the door inward, he immediately discovered that it was partially blocked. Likely, by a piece of furniture. The poor woman was trapped inside.

Using all his strength, he forced the door open, squeezed through the opening and made his way into the once-elegant quarters.

The draperies hung out at a strange angle. And yet there was very little light coming through the window. As his eyes adjusted to the darkness, he saw that the English oak furniture had slid downhill with the starboard list and was jumbled against the wall. The Persian rug had crinkled in wavy buckles. The mirrored armoire had skidded several feet before toppling over on the chairs.

He stepped on broken shards of glass and into the bedroom. Squinting, he made out the figure of Mrs. Donaldson huddled with Mr. Duns on the four-posted bed now resting against the downhill wall.

"Who's there?" Mrs. Donaldson's voice warbled.

"It's me. Curtis."

"Curtis? Please. Dinna be daft! Go! Save yourself, laddie."

"Not without you, ma'am."

"I'm an old woman. Don't waste your time on me."

Walking carefully on the slanting floor, steadying himself as best he could, he answered. "Josie would have my hide if I didn't rescue you." He stood beside the bed. Mr. Duns stared up at him, dark eyes seeming to understand Curtis was there to help. The dog rose, wagging his tail.

"Not yet," he said, reaching to pat his head. "First, we need to get a life vest on your master." Curtis bent down to the floor, fumbling through the contents of spilled perfume bottles, a silver-backed brush and mirror set, and an overturned chair. Two life vests – once stored on the armoire – had fallen nearby, wedged beneath the marble-topped table, yet easily pulled out. One for her and one for Curtis.

"Mrs. Donaldson?" a man's voice called from the bedroom door jam. "It's Thomas, ma'am," he said. "I've come to help."

"Thomas! Glad to see you, my friend," Curtis called. "Come in and get the dog. I'll carry the lady."

THE LIFEBOATS on the port side swung in over the deck, making them unusable for the evacuation. Those who had tried to push the heavy craft out over the ocean had given up...or had died trying, crushed when the lifeboat swung backwards as the ship rolled to starboard. The empty lifesaving crafts continued to bang hard against the stateroom walls, shattering windows, splintering off chunks of wood each time they slammed into the metal bulkhead. Lifeless bodies had rolled against the angled outside wall, their blood running down the deck.

"My God," Mrs. Donaldson whispered, turning her head away from the grisly sight.

"Don't look, ma'am," Curtis said. He knew the only possible route of escape was on the starboard side of the Boat Deck. Although the woman's body was thin and lightweight, it was a struggle to hold onto her and keep his balance. People slipped, fell, slid towards the front of the ship. Towards the sea. It was an obstacle course of sorts, dodging panicked passengers who ran and tripped and stumbled as if they had gone mad.

Once he and Thomas had reached the other side of the ship, Curtis saw that the bow and even part of the Bridge were completely underwater. And the aft of the ship had begun to lift. A vision filled his mind. Either, the *Lusitania* would roll over on its right side before making its final plunge to the bottom; or the lower decks would fill, one by one, and the ship would become more level before it sank.

The only option left was to get Mrs. Donaldson, Thomas and the dog into a collapsible boat. That, or they would have to jump into the frigid water, which was a terrible idea when attempting to rescue an eighty-something-year old woman, her Westie, and a teenaged boy.

Several Cunard crewmen had released a collapsible lifeboat that had been stored beneath the already launched Lifeboat Number 7. They had lifted the oiled canvas sides and cut the ropes. Sitting at their station, oars readied, all they could do now was to wait for the rush of water to lift them up as the deck flooded.

"Do you have room for more?" Curtis called to the sailor who seemed to be in charge of the make-shift craft.

"We can take the lady and the lad, but I fear you're going to have to find another way off," one of the men, dressed as a waiter, said in a regretful tone. "I'm sure you'll find another collapsible further aft."

"And my dog, too," Mrs. Donaldson said insistently, as Curtis handed her to the crewman with the handlebar mustache, one of the ship's barbers. *Was it only two days ago this same man had cut his hair in the Lusitania's own barber shop? Impossible.*

"I'll take good care of your lady friend," the barber said with a smile, sliding his arm around her back.

"I'm sure Thomas can hang on tight to the pup," one of the oarsmen assured. "I fear we're in for a jolly good ride."

Curtis yanked the tie loose on his life vest, pulling it off. "You take this, Thomas. I'll find another."

"No, sir. I'll be okay," Thomas said.

"Take it!" Curtis insisted. "I'm counting on you to help Mrs. Donaldson."

Thomas reluctantly reached out. His gaze lowered, he accepted the life jacket.

Tears flowed from Mrs. Donaldson's eyes. "Thank you, my dear," she said. "I shall not forget you."

CURTIS MADE his way to the next collapsible. And then the next. And the next. They were all filled to capacity, waiting to be lifted off the deck by the approaching flood of sea water. And then Curtis saw him. Mr. Van Camp. He sat in the last collapsible, head turned away as if he hoped Curtis wouldn't notice him. Catching his breath, holding onto the side of the rickety-looking craft, Curtis shouted at him. "You've got the papers, right?"

Van Camp remained still. Didn't even turn his head.

"I said, you got the documents, didn't you sir?"

Van Camp slowly twisted his head to face Curtis. "That was your responsibility."

"No, it was both of our responsibilities!" Curtis felt his temper boiling up from somewhere in his chest. "I've been busy rescuing people, you son-of-a-bitch."

"Then get them now or you'll never work on Wall Street again."

For a moment, Curtis wanted nothing more than to yank Van Camp out of the collapsible and drag him downstairs to the Purser's office. The reality was that the man could, and would, ruin his chances for a successful Wall Street career. He could even get Curtis fired at the House of Morgan.

"Damn it," he whispered through clenched teeth.

His facial features morphing into a strange, vacuous expression, Van Camp turned away.

Anger took over where determination for survival had been. "You bastard," Curtis spat.

Drawing a breath of strength, he made his way to the center stairwell. The loan documents were still in the Purser's safe one level down on the Promenade Deck. When he stepped on the top step, he froze in place. A froth of swirling green water had covered several of the bottom stairs. Hesitating, assessing the water's depth, he made an instant decision to give it a try. He bounded down the stairwell and waded, knee deep, into the main entry room. Everyone, passengers and crew, who had been below the Promenade Deck had surely drowned by now. The only ones still alive were up on the Boat Deck or in a lifeboat that had been successfully launched, or in one of the collapsibles waiting for the *Lusitania* to slip beneath the sea. Pushing off tilted walls, fighting the floor's slant, he managed to reach the Purser's front desk. No one – no crewman, no officer – remained inside. They were helping with the passengers. Or they had already escaped the ship.

"Hello?" he called, stumbling through the open door to the Purser's interior office. Sopped papers, pencils, spilled ink bottles, an overturned chair, and all sorts of debris floated around in the room.

"My God," he said, trying to calm a sudden urge to panic. The Purser's office was nearly mid-ship and was two tilting decks down from the top level of the vessel. His time was short. He had to get to a lifeboat. He glanced at the floor-to-ceiling safe door, still locked tight. There was nothing he could do now but to run. To save his life. To hell with the documents.

WHEN CURTIS and Josie had taken strolls together on the uppermost navigation deck, he had noticed a small collapsible secured to the deck behind the Bridge. With water surging over the decks below, it was too late to make another attempt at finding a spot in a larger collapsible. The one upstairs was probably meant for the officers on the Bridge to make their escape. Officer or not, he sprinted up the stairs.

"Room for me?" he hollered, approaching the half-filled canvas-sided boat.

"Yes!" Mr. Street, owner of numerous haberdashery shops in the New York City burroughs, shouted back. "Hurry! We don't have much longer."

Moving forward, Curtis sloshed through the rising tide. His shoes, lower portions of his trousers and overcoat were soaked through. His feet and toes had already numbed in the frigid water. Climbing into the simple patchwork of a vessel, he settled on the bench. The sea bubbled up around them, as the ship edged ever closer, nose down, to the bottom. "Why aren't we floating?" Curtis yelled at Petty Officer Winters, one of the two crewmen holding the oars.

"We can't get the line loose," a third Cunarder, a Scot who sat in the rear of the collapsible, said. "I'm hoping the rope will swell and soften with the surge. Otherwise...."

"Some idiot painted right over the knotted rope," Mr. Winters said with a scowl. "Guess he didn't figure out that would make untying it quite impossible."

Mrs. Street, an aging woman dripping with jewels, sat next to her husband. She held a lacy handkerchief, sniffing. Her cheeks, her eyes, were wet with tears. "Then, we're doomed."

"Now, Elizabeth. We're going to be all right," her husband assured her, patting her gloved hand. "They'll figure it out."

The front of the craft continued to lift, making it increasingly difficult to hang on. And then Curtis remembered. "Wait! I have a knife!" Fishing it out of his pants pocket, he opened the blade, leaned over the back of the boat, and began to saw the rope.

"You're an answer to our prayers," the petty officer said.

The water was elbow-deep now. Curtis' fingers burned in the freezing water. It wouldn't be much longer before it would pour into the boat. Using both hands, Curtis yanked and pulled with all his might, continuing to slice through the stubborn cords.

The front of the collapsible lifted even higher as seawater rushed over the ship's superstructure. But with the back of the collapsible still attached to the deck, water began to spill over and inside.

"Hurry, please," Mrs. Street cried, her arms wrapped around her young daughter.

Curtis glanced at the Bridge. A foamy wave approached, pushing papers and charts and miscellaneous things that had obviously spilled out of the Bridge offices' doors and broken windows. The surge of flotsam came rushing towards them.

Leaning over the collapsible, the Scotsman pulled the rope taut. "Come on, laddie! We'll be going down with the *Lusy* if you can't get us free," he said, sounding desperate.

Curtis' heart pounded wildly. With a final slice, the knife cut through, snapping the line loose. The boat jerked and bucked. Curtis and the Scottish crewman were thrown backwards in a jumble, hitting one of the empty wooden seats. Curtis cried out, feeling the knife's sharp blade slash his flesh between his thumb and index finger on his left hand. The pain was searing. Blood ran from the gash in a thin rivulet, swirling a tiny red ribbon into the water on the little craft's floor.

At last freed from its confinement, the collapsible had begun to float evenly in the rising water.

"Are you all right, son?" A sooty hand held out a blue neck scarf. "Here. Take it. Wrap it 'round your hand to stop the bleeding."

Curtis took the kerchief. "Thanks." By the look of the man's blackened face, he was a coal trimmer, who had miraculously escaped from the stock hold in the depths of the ship.

"It's us who should be thanking you, sir," he said. "We'd be goners for sure if it wasn't for you."

Moving carefully so he wouldn't rock the boat, Curtis scooted up on a seat. Glancing over his shoulder, he saw around a dozen people hanging on to the railing of the Boat Deck. Mr. Frohman braced himself, a cigar in his mouth; Mr. Vanderbilt in his fine clothes; and… was it really the actress, Rita Jolivet? She clung to the railing with gloved hands, bawling hysterically.

"Swim for it!" Curtis yelled at them, cupping his hands around his mouth. "We have more room in here!"

Frohman glanced at him, smiling. He tipped his hat, shook his head. Removing his cigar, he called out. "Thanks, son, but I fear it's too late. We're off on a great adventure."

"Please!" Curtis begged, shaking his head. "Please try…."

A loud *ping* rang out. And then another and another.

"Duck!" Officer Winters shouted. Lines from the Marconi room had snapped as the vessel twisted and flexed on its slow descent to the bottom. Those were the very lines that had magically carried the dots and dashes from the ship to wireless receivers miles away. Now, as they wildly flailed about, they had become dangerous foes. The loose wires were brutal, striking at several men standing on the rear pilot's deck like a cobra's sharp tongue. Two had been slashed across the face, screaming in pain as they toppled over the railing and into the sea. The fate of the third man was just as terrible. He fell to his knees in obvious pain, sliding off the platform, his body ricocheting off a metal gate before he fell into the water.

It was hard to witness everyone – even the famous and the rich – swept off the ship as the wall of bubbling water washed over them. Mr. Vanderbilt, Frohman and Rita Jolivet were gone. The decks were devoid of life. Curtis gazed out at the water. There were hundreds and hundreds of people in the churning water. Hands waved in the air. Shouts for help could be heard from all directions.

Their small lifeboat began to buck and sway with the increasing gush of seawater.

"Hang on," the petty officer ordered. Twenty souls, including the Cunard crewmen, Mr. and Mrs. Walker and their two small boys; the Streets; a chamber maid, still in her crisp uniform; and two men he didn't recognize, had managed to make their way to the collapsible. Besides the two rowers, there were three Cunard crew on board with them. That left several empty places in the boat.

"Let's get the hell out of here!" Mr. Winters yelled out, paddling frantically.

"Lord, Jesus," Mrs. Walker said. "Help us."

CURTIS HAD been in rough seas on more than one occasion, but he had never experienced anything like this. It felt as if they were caught in a vortex, a vacuum trying to pull them down.

As the *Lusitania* began to slide under, taut lines from the smokestacks snapped, madly whipping about. Explosions continued inside the hull as the chilly water met still-lighted boilers. Glass windows blew out from the changing pressure underwater. No doubt the beautiful stained-glass domes in many of the public rooms had shared the same fate.

And then it was over. The ship was gone. Nothing could be done now. Nothing but save some of the people fighting for their lives in the unforgiving cold of the Celtic Sea. Curtis grabbed a spare oar and helped the two crew members, stroking furiously to get away from the whirlpool created by the vanishing ocean liner.

Most curious, was the ship had seemed to freeze in place for a few minutes. The aft end had stuck out of the water, propellers turning slowly. That had given the collapsibles time to get further away from the dying vessel. And then, the *Lusitania* continued its downward slide. The smokestacks submerged, pulling in wreckage…and people. A few moments later, that same debris and bodies were belched out in a grand puff of black soot.

Mrs. Street gasped. "God in heaven. Help them."

"There are too many to save," Mr. Winters said, shaking his head. "Too many…."

"Look! Over there!" Curtis said, pointing. "A woman with a child."

"Right on, gents. We can only pick up a few of them, or we'll sink ourselves from the weight. God help us. We shall have to make some life and death decisions in the next few minutes."

"Aye," said the Scotsman. "We'd better make it fast, or they'll all be dead soon. The water is too cold for them to live much longer."

"Women and children, then," the Petty Officer said in a stiff tone, his bottom lip quivering. "Women and children first."

PART THREE

Chapter 34

CURTIS STOOD on the Queenstown wharf, staring numbly across Cork Harbor. He scanned the opening to the sea for incoming boats. Hours had passed since the collapsible in which he traveled arrived in port. But where were the rest of the lifesaving vessels?

As the hours crept by, the sky morphed from a cloudless blue to shades of peach and lavender and, finally, into steel gray. Darkness descended rapidly, bringing with it a chilling breeze. Light from the street lamps and buildings along the waterfront glistened yellow streaks across the inky water that lapped against the wood pilings holding up the dock.

The rowing had been exhausting for Mr. Winters and the other Cunarders in charge. The sun had been warm and only a few of the collapsible's occupants had managed to keep their hats during the chaos. They had no food. No water. Curtis and another man had taken rotations with the oars. He didn't care how much the motion hurt his wound and made it bleed again. They had to get to the seaport town as soon as possible. That's all that mattered for now.

When their small craft had been around an hour from Queenstown, Curtis and his boatmates encountered a sorry little fleet of rescue boats. One of them, a fishing boat, had pulled beside their collapsible to see if they all wanted to come on board. When the vessel's captain explained he would proceed south to where the ship had gone down to pick up victims, Curtis and many of his fellow survivors decided to continue rowing towards Queenstown. Half of them had transferred to the motorized craft. Several of the ladies were just sure the collapsible would spring a leak, and they would wind up in the sea.

After transferring blankets and a large container of drinking water to Petty Officer Winters, the fishing vessel rejoined the ragtag armada enroute to the *Lusitania's* final resting place.

Only a few of the collapsible crafts, including the one in which Thomas and Mrs. Donaldson had journeyed, as well as one of the large conventional lifeboats, had reached Queenstown before Curtis' group.

Upon arriving, a Cunard representative had explained that most of the lifeboats had waited for rescue craft at the location of the sinking. Curtis couldn't imagine why they hadn't immediately rowed to Queenstown, when so many of the survivors had been injured and needed medical care. *Fear makes people do strange things*, he thought, shaking his head.

So, why was it taking the rest of the lifeboats and rescue vessels so damned long to arrive in Queenstown? Had they gone to the port in Kinsale instead?

The longer he waited, the worse Curtis felt. His head pounded, his cut throbbed, and he was exhausted. Not that he could sleep. He might not ever sleep again. He had seen such terrible things at the site of the sinking. So many dead bodies. People he recognized, had spoken with. Men from the poker games. Both of the Warwick girls, unseeing eyes wide open in death, floated a few feet apart. He had watched both Mr. Frohman and Mr. Vanderbilt desperately clinging to the railing as the *Lusitania* slid down. It had been too much; too much for anyone to bear.

After the collapsible made its escape from the sinking ship, he had used an extra oar to push dead bodies and small suitcases and chairs and everything else imaginable aside while they searched for people who were still alive. So many bodies were tangled in the wreckage; so many bodies covered the surface that, in some places, it was impossible to see the water. How many had died? Hundreds, for sure. More likely, over a thousand. He was grateful he hadn't seen Josette or her sister. Were they still alive?

If Josie's lifeboat had been damaged, if she had been spilled out like so many others, at least she was wearing a life jacket. And she knew how to swim. She told him she had learned as a child. Her father had insisted they all take lessons before he would allow them on his sailboat. Surely, she was in one of the rescue boats and on her way to Queenstown.

Unless…. He tried not to think the worst. But how could he not? So many of the dead and dying had suffered terrible injuries. Gashes oozing blood, broken limbs, burns. And worse. So much worse.

He blinked back tears, fighting the need to break down and sob. "No. Not Josie," he said softly, shaking his head. He wouldn't allow himself to think those thoughts. Yet, he knew too many of the lifeboats had something go wrong. Knotted lines, incompetent crew who hadn't received training in evacuating the ship, let alone having hands-on experience unleashing the heavy ropes, unchaining the craft, or using the davits properly. The entire evacuation process had been a complete debacle.

"Damn Captain Turner," he grumbled loudly. "Damn the bastards at Cunard who wouldn't authorize holding practice drills for the passengers. Damn them all to hell!" Clutching his fists, Curtis drew in a wrathful shallow breath. Giving in to his emotions, not caring what any passersby thought of him, he cried out. "Josette Rogers! Where are you, Josie?"

It wasn't fair that Josette was gone. Besides Mrs. Donaldson, Curtis had helped rescue five people. Pulled them into the little collapsible. Five people suffering from frostbite, fingers and lips the color of blueberries. He begged to continue their search; to save more people. To find Josette. But when their collapsible was so low that the water had nearly reached the gunnel, the craft's passengers made a unanimous decision to head for Queenstown. Clearly, they had done all they could do. Taking in additional souls would have likely capsized the collapsible, dooming them all to death.

Ambling to a nearby bench, Curtis sat, knees spread, head down. He was tired. Hungry. Cold. Several doctors and nurses had come to the dock in Queenstown to treat non-life-threatening injuries like his. The hospital transports were used for the seriously injured. The nurse who examined his hand sewed the gash together and bound the wound with a clean strip of bandage. She had given him a small container of morphine to help with the pain, but he'd found that it also dulled his senses. He had decided he would only use it at night to help him sleep. If he could ever sleep again.

"Oh, here you are, Mr. Carlson."

Blurry-eyed, he looked up. It was Thomas. "Hello, son."

"I figured your clothes were still damp, so I brung you a blanket and a sandwich, sir," he said, handing Curtis a paper bag. "It's lamb. Hope it's to your liking." Thomas placed the heavy wool blanket around his shoulders.

The instant warmth felt wonderful. "Thank you," Curtis said. Forcing a small smile, he hoped the young man couldn't see his tears in the darkness. "How are Mrs. Donaldson and Dunsy doing?" The boat carrying Thomas and Mrs. Donaldson had arrived in Queenstown shortly before Curtis' group had climbed onto the quay. Thomas, such a good lad, had escorted the Scottish woman and her dog to the Queens Hotel, one of the nearby accommodations taking in the first-class passengers.

Thomas sat beside Curtis. "Reckon they're both sleeping by now."

Curtis nodded. "That's good. Thanks for taking care of them."

"You should eat something, sir. Everyone else has been fed."

"Now that you mention it, my stomach is definitely rebelling." His digestive tablets were in his bureau drawer at the bottom of the sea.

"It's all they had left," Thomas said with a shrug. His gaze moved out to the bay. "The Cunard representative at the hotel said the rescue boats should be here any minute. You'd best be having a bite to eat, 'cause it's liable to get pretty hectic around here once they come in."

"You're right." He pulled a wrapped sandwich from the paper bag. "Lamb, you say?"

AT LAST, the trawlers, fishing boats, two well-worn and relatively small naval patrol craft entered the bay, running lights glittering in the blackness. Thomas followed Curtis, as he made his way through the growing crowd of onlookers gathering on the street and wharf.

Minutes later, Cunard employees assisted weary *Lusitania* survivors onto the dock and led them up the ramp. Curtis pushed his way to the top of the incline. "Please. Let me help," he said to the official who held a clipboard and pencil. "I was on the ship. So were my friends."

"Sorry, but you've got to wait here, sir." the Cunarder said in a flat tone.

With a frustrated grunt, Curtis took a step back.

Each person who passed gave his or her name. The official wrote quickly, straining to see the pages in the dim light emanating from a nearby street lamp.

Curtis watched. Waited. Blankets and crewmen's jackets were draped around the women's shoulders. Once perfect coifs hung in clumps. Most of the survivors' clothes were seriously rumpled. Some were still wet, by the look of them. He recognized many of the passengers, including Mr. Arturo Lorenzo. After he had checked in with the Cunard official, Curtis stepped over and spoke to the man.

"Excuse me, Mr. Lorenzo. Have you seen any of the Rogers family?"

The Italian wine broker was hunched over, his legs wobbling beneath him as he took each unsteady step. "Who?" He looked up with weary eyes. "Oh, yes. The Rogers." He paused and drew in a breath, shaking his head. "It's all so horrible," he said, his voice reflecting his anguish. "I'm sorry to have to tell you this, but I believe they were trapped in one of the lifts. Tragic…" His voice trailed off.

"On the elevator?" Curtis said. He felt his breath escape in a huff. "Trapped?"

"I fear so. Someone told me they were among those poor souls on the lifts when the power went out." His brow furrowed, as his mind had drifted back to the tragedy.

Curtis felt as if he had been hit in the chest. He couldn't breathe. "Dear God," he gasped. "Are you sure? I mean, how do you know?"

"I noticed that Mr. and Mrs. Rogers left the dining room a few minutes after the first explosion. I had to help my wife. She was knocked off her chair by the jolt. Hit by a few pieces of silver and a tea pot, you see. After the second explosion, when we lost power, we ran out the main doors and we could hear them screaming for help! They were stuck between floors. It was so dark," he said, his voice trembling. "I used my cigarette lighter to guide our way to the stairs. I could make out the figures of two waiters trying to get the lift down, pulling and pulling on the lift's floor. But it was useless."

Curtis closed his eyes for a moment. Such an unimaginable horror. "How about Yvette? One of the twin daughters. She wouldn't have used the elevator. She would have taken the stairs."

"Hurry it along," the Cunarder with the clipboard shouted at them. "You're holding up the queue. We've got to get some of these folks to a hospital."

"Condolences to all of us, my boy. My wife and son are missing, too." Mr. Lorenzo's voice was soft. Weak. "I shall pray to Holy Mother we find all of the ones we love."

Curtis managed to say, "I hope you find your family, Mr. Lorenzo."

Nodding, the man continued walking with the other survivors.

Curtis was stunned. Trapped in the elevator. Water rushing in, and nothing they could do to escape. It was beyond anything he could imagine. He hoped Josette and Yvette would never find out how their parents died…if either of the girls was still alive.

"Mr. Carlson?"

In the shadowy light, he saw Georgie's nanny and sister approaching. "Hello," he said. "I'm very happy to see you both made it. And Georgie?"

She shook her head, her bottom lip quivering. "We don't know."

BY DAWN, the last of the rescue boats had docked. Neither Josie nor Yvette were among the survivors who had been picked up. Once the living had been dropped off, several of the larger craft had made multiple trips to the accident site to gather as many bodies as possible. Hundreds of people, it was feared, had gone down with the ship. Like

Mr. and Mrs. Rogers, they would spend eternity at the bottom of the sea.

Curtis fought the pictures in his head. He could still hear the screams, see people washed off the ship, hear the groans of those in the last throes of freezing to death in the ice-cold water. Curtis closed his eyes and breathed in fresh air. He couldn't give up hope. Couldn't allow himself to believe Josie was gone. She was still alive. He knew it. Felt it.

Cunard representatives walked among the crowd lingering near the quay, announcing all the passengers who were alive were finally on shore. Kind-hearted local citizens had come to help, bringing with them blankets and coats. The local hospitals were filled to overflowing, they had said. Those who with less serious injuries were taken to nearby hotels.

For hours, a constant parade of lorry trucks, horse-drawn wagons, and private motorcars picked up *Lusitania* survivors. Curtis was told that families from throughout County Cork took survivors, even some with minor injuries, into their homes or to their farms until further arrangements could be made for them.

Things didn't die down until the wee hours of the morning. Even then, Curtis watched the steady flow of trawlers and larger vessels returning to port with the dead.

By the time the sun began to rise, hundreds upon hundreds of corpses had been placed in rows along the walkway and the wharf. Men, women, children. They had been grouped by those categories. Curtis had tried to make out their faces before they were covered, but there wasn't enough light.

Every extra sheet, blanket and tarpaulin in Queenstown had been utilized to cover the deceased. It was a shocking sight. Unreal. Curtis had seen so much death, he felt dazed, as if he was dreaming the whole sickening thing. He didn't know where he was going or why he was walking aimlessly, but he had to keep moving. He paced, meandered, sat, and then wandered around town some more. Until dawn, when the official task of identifying the dead began.

Those with family in the British Isles were lucky, if one could call any part of this tragedy lucky. They would be taken home to be buried by their loved ones. But the rest, Canadians, Americans, French, Italians, Belgians – there wasn't sufficient time for their friends or relatives to make the trip to Ireland to claim bodies and return them to their homelands. Cunard officials had already posted a notice that there would be a mass burial on Monday. Those who had been identified were taken to one of the make-shift morgues, if the families wished to have them embalmed before shipping them out of Ireland for burial.

Like a strange procession, mothers, fathers, brothers and sisters, friends and lovers – most of them survivors themselves – they filed down the rows of corpses, squatting and carefully lifting the fabric coverings to view each face. Curtis joined in the line, his emotions a complex mixture of hope that he wouldn't find either Josette or her sister, and hope that if they were indeed dead, he would be able to identify their bodies in time to have them sent back to Manhattan.

A mass burial. *Death knows no class distinction,* he thought repeatedly, recognizing the pale, waxen face of Lady Begnell, wife of a distant cousin to the King of England. How ironic that so many of this group of the dead, so staid in their belief that humans should be separated by class, by wealth, by social status, should wind up in the ground together with the working class that had traveled in third class. Possibly, Lady Begnell and other British dignitaries would be claimed by family members. Yet, most of the rich and famous Americans and other foreigners would likely wind up in the huge pits being dug in the cemetery a few miles away.

Moving slowly in the line, one by one, he glanced under the coverings. One by one, he saw people with whom he had chatted over lunch and dinner. Young and old, pretty and privileged. Rich and poor. The hardest to see were the mothers still holding their babies. And then it happened. A patch of curly brown hair peeked from the piece of broadcloth covering a small corpse. "Oh my God!" He lifted the edge of the fabric, dreading what he knew he'd see. Falling to his knees, tears welling, his heart, his soul were broken. "Oh no. Georgie," he whispered, lowering the cloth draping. "I'm so sorry. So, so sorry."

His knees shook as he stood. Wiping his eyes with his soggy coat sleeve, Curtis knew he had to pull himself together. Neither of the girls was under the tarps. That could only mean one of two things: their bodies hadn't been recovered, or perhaps they were among the injured who hadn't been identified. Nor did he find Mr. Vanderbilt, Mr. Frohman, or Mr. Hubbard. Even Mr. Van Camp wasn't there. The realization Van Camp was likely dead suddenly struck him. The man had always landed on his feet, undeservingly climbing the ladder of success at Morgan and Company. Perhaps, he wasn't lucky this time.

Making his way back along the main thoroughfare paralleling the waterfront, Curtis entered the brick building on the quay where Cunard had its offices. He wanted to double-check the listing of the injured. To question anyone who would talk to him and maybe find a clue about Josie's or Yvette's fate.

Inside, it was sheer mayhem. Swarms of survivors were still looking for a place to sleep, and to receive vouchers for food and clothing. Lines of people waited impatiently to send telegrams. Newly arrived family members shouted, crying, begging for information about their loved ones.

Zigzagging through the chaos, Curtis recognized one of the Cunard staffers who had worked in the *Lusitania's* Purser's office. He grabbed Mr. Monroe by the shoulders as he passed by. "Please, sir. Have you seen the Rogers' girls? You know, the pretty twins." Curtis had to raise his voice to be heard over the commotion.

Mr. Monroe thought for a moment. "I do recall seeing a girl, possibly one with blonde hair. She had sustained severe injuries."

"Was she taken to one of the hospitals?" Curtis begged, a sense of hope rising in his chest. He resisted the urge to grab the lad by his lapel, to shake him, for no good reason. "Was it one of the Rogers' girls?"

Monroe thought for a moment. "I believe someone said she was Yvette Rogers."

"Yvette? Not Josette? Are you certain?"

"She was apparently identified by several survivors, including someone who was on the lifeboat that picked her up."

Curtis shook his head. "Who? Who identified her?" he shouted.

The Cunarder pulled back. "Please, Mr. Carlson! That's all I know."

"How did they know her? The girls looked a great deal alike and—"

Mr. Monroe reached out, a compassionate expression suddenly covering his face. He took Curtis' arm. "I understand, sir. Please wait for the list before you give up hope."

Swallowing hard, realizing he was out of line, Curtis nodded.

"Would you be wanting to, to take a look among the victims? To see if you can find the other one, I mean." Mr. Monroe glanced in the direction of the door leading outside…to the laid-out bodies.

Curtis frowned. "I already did."

Monroe's gaze dropped. "I see. Quite sorry, sir." He looked up. "If you can make any positive identifications of the victims you have seen, please give your information to the clerk. Mr. McGillicuddy is making the list. We'll be posting it as soon as possible."

Curtis let out a slow sigh. "Of course."

"If you don't mind me saying so, Mr. Carlson, you look like you could use some rest. And, well, sir, we are handing out vouchers for new clothes for the first-class passengers, courtesy of Cunard. You may obtain what you need at the shops here in town. Why don't you get yourself over to one of the local shops for a new suit of clothes. The Queens' Hotel is expecting you. There are vouchers for local restaurants in the envelope, too. Please get something to eat and some sleep. We'll send word to let you know if there are any changes."

AFTER SHOWERING and changing his bandage, Curtis found a bed in a room where three other men from the *Lusitania* had also been assigned. When he arrived, they were just leaving. Curtis welcomed the privacy and an opportunity to sleep.

The bed was small and the mattress soft, but it didn't matter. The hotel had provided him with a long flannel night shirt. His damp, salt-crusted suit, coat, under garments, trousers, socks and shoes still smelled of the sea. He spread everything he could on the steam radiator to dry. Later, he would shower and shave and try on the new clothing he had picked up at a nearby tailor's shop. Now, all he wanted was a nap. He took a sip of the morphine and was out cold almost as soon as he laid his head on the pillow.

Chapter 35

"MR. CARLSON. Wake up, sir. The survivors' names have been posted at the Cunard offices."

Curtis rolled over, blinking his eyes to focus. "Thomas?"

"Yes, sir. You've been asleep for hours. I thought you'd want to know. The hotel clerk said I could come upstairs and wake you. He gave me a key. I hope you don't mind, sir."

Curtis threw back the bed covers and sat straight up. "Did they find Josette? Is she alive?"

Thomas' face changed, his lips drooping into a frown.

"What? Tell me, boy!"

"I'm sorry, sir. I saw Miss Yvette Rogers' name as a survivor. But not Miss Josette. She...she is officially listed as among the missing."

"The missing?" He felt tears welling and bit his bottom lip to keep it from quivering. He worked to gather himself. He couldn't let the young man see him like this. "She isn't dead. I would know it if she was."

"Miss Yvette was apparently on one of the first boats into port yesterday." Thomas glanced down at the floor. "Mr. Monroe said she's at Queenstown Hospital just outside town."

"Did he say how badly she was injured? Or what happened?"

"No. He did say she's still unconscious, though."

Curtis got out of bed, turned his back to Thomas, yanked off his nightshirt, and grabbed the new pair of heavy wool pants. Sliding his legs into the trousers, he said, "I'm going to see for myself." He felt a sense of emptiness in his chest. "They must have made a mistake. There was so much confusion. What if they misidentified her?"

His shirt was still folded inside the brown paper wrapping. He tore open the package as he spoke, crossing the room. "It's Josie in that hospital bed. I'm sure of it. She's the one who knew how to swim, for God's sake. Not her sister." Tucking in his shirt, he used his old belt to hold up the trousers.

"It's, it's possible...I reckon," Thomas said in a halting voice.

Anger built up where hope had been. "What in the hell do those so-called witnesses know about identifying the twins, anyway?" Curtis sat on the edge of the bed. Pulling on his new socks, he added, "What about Mrs. Donaldson? Did you tell her?" The shoes that had been given to him were about a size too big, but they would have to do for now.

"Yes. She left for Queens Hospital a couple of hours ago. She said I should tell you that when you're ready, you should join her there."

"Thanks, Thomas. Would you please ask the front desk to have my clothes washed and pressed as soon as possible? These goddamned woolen garments are itchy as hell," he said, slipping into the dark green jacket. And ask them to please pick me up a tie that will match. Cunard is footing the bill."

CURTIS CLIMBED out of the back seat of the cab, a black Napier taxi that looked as if it had sat outside in the wet Irish weather for years. After giving the driver a Cunard voucher in payment, he bolted for the hospital's front door.

Compared to the hospitals in New York, the Queen's Hospital was quite small. The three-story structure could have been mistaken for a hotel or a university lecture hall. Ivy climbed up one of the exterior stone walls, trimmed back around the windows and chimney.

Inside, the receptionist directed him to the second floor, where the injured women had been taken.

Christ, how he hated hospitals. He'd spent too much time in one back in New York – when his grandfather died a few years ago. Hospitals all smelled of rubbing alcohol and urine and God knew what else.

Exiting the elevator, he went to the open door at the end of the corridor where the sign read, "Women's Ward." He paused at the entrance, gazing into the long room. The beds were lined up in parallel rows only a few feet from each other, like photos he'd seen in the newspaper of military field hospitals in France. But, then, this, too, was an emergency situation like none other the area had ever seen. Civilians, not soldiers. Women, mostly. Some older children, too.

From what the clerk at the Cunard office said, only a few infants had survived. Ironically sad, since the directive had been women and children first. And yet....

Unbuttoning his new overcoat, Curtis drew in a shallow breath and slowly entered the room. Strolling down the center aisle, he glanced at the faces, some bruised and scraped, some bearing stitched-up gashes. Closed eyelids circled by purplish flesh, swollen lips, cracked and bloody from the sun and salt water. Heads and limbs and faces bandaged with gauze held together by strips of white tape.

First-class lady passengers lay in beds beside third-class nannies and second-class members of the choir. All had experienced the terror of the sinking. *At least they were alive*, he thought, his mind flashing to the bodies lying there in the street. And to the ones he'd seen floating lifelessly at the site of the disaster.

Curtis paused, swallowed hard and tried to put the ghastly images out of his mind. He had to focus on his mission. To find Josette.

Family members, or perhaps friends who had survived the ordeal with fewer injuries, sat in chairs crammed between the beds where they could comfort their loved ones. They were likely still in shock themselves; grateful to be alive, that their injured wife or daughter was alive.

At the end of the long room, under a curtained window, sat Mrs. Donaldson. She turned and smiled.

He nodded and proceeded forward. He saw the figure under the blankets, her head on the pillow, butterscotch locks of hair fanned out. Curtis wasn't a religious man; yet, he found himself praying that the girl lying in the bed was his Josie. Each step closer made him more apprehensive.

"I came as soon as I got your message." Though he was talking to Mrs. Donaldson, his eyes were locked on Yvette. Or was it Josette? He strained to look at her features.

"How is she?" he asked. The girl's petite form was visible under the blanket, a white sheet drawn up to her chin. "Is she going to be all right?"

"Aye. In time." She turned back to Yvette. "Poor wee girl hasn't woken yet, though. The doctor said a blow to her head has left her in a coma. The doctor supposed whatever struck her was quite heavy."

Curtis stood at the foot of the bed. He gasped audibly. Shocked, he scanned her face…looking at the places that weren't bandaged. Her left eye and cheek, and her mouth and chin weren't covered but were swollen and bruised. The pitiful creature in the bed was barely recognizable as the pretty young woman she once was. It was worse than he had imagined. Curtis rubbed his temples. "I don't know how many times I've said 'Oh, my God' today."

Mrs. Donaldson let out a sad sigh. "It is heart-breaking and hard to see. The good news is the doctor says she will survive. The question is, how much will she remember?"

"Do…do they know which lifeboat she was in?"

"The Cunard lad said she was pulled into a lifeboat shortly before the ship went under. He said she was unconscious and half-frozen. Nearly drowned, too."

Curtis stepped closer. "The whole thing was ridiculous. Cunard didn't do a thing to keep this from happening. And where was the Royal Navy escort? Why in the hell weren't the passengers given a drill so they'd know what to do?"

He realized that he had sworn and apologized before continuing. "She must have been hit by another lifeboat that came down on top of her. Or maybe something like those big potted palms in the Verandah Café." He nodded. "Yes. That would make sense. I saw a couple of them rolling around on the deck before they finally fell overboard." He shook his head at the image. "Poor devils in the water below would have been hit."

"No one knows for sure, Mr. Carlson."

He stepped to the head of the bed and bent over her, scanning her face closely. It was difficult. Whether it was Josette or Yvette, it looked as if she had been in a battle. But was it really Yvette? How could anyone be sure with her once-beautiful features in such a condition?

With a heavy sigh, he stood upright again and turned to Mrs. Donaldson. "I have to ask. Are they sure it's Yvette? I mean…how could they tell for sure? Even I don't know."

"Several people have identified her."

"But they look so much alike. Josette told me how she and her sister even fooled their teachers when they were little girls. Couldn't you all have been mistaken?"

"No, laddie. I'm afraid not. This is Yvette. She was wearing several items that helped with her identification." Mrs. Donaldson raised her hand and placed it on his arm. "I am so very sorry. I believe Josette had a real fondness for you, too. I could see it in her eyes. If you can stay in Queenstown for a while, until Yvette wakes up, maybe you can speak to her yourself. That way, you can be certain. Not that it will bring you peace. But at least you'll know for certain. It may bring a bit of calmness to your heart."

Shaking his head, he sighed deeply. "I doubt anything will bring me peace now, Mrs. Donaldson." Discouraged, he stepped away from the bed. "I wish I could stay. Unfortunately, I have to get to London to take care of some important business. My uncle and I had been scheduled to meet with businessmen in London on Monday. I'm afraid it can't wait."

"That's a pity." A sad expression swept across her tired face. "And what of your uncle?" she said, changing the subject. "Any news?"

He shook his head. "The clerk at the hotel stopped me as I was leaving this morning. He told me my uncle didn't survive. His body washed ashore and was recovered on a beach with quite a few others early this morning. The Cunard men were able to identify him, since he was wearing his money belt and had his passport tucked into his trousers pocket."

"But they still have not found your Josette, I assume."

"Not yet." He swallowed hard and cleared his throat. "I haven't given up, though."

With a woeful nod, Mrs. Donaldson reached out her hand. "Please accept my sincerest sympathy for all of your losses." Her mouth twisted into an odd smile. "My husband will likely haunt me for not burying his ashes in Scottish soil. He, too, lies with too many of our compatriots inside the hull of the *Lusitania*. Perhaps it would have been better if I, too, had gone down with the ship…with my dear husband."

"Don't say that, ma'am. I'm sure Mr. Donaldson wouldn't have wanted that."

For several moments, she quietly contemplated his words. She lifted her gaze. "Aye. You're right, lad. And I thank you again for risking your life on my behalf." She cleared her throat, sniffed, and asked, "And will you be returning here after your time in London?"

"I'm not sure about anything at this moment." He shook his head. "I suppose there's no reason to return to Queenstown, since Josette—" He paused and looked at Yvette's face again and let out an audible sigh. "Well, it would seem there's no reason to come back here. Besides, I'm sure my employer will want me to get back to America as soon as possible."

She blinked several times, wearing a befuddled expression. The dear woman looked as if she had aged another ten years since the tragedy. "And is it your university that is waiting for your return? Surely they would be willing to allow you more time."

"I'm so sorry. I fear I can't say more on the subject." He placed his hand on her shoulder, realizing she was still wearing the same tan lace dress she had worn during her escape from the *Lusitania*. "Thank you. And please promise me you will take care of yourself. Go back to the hotel and get some rest. And you might want to do a bit of shopping. I'm sure you'd like to get a fresh dress to wear."

"Aye. And Mr. Duns needs to be walked. No telling if he's done his business inside the room by now."

"You do know that if I could stay here, I would." He pulled a folded piece of notepad paper from his coat pocket. "This is my home address. Please, Mrs. Donaldson. When Yvette wakes up…if everyone was wrong. If she's my Josie, please send me a telegram immediately. Frankly, I would appreciate it if you would write to me one way or the other. If it's indeed Yvette, then I will have to move on with my life. But if it's not…"

Eyes lowered beneath hooded lids, Mrs. Donaldson didn't respond.

He leaned closer to the Scottish woman. "I know it sounds like wishful thinking, ma'am, but I put Josette into a lifeboat myself. She said her sister had gone back to their stateroom." He felt those damnable wetness welling in his eyes again and took a quick swipe at an escaped tear. "I thought Josette would be safe in that lifeboat. I should have kept her with me, where I could protect her. I thought—"

"It's not your fault. No one knew things would be so dreadful."

He drew in a shaky breath and nodded. Then Curtis reached for Yvette's limp hand. "I'm so sorry. If only you would wake up. I have so many questions." He gave her hand, reddened from the near-freezing water, a gentle squeeze. "Your sister told me about the young man you have waiting back in the States. The piano player. You need to get well for him."

A heavy-set nurse approached, her footsteps hammering on the bare wood floor. "Hello. I'm Mrs. Flanagan. I'm afeared you both best be leaving now. 'Tis time for me to be changing Miss Rogers' bandages."

Curtis had an instant thought. "Of course, Mrs. Flanagan. But I have a quick question for you. Have you been her nurse since they brought her here?"

"That I have."

"Do you recall what she was wearing when she was admitted? Was it a light blue dress?" That's what Josie had worn under her coat.

The nurse thought for a moment, her brows furrowing. "I'm sorry. I cannot recall. There were so many."

"But do you know how they identified Miss Rogers?"

Her face took on a look of impatience, which reflected in her tone. "Please, sir. You must be going. I have too much work to do to be answering your questions."

Mrs. Donaldson rose. "Come, Mr. Carlson. Mrs. Flanagan is right. We should leave."

Curtis nodded, helping Mrs. Donaldson out of the chair.

Arm in arm, he led her down the center aisle. Curtis glanced over his shoulder, as the nurse pulled a curtain to cordon off Yvette's bed from view. He felt worse than ever. If only he could find a way to be completely certain it was Yvette and not his Josette lying there in the bed.

And yet, they said she had been positively identified. But how?

"Promise you'll let me know if there are any changes in her condition. Especially, if she wakes up."

"And if it's not Miss Josette, lad, will you be all right, then?" the Scottish woman asked.

"I honestly don't know, ma'am. I had just found Josette. I've never met anyone like her. She challenged me. She was my equal in intellect and interests." He paused for a moment. "We were falling in love."

"I know, lad. You will grieve. And then, you must go on living your life. I know all this misery, the horrors we've all seen, could easily ruin your future if you let it. But you're a strong lad. And you must believe Josette and the rest of them are in a better place. And that you two will meet again one day in heaven."

Curtis didn't answer but helped her into a waiting taxi. Settling into the seat beside her, he asked, "How long will you stay here in Ireland?"

"I shall stay with Yvette until her fiancé arrives. I'm certain he has heard about the tragedy and may very well be on his way by now."

"And what if President Wilson suspends travel for passengers between here and the United States? What if Yvette's fiancé can't get here?

"If that were to happen, then I suppose you wouldn't be able to get home either, would you now?"

"That's a possibility, I suppose. I'll have to check with my employer's office in London regarding what to do next. And then we shall see."

Chapter 36

SATURDAY AFTERNOON when he had finished rehearsal at the Claremont Theater, Jonathan Franklin stepped out the side door and headed down the alley towards Broadway. As he rounded the corner to the street, he noted a newsboy standing beside a neatly arranged stack of papers. A small crowd had gathered around, tossing coins in a bucket as they pulled off the top copy.

"*Lusitania* torpedoed!" Hundreds dead!" he shouted. "Get your paper! Germans sink the *Lusitania*!"

Jonathan froze in place. His jaw slackened, and he tried to breathe. "My God," he managed in a whisper. Without thinking, he darted forward, his heart pounding hard and fast, pushing his way past a man walking a Golden Retriever.

"The *Lusitania* sank?" he half-yelled, frantically grabbing a newspaper. He unfolded it and read the headline. Then he scanned the article that took up most of the front page.

"No, no, no!" he cried out, breathing hard. The names of the victims weren't mentioned. Tossing the newsboy a coin, he haphazardly stuffed the paper under his arm and hailed a taxi.

The *Times*' article reported that Cunard's office in Britain would telegraph the names of the dead, the living, the injured, and the missing to their New York office every few hours.

"Please take me to Pier 54," he ordered sliding into the back of the cab.

"Cunard, sir?"

"Yes."

"The *Lusitania*," he said in a tone that reflected his understanding. "A friend of yours was on board?"

"My fiancé."

"Oh. So sorry, sir. Things don't look so good for the folks traveling on that ship. I heard she went down fast. Not like the *Titanic*. They had a couple of hours to try to get off, but the *Lusitania*, well, they're saying she sank in minutes."

"That doesn't mean my Yvette isn't safe," Jonathan snapped back. "I'm certain her Father made sure his family made it safely to a lifeboat." He closed his eyes pictured her face. And he prayed.

THE CUNARD Office was located inside the large building where the *Lusitania* had docked. It felt odd to Jonathan to be in the last place where Yvette and her family had been before boarding the ship. *I should have been here the day she left*, he admonished himself. *Damn it. Damn the Germans and their damnable torpedoes*. Fists clenched, he headed to the counter.

Hundreds of people – friends and family of the passengers, reporters and photographers – crowded around. Names of some of the passengers had already been posted on the enormous chalkboard covering much of one wall – one column for drowned, one for injured, one for saved. None of the Rogers' family was listed.

When the newest identifications were received by wire, a Cunard employee climbed a step-ladder. A hush fell over the otherwise noisy interior as he wrote out their names. With each new entry, there were reactions – too often sorrowful cries, sometimes angry words directed at the Germans and, more frequently, at Cunard's management and at Captain Turner.

Like so many others, Jonathan stayed through the night, waiting, hoping, praying. His job, be damned. He couldn't focus on anything but Yvette. Thoughts, memories filled his head. Visions of his pretty princess – he liked to call her that, though she wasn't too keen on the princess part – in one of her pink dresses as she walked beside him. He thought of her beautiful hair, her soft lips, her silly laugh.

Hours later, Jonathan held his breath as the latest telegraphed list was carried to the chalkboard by an employee. He watched impatiently as the man wrote several more names in the survivors' column. And when the man drew a rather fancy "Y" in the "Injured" column, his heart raced. The rest of the name was scrolled. "Yvette." And then, "Rogers."

"Oh, my Lord! She's alive!" he shouted out loud. Jonathan couldn't help himself. "She's alive!" he said, laughing this time. "Injured, but alive!" He turned, smiling, as he pushed his way to the front desk. "Is there any way to know how critically my fiancée is injured? She's listed as alive but injured. How can I find out where she is, or if she's going to be okay? Or if her family made it, too?"

"I'm so sorry, sir. We realize the waiting is terrible. But the gents over in Ireland are doing their best to wire us as soon as anyone from the U. S. is identified," he said. "I'm certain there will be more information as the days pass. But for now, go home and get some sleep. It has been a very difficult time for all of us."

MUCH TO Jonathan's surprise, passenger liners didn't stop their crossings between the United States and Great Britain, including British-owned Cunard liners. Even more surprising to him was that so many people were trying to get to England. He was finally able to book a third-class cabin on the SS *New York* leaving in another week. Bound for Liverpool, the ship was American-owned, and it flew the American flag. Not that it was a guarantee the German U-boats would leave ships owned by the U. S. alone. After their calloused aggression against the *Lusitania*, what would happen next was anyone's guess.

"EUSTON STATION! End of the line," the uniformed conductor bellowed as he walked through the train car.

Curtis had managed to doze off and on during the trip. God, he needed a shower and shave. The journey was long and tiring. By train and ferry from Ireland to Liverpool, then by rail to London. An employee of Morgan and Grenfell, Ltd., Morgan's London's office, would meet him at the station.

Before leaving Queenstown, Curtis had wired Mr. James Stephenson, a respected high-ranking company executive, the man to whom he and Van Camp were to have delivered the loan documents. Curtis had reported that, together with several other corpses, including the producer, Charles Frohman, Mr. Van Camp's remains had washed up along a rocky beach south of Queenstown. Van Camp's remains, Curtis was told, were to be buried in Queenstown.

284

Morgan and Grenfell's representative had telegrammed Curtis in Ireland requesting he bring the loan documents to the office in London as soon as possible. He had responded that he would arrive in London in two days. He didn't mention the loss of the vital papers on the *Lusitania*. That would have to be done in person. It deserved a lengthy explanation, he felt. Nothing short and sweet like "PAPERS LOST." Tempting, but it would have been cowardly.

Exiting the railcar, Curtis spotted a balding, thin-faced man waving his hand. "Here we go," Curtis said under his breath. There was no way out of this one. He had dreaded facing the firestorm of criticism, even though it had been Van Camp's decision to cloister the crucial documents in the Purser's safe. Van Camp was accountable. But, then, he was gone.

"Hello there! Mr. Carlson, I gather."

"I am. And you are?"

"Mr. Wade. I've been driving for the Morgans here in England for years." Curtis forced a smile. He carried a brown leather valise, which he had purchased in Queenstown, in his left hand, still bandaged; and a small suitcase with a new shirt, fresh undergarments, a toothbrush, comb, razor and hair cream in his right hand. Wearing the cleaned clothes he'd been in on the ship, he had donated the scratchy Irish wool trousers and jacket to a third-class passenger before he left Queenstown.

"I'd like to freshen up and shave before heading over to Morgan's office," Curtis explained. "Please stop by a pharmacy...I mean a chemist's, before we go to the hotel."

"Of course, sir." Mr. Wade took the suitcase from Curtis and led him towards a shiny black Rolls Royce. What Curtis didn't mention, and the true reason he needed to see a druggist was he wanted to purchase medicine to soothe his churning stomach.

CUNARD'S OFFICE had given him a voucher provided by Mr. Morgan for a free stay at the Savoy, one of London's most prestigious hotels. The Savoy's rooms had been occupied by royalty, actors, and diplomats from all over the globe. Mr. J. P. Morgan himself had stayed there many times. Strange, it seemed, that the Savoy was where Mr. Frohman said he always stayed on his visits to England. He even had a favorite table in the hotel's dining room. *How many of Frohman's party are dead now?* Curtis wondered. *Rita Jolivet is alive, but what about the rest of the producer's famous friends?*

Curtis wondered what, if anything, Cunard had done to assist the survivors who hadn't traveled in first class. An anonymous British philanthropist had provided some money for them to buy new clothes and food, and the Irish people had helped with lodging passengers from second and third Class. But, how would they get home? Was Cunard paying for their transportation? It was troubling.

As the Rolls Royce pulled up to the hotel, Curtis told the driver he would need at least an hour to get ready. "Two hours would be even better."

"Afraid not, Mr. Carlson" the driver said, opening the rear door. "Sorry, but Mr. Stephenson awaits your presence...most impatiently. I'll be back at three."

While the Savoy was simple on the outside, the interior was another story. The lobby felt more like a French palace than a British hotel. Walking into his suite behind the bellboy, Curtis searched his jacket pockets, finally finding an Irish coin. Not worth much, Curtis realized. "Sorry, lad," he said with an embarrassed shrug. "This is all I have for you at the moment. I'll get back to you when I've had a chance to visit the bank to get some British pounds."

"No worries, sir," the young man said, lowering his head in a respectful manner. "If you don't mind, I'd rather have a shake of your hand, Mr. Carlson, with what you've been through and all. Me name's Jimmy. Jimmy Winkle."

Embarrassed, surprised, Curtis held out his right hand. "Sure, Jimmy. I'm just curious. How did you know? About me being one of the survivors, I mean."

"Blimey, sir. We all know. The Prime Minister instructed the hotel management to treat the survivors with the greatest of respect. Especially you Americans. They're checking in a dozen today, I reckon."

"I see."

"If you ask me, sir, that ship was doomed before she ever left port. The British government should take the blame for what 'appened to all of you. The newspapers said they should, they did." Jimmy stepped closer. "Some folks think Churchill and the bunch let the whole thing 'appen, if you know what I mean."

He didn't. "Why would the British Admiralty let something like that happen?"

"To get you Americans into the muddle." The bellboy tugged down on his uniform jacket. "Quite a few Americans died, from what they said. If you Yanks get riled up, your president will join in the war effort."

Surprised, Curtis drew back. "That sounds crazy. I mean, to let so many people die. Not just Americans, but—"

"They're saying the British Admiralty didn't think one of them German subs could actually sink the *Lusy*, what with the big ship being so fast and all. Reckon it surprised the old boys that the torpedo hit the ship at all. It's criminal, I jolly well say."

"Are you saying the Prime Minister knew the *Lusitania* would be torpedoed?"

"Not me, sir. The newspapers. They said there was no naval escort ships sent to protect the *Lusy*, the way it's been done since the war started. And they said a couple of other cargo ships had gone to the bottom a short time before the *Lusy* was blasted. They bloody well knew there was a German submarine mucking about in the area. I wonder if they warned your captain."

Curtis felt like the wind had been kicked out of him. "I had no idea." He searched Jimmy's face. "Of course, this is just rumor, right?"

"I reckon. Depends on if you believe what you read. And it does seem like the P. M. and Churchill are determined to get you Americans involved. Blimey, sir, I can't think of a better way to do it. Can you?"

AFTER CLEANING UP, Curtis hurried back to the Rolls Royce and its impatient driver. The Morgan and Grenfell office was situated in north-central London in the main business district across town.

Curtis had never been to London. The historic city was impressive, though the decorative friezes in the facades of the old buildings were black with centuries of coal soot. He hadn't imagined his first trip to Mr. Morgan's London office would be under such difficult circumstances. He would have to single-handedly explain what happened to the loan documents and convince Mr. Stevenson that losing the papers wasn't his doing. Stevenson would then send a wire to Mr. Morgan in the Manhattan office regarding the reason the crucial papers had gone down with the ship. Curtis would make it perfectly clear that he had tried to retrieve the loan papers after the torpedo struck; and that he had risked his life to fulfill his duty and his promise to Mr. Morgan.

But how far should he go with disparaging Van Camp and his cowardly actions? Should he tell Mr. Stevenson the truth? *Geez*, he thought, squirming uncomfortably as the driver pulled up in front of the office. He'd have to avoid mentioning he'd saved an elderly woman and her dog before he ran to the Purser's Office.

Nervous, Curtis climbed out of the motorcar. Drawing in a breath of courage, he stepped inside the office.

"Is it you, Mr. Carlson?" A nice-looking man of around forty approached. "We've been expecting you."

"Yes, sir. I'm Curtis Carlson."

"Jolly good! I'm Charlie Winters. So happy to meet you." He reached out to shake Curtis' hand, a wide grin covering his round face. His eyes glanced at the bandage on Curtis' injured hand. "Oh! I'm ever so sorry, old chap," he said, withdrawing his right hand. "Was it from the...the tragedy? I mean, were you injured making your escape?"

"Yes. But I'll be fine."

Winters' gaze dropped. "Don't mean to pry, sir, but we've heard so many reports about the deaths. Terrible. Simply terrible."

Curtis reached up and patted Mr. Winters' shoulder. "I'd say I got off pretty easy, compared to most."

A distinguished, clean-shaven man with silver hair approached. "Greetings, Mr. Carlson," he said in an enthusiastic, albeit loud voice. He introduced himself as James Keegan. "Everyone. This is Mr. Carlson from the New York office. A survivor of the *Lusitania* disaster."

Applause erupted, and literally, everyone in the open-floored office rose. "Here, here, my good fellow!" someone yelled.

Curtis felt his cheeks burning. "Thank you, gents. But that's not necessary."

"Please, sir. You must tell us all about it," one of the typists, a middle-aged woman with dark hair set with finger-waves, said. "The

288

Germans have done so much evil," she added. "This has been such a difficult time for everyone in Great Britain."

"Perhaps Mr. Carlson can share his stories later," Mr. Keegan said. "At the moment, Mr. Stephenson is waiting for Mr. Carlson's arrival."

WITH PROPER introductions made, Curtis settled into a chair in Mr. Stephenson's office and broke the news about the fate of the crucial loan documents.

"I'm rather not surprised, Mr. Carlson. According to the newspaper accounts, the *Lusitania* went under quite fast. Not much time to save anything but yourselves."

Curtis felt slightly relieved that Stevenson understood the predicament. "Yes, sir. It was mere minutes. Something around fifteen or sixteen, though it seemed like it was even less. Everything happened in a blur."

"And you say Van Camp ordered *you* to retrieve the documents from the Purser's Office?" Mr. Stephenson pushed his wire-rimmed glasses back up his rather large Roman nose. "And where was he when the torpedo hit?"

Curtis shrugged. "All I know is that he managed to get a seat on a collapsible, as did I, though mine was the last one available."

"I see." Mr. Stephenson's brow furrowed. "His was one that overturned, then?"

"Yes. Too many were in disrepair and took on water. I was told that many couldn't be launched. I had to cut the one I was in loose with a pocket knife. It was almost impossible to launch. Cunard should have to pay dearly for the death of so many innocent people."

"And they found Mr. Van Camp's body. Did his family ask to have his remains shipped home?"

"I believe he was buried in one of the mass graves in the cemetery near Queenstown." Curtis swallowed hard. "Most of the dead were buried together. There was no time to—"

"I read that Mr. Vanderbilt hasn't been found."

"No, sir. Hundreds of people are unaccounted for and presumed dead." Curtis held back his emotions. All he could think of was that Josie was among the missing. That she had drowned and washed out to sea and… He closed his eyes, trying to erase that image from his head. "Sorry. It's still too painful."

Mr. Stephenson smiled gently. "I understand, son. Such a waste of life." His expression changed. "Damnable Germans!" He rose, his jaw clenched, eyes narrowed. "After this travesty, I feel certain your President Wilson will jump in and help our Allied forces."

"What will happen now that the loan papers are gone?" Curtis asked.

"I'll discuss it with Mr. Morgan and the others involved in the transaction. It's imperative England and France obtain the money as quickly as possible. Ammunition is running low for the Allied troops. So is food. Without the Morgan loan, we will likely lose this war. And if we lose, America will lose with us, whether or not they're participating in the fighting. After all, we are trading partners with the United States. Wilson should have a better handle on things. He cannot simply brush aside what's going on over in Europe. America needs the Allies to win, or the American economy will be in turmoil."

CURTIS WAS SURPRISED to learn that passenger ships – even British owned ones – were still making the crossings between Liverpool and New York. Like the other passengers on board the SS *St. Louis*, Curtis was in a hurry to get to the United States. The ship was a much smaller vessel than the grand *Lusitania* had been. The amenities were few, the décor was simple, and the food was marginal, at best.

It was nerve-racking to be out on the open sea again. Curtis found himself scanning the waters, half expecting to see the conning tower of a submarine or the trail of bubbles left by a torpedo. Mr. Stevenson had informed him that after the *Lusitania* sank, President Wilson admonished the Germans for attacking a passenger liner. He quickly negotiated a guarantee from Kaiser Wilhelm. American ships would be safe on Atlantic crossings, as long as the United States stayed out of the war. And if they didn't transport munitions to England or France. Still, the vision of the torpedo blowing up inside the *Lusitania*; the ensuing catastrophe; the dead and dying, and most especially, the loss of Josette, haunted him.

The hours aboard the ship ticked by slowly. At night he laid in bed, rolling with each pitch of the ship, imagining what might have been. Remembering Josette's delicate features: slightly turned up nose, full lashes, tiny dimples when she laughed. Life with Josette would have been an adventure. He turned on his side, adjusting the blanket, too short for his six-foot-two height.

And when his eye lids became heavy and drifted shut, visions of dead faces stared up at him, startling him awake. Damn. Would he ever get past this misery? As much as he tried to act like a normal human being, as much as he tried to be friendly and smile at his fellow passengers on the *St. Louis*, the faces on the Promenade Deck and in the dining room seemed to morph into the faces he had become so familiar with on the *Lusitania*; the same distorted, paper white faces he had viewed in the morgues and on the quay.

Each time he left his small, sparsely decorated stateroom, Curtis attempted to gather himself. To put those thoughts out of his mind. Like Mrs. Donaldson had said, he had to get on with his life. What other choice was there for any of them – the *Lusitania* victims, as some people called them? They were survivors, not victims. They were individuals who had lost their children, widows grieving their now-dead husbands and vice versa.

Despite the crew's words of comfort and the captain's personal guarantee the 'Huns' would not repeat the *Lusitania* mistake, there was no peace of mind for Curtis or any of the other dozen men and women on board who had survived the horrors of the *Lusitania*. And yet, there was no other way home. Back to America. Back to their so-called normal lives.

Chapter 37

IT TOOK JONATHAN nearly three weeks to get to Ireland, and when he finally arrived in Queenstown late Thursday afternoon, he was exhausted. Paying the taxi driver, he picked up his suitcase and wandered down the street bordering the waterfront in search of the hotel where he had booked a room.

Queenstown was far from the quaint village he had imagined. He had expected cobblestone streets and white-washed cottages and thatched roofs. Instead, the hills surrounding the port were covered with painted houses that looked like children's building blocks stacked up the streets running perpendicular to the bay. Along the main thoroughfare, picturesque little hotels, restaurants, and a variety of shops faced the bay. Dominating the setting was a large church with a tall spire.

"Excuse me," he said to a stout, older man wearing a dark tweed cap. "Can you please direct me to the hospital where the injured *Lusitania* passengers were taken?"

He squinted, surveying Jonathan suspiciously. "Another American reporter, are ye?"

"I'm no reporter, sir." Then Jonathan explained his reason for coming to Ireland.

The man's demeanor changed. "Let me introduce meself. I'm Tavis Conner. 'Tis been a terrible time for all of us here. The newspapers 'round the world are calling Queenstown 'the port of the dead,' what with the mass burials and coffins and hearses."

"I can't even imagine how awful this has all been for you and your fellow residents, sir. My fiancée's family is among the missing. Presumably, they're dead and perhaps now lie in one of those mass graves in your cemetery."

"That, or they're calling the sea their final resting place."

The image made Jonathan's skin crawl. He thought about haughty Mrs. Rogers and her phony French accent. Stern Mr. Rogers, a man who worked hard and loved his family. And Yvette's identical twin, Josette. Beautiful, feisty, stubborn. They were all missing. Surely, they were dead. Poor, dear Yvette. She would have to live with the terrible fact. And he would have to help her through this.

After the Irishman gave him directions to the hospital, Jonathan expressed his gratitude and headed to the hotel at the end of the block to drop off his suitcase. The main thoroughfare bustled with wagons carrying wooden crates and large boxes of freight that had been loaded from the ships that docked along the quay. Automobiles were few in number compared to various horse-drawn conveyances. Queenstown had seemingly begun to return to normal after such a great tragedy had interrupted the lives of so many of its local residents.

BY THE TIME he reached Queen's Hospital, the sun had dipped low in the sky.

"May I help you, lad?" the woman at the front desk asked.

"Hello, madam. I'm Jonathan Franklin, and I'm here to see—"

"Ah, yes. Miss Yvette Rogers," she said with a wide grin. Which Jonathan found odd, given the circumstances. The woman, a slight creature with large eyes and dark hair secured into a small bun on the nape of her neck beneath the edge of her white cap, called to one of the nurses. "Oh, Sister McGrath. Please escort the gentleman up to see our Yvette Rogers. 'Tis the lad we've all been expectin.'"

The nurse, who had crossed the room and was heading for the stairs, turned and smiled. "Saints preserved! So you're here at last! Follow me, Mr. Franklin. We have a surprise for you, we do."

Yvette was in a bed near the back of the long room, sitting up, leaning against a pile of pillows. She turned towards him as he approached.

"She's awake!" Jonathan shouted to the nurse. Then he sprinted to Yvette.

Her head was partially bandaged on the right side, but she was still beautiful, despite her injuries.

"Yvette!" Jonathan said, hesitating momentarily at the sight of her. He drew in a sharp breath. "Lord in heaven!" He felt tears forming in his eyes. "Yvette! Yvette!"

The nurse trailed several feet behind him.

Reaching her, Jonathan reached out and took her hands.

"Oh, my dearest! I thought...I thought you were in a coma." He scanned her face. The scratches seemed to be healing, though there was still a bit of bruising on the right side above her eye. "How are you feeling, my love?" He leaned closer to kiss her.

"No!" Yvette looked frightened.

Jonathan drew back, confused.

Yvette's gaze moved to the nurse. Her brows furrowed deeply as she looked at him again. "Do...do I know you, sir?"

"Of course! It's me, darling. Jonathan."

"Don't you be worrying yourself, Mr. Franklin," Sister McGrath said in a comforting tone. "She's suffering a bit of memory loss. The doctor said it's not unusual for someone who has experienced a head injury the way she has."

Jonathan stood up straight and addressed the nurse. "How long will her confusion last?"

"'Tis up to the good Lord," she said. "She'll be healing in her own good time." Sister McGrath placed her hands on her generous hips. "And havin' you here, well, I'm sure it'll help with the process. Just be remindin' her of all the t'ings she's forgotten, and you'll be seein' miracles happening."

THE RIDE BACK to the center of town was miserable. Jonathan didn't know what to do. Should he cry or scream or...? Yet, his pink princess was alive, and she would recover. Before he left, the doctor had taken him aside, explaining it could take months or even years for patients with severe concussions to recover their memories. On top of that, something as horrific as the *Lusitania* disaster could have caused her mind to deliberately shut out hurtful memories – things like recalling her sister and parents, for instance. Yvette, he said, would need to remain in the hospital for a few more weeks before she could be moved to London.

Jonathan realized just how difficult that would be for Yvette. As the only remaining family member, she would need to take care of business matters, including her father's inheritance, once she was well. There was also the matter of the Rogers' mansion in London and Yvette's father's will. So many details, and she couldn't even remember her name.

After wolfing down a large plate of fish and chips and a glass of dark ale at the local pub, it was back to the hospital. To Yvette. This time, an elderly woman sat next to the bedside.

"I've been expecting you lad." She introduced herself as Mrs. Donaldson. "And now that you're here, I'll be heading to my home in Scotland. Unless you need my continued support, Yvette," she said with a worried look.

Yvette didn't say anything, but her face reflected utter bewilderment.

"From what the nurses told me, you've been an angel, madam. You've stayed true to your word and visited her every day."

"Mrs. Donaldson has been a good friend," Yvette managed. "I don't know how I shall ever be able to repay you for your kindness, ma'am."

"Och!" she replied with a wave of her hand. "You dinna owe me anything."

"How long has she been awake?" Jonathan asked. He stood on the opposite side of the bed across from Mrs. Donaldson.

"Less than a week," she responded. "I believe I sent you a telegram, but you must have already been enroute to Ireland." She suddenly looked confused. "Or did I send it to Mr. Clark, my estate overseer?"

"Well, it doesn't matter now. I'm here," he said with a smile, gazing down at his beloved. She was too thin and pale as milk. The bandage on a portion of her head was clean, but the hair around its edges was caked with dried blood. "Oh, my poor darling," he whispered, reaching down with his hand to touch her cheek.

She recoiled. "I'm sorry, Mr. Franklin. Jonathan. But I would appreciate it if you could keep your distance. Please give me time."

"You must remember, you're a stranger to her," Mrs. Donaldson said in an understanding tone.

It was a painful reality for Jonathan. He let out a deep sigh.

"Oh, lad. Don't give up hope. Your love will shine through. I'm certain of it. She spoke of you so often on the *Lusitania*." She glanced up, "Who was it who said love conquers all?"

"It's a painting by Caravaggio. *Amor Vincit Omnia*," Yvette whispered.

Jonathan's jaw slackened with surprise. "My gosh, Yvette. How did you know that?"

"I don't know. I believe I remember reading about that painting. I think it was done around 1602." Yvette blinked several times, then continued. "The artist was Italian. Quite famous, especially in Rome. And, and the painting itself is a nude cupid with wings." She looked up at Jonathan. "Yes. I remember. I read about it in an art history class."

Baffled, Jonathan drew back. Forced a smile. "Art history? I didn't realize you studied it."

"I believe I did," Yvette said with a little smile and a strange look.

Jonathan felt as if his heart had stopped beating. Yvette – his Yvette – wasn't the least bit interested in such things. *Oh my God. Is this Josette?*

AFTER A QUICK BITE of breakfast, Jonathan accompanied Mrs. Donaldson and her adorable Westie dog to the train station. Saying goodbye to Yvette last night had been difficult for the Scottish woman. And for Yvette, too, who teared up as she thanked Mrs. Donaldson for her unwavering kindness.

Although he hadn't said anything to Yvette about her uncharacteristic and sudden interest in art history, he couldn't forget the matter. Walking helped him think better and clear his mind. And he certainly needed to mull over yesterday's events.

The morning air was quite agreeable; perfect for a stroll around town. Passing by Cunard's office, he decided to go inside to see if any other bodies had been recovered or identified. Josette, as far as he'd last heard, hadn't been found yet. Stepping close to the updated list of names on the counter, Jonathan scanned the pages. Unlike Cunard's New York office, the entire passenger register had been posted. And it had been alphabetized. Notations were made in small print beside those who had been saved and those who had been identified among the dead. The rest of the people – those who were still missing or had not been identified as of yet – didn't have any markings beside their names. Thumbing to the pages containing the "R's," he saw that Henry Rogers, Mildred Rogers, and Josette Rogers were still among the latter grouping.

Leaving the front counter, Jonathan turned and stepped towards the exit, glancing through an open doorway as he passed. Inside the office, a woman sat in front of a clerk's desk as he spoke to her. Her back was to him. She wore a straw hat, and a braid hung on her back. Her hair color was much like Yvette's – golden with a caramel hue.

And then he heard her voice.

"You are not listening to me, sir!" she said in an angry tone to the man behind the desk. "Good heavens! You've listed me as a patient at Queentown Hospital. Obviously, that's not true. I'm sitting right here! You have made a mistake. I've never been at that or any other hospital in Ireland. I have been recuperating at the Downing family's farm."

Jonathan's jaw slackened. Goosebumps tingled on his arms, neck and head.

The young woman continued. "The patient in the hospital has to be my sister, Josette Marie Rogers."

"Yvette?" Jonathan said, storming into the room. "Dear God! Is that you?"

The young lady twisted around, still sitting. "Jonathan! You're finally here!"

He rushed to her, arms outstretched, walking to the front of her chair. "Oh, my darling. I found you!" He stopped when he saw the cast on her left foot. A pair of crutches leaned against the edge of the desk. "You've been hurt!"

"Yes, I know!" She struggled to stand, her cheeks flowing with tears. "I broke a bone or two in my foot when I jumped from the ship. I hit a piece of wreckage and—"

Jonathan reached out and helped her up, drawing her to him. "Oh, my poor darling." He stroked her head, her back, kissed her forehead and cheeks repeatedly. As she drew back to look up in his eyes, he kissed her gently on the mouth.

Mr. Adams, the clerk, cleared his throat several times, as if to interrupt. Finally, he spoke. "I presume this is your fiancée, sir."

Without moving his gaze from Yvette, Jonathan said, "How did you figure that one out?"

OUTSIDE THE CUNARD building, Jonathan helped Yvette to find a bench. Sitting beside her, he took her hand, giving it a gentle squeeze. "I'm so sorry about your mother and father, my darling."

Biting her bottom lip, Yvette nodded. "Thank you," she whispered. "But I believe my sister is still alive! I saw my own name among the injured that had been admitted to Queenstown Hospital. There must have been a mix-up, because I was taken to a farm outside of town to recuperate."

"I know, my love. It's Josette. I saw her yesterday. They told me she was you, but I knew it wasn't."

"You saw her? How is she? Is she going to be all right?"

He helped Yvette stand again, sliding the crutches under her arms. "She's lost a lot of her memory. The doctor believes it was because she was struck on the head by something during the time she was in the water. She had a bit of hypothermia but no permanent damage. Luckily, she was pulled into a lifeboat before she froze, unlike so many other poor souls."

"Please, my love. Take me to her. I can't wait another minute."

JOSETTE SEEMED to be dozing when Jonathan and Yvette approached her bedside. Yvette reached out and laid her hand on her sister's arm. She leaned down and spoke in Josette's ear.

"Sister. Wake up. It's Yvette."

Josette's eyes fluttered open.

"I'm here, Josette. Do you know me?"

Josette's expression was one of confusion. She narrowed her eyes, searching Yvette's face. "You do look familiar."

Yvette burst into laughter. "Well, sister, I should hope so."

"Sister? You're my, my sister?"

"I am! Wait a minute. I have something to show you." Yvette fished into her handbag and retrieved a small gold trimmed mirror. She held it low, in a place where Josette could see her own reflection. "There. Take a look at yourself."

Josette lifted her head, gazing into the mirror. "Oh my," she gasped. "I look terrible."

"Don't worry about that, sister. As soon as they get that bandage off your head, we'll shampoo your hair and give you some curls. Now look at yourself and then look up at me."

Josette appeared confused. Staring into the mirror, she glanced at Yvette and then back at the mirror. Her brows lifted. "Oh, my goodness. We do look quite alike," she said in a barely audible tone.

"That's because you're twins," Jonathan said. "Do you remember? Even a little?"

Josette laid her head back on the pillow." "My heavens. I have a twin." She looked over at Yvette again. "Please. Sit with me and tell me about everything. I must remember my life."

AFTER LEAVING THE HOSPITAL, Jonathan and Yvette made their way into the cozy restaurant inside the Queen's Hotel. A fire crackled in the fireplace, totally unnecessary considering the agreeable weather. Fortunately, their table was pushed against the windowed wall overlooking the street where they had a slight view of the bay.

Yvette wore the ill-fitting green checkered dress that had been provided by kind Mrs. Downing. She removed her shawl, folding it and hanging it over the back of the chair. Jonathan took the crutches from her and helped her sit.

"Let's order wine," Jonathan said. He leaned the crutches against the wall and sat facing Yvette. "We need to celebrate our good fortune."

"No wine for me. And I don't know that it's such good fortune, Jon." Her voice wavered, eyes tearing. "My parents are gone. Too many good people died in that tragedy. It was so horrible, and I was so frightened."

"I can only imagine, my dear." He fished a handkerchief from his coat pocket and offered it to her. "But you and your sister are both alive. And I'm here and I'll take care of you. Everything is going to be all right."

Yvette stretched her arm across the table, accepting the handkerchief. "What are we going to do?"

"Have you heard from your father's company?"

Yvette shook her head, dabbing her eyes. "I suppose I should send them a telegram. Most likely, they read that Yvette Rogers was unconscious in a hospital here in Queenstown," she said, rolling her eyes.

"Don't worry, darling. You'll spend time helping your sister get her memories back. I'll take care of everything else. You needn't worry your pretty head with business matters."

Yvette abruptly leaned back, frowning. "I'm no frail flower that must be taken care of, Jon. I've just survived an unthinkable tragedy. I believe I can handle working with my father's business associates and his barrister in London to settle the estate."

Jonathan was taken aback. This was a much stronger Yvette. "Well, well. I can see you are going to be fine, my dearest. Still, I shall be with you to help, should you need me."

Yvette smiled, her features softening. "Did you get my wire about Mr. Frohman's offer for employment in London? I left my message with the Marconi operator on the Lusitania just before I went to the stateroom."

"Mr. Charles Frohman, the producer?" Jonathan answered, taken aback. "I read he died. You met him?"

"Yes! I did. He…he was a wonderful man, Jonathan. It broke my heart when I learned of his death."

"I never received the message. He offered me a job?"

"He did, indeed," she said. "He told me he wired his business manager in England. You are to be hired to play for their theatricals." She let out a sigh. "You see, most of the musicians in Great Britain have already joined the military and are fighting overseas. Many have died at the Front."

"Yes, I know. Too many young men have already been lost, my dearest." Jonathan heaved a sigh. "Don't worry," he added, hoping to lift her spirits. We can contact Mr. Frohman's office in London. They'll help us sort everything out." He paused. "You must tell me all about Mr. Frohman when you're up to it. How you met. What he said. Meanwhile, let's not worry about employment right now. There are things we need to take care of first."

A plump waitress wearing a crisp white apron over her dress placed two menus on the table.

"Two teas, please," Yvette told her. "Bergamot, if possible."

As she walked away, he leaned forward. "This is a very nice hotel, Yvette. A perfect place for a honeymoon. I've spoken to the front desk manager, and he has a large suite available. All we need to do now is get married."

Yvette's eyes widened; her mouth fell open. "Married? But, I'm not of legal age yet."

"I know, my darling, I know. But who's to question? Your passport papers were on the *Lusitania*, and your father— Well, we shall simply tell them you're twenty-one."

"Lie?" Her eyes were as round as tea cups.

"Why not?" Jonathan smiled. "Desperate times call for desperate actions. Besides, it'll be easy. The hotel clerk said there's a place in Casement Square where we can register to be married. We can have a quick civil ceremony. Tomorrow."

She pulled her hand back. "Tomorrow? But you know I want to be married in a Catholic church. And perhaps my grandmother can give permission."

He shrugged. "Yes, though that would take time. You see, we can get married here. Now. And then we'll marry again in a Catholic church in London once things settle down. After I have a chance to convert to your religion. Your grandmother can come then." He reached into his pocket and pulled out the ring box he had been hiding. "I bought this in New York the day before my ship sailed." He removed the lid and held it for her to see. "I realize this is ridiculously fast, and it's quite unusual. But, then, these are unusual circumstances. So? What do you say, sweetheart?"

Yvette studied the diamond ring glittering inside the small velvet box. "Oh, Jon. It's beautiful." She raised her gaze, smiling. "And what about tonight, Jon? Will we stay in that big hotel room together?"

He could tell that the thought of having sex before they were officially married troubled her. "Yes, but we'll sleep separately. I'm sure there's a couch that I can use."

Yvette's face turned a shade of pink. "Perhaps," she said coyly, "that won't be necessary."

Chapter 38

"CURTIS! WOO HOO! Curtis Carlson!" A woman's voice rang out, louder than most other well-wishers who had come to greet the S.S. *St. Louis* on a pier near the Cunard wharf where the *Lusitania* had once moored.

Squinting, sunlight in his face, Curtis realized that it was Liliana O'Toole waving a white handkerchief from the crowd that waited on the quay. *Oh, crap. What in the hell is she doing here?*

Standing beside Liliana were his father, mother, and his fifteen-year-old sister, Margaret. Curtis' spirits immediately lifted at the sight of his family. He found himself grinning and waving back.

As the first passenger, another of the *Lusitania* survivors, made his way down the gangway, a cheer arose from the massive assemblage. Newspaper photographers had set up their cameras to record their return to American soil. Safe soil. Home.

A middle-aged woman in a cranberry-colored dress and matching hat pushed through to the front of the pack. "Lloyd!" she cried, waving a gloved hand in the air.

The man called out, "Henrietta!" half scrambling the rest of the way down the sloped gangway. The pair was reunited a few moments later, locked in a tearful embrace.

Newsmen flashed photographs of each passenger they thought was one of the survivors. They swarmed around them, throwing questions rapid fire. "What was it like?" one asked Curtis. "Did the Germans shoot at the people in the water like we heard?" another shouted.

"No. Not that I saw," Curtis answered. "Look, gents. It was a harrowing experience for all of us. We just want to go home and get some rest. Now, if you'll excuse me."

He elbowed his way towards his family and, unfortunately, Liliana.

His mother and sister sobbed. One by one, Curtis hugged each of them. When he paused in front of Liliana, he dropped his hands to his side. "Hello, Lil. How did you know I was going to be on the *St. Louis*?"

Throwing her arms around him, she shouted, as if to be heard over the crowd. "I was sooo worried about you, sweetheart. I kept checking and checking with the Cunard office, but they wouldn't tell me nothing at first." She drew back, looking into his eyes. "Can you believe they made me read your name in the list of survivors in the newspaper?"

Curtis almost said, 'You actually read?' He didn't. "Ah. I see."

"So, then, I telephoned your *da*, here," she went on, releasing Curtis as she glanced at his father. "And he was kind enough to tell me when you'd be arriving." Grinning, she flipped her hands up at the wrist. "So, here I am!" she boomed.

Curtis looked at his father. "Gee, *da*, thanks. That was certainly *nice* of you."

Looking a little sheepish and as if he understood Curtis wasn't at all pleased, his father simply answered with an "Uh. You're welcome, son."

Liliana smiled, completely missing the underlying meaning of the conversation. She slid her arms around Curtis' neck and leaned in close to his right ear. "My poor baby. Your *da* said you were injured. How's your hand doing? I'm so glad you're finally home," she whispered in a long ramble. "I'll come over to your apartment later. I'll bring dinner. Spaghetti and meatballs, like I know you love."

Curtis made no attempt to lower his voice. "Thanks, Lil, but I'll be spending the evening at my parents' house." He turned to his father, breaking loose of Liliana's grip. "Hey, Pop. Where's Wil?"

His father glanced down at Curtis' hand, still donning a small bandage. "Yes, my boy. How *is* your hand? Are the stitches out yet?"

"It's healing just fine. The doctor said I should be back rowing in a few weeks. So? Where did you say Wil is?"

"He's minding the store. Literally. But he said he'd be home tonight for dinner. He has some big news to share with us," his father said with a broad smile.

Liliana, on the other hand, wasn't smiling. She stepped back, obviously hurt. Her eyes were tearing, in fact. Curtis smiled at her and said, "Thanks for coming to welcome me home, Liliana."

His words did little to comfort her. Obviously, she had other plans for him.

"Of course," she said, wiping a wayward tear that had escaped her heavily mascaraed left eye. Pink rouge smeared on her white glove as she drew her hand across her cheek. "I'll see you soon, then. And if you need me to come by tonight, I'll even change your bandage. Nurse Lil, here," she said in a joking manner with a shrug. Then she smiled at his parents, moving her gaze back to Curtis. Excusing herself with a "See ya later," she disappeared into the crowd.

"What in heaven's name was that, son?" his mother asked with a perplexed expression. "When she telephoned, she told us she's your girlfriend. Is it serious?"

Curtis rolled his eyes and shook his head. "She only imagines she's my girlfriend, Mom. She's a neighbor, and a nosy one at that."

"Glad to hear that, son," his father said with a look of relief. "Girls like her aren't exactly wife material, what with the short skirt and painted face and all."

"Her skirt must have been six inches above her ankles," his mother added with a cluck of her tongue.

"She's a model. I guess shorter skirts are the fashion now. More modern, I was told."

Margaret lit up like a lamp. "Wait a minute! Oh, my gosh! That was Lilly May, wasn't it? I've seen her in all the fashion magazines."

Chuckling, Curtis answered. "Yes, that's her, all right. Bobbed hair, red lips and all."

"Golly, Curtis. Why didn't you tell me your neighbor was Lilly May? She's famous. And she likes you! Good grief. She's so pretty. Why isn't she your girlfriend?"

"Long story, kid. I'll tell you about her one of these days."

"Gosh and by golly," Margaret said with hopeful eyes. "I want to be a model one day. Please, Curtis. You simply must bring her over some time. You just have to."

CURTIS' YOUNGER BROTHER, William, was about as different from him as night and day. Wil had no interest in pursuing a university education and had always intended to take over their family's store when the time came. And that time came early. As soon as he graduated from high school, Wil became more than a full-time employee.

Curtis often teased his brother that he was smarter than he looked, a sure-fire way to irritate him. Wil would always fire back that he had no interest in politics or economics or history or travel like his bookish big brother. Wil's goal in life was to stay close to home and hearth. To marry a nice girl and have a wagonload of kids. And most of all, to follow in his father's footsteps with the business, something Curtis had never given a damn about.

With William at his side managing the business, his father had opened a second hardware store in Brooklyn. A third would soon open near Greenwich Village.

Sitting around the dinner table in the family's new house on the Upper East Side, Curtis looked around the table. "It's so good to be here. I can't even express how much I love all of you."

At fifty, his mother looked much younger. She dabbed the napkin at the corner of her eyes. "We were so frightened, son," she managed to say between sniffles.

His father shook his head. "Our country is in a real bind. Since the *Lusitania* tragedy, there have been protest movements all over the country insisting that we join the war effort."

"There are just as many Americans who don't want us in that war," William added. "We've all seen the newspaper reports about the

German atrocities and how many soldiers have died a terrible death. Young men my age don't want to go to Europe to die in a war that has nothing to do with us."

"Who can blame them for that?" his mother said. "I, for one, don't want my boys going over there to fight."

William poured himself a glass of red wine. "The experts say it should end pretty soon, so we might not have to make decisions about whether or not the United States should get involved."

"I wouldn't count on that," Curtis said, reaching for his stemmed glass. "The so-called experts predicted it would all be settled before last Christmas."

Father added his two cents. "Yes. And that the Germans would capitulate and things would get back to normal before Santa Claus made his rounds."

Curtis grinned. "You can see how well they did with that prognostication."

"Ooh. Such big words, brother," Wil teased.

Their father shot a familiar "quiet boys" look at them. "Be that as it may, most of the products we sell are produced here in the United States. But some of the manufacturers who once focused on things like nails and buckets – you know, things made out of metal, which is a lot of our inventory – have changed their tooling to make bullets and guns to sell to the British or the French governments."

"Or, most likely, anyone else willing to pay a hefty price. Including the German government," his mother added sarcastically. "Do you think your Mr. Morgan would do that to turn a big profit?"

"They wouldn't do that, would they, Curtis?" Wil asked with a shocked expression. "I mean, we're all on the side of the Allied countries, aren't we?"

Taking a sip of his wine, Curtis shrugged and swallowed. "I'm afraid you all don't understand the world of large corporations. It's all about making huge profits and getting rich. Especially with our cowardly president keeping America neutral right now."

"I still can't believe that horse's ass didn't declare war on the damned Germans after what they did to you and all those other innocent folks on that doomed ship," Father said in an angry voice. "What the hell is he thinking? What is he waiting for? Hell to freeze over?"

"Father. Watch your language please," Mother cautioned.

"Well, it's true. We have Germans spies right here in New York setting off bombs. I guess they'll have to kill more Americans before he takes any kind of action."

"Tell us about the *Lusitania*, Curtis. Where were you when the Huns attacked?" Wil asked. "Did you see the dead bodies?"

The image of a woman still holding her babe to her chest flashed into Curtis' mind. Her dark hair swayed with the ebb and flow of waves, her eyes closed. She looked so peaceful; like she was asleep. He had leaned out of the collapsible to see if he could rouse her. If she was alive. He had tried to pry the child from her rigid arms. Both were dead. Curtis drew in a sharp breath. "Yes," he answered softly.

Father cleared his throat. "Now, William. We all agreed we wouldn't discuss the…incident. Curtis doesn't need to be reminded about what happened."

"I want to know everything," Margaret interjected. "What was Rita Jolivet like, Curtis? Was she gorgeous? Did you talk to her? The newspapers said she almost drowned and that she had to jump into the water as the ship sank. Is that right? Did you see it? She's alive, right?"

Curtis smiled at his sister. "Dad's right. I'll tell you all about it in good time. Right now, I just want to have dinner and catch up on all of your news." He set down his glass.

Margaret huffed her disappointment, crossing her arms.

Thankfully, before the conversation went any further, two uniformed servants—Curtis didn't recognize either of them and surmised they were new—entered the dining room carrying trays of food. It smelled like a pork roast, one of Curtis' favorite dishes.

"Geez, it's great to be home," he said.

FINISHING HIS SLICE of apple pie, Curtis leaned back in his chair. "So, little brother. I understand you have a big announcement for us tonight."

William flashed his baby-blue eyes at Curtis, and then moved his gaze around the dinner table. "I do have some news to share. But let's wait for Mom."

"Wait for me to do what?" their mother said, entering with a small box tied with a red, white, and blue ribbon. She set it on the table, took her seat, and said, "Go on, Wil. Tell us. We've been dying to know."

"Okay, okay." William laughed, waving his hands. "I'll tell. I've asked Barbara to marry me, and the foolish girl said 'yes.' She was going to come tonight to share the news, but, unfortunately, she wasn't feeling well."

"You're getting married?" Mother said, her eyes instantly flooding with tears.

"We haven't set the date yet, but sometime next year."

"Nicely done, Wil," Curtis said.

Their father pushed back from the table and walked to William's chair. "Congratulations, son. That's wonderful news." He turned to the rest of the family. "First, we got Curtis back in one piece, and now this. Wil is getting married. Let's all lift our glasses and have a toast. To William and Barbara. And to our Curtis. May you all be as happy as your mother and I are tonight. Welcome home, Curtis."

After the toast, his father reached for the box and pushed it over to Curtis. And now we have one more piece of business to discuss. "Son," he said to Curtis. Your mother and I have been blessed in so many ways. When we heard the news about the *Lusitania,* we were frantic. I promised God that if he had spared you, I would do something wonderful to celebrate your safe return home."

Mother grinned. "Go ahead and open the box, son."

"What is this?" he asked, fumbling with the ribbon, a slight challenge with his injured hand.

"Oh, for heaven's sake, Curtis." Always an impatient child, Margaret grabbed the box and untied it for him. She opened the lid and handed him a piece of paper that had been folded several times... presumably so it could fit into the box. "Here," she said, presenting it to him.

He opened the page and read it. "It's a bill of sale." He felt like someone had punched him in the gut when he saw the word 'sloop' listed. "Holy smokes!" he gasped. "What's this?"

"Not just any boat, son," his father said. "It's the one you've had your eye on for more than a year. We thought you had endured so much, you deserved something good to happen."

"You bought the Herreshoff for me? I don't know what to say. Thank you so very much. I'll never forget this."

BACK AT HIS APARTMENT, his stomach full, his spirits lifted, all he wanted now was to sleep. Seeing his family had certainly made him feel happy for the first time since…since that ghastly day. And the sailboat. That would be his respite from the world. He would take her out as soon as possible and spend the day on the water.

After peeling off his jacket, he settled himself onto the couch.

A faint rap on the door interrupted his thoughts. "Curtis? Are you still awake?"

He drew in a frustrated breath. *Ah, nuts….*

"Curtis? I heard you come home. Can I please come in? I promise I'll only stay for a minute."

"I'm resting, Lil. Maybe some other time."

After a long silence, she answered. "I really need to see you. Please let me in."

Curtis groaned. "Sorry, Lil. I'm too tired for company."

Liliana didn't say anything else, but he could feel her presence, still standing on the other side of the door. Minutes passed, and she was still there.

"Please Curtis. It's real important."

"Oh, crap," he muttered under his breath. With a frustrated sigh, he walked to the door, unchained it, and pulled it open.

"Can't this wait, Lil? I'm exhausted."

Her eyes were red, swollen. "No. I have to talk to you."

"All right, all right. Come in."

Liliana was dressed in a flimsy pink silk robe, tied tightly around her waist, and heeled bedroom slippers.

"Have a seat," Curtis said, pointing to a chair.

She draped herself on the couch, the slit in her robe exposing her bare legs.

Curtis stood. "Now, then. What is it that couldn't wait until tomorrow?"

Pulling a handkerchief from her robe pocket, she dabbed her eyes, sniffing a few times. "I think you know how I feel about you, Curtis."

He bit his lip, nodding. "Yes. I believe so."

"And do you even care about me, even a little bit? I…"

Christ, he thought. Would he have to get blunt with the woman?

"I love you so very much. Please say you love me, too." God, how he hated being in this position. He didn't want to hurt her, but…

"Look, Liliana. We really don't know each other all that well."

Her expression hardened. "What?" Her voice was loud, sharp. "Don't know each other? Oh my God! We've slept together, Curtis Carlson."

"Love? That wasn't love. That was having too much to drink."

"It was more than that for me."

He slapped his forehead, pacing. "You can't love me, Liliana. We have nothing in common. I'm just a silly bookworm. An academic, who loves sailing. You live in a different world than I do. An exciting world with celebrities and bright lights. You want to get into the moving pictures."

"That's all over, Curtis. I've quit my modeling job."

"What? Why in God's name would you do that?"

"Because…" Tears flowed heavily, dissolving the last bits of mascara from her lashes, streaking dark stripes down her face. "Because I'm carrying our baby."

Chapter 39

July 1915

SINCE CURTIS HAD RETURNED to work at Morgan and Company, he had seen little of Jack Morgan. But today, the millionaire entrepreneur had returned to his Wall Street office. Curtis worried Mr. Morgan would reprimand him about losing the loan documents to Davey Jones' locker. And when Curtis was told Morgan wished to see him in thirty minutes, his stomach rebelled from too much coffee and no breakfast. He pulled out his top desk drawer, grabbed two digestive tablets and swigged them down with a gulp of lukewarm coffee.

On his first day back to work, Curtis met with the senior partners in a lengthy discussion about what had transpired on the *Lusitania*. Eight of Morgan's long-time associates stared up at him from their seats in the conference room as he explained, step by step, about the three German spies and why Mr. Van Camp had made the unfortunate decision to keep the papers entrusted with the Purser.

There hadn't been any further discussion or repercussions in that regard in the past weeks. Was that about the change? Standing outside Mr. Morgan's office at precisely ten o'clock, Curtis drew in a deep breath and rapped on the door.

"Ah, Carlson. Come in," Morgan called. As Curtis entered, Mr. Morgan smiled and instructed him to have a seat. "I hear congratulations are in order. How's the blushing bride? You married the lovely Lilly May, didn't you? My daughters were thrilled when I told them you married the famous fashion model."

"Yes. Lucky me. I married Lilly May," Curtis said with a half-smile, stepping to a chair facing Morgan's ornate desk. "I'm afraid she hasn't been feeling well these past days." Curtis was uncomfortable having to explain she was pregnant. "You see, we decided to start a family right away."

He leaned back, nodding. "Say no more. My wife had the same problem with the morning sickness for our first child. We worried about Mrs. Morgan's health, but she was fine, and Junius came out healthy and strong."

"Thank you. I'll pass that along to Liliana."

"I hear you've moved to the Upper West Side. To the impressive Ansonia Building."

"Our new apartment is certainly a big step up from the old place. It's near Central Park, so when the baby comes, my wife will be able to spend sunny days there."

"Good investment," he said with an approving nod. "And a good place to spend the bonus money and raise that I authorized for you, right, son?"

"Yes, sir. I certainly appreciate the gesture. I mean, not a gesture, but—"

"Nonsense, my boy. You deserve that and more. You risked your life to do your job for me. If that's not going the extra mile, then I don't know what is. You'd never catch someone working for that damnable Rockefeller doing something like that for his boss," he said, snickering. "You're a downright hero, tried and true. The *Tribune* interview they did with you reflected quite well on the House of Morgan."

Together with several other survivors who lived in New York City, Curtis' photograph had appeared in the newspapers, as well as quotes about the final moments of the *Lusitania*.

"Let me tell you why I've asked to see you, Carlson. As a sailing enthusiast, I'm sure you're aware we've canceled the annual America's Cup because of the situation with the war."

"I wasn't surprised. Sir Thomas Lipton didn't have enough young men to crew his vessel."

"Precisely. Too many left for the Front when Britain went to war." Morgan shifted in his chair, his dark eyes locked on Curtis. "Cornelius Vanderbilt, Alfred's brother – I believe you said you met the late Alfred Vanderbilt on the Lusitania – chartered a yacht, the *Vanitie*, to race against the *Resolute* off the coast near my house on East Island. I have financial interests in the *Resolute*, you see, so I do have some of the say-so about the crew."

"Are these official races or preparatory races, sir?"

"More for the fun of competition," he said with a wink. "Our friends over The Pond aren't exactly thrilled that we're doing this, since they can't participate. So, here's where you come in, my boy. I need another man to crew. Bill Tracy usually handles one of the jib winches, but he was in a motor car accident out on Long Island last weekend and broke some bones. Too much drinking, I believe." He looked disgruntled at the thought. "Think you could fill in his spot?"

Curtis chuckled, shaking his head in disbelief. "I'd be thrilled, sir. Racing one of the America's Cup yachts will be a dream come true."

Opening his fancy wood cigar box, he retrieved a fresh stogie. "Now, now. Don't get too excited. I need you back here at the office next week. There's a lot of work for you to catch up on." He glanced down, sliding the tip of a cigar into the cutter.

"Of course, Mr. Morgan. I'm honored."

"Excellent. Then you shall stay at Matinecock Point, my home on East Island. I have an extra guest bedroom, though you'll have to put up with several other guests, as well as my own family."

"Sounds terrific!"

"Go down and see Mrs. James, our new typist, for the details. I'll send a car for you in the morning. The crew has the boat readied. They'll get back to practice runs as soon as you arrive."

"Thanks so much, Mr. Morgan. I promise I won't disappoint you."

He turned to leave when Morgan said, "By the way…about the lost loan documents."

Curtis felt his stomach tightening. "Yes, I know. If I could do it over again, I would insist that they remain hidden in Mr. Van Camp's stateroom."

He shook his head. "No, son. That decision was Mr. Van Camp's. And it cannot be undone. I wanted to tell you that representatives from England and France will be coming here in the Fall to sign the new loan agreements. I suppose they'll have to come on an American ship. Hopefully, those damned Germans will keep their U-boats from launching torpedoes at the U. S. passenger ships."

PLACING HIS BRIEFCASE on the table in the entryway, Curtis sauntered further into the apartment. "Hello! I'm home!"

He paused long enough to hear clanking pans and the cook's footsteps through the closed kitchen door down the hall. He had hired a maid and a cook, since Liliana decided she hated preparing food and cleaning was out of the question while she was pregnant.

"Liliana?" he called. No response.

Entering the parlor, he saw that Liliana was draped across the settee in her silky, black Japanese kimono embroidered with red and yellow flowers.

"Are you all right?" he asked, baffled about her silence.

She shrugged. "I want you to stay home tomorrow to keep me company." She sat up and swiveled around. Three and a half months of pregnancy had barely changed her figure.

"You know I can't do that. I have to work. We have a baby coming, and money doesn't grow on trees." He stopped short of saying she was spending his earnings almost as fast as he earned it. Expensive clothes, bric-a-brac for the new house, things for the baby.

"What am I supposed to do while you're gone all day?"

Every time she whined, her lips pouted as if she were a child. It drove him nuts. "I don't know, Lil. Go visit your mother. Or volunteer a little time at an orphanage. Read something interesting." Lil and books, he mused. There was an odd pairing. She occasionally read the newspaper's society page, but books….

"Dinner is served, Mr. and Mrs. Carlson," Mary, the cook, announced at the doorway. "I've made Mr. Carlson's favorite. Pot roast."

"Oh, good God. Not again?" Liliana snipped. "Don't you know how to make nothing else? Spaghetti, for instance?" She stood up, pulling the robe closed.

Mary's face reflected her displeasure. "Yes, ma'am. I've made you spaghetti several times, and you said it made you sick, so I thought—"

"Well, Mary quite contrary," Liliana shot back. "You just don't know how to cook it right."

Curtis intervened doing his best to sound patient. "Thank you, Mary. Let me wash up, and I'll be in the dining room momentarily."

Mary nodded, turned and walked away.

"I'm not hungry, Curtis. You go on ahead."

"You need to eat, Lil. You have a baby growing inside you that needs healthy food."

"A baby that will make me fat and undesirable," she said with a sour look.

"For the hundredth time, you're pregnant. You'll still be beautiful. Believe me. You'll be able to get your figure back after the baby is born. But if you don't eat, the baby won't be healthy. And if you don't want pot roast, hell, Mary can make you something else. Eggs, maybe."

Liliana heaved a sigh. "Oh, all right. But I'm not eating nothing that's gonna make me fat."

THE NEXT MORNING, Curtis packed a suitcase for his trip to Long Island. He hadn't mentioned he would be staying at the Morgan's mansion. More than likely, she would have insisted on going with him. Instead, he jotted a note to her saying that Mr. Morgan had called, ordering him to go on a business trip. It was a lie, but a lie was better than another confrontation with her. He tiptoed into the bedroom, set the envelope on Liliana's dressing table beside her sterling silver brush and mirror set, and quietly left the room.

Walking down the front hall to the door, he took his hat from the rack and wished the maid the best of luck. "I promise I'll bring you and Mary back something special from my trip."

Anything, anything he could do to keep them from quitting. Bribes, perhaps, to show his gratitude for putting up with Liliana's constant complaining and badgering. "And just remember, she's pregnant. I'm sure things will be better once the baby comes."

THE NEXT THREE DAYS passed quickly. It had been close to a year since Curtis had sailed in a competition. Two days of practice was all it took for him to get his brain back into racing.

Despite of the light breezes, the crew of the *Resolute* was in fine form. Curtis' hand had healed completely, though he struggled with cranking the winch the first time out. Working through the discomfort, by day three, he felt like his strength had returned, and his determination to please his boss and win the race outweighed any pain or gripping weakness he experienced.

On Friday, they had their last practice, finishing with plenty of drinking and laughter on the yacht while it sat at anchor. It was heaven, tried and true; especially, being away from Liliana. Curtis felt suffocated by her. He would only escape for a few days, but he would enjoy his time on the *Resolute* to the utmost. And after the baby was born, he'd have to wait a few years until the child could don a life jacket. Then he would take him or her sailing on his new yacht. Curtis gazed up at the night sky, smiling at the thought. The closest stars sparkled blues and pinks…and he remembered the night on the *Lusitania*. Josette. Walking together on the Boat Deck. Standing at the guard rails and looking up at the constellations. Tears welled in his eyes. Sniffing, he finished off the rest of the Scotch in his glass. God, how he missed her.

SO HERE HE WAS, waking up in a guest bedroom on the second floor at Jack Morgan's grand East Island estate. The guestroom was furnished beautifully. It wasn't his taste, not at all, with its soft blue silky draperies, canopied bed, and what he guessed was French-styled furniture. Even the marble fireplace was a jumble of carved swirls topped with a mirror edged in gold gilt.

Curtis chuckled. He couldn't believe his good fortune, staying under the same roof as the British Prime Minister and his wife, the Morgan family, and assorted high-ranking dignitaries who had come to the mansion for the holiday to see the race. Not exactly the America's Cup, but a close second.

"Mr. Carlson? I have your breakfast tray," one of the servants said outside his door. "May I come in, sir?"

"One moment," he called. Quickly dressing in trousers and a shirt, he walked to the door, opened it, and took the tray out of the girl's hands. "Thank you, Miss…?"

"Miss Rooney," she said with a tiny curtsy.

A curtsy! To the son of a business proprietor.

"Would there be anything else I can get you, sir?" Her Irish brogue was charming.

"This will do nicely, Miss Rooney. And thank you again." When he gave her a little wink, she began to giggle, turned on heel, and then flitted down the hall.

Laughing, Curtis used his foot to close the door. He walked across the room and placed the tray on a small table under the window and poured a cup of coffee from the silver pot. He glanced outside to the sweep of lawns, neatly trimmed hedges, and a rainbow of colorful flowers that rimmed the long driveway. It was a glorious day.

A taxi entered the estate through the open gates, likely a late-arriving guest. He took a sip of coffee, watching as a pencil-thin man dressed in an ill-fitting gray coat climbed out of the motorcar. He certainly wasn't up to Mr. Morgan's usual standards for visitors. Nonetheless, he walked to the front door, disappearing from Curtis' view.

While the more important guests breakfasted downstairs, Curtis had decided to have a quick bite in his room. He would meet the yacht's crew at the dock in an hour for another practice run. Some stayed in the Morgan's guesthouse near the front gates. Others stayed at a nearby inn.

As he picked up the cup of coffee, he heard a commotion in the hallway. He suddenly heard shouting. Loud shouting. A woman let out a blood-curdling scream.

"What in the hell?" Curtis scrambled to his bare feet and headed for the door. Stepping into the hall, he saw the odd visitor, who had arrived in the taxi, standing at the top of the stairs.

"Holy crap!" he whispered. The man held a pistol in each hand. And they were aimed squarely at Mr. and Mrs. Morgan!

"Who are you?" Morgan shouted. "What do you want?"

"I have you, Mr. Morgan!" was the intruder's strange response.

Two of the Morgan's children stood behind the hawk-faced man. The young girl cried out. "Mother!"

"What do you intend to do with the children?" Mrs. Morgan said in an angry, insistent tone. Leaning forward as if ready to pounce on the gaunt intruder, her expression was one of a mother tiger protecting her cubs.

"Stay back, Jane," Morgan instructed his wife.

In a flash, Mrs. Morgan leapt in front of the man, putting herself between her husband and the intruder.

"Jane!" Mr. Morgan hollered, pushing his wife out of the way as he tackled the gunman.

Curtis raced forward just as the man pulled the trigger. Twice. "Run!" He yelled to the children. "Get help!"

Mr. Morgan groaned, obviously hit by the bullets. Still, he struggled with the would-be assassin, knocking the gun from his right hand.

Curtis was at the wounded tycoon's side. Blood had spread out rapidly across his waistcoat. Morgan had pinned the shooter down with his body. The intruder's left hand, still wielding a second gun, fought to shoot Morgan again.

Curtis dropped to the floor, prying the gun from the man's grasp. Several other men, including Mr. Physick, the butler, had rushed up from the first floor. Mr. Physick held a lump of coal in his hand. Gritting his teeth, he pounded the assailant's head.

"Stop!' Curtis shouted. "You'll kill him!"

He glanced up, dropping the black chunk. "That was my intent, sir."

"We need to know who sent him," Curtis said, pulling the injured Morgan off the shooter.

Mrs. Morgan rushed to her husband's side. Sobbing, she held his hand. Morgan's clothes were soaked with boood. He had been severely injured, but was conscious.

Curtis jerked the would-be killer onto his stomach, pinning his arms together. Something large and heavy had flopped out of the intruder's bulky jacket pocket.

"Dear Jesus. It's dynamite!" someone cried out.

Without thinking, Curtis handed the guns to one of the men, a guest from downstairs, who had heard the shots and came upstairs to help. Swallowing hard, Curtis reached out, carefully picking up the bundle of explosives.

"Good God, chap! Get it into a pail of water or something," Prime Minister Spring-Rice, said in a frightened tone. "It looks as if he set it with one of those timing devices."

"Follow me, Mr. Carlson," Miss Rooney instructed, surprisingly calm. She led Curtis to the bathroom at the end of the hall. He placed the dynamite sticks in the tub, while the maid turned on the faucet.

"Please make sure it's completely covered before you turn off the water," Curtis instructed.

Then he was back out in the hallway to check on Mr. Morgan. He was still awake. Mrs. Morgan and several others, including the Prime Minister, knelt beside him.

"Did someone call for a doctor?" the Prime Minister asked.

"Yes, sir. He's on his way," another man responded. "The police have also been notified."

The Morgans' burly chauffer had arrived with a length of rope and tied up the attacker. In spite of the blood oozing from his skull, he managed to yell. "I have been living in hell. I did not intend to shoot Mr. Morgan." His voice quivered, his German accent quite obvious. "I want to say to him, he should *not* be contributing to the British war effort. The weapons you send kill German men. They are human beings, just like you. This must stop, Mr. Morgan! If not, you should kill me now!"

ALTHOUGH MR. MORGAN had been shot twice, he insisted that he wasn't seriously hurt. And yet, he had lost plenty of blood. Morgan's private doctor found both bullets had passed through his body without so much as hitting bone or a vital organ. It was a miracle of sorts, Curtis thought. The gunman had shot directly into the financier's body at close range. Morgan had been lucky throughout his life, and today was further proof of his good fortune.

Not that Mr. Morgan saw it that way. He brushed off the incident as an unfortunate interruption to his holiday party. He angrily fought his doctor's order to stay in bed to recuperate.

Most surprising to Curtis was that Mr. Morgan insisted the yacht race go on as scheduled. It was a long-standing Independence Day tradition, and a couple of gunshots to his groin didn't change that. The race would take place on July 5th.

Although their spirits were low, each member of the *Resolute's* twenty-five-man crew pushed extra hard to secure victory to honor Mr. Morgan's bravery. Unfortunately, they lost by three minutes. Curtis wondered if things would have been different if the team hadn't been so distraught by the attack on the Morgan family.

Nevertheless, celebrations went on as scheduled. After the race and picnic-style dinner, Curtis was driven home. Back to the confines of his marriage. Back to reality. It was almost ten o'clock. As usual, Liliana sat in the parlor in front of the ornate marble fireplace, glass of red wine in hand, watching the dance of the flames.

"You really didn't need to wait up for me, Lil."

She took a sip from the goblet and looked up at him with narrowed eyes. "So, where were you, Curtis? Gone for days without so much as a telephone call." You look like you got some sun." Her tone was even more brusque than usual.

He let out a slow breath, walked to a chair on the other side of the fireplace and sat down. "There's something I have to tell you."

"What? That you were in the country with Josette?"

Curtis was stunned. "Josette? Why would you think that?"

"She's your mistress, isn't she?"

"No. I don't have a mistress. And why would you think of the name Josette?"

Liliana's face contorted. "You've made it pretty damned obvious you don't love me. You don't touch me. We don't have sex. Half the time, I feel like you don't even see me. And sometimes…you call out her name in your sleep." She spat the words.

Curtis answered reluctantly. What could he say at this point that wouldn't be hurtful? Or did that even matter now? "Look, Liliana. You knew I didn't love you when I married you. But I promised I would take care of you and the baby, and that's what I'm doing. And as far as Josette is concerned…" Even saying her name was like an arrow to the heart. "I knew her on the *Lusitania*."

Grunting, she said, "Does she live here in New York?"

"You don't understand, Liliana. Josette Rogers is, is dead."

"Oh." She paused. "But you still have a thing for her, right? She must have been a real dish. Did you have sex with her? You must have, or why else would you be dreaming about her."

Curtis was reaching his boiling point. "Of course not! Why would you even think that? She was a real lady."

"And I'm not, right?" Liliana took another sip from her glass. "I trapped you into a loveless marriage. That's what you think, right, Curtis?"

That's exactly what she had done, but saying those words would be useless. "Look, you're my wife. You're having my baby. I'm here for you. Isn't that enough?"

Without another word, her mouth set in a hardened frown, she set the glass down, walked past him, and went to bed.

Curtis sat up for a while, sipping a glass of his favorite single malt. Sleeping in the guest room was something he often did, especially when his wife was angry. And that was often. Dreaming about what could have been, should have been with Josie was where he found solace. And if he called out her name in his sleep, he didn't care what Liliana thought. He would move his things into the guest room. Permanently.

Chapter 40

WHEN JOSETTE was released from Queenstown Hospital in June, she accompanied Yvette and Jonathan to London, to the large, four-level house near Kensington Palace they had inherited from their father's estate. A Rogers and Rogers representative had already hired maids and a cook, who made sure the interior was spic and span and ready for their arrival.

"This place looks like a museum," Jonathan said, as they sauntered through the downstairs rooms.

Not surprising, the first thing Yvette had done when they walked inside the house was to search for a piano. "The Steinway is stupendous," Yvette said, entering the music room. "I wonder if it needs tuning?"

"We need to update the decorating to a more modern style," Josette said, scanning the room.

"When we get back to Compton House, we'll make changes there, too." Yvette pulled her fingers from her gloves as she spoke. "Mother loved her French Provencial décor. She always said it reminded her of her visits to the French palaces in the Loire Valley." Glancing around, she added, "I wonder how she would have liked this dingy place."

"At least it's been wired for electricity," Jonathan commented sarcastically.

Josette shrugged, glancing around the room. Red flocked wallpaper ran from the wainscoting to the high ceiling, while dark walnut paneling covered the lower portion of the walls. That, and the fact the ceiling-to-floor draperies were brown, made the room seem especially gloomy. "I suppose this will provide a good project for me to fill my time."

Yvette turned to her. "And when you're feeling better, perhaps you can continue writing your sociology paper. In time, some of what you wrote on the ship will probably come back to you." She smiled. "You have important things to do with your life. And I can guarantee that doesn't include the goal of redecorating old houses! On the other hand, I'm happy to have you take over the project."

IN THE WEEKS that followed, Josette and Yvette not only shopped for new wall coverings and furniture more suitable to their taste, they purchased new wardrobes at Harrods's and Selfridge's, had afternoon tea at the Savoy Hotel and the Ritz, and strolled around Trafalgar Square. The history of the city was preserved in its stone buildings, in massive statues, and in the Royal guards wearing crimson jackets and cylindrical hats that reminded Josette of a pile of black cotton candy. There were landmarks like Big Ben, London Bridge, and the infamous Tower, where famous people had lost their heads.

Indeed, London proved to be a fascinating city. Yet, the new blackout rules imposed by the War Cabinet made living in the glorious locale unbearable and too nerve-racking for Josette.

It was the fall now, and the sun disappeared each day around four o'clock. There were no sidewalk lamps to light the streets. No electric fixtures in the department stores' windows along Brompton Road in Knights Bridge to illuminate the delightful holiday displays. Lights, even the smallest lanterns, British officials said, would help guide German Zeppelins as they crept across the sky dropping aerial bombs and incendiary devices on the towns and cities of the British Isles. The huge gray, hydrogen-filled airships kept the civilian population on edge, no doubt part of Germany's plan to conquer the British Isles. Psychological warfare, the newspapers called it. And their strategy seemed to be working.

Zeppelins often came at night, when the darkness shielded them from view. Their bombs seemed to drop on random targets, rather than places like weapons factories or military bases. And when one was spotted approaching, Boy Scouts stood on street corners blowing their bugles to signal that residents should take cover. British soldiers launched maroons, extremely loud, exploding fireworks that made effective warning devices. On several occasions, Jonathan, Yvette, and Josette hid in their basement when the warning signals sounded.

The tension, the fear. It was all more than Josette could bear. Her nightmares were frequent. More often than not, she woke up in a cold sweat, startling herself awake while screaming. Faces were clear in those dreams, but she still couldn't identify who the people were. She had visions of being in the water; of people running and jumping from the sinking ship. But they were only bursts of pictures, gone in seconds. Were any of the faces her parents? If only she could remember.

To help her with her recovery, Yvette talked at length about their lives together growing up in Manhattan. About Compton House, and her school and her friends. Most of all, her sister shared stories about their mother and father. Sadly, they didn't even have a photograph of them. All their personal possessions had been in freight boxes on the *Lusitania*. Their only consolation was that there might be additional family photographs at their home in Manhattan.

As well-intentioned as Yvette was, it wasn't enough. Josette's doctor in Queenstown had referred her to Dr. Floyd Marsh, a renowned London physician specializing in brain injuries.

On Tuesday after lunch, she took the Underground to his private office near King's Cross.

"Look, Dr. Marsh. All I want is to go back home to New York. I'm sure I'll remember a great deal more if I do." Josette preferred to sit on the edge of the fainting couch, rather than lying down.

The doctor, an older man with thinning white hair, spoke in a calm voice. "While it's true familiar things and surroundings stimulate the brain, sometimes our minds shut out things that are simply too painful to remember. We can remember basic things, like how to walk or sew or to write. You've remembered your sister. True?"

"Yes. And her husband, Jonathan. It took a while, but spending time with them, well, some of the memories returned. Not as much as I'd like, though," she said with a shrug. "But I don't recall much about the *Lusitania*. I'm beginning to remember a few things about my mother and father. Just small things."

"That's quite typical of your type of trauma, Miss Rogers." Dr. Marsh sat behind his desk, tapping his pencil. He leaned forward with a serious expression. "Your memory loss is protecting you. At least for now. Be patient. In time, I'm certain some of the events on board the ship will return. And if they do not, would that be such a dreadful thing?"

Josette shrugged and drew in a slow breath. "I'm not sure. My sister said I fell in love with a man on the crossing. I would like to remember him. I *need* to remember him."

"I reckon the whole event is still too painful. And, subconsciously, you may be worried about his fate? Am I correct?"

"No, doctor. He survived. I was told he actually visited me while I was still unconscious in the hospital. Of course, he thought I was Yvette."

"Then, perhaps you should find him. Write to him. Or send him a telegram. Good heavens. Does he even know you're alive?"

Josette nodded. "A friend of mine wrote to him with the news a few months ago."

"And has he responded?"

She folded her hands in her lap, gazing down as she did so. "No. I fear not."

"I see. You must be worried your sister was wrong about the gentleman's intentions."

"Oh, I don't know." Frustrated, Josette sighed, wringing her hands. "From what my sister said, he lives in Boston…though something deep inside of me says he lives in New York City." For an instant, she fought to remember him. She could not.

The doctor paused. "That could be a signal that your subconscious is trying to break through your memory loss. Tell me, then. Why don't you simply return to New York, Miss Rogers?"

"I do want to go. But, but the reality of traveling across the ocean on the same route the *Lusitania* traveled – in reverse, of course – frightens me." The very thought of being on a ship sent a shiver through her. Would the vessel pass over the area where the *Lusitania* lay in its watery grave? The very spot where her parents and all those other people were entombed inside the hull? She closed her eyes and drew in a shuddering breath.

"Are you all right, Miss Rogers?"

"I don't know if I'll ever be all right, Dr. Marsh." She opened her eyes when he approached holding a handkerchief in his outstretched hand. "Thank you," she said, accepting it. She dabbed her eyes. "I still see faces in my nightmares, doctor. I wake up screaming."

He nodded, his gaze fixed on her face. "Truthfully, I don't believe you're in good enough health to make the sea crossing just yet, Miss Rogers." He returned to his desk and shuffled through his papers until he found what he was after. "Ah, yes. Here it is. Last week you told me your friend, Mrs. Donaldson, invited you to stay with her in Scotland. I believe you should take her up on her kind offer. Go, Miss Rogers. Go to Scotland. Get as far away from London as you can. I believe inland Scotland would be the perfect place to find peace and quiet. Stay away from the coastal cities. From the ocean. Anything that would remind you of the war and the trauma you suffered. Be patient with yourself. Spend time in prayer and contemplation and the memories will most likely return."

ON OCTOBER FIRST Josette made her escape, boarding a train headed to Edinburgh, where she would be met by Mrs. Donaldson's chauffeur and driven to the town of Duns.

Even as the train clicked rhythmically over the rails on its way north, Josette felt a sense of peace, something she hadn't experienced in a long time. Peering out the window, the countryside was every bit as beautiful as Mrs. Donaldson had described. Vast green meadows dotted with grazing sheep; low stone walls demarking property lines; and the ruins of abbeys and ancient stone towers and shepherd's cottages could be seen here and there. Patches of forests had begun to morph from green to gold and orange. The train crossed over rivers and streams and a sweeping view of the North Sea. Josette leaned her head against the window and fell into a deep sleep.

The weeks she spent with Mrs. Donaldson were peaceful. Divine. Josette read the books her sister had packed for her – two Jane Austen novels and one written by Charlotte Bronte, called *Jane Eyre*. Josette enjoyed them immensely. Light reading, very romantic. Had she read them before?

She enjoyed walks with Mr. Duns and took long naps. The Westie was her constant companion, curling up beside her feet or lying next to her on the couch when she slept.

By mid-November, Josette was feeling stronger. She had read Yvette's books and everything in Mrs. Donaldson's library. She was sleeping better...and she had become quite bored.

More frequently, pictures began to pop into her mind. Past events, conversations, her father's voice booming out the words, 'damnable' and 'hell.' Her mother scolding him for cursing. As the bits and pieces of the puzzle began to fit together, Josette knew she was on the mend. Christmas was about five weeks away, and she wanted to spend the holiday with her sister and Jonathan. It would be their first Christmas without their parents, and although Josette didn't recall enough to have it affect her deeply, she knew it would be especially difficult for her sister. As much as she would miss Mrs. Donaldson and Dunsy, it was time to return to London.

Josette told Mrs. Donaldson about her plans at lunch. She took the news graciously, as Josette knew she would.

"But I don't want to leave you alone," Josette said, fighting back tears. Mrs. Donaldson seemed to have aged rapidly since Josette had arrived. She had noticed the dear woman had become increasingly forgetful, and her balance had grown worse, making it difficult for her to walk. Likely the tragedy, the shock, had taken its toll on Mrs. Donaldson, too.

"Och, don't worry about that," she said with a wave of her hand. "My niece, Jeannie, would like to come stay with me. Her fiancé has gone off to war, and she's been keen on moving away from her parents' home in St. Andrews."

"Are you sure you'll be all right?"

"We'll miss you very much, my Dunsy and me, but you can come back for a visit whenever you'd like." She picked up a slice of grainy wheat bread from the bowl in the center of the table. "And what will you be doing next, then?"

Josette set her soup spoon down, looking across the table at her hostess. "I'm not certain. I can't leave Britain until Yvette and I settle our father's estate. Remember? We talked about this a while ago."

Mrs. Donaldson placed her elbows on the table, her eyes narrowed. "Oh, aye. Now that you mention it. So, it's back to London for you, then?"

Oh goodness, Josette thought, trying to hold back the sadness she felt inside. She had explained her plans to Mrs. Donaldson not five minutes ago. "Yes. London. I'm afraid so."

Mrs. Donaldson broke off a small piece of bread and dipped it in her lamb stew. "As I recall, when we talked on the ship, you often spoke about helping widows and children."

"Yes. My sister has talked about that at length. We shall eventually convert our town home in Kensington. It has quite a few bedrooms. It will be perfect. I'll hire some help to manage it."

Mrs. Donaldson took on a serious expression. "The winds of change are surely blowing, lass, especially in the direction of women's rights. Just look at how the war has already affected change here in the U. K. More women are working than ever, since the men have gone off to the Front. They're becoming nurses and ambulance drivers and all sorts of other jobs that they have haven't been privy to in the past. Do you no' think you could study business and step into the professional role at your father's company sometime in the future?"

That was the most rational thing Mrs. Donaldson had said in hours. She seemed to slip in and out of reality. Strange, these memory tricks played on the elderly woman. Picking up her cup of tea, Josette pondered the question. "I don't think I want to, ma'am. I think I should put my time and energy into making changes in the world. Perhaps I can make those winds of change blow even harder in another direction. I'll have enough money to do good things to help the needy."

Mrs. Donaldson snickered. "Aye. And if anyone can do it—" Cocking her head to the left, she asked, "And will you return to your home in Manhattan or remain in London?" Another question that had been asked and answered several times in the past days.

"In time, I'll go back to Manhattan." She took a sip of tea. "I'm quite sure there are plenty of women who need a helping hand there, too."

"And will you look for your Mr. Carlson?"

"I suppose so…though I still can't remember him. On the other hand, both you and my sister have said he acted as if he was in love with me." It felt awkward saying those words.

"Oh, aye. Clearly he was."

"What I don't understand is, if he truly cared about me, then why do you suppose he never responded to your letter telling him that I'm alive?"

"Letter?" It was evident Mrs. Donaldson was confused. Then flustered. "Oh dear. Oh dear. Did I not write to you about that matter?" She raised her hand to cover her mouth.

Setting down her cup, Josette straightened in her seat. "About what matter?"

Mrs. Donaldson tapped her index finger on her cheek, her eyes blinking as she gazed up, as if the answer was somehow on the ceiling. "Let me see, now. As I recall, I had a slip of paper with Mr. Carlson's address on it. But, I could never find it. I think I placed it in my waistcoat jacket when we were in Queenstown the day he left the hospital. I was supposed to send him a wire if you were found… perhaps." She paused. "Yes. Yes. He was rather insistent a mistake had been made. He thought the girl in that hospital bed was you, and not your sister."

This was the first time that Mrs. Donaldson had shared this information. "I wonder how he knew that? I was bandaged and quite a sight, from what you've told me."

"Aye. That you were." Mrs. Donaldson said. She lifted her shoulders in puzzlement. "I don't know, lass. He was quite adamant about it, though. But by the time I heard from your sister regarding the situation – the mix-up with your identity, that is – I believe I had thrown away the clothes I was wearing on that dreadful day, including my waistcoat with his note."

Josette gasped. "So, it was lost?"

She nodded, looking upset. "I'm so sorry, my dear. I had forgotten all of this. I don't think of that terrible time very often. I believe I've done you a true disservice."

Josette was shocked. "Then, he doesn't know I'm alive?"

"I wrote to your sister telling her what happened. And that I had no way to contact Mr. Carlson." She paused. Her eyes took on a bewildered look. "At least, I think I wrote to her. Oh, my goodness. Forgive me, lassie. I'm not sure if I ever wrote to her. My memory isn't good these days."

Josette knew her sister had never received such a letter. Poor, Mrs. Donaldson. She looked like a frightened child.

Letting out a long, slow, frustrated sigh, Josette asked, "Please. Think hard. Was there anything Mr. Carlson may have said to you on the ship that would indicate where he lived or if he was still teaching at Harvard?"

"Not that I recall." Mrs. Donaldson said, looking suddenly pleased. "On the other hand, I do remember that nasty uncle of his was a real braggart. He went on and on about his business ties to J. P. Morgan's company on Wall Street, like he was somebody important." She sniffed, pulling out the handkerchief she kept stuffed into her skirt pocket. "I'm sorry, but don't recall exactly what he said...but if I were you, I'd check with someone at the House of Morgan to track down Mr. Carlson's uncle." She added, "God rest his ornery soul."

Chapter 41

London, England
December 23, 1915

A LIGHT SNOW had fallen all day, making the sidewalks slippery and wet. Josette and Yvette both bundled up in their warmest clothes and headed out for dinner at a restaurant near their home.

"Kidney pie? Again? Really, Yvette," Josette said to her sister when the steaming pastry was served. "That pie is made out of an actual animal's kidneys. Disgusting."

"When in Rome," Yvette said with a shrug. "Besides, as you know, there are food shortages, and rationing on some items has already begun."

"I know, I know. But there are still plenty of fish in the sea. And if you haven't noticed, there's abundance of sea around here." Josette had grown fond of fish and chips. Potatoes were a staple that seemed to grow well in English and Irish soil, and the crispy deep-fried segments were delicious.

"I'm so excited," Yvette said in an enthusiastic tone, a wide grin on her face as she stabbed a piece of meat. "It's the Duke of York Theater, for heaven's sake. I heard so much about it from Mr. Frohman." Her smile faded for a few seconds, likely remembering the producer who died when the ship went down.

"I still say you should be doing more auditioning, Yvette. Even Mr. Frohman encouraged you to have your own career. I know you could do it."

"Anyway," Yvette continued, forcing a smile, "Jon said there will be a small orchestra – mostly women and a few men too old to fight in the war."

Frustrated that her sister always took a back seat when it came to Jonathan's career, Josette sprinkled her fried fish with malted vinegar. "One of these days, you'll realize you can have a career as a musician, should you so choose."

As usual, Yvette ignored her.

After they had finished eating, Josette and Yvette took a taxi to the theater. As promised, Mr. Frohman's British representative had auditioned Jonathan the week following their arrival in London. Since then, he had been working on a regular basis. While many of the theaters were closed until the end of the war, there were still performances held here and there; mostly, to encourage patriotism with uplifting songs, anti-Kaiser Wilhelm plays, and to entertain the soldiers who had come home for a break from the war.

The Duke of York Theater had been draped in blue, white and red bunting, both on the inside and the outside. British flags hung on poles on each side of the stage, while smaller versions of the Union Jack were pinned to the side walls. Jonathan had arranged for "his girls," as he called Yvette and Josette, to sit in the front row, dead center.

The theater filled quickly. Josette turned to scan the audience. The seats were a sea of khaki, dark blue, and even a few volunteers wearing gray uniforms, interrupted by young women wearing their finest dresses—girls who were accompanying their beaus for a night of merriment…and diversion.

Several men sat in wheelchairs along the aisles and at the back of the theater. Josette couldn't help but notice many had missing limbs. Empty jacket arms and pant legs were folded at the point where flesh and bone no longer existed; the fabric pinned closed to lessen the acknowledgement of their absence.

The house lights went down. The red velvet curtain lifted. And there he was. Jonathan sat at the grand piano, the back of his long split-back jacket hanging over the bench. A very small orchestra, if one could call it that, considering there were only two women playing violins, a boy with a snare drum, a girl holding a metal triangle who stood behind a table covered with varied sizes of bells, and an elderly woman sitting before a massive harp. Six women, who made up the choir, stood to the right of the piano, holding their song books.

"He looks so handsome. Don't you think so, sister?" Yvette said, looking as if she would burst with pride.

Josette nodded, smiling.

After the applause died down, the Christmas carols began. The audience joined in the singing; but not Josette. She couldn't remember the words. Not at first. But then, something changed. She mouthed a few words to *Silent Night*. When the choir sang, *O Holy Night*, Josette began to tremble. She turned to her sister, whispering in her ear.

"That was our mother's favorite Christmas hymn, was it not?"

Yvette drew back, her brows arched with surprise. "You remember that?"

Swallowing, Josette nodded.

Yvette's mouth was agape. Then she smiled. "Oh, my goodness," she mouthed, grabbing Josette's arm. "That's wonderful!" she managed to whisper.

And when Jonathan played the opening to *Deck the Halls*, Josette remembered. She closed her eyes and saw the visions in her head. Her sister sitting at a piano playing these same songs in the music room at their home in New York.

Oh, my Lord in heaven. It's all coming back. She pulled a freshly laundered handkerchief from her purse, dabbing her eyes.

Next were the patriotic songs. The men certainly loved them, clapping to the rhythm, belting out the words.

Josette had flashes of hearing these same songs recently. Her mind swept back. There was movement beneath her feet. The ship. She had been on a ship. Josette felt it lift and settle, rock and lift again.

Yvette continued to glance at her. She, too, was sniffing, wiping away tears with the understanding that Josette's mind was, at last, healing.

The final song was meant for Yvette. Jonathan stood up and introduced his wife and acknowledged his love for her. Then he sat down and began to play.

The music was beautiful, soul stirring. Josette knew she had heard it before. Another picture flashed in her mind. She was with…him, standing on the ship's deck while Yvette played *Clare de Lune*. The fluid sounds wafted through a doorway or, perhaps, a window. She looked up at the stars. He stood beside her. "Curtis," she whispered, so taken by the scene that she began to weep audibly.

"What is it, Josette?" Yvette said softly, her face reflecting her concern.

"I…I," she stammered. "I remember, Yvette. I remember everything."

ON CHRISTMAS EVE, snow began to fall in the afternoon, dusting Manhattan's sidewalks and trees with a glistening white blanket. Curtis left the office at six o'clock, promising Lilianna he would be home in time for dinner. But this evening, his taxi ride home from the office was even more precarious than usual. Between the throngs of pedestrians darting across busy streets to do last-minute shopping, the more-than-usual swarm motor cars and trucks, and traffic accidents caused by slippery roads, it had taken an extra forty minutes to arrive at his apartment.

He entered, placing his satchel on the side table in the hallway and walked into the parlor. The place was quiet. The eight-foot Christmas tree he had purchased three days ago stood in the corner beside Liliana's new piano. The tree had been exquisitely decorated by his maid and her sister, strewn with big red bows, strung popcorn, and shiny gold balls. A new invention, small, colorful lights strung on long wires, had been wound around the tree numerous times, creating a delightful effect.

And yet, there was no sign of Liliana. A strange sensation washed over him.

"Lil? he called. She rarely left their apartment these days. "Are you here?"

"Mr. Carlson! Please come into the bedroom!" It was the new cook's voice.

He raced down the hall. The door was open. Liliana was lying on the bed. Her face was as pale as white bread. The circles under her eyes were so dark, she looked as if she had been in a fist fight. And lost. She hadn't even bothered to comb her hair or put on her usual layer of lip paint and mascara.

"What's happened?" he asked Miss Dominico.

Her face reflected her concern. "I'm so glad you're home, sir. I believe your wife is going into labor."

At that moment, Liliana cried out, grabbing her protruding abdomen, writhing in pain.

"Have you called the midwife?" he asked.

Andrea Dominico was an Italian immigrant, who not only made spaghetti that even Liliana would eat, but she had become a sort of companion for his wife these past weeks. She shook her head, her face reflecting concern. "I'm so sorry, sir. Mrs. Carlson didn't know how to get hold of her. Your wife is in a poor way. Her water has already let go."

Curtis glanced at the pink-tinged stain that had blossomed across the white satin bedspread from under Liliana. "When did this happen?

"About hour ago. I didn't know what to do. We expected you home earlier and—"

"An hour ago! And you didn't call for help? Don't you know how to use the telephone?"

She nodded, her eyes wide with fear. "I thought I should wait for you, Mr. Carlson."

"For God's sake, then do it now! Ask the operator to connect you with Dr. James Hansen. He lives on Park Avenue. Tell him to hurry."

Liliana doubled over as best she could, screaming. "Get this thing out of me! Help me, Curtis!"

Removing his bowler, he tossed his hat on the floor and perched on the edge of the bed next to Liliana's head. "Hang on, Lil. The doctor will be here soon. He'll call your midwife."

Gasping to catch her breath between contractions, Liliana blinked up at him. "Please take care of the child, Curtis."

"I'll take care of both of you, just like I promised."

"I know you never wanted a kid, but if I die…"

"Don't talk like that. You're going to be fine."

"I don't think so, Curtis. I can tell. Something's wrong." Her eyes suddenly closed tight, her features contorting into a pain-affirming grimace. "Aaaaah….!" she cried. "Make it stop! Please. Help me."

Curtis brushed several stray hairs from her forehead, then took her hand. "Hang on. Hang on. Everything is going to be fine."

Liliana thrust her head back on the pillow and let out a blood-curdling scream.

Chapter 42

April 1916

ON FEBRUARY 5TH Josette and Yvette had turned twenty-one. It wasn't a joyous occasion, though it certainly meant they could finally move forward with their plans to sell their father's company. They chose not to celebrate their birthday, however, for it was the first time they had been without their parents. Even worse, Jonathan had traveled to Edinburgh for a performance at the university; not for the students, but for military personnel on leave from the Front.

In the months since their parents' death on the *Lusitania*, Rogers and Rogers Import/Export Company had made deals with The House of Morgan to purchase much-needed American-made goods and transport them to Britain. Josette had attended several board meetings at the Rogers' office in London to discuss what to do with the business.

Not surprising, the Board of Directors was delighted when Josette and Yvette announced they wanted to sell the company. They had one stipulation – that Rogers and Rogers branch office in New York City would continue to be operated by the current management staff, and that Mr. Herrmann and the other employees hired by their father must remain with the company.

Arrangements were made for Josette and her sister to receive a lump sum – a fortune – for the sale of the long-established and profitable Rogers and Rogers Company. When the money was transferred into the girls' individual bank accounts, Josette set about plans to return to New York.

For now, Jonathan and Yvette planned to continue living at the family's historic mansion in London. Eventually, when her sister and brother-in-law moved back to America, the house in Kensington would also be used to house the families of dead soldiers.

The war had dragged on longer than anyone had anticipated. Estimates of the dead had already soared into the millions. And that was just the Allied troops. Heaven knew how many Germans, Austrians, and Turks lay dead on the muddy fields in Europe. Poisonous gas attacks along the Western Front in France were nearly a daily occurrence, and Zeppelin raids in England had become a recurring, overwhelming threat. German Imperial warships had launched bombs into coastal cities, like Scarborough and Whitby.

Josette's nerves were still raw, and every time explosions from German bombs or cannon fire from the British military rattled through the house, she felt as if she was set back in her healing process. She had had enough of this God-awful war. It was time for her to return to her home in New York City. And to find Curtis Carlson. Could she brave the voyage, now that she recalled everything that had happened on the *Lusitania*? How would she be able to go back home, where she would be surrounded by reminders of her mother and father? And, foremost, would Curtis still have feelings for her?

GETTING THROUGH Liliana's funeral the day after Christmas was difficult. Her mother, her brothers...they had all held Curtis accountable. In her grieving stupor, Mrs. O'Toole, had stood beside

Liliana's flower-draped coffin and shouted at Curtis, "You killed my beautiful daughter. My Liliana died of a broken heart."

Apparently, Liliana had confided her unhappiness to her family. Of course, they would never know the truth about what happened; that Liliana had deliberately gotten herself pregnant to trap a man she saw as a successful Wall Street investment banker…her future meal ticket. Mrs. O'Toole had even proposed that Curtis turn his child over to her to raise. He refused, though he agreed he would allow Liliana's family to spend time with Georgie occasionally.

It hadn't taken long for Curtis to realize that dealing with a newborn baby was extremely difficult, especially, when the infant didn't have a mother. Doctor Hansen had arranged for a wet nurse to feed the boy. Besides the cook and maid, Curtis hired a full-time, live-in nanny to care for little Georgie.

Most surprising was how fast he became attached to the baby. Saturdays, weather permitting, he pushed Georgie through the park in the fancy baby carriage he'd purchased before the child was born. Evenings, when he returned home, he spent time with his son, though he drew the line at changing the dirty diapers. He left that chore to Nanny Beatrice Clark, an older woman who adored children and had once worked for the Morgan family.

Curtis' increasing sense of peace, of happiness often gave way to feelings of guilt about his marriage. Liliana had been as unhappy as he was. If she had survived, they would have surely divorced. He reminded himself that there was nothing he could have done to change what happened to her. Liliana died from what Doctor Hansen called *septicemia*, child birth fever, an infection within the uterus. He said it was a miracle the newborn could be saved. Thank God the boy was healthy, despite the terrible circumstances in which he entered the world. Now Georgie was his responsibility. The least he could do was be the best father he could.

Chapter 43

PERHAPS DR. MARSH had been right. Maybe it would have been better if her memories hadn't returned. Moving back to Compton

House had been difficult for Josette. Every nook, every doorway, every piece of furniture generated recollections of her life there with her family. She left doors shut to several of the rooms, including her father's office and her parent's bedroom. Leaving everything exactly as it had been before they left for England, the maids merely kept the closed-off rooms clean. For now. When Jonathan and Yvette came home, the interior of the house would be remodeled to a style more suitable to their taste.

Visiting Grandmother Murphy for the first time since her return had been incredibly emotional. They sobbed together, exchanged stories about Mother and Father – especially Father – and discussed what would happen next for Josette.

"I have an idea, dearest girl. We can live together," Grandmother Murphy said insistently. "I can move in with you. Or, if it's too painful for you to be at Compton House, you can stay here with me."

"I'm doing all right for now, Grandmother. Thank you," Josette had responded. As much as she loved her grandmother, the woman was something of a chatter box and, at the moment, Josette needed a more tranquil surrounding. "But I shall come to visit you every Tuesday and Thursday. We can go shopping and have lunch at Macy's. Or, perhaps we'll have afternoon tea at the Plaza Hotel. I do miss scones and clotted cream."

AFTER THE FOG had finally lifted from her mind last December, Josette had written down each and every memory that had come to her in her dreams, in the bathtub, and most especially, when she had walked along the Thames River in London. Over the course of weeks, she had recalled portions of conversations she had with Curtis on the *Lusitania*. Had he really told her that he had left his teaching position at Harvard University to take a job with the famous Mr. J. P. Morgan's establishment in New York City's financial district? Or was it simply that his uncle had investments with the House of Morgan, as Mrs. Donaldson believed?

After another restless night of trying to sleep, she was up and dressed early. She had changed clothes several times, wanting to find just the right thing to wear. She settled on her tailored navy blue and white skirt and fitted jacket, and a serious white hat, an appropriate ensemble for a respectable woman to wear to the prestigious House of Morgan.

When Josette's father had spoken about Wall Street, it was with reverence and awe. The narrow street packed with banks and offices occupied by many of the most important men in the country had overtaken London as the world's most important financial center.

Josette paid the driver, stepped from the cab in front of 23 Wall Street, and walked to the entry on the corner. Drawing in a deep breath of courage, she paused and looked at her reflection in etched-glass door to make sure her hair, her hat, everything, was in place. Nervous, she gathered her courage and reached for the brass door handle. A sudden gust of wind blew through the narrow street, loosening a curl from under her hat. "Oh dear," she said, looking back at her reflection. As she tucked the wavy strand behind her ear, a gentleman appeared from behind her.

"Excuse me, miss," he said as he passed. Stopping, he opened the door, tipping his hat brim in respect. "There you go," he said with a half-smile. "Are you certain you have the right address? We don't have many ladies visit us here at Morgan's."

"Thank you. Yes, I'm certain." She glanced up at him with a smile, then walked through the door and looked around. The interior of the building was rich with marble, potted plants, and beautiful paintings. Rows upon rows of desks dotted the area behind a low panel. The place was simply alive with the click-clack of typewriters, ringing telephones, and men speaking into their phones' mouthpieces in loud voices. Josette found it exciting, albeit a little overwhelming.

"May I help you find something?" asked the gentleman who had escorted her inside. He pulled a warm gray scarf from around his neck, hanging it on a wall rack in the lobby area.

"Yes, please." She found herself raising the level of her voice. "Do you know if there's a Mr. Carlson working here? Curtis Carlson, that is."

He smiled. "Indeed, there is. And do you have an appointment with him?"

Her mouth opened with a gasp. She fought to hide her excitement. "No...but I'm certain he would want to see me. We're old friends."

He eyed her suspiciously. "And your name is...?"

"Josette. Josette Rogers. We were both on...on the *Lusitania*."

His expression softened. "Oh, my dear. I see. From the *Lusitania*. I'm so sorry." He quickly removed his coat, placing it on the hanger beside his scarf.

"Let me introduce myself, Miss Rogers. I am Mr. Henry Davison, one of the Senior Partners here at Morgan and Company. Mr. Carlson works with me now, since Mr. Van Camp, senior, passed away when your ship sank."

"Mr. Van Camp worked here, too?"

Mr. Davison's face took on a look of confusion. "Why, yes, miss. He was a senior partner. And did you meet Mr. Van Camp?"

"Yes, I did. I just didn't realize he was...who he was."

"Terribly sad, the whole *Lusitania* calamity," he said, shaking his head. "Thank God you made it, Miss Rogers. And thank God Mr. Carlson survived, too."

Josette made a quick decision not to say anything else. This wasn't the time nor the place. "Thank you, Mr. Davison. It was indeed a tragedy."

"Please. Have a seat." He pointed to a nearby bench. "I believe Mr. Carlson is upstairs. I'll let him know you're here."

"Thank you, sir." Smoothing her skirt, Josette sat down, resting her pocket book on her lap, as Mr. Davison disappeared into an elevator. As she looked around the room, she noted there was only one female seated at a desk, her hands busily typing. The middle-aged woman glanced up each time the machine dinged. Raising her hand, she pushed the metal arm to slide the platen back.

"Mr. Wells!" a rotund man with the most unusual shade of reddish hair shouted as he exited his office door across the foyer from where Josette sat. His beard, eyebrows and head were all a combination of apricot and copper, a color not often seen on what people called 'ginger heads.' He crossed to the low room partition and hollered. "I thought I told you to bring me the Bostitch file immediately!"

A young man, who she assumed was Mr. Wells, jumped from his chair on the left side of the sea of desks. "Yes, sir. Sorry, sir. It's nearly ready." He looked eighteen or nineteen.

"Bring it to me now, you incompetent buffoon!" the man, his superior, said in a vulgar tone. "You've taken far too long to get it typed up. I shall see to it your paycheck suffers."

Josette straightened. Who was this horrible creature? She glanced from the young man to the ruddy-faced boss and back again. The employee was obviously frightened. Strange that no one else seemed alarmed. Heads stayed down, eyes focused on their work.

"Very well, Mr. Van Camp," young Mr. Wells said, looking quite dejected.

Then it struck her. Josette drew in a sharp breath. Had the lad really called him Mr. Van Camp? "Mr. Van Camp?" she questioned. "You're Mr. Van Camp?"

"What's that you say?" He turned towards her and took several steps closer.

There was something familiar about him. "You're Rudy Van Camp, aren't you?"

He eyed her carefully. "Yes. I'm Rudolph Van Camp. And who are you?"

"Miss Josette Rogers." Standing, she said, "Curtis mentioned that his Uncle Phineas – your father, I presume – had a son named Rudolph." Josette walked to him. "I'm sorry about your father's passing, Mr. Van Camp. I presume you're Curtis' cousin."

He stared at her for the longest time, his eyes narrowed. "So, you were on the *Lusitania* with my father and Curtis Carlson?"

"Yes. I fear I was."

"Hmm." Most surprising, his expression wasn't one of sadness. Instead, he simply said, "Have we met before? You look very familiar."

Josette narrowed her eyes, tilting her head as she thought. The odd way he looked at her, with such intensity made her quite uncomfortable. "I don't believe so. On the other hand, you see, I was injured on the *Lusitania* and have been suffering from memory issues...though I must admit, you are familiar to me, as well." She looked directly at him. "Perhaps it's because you resemble your father."

Hurried footsteps echoed from the nearby stairwell opening. She turned to see Curtis exiting. Her heart pounded wildly. "Curtis!" She couldn't hold back her tears.

Seeing her, he froze in place for a moment, his mouth gaping open. "Josie!" he yelled. Is that really you?"

She nodded. Clutching her purse handle, she rapidly moved in his direction.

He sprinted to her, stopping inches away. "Josette? Is that you?" he said again, searching her face. His breathing was rapid, his lips parting as he shook his head.

"Yes, Curtis. It's me."

"I can't believe it. How is it possible?"

Josette's heart pounded so loud, he could surely hear it. She laughed. "It's such a long story. We have so much to talk about," she said, tears welling. "Is there somewhere private we can—"

He gathered her into his arms, squeezed her, then pulled back, gazing into her eyes. "I thought you were…. Oh, Josie girl. I can't believe this! Why didn't Mrs. Donaldson write or send me a wire or—?"

"Well, well, Carlson?" Rudy interrupted as he stepped closer. "A long-lost love? A shipboard romance? I'm sure Miss Rogers will be happy to meet your son."

Josette almost stopped breathing. "What?" She pulled loose of Curtis' arms, brushing tears from her cheeks. "You have a wife? And a child?"

He shot Rudy Van Camp a nasty glance and returned his gaze to her. "No. Well, not any longer. I mean…" He shrugged oddly. "She died, Josie. In childbirth."

"I…I…" Josette stepped back. "I'm very sorry, Curtis. I didn't know you were married."

"I wasn't when I met you. It all happened when I came back from England."

It was too much for Josette. She shook her head, expelling a discouraged breath. "I really should be going."

Curtis reached out, placing his hand on her shoulder. "Please, Josie. Hear me out. There's an explanation."

She shook her head, pulling away. "I understand. You thought I was dead. I can't blame you for moving on. Now, if you'll excuse me, I really must be going, Curtis." Scooting past Mr. Van Camp, Josette headed towards the entrance.

Curtis walked beside her. "You can't leave, Josie. We need to talk. I have so many questions." He wore a look of desperation. "I have to explain everything to you. Let's go to my office where we can have some privacy."

Still feeling shaken and as if she needed to flee, Josette continued her charge to the front entrance without uttering another word.

"My God, Josie. Please tell me what happened. What about your sister? Is she—"

Josette stopped, fighting to keep her bottom lip from quivering. The last thing she wanted to do was make a further scene in the prestigious House of Morgan. Gathering herself, she managed to say, "Yvette is alive and well. She injured her foot when she jumped from the ship. She was taken in by an Irish farmer and his family."

"So, it *was* you in the hospital!"

She nodded. "Everyone thought I was Yvette."

"Ha! I knew it was you. I knew it! I felt it in my soul. Please, Josie. Come up to my office, so we can talk in private."

Before she said another word, Rudy Van Camp strolled closer, seeming to enjoy his interfering. "Why don't you let the lady go, Carlson? It's obvious she doesn't want anything more to do with you. In fact, I would be happy to drive you home, Miss Rogers."

"Thank you for your offer, Mr. Van Camp, but my driver is waiting for me," she lied. She wanted nothing to do with this obnoxious tyrant.

"Suit yourself." Rudy gave her a 'you don't know what you're missing' smirk. "Good day, then, pretty lady."

An alarm went off in Josette's mind. She was suddenly swept back to the day she and her sister visited the bakery in Little Germany. Josette squinted her eyes, searching Rudy's face.

An involuntary gasp escaped her lips. She remembered him. The bakery. Yes! That was it. His unusual hair color. The tone of his voice. He had spoken to his friends in German and, when he walked past Josette and Yvette, had uttered that same phrase with the same inflection to her and Yvette as he held the door open for them.

Rudy Van Camp stared at Josette in a strange silence. She knew he was the fourth man that had been at the table with the Germans. He was acquainted with at least two of the spies arrested on board the *Lusitania*. Was he, too, an undercover German agent? Most importantly, did he notice the fear in her eyes…or, God forbid, did he recognize her?

"What is it, Josie?" Curtis asked with a look of concern.

Josette glanced at Curtis. "It's nothing. You're right. Perhaps we need to talk, Curtis. But not here."

"Great!" he said with a relieved grin. He moved his gaze to Rudy, giving him an angry glare. Then he turned to Josette again and said, "Please come with me, Josie."

Without another word, she followed him into the elevator. The operator closed the doors and moved the lever to the second floor. As they ascended, Josette turned to Curtis. "I do apologize for bothering you here at your place of employment. But I had no other way of finding you."

"Oh God no. Don't apologize. I still can't believe you're here. I've had so many dreams about finding you." His brows knit into a deep furrow. "Why didn't Mrs. Donaldson write to me?"

"She lost the note you gave her."

He let out a soft groan. "I suppose I should have tried to contact her, but I thought you were...well, you know."

She gazed up at him, biting her lower lip. She desperately wanted to blurt out her recollection of seeing Rudy Van Camp at the bakery, but didn't dare...until they were alone.

"Second floor," the operator announced, opening the elevator's doors.

Still silent, Josette and Curtis walked down the hallway and stepped into his office. Closing the door after she entered, Curtis placed his hand on her shoulder and turned her around to face him. "I've missed you more than you'll ever know, Josie girl. Can't we pick up where we left off?"

"Please, Curtis. Before we talk about us, I must speak to you regarding Rudy Van Camp.

"Rudy? What about him? Other than he's a horse's rear."

She lowered her voice. "I believe he's a German agent."

A shocked look swept across Curtis' face. "What? Good grief!"

Josette went on to describe her encounter with Rudy in Little Germany. "Yvette and my butler's wife – she worked in the bakery – we will all be able to identify him as the man who interacted with the Germans my sister and I identified on the ship."

"Oh my gosh!" Curtis said, his eyes wide with excitement. "This makes so much sense. You have no idea how important this information is, Josie. I've always suspected there was a leak in Mr. Morgan's network, especially among the men who worked on the loan documents that Rudy's father and I were taking to London."

"Loan documents? So, that's why you were going to England!"

"Yes. It was for an enormous amount of money for shoring up the British and French governments. That's what I couldn't tell you about. I wanted to explain everything, but I was sworn to secrecy." A surge of determination swept across his face. "You wait here. Call the police and ask for Captain Tunney." Curtis headed for the door.

"Wait! Where are you going?"

"If you think there's even the slightest possibility Rudy recognized you, then he's likely to make a run for it. I'm going to make sure he doesn't."

Chapter 44

BYPASSING THE ELEVATOR, Curtis bounded down the stairs. Should he yell to everyone on the office floor? Should he warn them the police were on their way? *My God. There could be shots fired.* But if he called out to warn everyone, Rudy would hear, too.

Moving as fast as he could, trying not to call attention to his hurried pace, he stopped in front of Rudy's office door. It was closed. Without knocking, he slowly turned the knob and peered inside. Rudy had opened several file drawers, rummaging through the folders as if searching for something. Sheets of paper were strewn across the floor. His open valise sat on his desk.

Curtis swung the door open, startling Rudy. "Carlson. What do you want? Get out!"

"That's not going to happen, Rudy." Curtis entered, closing the door behind him. "What could you be looking for, hmm? Could it be information to take to your German associates?"

Rudy looked startled. "What are you talking about, you son-of-a-bitch?" His face had reddened. With a sudden move, Rudy lunged at Curtis, taking a swing at his face.

Curtis ducked to the side and grabbed Rudy, brusquely yanking him forward. He balled his fist and threw a hard punch, connecting with Rudy's left jaw. Rudy fell backwards, knocking over a chair as he toppled to the floor.

For a long moment, Rudy was dazed. Making a loud growling sound, he was up again, surging forward, leaping at Curtis. Rudy Van Camp must have outweighed Curtis by at least fifty pounds. Using his girth, he knocked Curtis to the floor, dropping on top of him. But Curtis was much stronger and in better shape. They rolled and punched and struggled, their bodies banging into furniture.

Curtis wasn't aware that someone had entered until Mr. Wells attempted to pull them apart. Another pair of hands assisted him.

"Get this ass off of me!" Rudy yelled. "He's crazy!"

Mr. Bixby, one of the partners, stood over Curtis. "What is going on here, Carlson?"

"He attacked me!" Rudy hollered, getting to his feet.

"He's a German spy, sir. He was gathering documents to steal." Curtis stood up.

Mr. Bixby's mouth fell open. "Someone call the police," he instructed. "We'll let them sort this out."

"I already spoke with one of the detectives." Josette had entered the room. "They're on their way."

Rudy shot her a cold stare. "It *was* you, wasn't it? At the bakery. There were two of you. Twins."

"Yes. And I'm prepared to testify that you were talking to those Germans who died on the *Lusitania*."

"So, you're an undercover German agent," Curtis stated with an angry huff. "You told the German government about the loan documents that were on the *Lusitania*. You knew it would be torpedoed. My God! Your own father was on board. You're responsible for the deaths of over a thousand people."

Rudy's expression remained defiant.

"Is that true, Mr. Van Camp?" Mr. Bixby asked in an astounded tone.

Rudy didn't say anything.

Josette crossed the room to stand in front of Rudy Van Camp. "You're responsible for killing my mother and father, you monster. And all those children. How could you?"

His eyes flashed his hatred. "The *Lusitania* was carrying ammunition. Thousands of bullets that would have killed German soldiers. Those passengers were merely casualties of war. They died for the greater good, including my bastard father."

Fighting tears, Josette slapped Rudy's cheek so hard, it made a smacking sound.

Rudy lunged for Josette, taking hold of her arm. "You were on the ship, weren't you? Did you identify my friends? Did you have them arrested?"

"Let her go!" Curtis grabbed Rudy's upper arm.

Josette yanked away from Rudy. "Yes! And the captain locked them up!"

"Bitch! You're responsible for their deaths. They planned to escape the ship before it was torpedoed."

Curtis shoved Rudy, pinning him against the wall. "Get something to tie him up," he instructed Mr. Wells.

"This isn't over!" Rudy nearly spat his words. "I'll find you both and make you pay!"

AN HOUR LATER, after the police had taken Rudy to police headquarters and things had calmed down, Curtis escorted Josette to his new Ford motor car and drove her to Lesser's Deli for a bite to eat.

"Are you sure you don't want me to go with you tomorrow to see Captain Tunney?" he asked.

"It's not necessary. Mrs. Herrmann will be with me. All we have to do is sign formal statements. The officer said we may not even have to testify at Rudy's trial. He's being charged with treason, and with the statements he made in front of everyone today, the police already have a strong case against him."

Curtis held the door open for Josette, and they entered the crowded delicatessen. Smells of strong coffee and cooking meat wafted from the kitchen. On one side of the glass case, plates of sliced meats and cheeses were displayed on top of shaved ice. Rows of pastries were laid out on the other. He pulled out a chair for her, and they settled at a small table in the back corner where they would have a little privacy.

He wasn't quite sure what to say. It had been so long since they had been together. Everything had changed in both their lives. "I hope you like pastrami sandwiches. They do have other things on the menu, if you don't," he blurted, suddenly feeling foolish.

"I do…though I've only tasted pastrami once when Yvette and I had lunch with…." Utter sadness radiated from her gaze. "With my father."

"I'm so sorry about your parents, Josie. There aren't any words to express—"

"It's so dreadful," she muttered, her eyes misting. "Such a terrible way to die."

"I'm truly sorry. I wish I could have been there for you." He hoped she hadn't learned the details about their deaths from other survivors she might have encountered in Ireland or England who had seen them trapped in the elevator.

"I probably wouldn't have remembered you at that time. But thanks." She smiled gently, brushing away a tear.

"But I'm here now," he said softly.

An awkward silence followed. Her expression changed. "Oh, crackers! I forgot to tell you that Yvette is with child," she declared.

"That's terrific news, Josie. I'm so happy for all of you." He chuckled. "We have so much to talk about, don't we?"

"Yes, we certainly do." Josette leaned forward, placing her elbows on the table. "Curtis, I think I know why I was mistakenly identified as my sister in Ireland."

"Really? You have a theory?"

"Yvette and I gave it a great deal of thought. I borrowed my sister's monogramed gloves at lunch before I met you on deck that…that terrible day. You see, Yvette's initials were on the gloves!"

Curtis expelled a gasp. "Of course! Embroidered gloves. You've solved the mystery. And to think a pair of gloves caused so much trouble." He shook his head. "If I had known, I wouldn't have left you. But Mrs. Donaldson was so sure you were Yvette and that her fiancé would arrive soon."

"Ah, yes. Mrs. Donaldson," she said with a shrug. "As I said, the poor darling has memory problems. She hasn't been the same since the *Lusitania*. She completely forgot about the note with your address."

"If only she had contacted me, things might have been quite different.' He smiled, leaning forward. "But we're together now and that's all that matters."

THEY SPOKE FOR HOURS, reminiscing about the good things that had happened on the ship. Josette talked about her life in England, her time with Mrs. Donaldson, Yvette's marriage and pregnancy, and the night at the Christmas performance when her memories began to return. Curtis told her about the attempted assassination of Mr. Morgan, about his new sailboat, and about how he got mixed up with Lil. That was the hardest topic.

"I hope you will join us at the park. I'd like you to meet Georgie. We're there most Saturdays. Under the cherry trees."

Josette cocked her head, eyes narrowed. "Georgie? Wasn't that the name of the little boy on the ship? The one you threw the ball for?"

"Yes. You remember him?"

"I do." She sat back in her chair. "I remember he wore a sailor suit. He was delightful." Her expression changed. "Oh dear. He didn't survive, did he?"

Closing his eyes, taking a deep breath, he told her. "I fear it's something I'll never forget, seeing the boy's lifeless body like that. I wanted to honor him by naming my son, George. I figured it was the least I could do to preserve his memory. Somehow it gave me a little solace."

IT WAS DUSK when Curtis drove Josette home to Compton House. He parked in the driveway in front.

"Is that your father's Ford?" he asked, noting the auto parked nearby.

"Yes. My father's Model T has been outside in the elements since we left for England. I shall send it to a garage to be cleaned up. Then, I intend to learn how to drive it."

Curtis smiled, nodding. "I'm certain you will! In the meantime, are you sure you don't want me to drive all of you to Police Headquarters in the morning?" he asked, as they walked up the flagstone steps to the front door.

"Don't be silly. I can take care of the situation. I'm quite strong, you see."

"That's one of the things I really like about you."

Josette smiled. "I must go in now."

"Wait. When can I see you again?"

"Please, Curtis. I need time to think, to absorb all of this. It was a bit of a shock, you see."

Curtis stood there for a long moment, shifting his weight from one foot to the other. "I won't let this be the end, Josie. We had something special between us. You felt it too. I know you did."

She reached up and touched his cheek. "Oh, my dear, Curtis. You're right. Yet, this is a lot to take in."

He opened his mouth to object, when Josette turned and reached for the door handle. She slowly turned around. "You have a motherless child to care for, and his needs must come first."

He nodded his understanding. "I'm so sorry I've put you through this, Josie. I know it's a lot to ask, but please understand. I thought you were dead, and I felt that marrying Liliana was the gentlemanly thing to do. I never loved her. And I never stopped thinking about you."

"I'm sorry, Curtis. But I'm simply not certain about what comes next for us." With that, she opened the door. "Good night. And thank you for lunch."

ON THURSDAY AFTERNOON, Police Captain Tunney came to The House of Morgan for a meeting scheduled with Jack Morgan. Curtis was called into the boardroom upstairs, together with several senior partners.

"We have intercepted communications between operatives in New York and Berlin." Captain Tunney said. He sat at the opposite end of the conference table from Mr. Morgan. "I don't know how much longer we'll be able to protect the shipping docks, Mr. Morgan. A great deal of the military cargo you're shipping overseas is under threat. We know there are both covert German operatives and Irish sympathizers working as stevedores at the shipyards. We could have an entire army guarding those areas, and we still wouldn't be able to stop them from planting explosives."

"What kind of incendiaries, captain?" Morgan asked.

"That's part of the problem. They're quite clever, these Germans. They continue to come up with new devices. If it was just dynamite sticks they're using, we'd know what we're looking for." Tunney heaved a sigh, leaning his elbows on the table. "Apparently, they're using all sorts of ways to disguise their bombs. We believe they've found some way to pack powerful explosives into small devices and a way to time their detonation. That's why so many vessels have gone up in flames in these past months, despite the department's efforts to inspect the cargo."

"It would certainly explain the second explosion," Curtis said. "It was so loud and destructive. I truly believe the ship could have survived the first blast, but that second one, well, it blew up like a volcano."

"According to Cunard's representatives, their on-board detectives searched the *Lusitania's* cargo hold for explosives after the young German's were arrested," Mr. Morgan commented. "Do you believe they might have missed one of these unique types of combustible devices? That the detectives might not have known exactly what they were looking for and missed it?"

"Very possibly…not that we can ever prove it one way or the other," the police captain explained.

"What kind of bomb did Eric Muenter use at the U.S. Capitol Building?" Curtis asked.

"I'm afraid he took that secret to the grave. All that the bomb squad detectives in D. C. found was some sort of melted metal chunks among the rubble."

"I'll never understand why your police officers let the bastard who shot me jump out of a window. How does that happen when a would-be killer and German spy is in police custody?" Mr. Morgan said with a stern stare.

Tunney cleared his throat. His face reflected his embarrassment regarding the department's failure to prevent Muenter's suicide. "Yes, sir. I know. It's unfortunate. And I can assure you measures have been taken to make sure nothing like that happens again."

"Have you been able to get any information out of Rudy Van Camp?" Curtis asked.

"Not much, though Van Camp admitted the undercover espionage network is meeting at one of the beer gardens in Little Germany. But he stopped short of telling us exactly which one. So, we're having some of our double-agents working undercover in the beer gardens to see if they can pin down the culprits."

"Meanwhile, what in the hell are we supposed to do to protect our shipments?" Mr. Morgan blurted.

Captain Tunney flashed an impatient look around the table. "Mr. Morgan…and the rest of you. We intercepted a message designating this company as an enemy to Germany and the Kaiser. Mr. Morgan, you are believed by many Germans to be the devil himself; an evil mark upon the world that must be erased."

Jack Morgan stiffened in his seat. "Erased? You mean, kill me?"

"Yes, I'm afraid so. Eric Muenter is dead, but there are likely many other agents who have targeted you. You are a blessing to the Allies, but hated by millions in Germany and several other countries, not excluding our own U. S. of A. Do not let down your guard, sir. Body guards should accompany you everywhere. Though my officers are working day and night to stop these undercover operations, there's a great deal of buzz that something big, something terrible is being planned. We hope to stop it before they can carry out the plot."

Chapter 45

June 1916

THE WARM WEATHER had finally arrived, bringing hordes of winter-weary New Yorkers to Central Park. Pushing the baby carriage through the onslaught of bicyclists, runners, and people strolling at a leisurely pace, Curtis stopped beside his favorite bench next to the stand of cherry trees. He reached into the carriage and lifted out six-month-old Georgie. "See the pretty pink flowers?" he said, sitting down. He held his son high enough to look over his shoulder, cradling the back of the baby's head with his hand.

A woman's heels clicked on the paved walkway. He turned.

"Good morning, Curtis."

"Josette!" A sense of elation, of relief that she had finally decided to come flooded through him.

She smiled gently. "Hello, Georgie," she said, settling on the bench beside Curtis and the swathed infant.

Balancing the baby on his lap, Curtis turned him to face Josette. "May I introduce Mr. George Carlson."

Letting out a giggle, Josette leaned over for a closer view. "Oh, my goodness. He's adorable."

"That he is," Curtis said warmly, gazing at his child. The baby smiled and made a gurgling sound. "That's how he greets people he likes."

"Well, thank you, Georgie," she said with a laugh. "My, my. Just look at your long eyelashes! You're going to be a handsome young man, just like your daddy, aren't you?"

"I'm afraid I have to give Liliana credit for those pretty eyes. Her Italian blood, I guess."

Josette suddenly looked uncomfortable, clearing her throat.

"Sorry, Josie. I won't mention her name again."

"Don't be silly. She was Georgie's mother. And I'm at peace with that."

Curtis smiled. He still didn't know how to respond. Instead, he rose and placed the baby back in the carriage. Then he sat down. "So... you've come to see us. Does this mean you've made a decision, Josie?"

Nodding, she scooted next to him and gazed into his eyes. "I had forgotten you for so long, but I still knew – deep inside – that something, someone was missing from my life. And when my memories finally returned...when I remembered you and our time together on the ship, I couldn't stop thinking about you. I want to start over, Curtis. I want to know everything about you; to spend as much time with you as possible. And your child, too, naturally."

For the first time since he had been on the *Lusitania*, Curtis felt a sense of peace. "I'm so relieved, Josie. I thought I'd lost you for a second time."

"I do have one condition, however." She grinned mischievously. "No more lies or secrets."

"I promise, my darling. He picked up her hands, lifting them to his lips, then delicately kissing the top of her left, then her right hand. His gaze held hers for a long moment. Turning her right hand over, he traced the shape of a heart on her palm. "I love you, Josie girl," he whispered.

He felt her trembling and released her hands. They leaned closer, their lips so near he could feel the warmth of her breath. He slid his arms around her back, drawing her to his chest.

Then Georgie began to fuss.

"Oh no! he said, sighing. "Are you sure you want to take on both of us?" he joked.

"I've survived the *Lusitania*. I do believe I can survive a little boy," she said with a laugh.

Shaking his head, Curtis stood, speaking as he rummaged through the blankets in the carriage. "If there's one thing I've learned, it's that having a child requires a lot of patience. I'm so grateful I have a good nanny to help take care of my son." Locating the baby bottle, he lifted the infant. He returned to the bench and removed the cap. He offered the nipple to Georgie. Looking quite contented, the baby suckled, making faint cooing sounds. "Speaking of babies, when are Yvette and Jonathan returning here from England?"

"She wants to have the baby here in New York. Jon is still performing for the soldiers, so he's not sure when he'll return home. So, I suppose we'll be searching for a nanny, too, though I plan to help when I can."

"And will they move in with you at Compton House?"

"Yes. Eventually, they hope to build a home on Long Island."

"And you, Josie? You've finished your college degree and, from what you've said, you've settled the business pertaining to your father's company in England. What's next?"

Josette lifted her shoulders in the smallest shrug. "As you know, I've always wanted to go into social work, so after Yvette and Jon move out, I would like to buy my sister's half of Compton House and convert it into a home for widows and their children." She added softly, "And if America enters the war, I fear there may be an even greater need for the families of dead or injured soldiers to find a place to live."

"That's my girl," Curtis responded. "Your generous heart is just one more reason I adore you."

Josette took on an embarrassed look. "I couldn't live with myself if I didn't help those less fortunate than I am. I have experienced terrible loss, but because of Father's estate, I shall be able to use my inheritance to make a difference in many women's lives."

Georgie had fallen asleep in his arms. Giving Josette an approving nod, he whispered, "That's wonderful, Josie." He stood up, carefully pulling the bottle's nipple from the baby's rosebud lips. He lowered the infant into the carriage and covered him with a blanket. Then he turned back to Josette. She hadn't yet told him she loved him...which began to cause him concern. "And what about us?"

She got to her feet, a smile crawling across her lips. "I love you, Curtis Carlson," she said softly. Josette drew in a breath, her eyes rimmed with moisture. "We've been through so much together, haven't we? We've earned the right to have happiness."

He searched her face – the face he had seen so often in his dreams. "I've never been so happy, my darling." He slid his arms around Josette's back, holding her so close he could feel the rise and fall of her breathing. "I'll never let you go again."

As they embraced in the dappled sunlight streaming through the branches of the cherry trees, the world seemed to stop. The pain of the past that had haunted Curtis began to recede. Nothing else mattered at that moment. Nothing.

•

Author's Notes

My fascination with the RMS *Lusitania* began many years ago when I worked at a university as a research and oral historian. In an interview with pioneering deep-sea diver Col. John D. Craig, he discussed his 1930s efforts to dive to the wreck of the luxury liner, which had been torpedoed by a German submarine off the coast of Ireland in 1915. My curiosity was piqued by his descriptions of the once-beautiful "Greyhound of the Seas" lying on the bottom of the sea around ten miles off the Irish Coast. Of the nearly 2,000 passengers and crew on board, 1,198 men, women, and children died in the tragedy, including 128 American citizens. I knew I had to write a novel about the event, the people on board the ill-fated ship, and the circumstances that had led the Germans to commit this heinous war crime. Why did the Germans torpedo a passenger ship? Who were the passengers? And what were the repercussions of the sinking?

I traveled to Cobh (formerly Queenstown), Ireland, where both the rescued survivors and the dead were bought to shore. I visited the cemetery just outside of town and placed flowers on the mass graves of the victims; spent time at the Cobh Heritage Center, where artifacts from the wreckage are exhibited; and stayed in one of the first-class suites at the Queens Hotel where half-frozen, water-logged survivors were lodged. Sitting in a pew at St. Coleman's Cathedral, the church where a requiem service was held shortly after the sinking, I imagined I was there with the survivors and their families for a solemn service dedicated to the *Lusitania's* victims. Just being present in this quaint town that had once been called 'the town of death' was an emotional experience, once again inspiring me to write this book.

The deeper I dug into the World War I era, the more I discovered fascinating facts that simply aren't included in most history text books, such as the large number of German spies committing acts of espionage in America and particularly in New York. Although this is a work of fiction, I have woven many of these actual events and people into the novel. *In the Shadow of War* is a story that might have been. Were Mr. Morgan's loan documents on the *Lusitania*? Did the German submarine simply happen across the *Lusitania* on the liner's way to Liverpool? Ship routes, dates, times, and other information were no secret. Numerous submarine attacks had already occurred in the area where the German U-boat laid in wait. Was it merely a stroke of luck for the U-boat captain, as Germany claimed, or was it a planned attack as many World War I experts believe?

I have woven factual incidents into the novel, such as the attempted bombing of St. Patrick's Cathedral; the information about the Great War which is discussed by my characters; the bomb set off in the U. S. Capitol Building and subsequent shooting of J. P. Morgan, Jr., by a German spy; the half-billion dollar loan made by Morgan and other American banks to the governments of Britain and France; and the events that occurred on the *Lusitania* leading up to the torpedo attack by a German submarine.

There are many people and institutions to thank: The staff at the Queen Mary in Long Beach graciously allowed me access to their enormous model of the *Lusitania*. The cutaway portion of the model allowed me to accurately move my characters and scenes around the ship and to understand where sections of the ocean liner were located, as well as how those places were accessed. Kathleen Sabogal, Assistant Director of the Carnegie Hall Archives, helped with the scene at the theater the night before the ship sailed. The Cobh Heritage Center in Ireland has been a great research resource for historical data in 1915 Queenstown. Chloe Pascual, Archivist and Special Collections Librarian, California State Long Beach, located my lengthy interview with Colonel Craig in the university's archives and made a copy for me. And the late Alison McClay, my mentor and an extraordinary novelist, spent countless hours combing through historic British newspapers and archives for details about the *Lusitania*.

I also wish to thank Carol Amato, Rebecca Anderson and Linda McLaughlin for their editing and suggestions; proofreaders Michael Barry, and Deborah and Fred Borad; my husband, Rick, who helped me extensively every step of the way; Alfredo Cuellar, who drew the map; and of course, the late Col. John D. Craig, without whom this book would not have been written.

Two excellent nonfiction books that I recommend for further reading are *Dark Invasion* by Howard Blum, and *Dead Wake* by Eric Larsen.

About the Author

Award-winning author, journalist and historian, Colleen Adair Fliedner, has written three nonfiction books, radio and T.V. commercials, screenplays, and hundreds of articles for newspapers, magazines, and online publications. She was a staff writer for the *Orange County Register* newspaper's online travel publication and was a regular contributor for Talking Travel Radio Network based on the East Coast. *IN THE SHADOW OF WAR: Spies, Love and the Lusitania* is her first novel. She lives in Orange County, CA, with her husband/research helper extraordinaire, Rick.

www.colleenfliedner.com

CPSIA information can be obtained
at www.ICGtesting.com
Printed in the USA
FSHW012356030219
55416FS